"Yes, Major Malcolm Wheeler-Nicholson is one of the very, very few people responsible for the birth of the comic book industry as the visionary founder of what we today call DC Comics. And, yes, Major Malcolm Wheeler-Nicholson is one of the very, very few people responsible for giving the world *Superman*. But The Major is also one of the very, very best writers of authentic American history-based adventure stories who, along with the likes of Dashiell Hammett, Edgar Rice Burroughs, and Robert E. Howard, elevated the pulp magazines of the early 1900s into one of the most popular forms of reading in the history of this country. How lucky we are that John Locke, working with The Major's dedicated granddaughter, Nicky Wheeler-Nicholson, has hunted down and preserved The Major's finest work in this important and vastly entertaining book collection, moments before they might have been lost to the black hole of time."

MICHAEL USLAN,
   Executive Producer of all the *Batman* movies,
   Comic book historian,
   And author of his memoir, THE BOY WHO LOVED BATMAN.

The Texas-Siberia Trail

adventure stories by
Malcolm Wheeler-Nicholson

Off-Trail Publications
Elkhorn, California

ABOUT THE COVER

Guidons are flags carried by military units with designs representing unit traditions. Major Malcolm Wheeler-Nicholson rode under guidons in his US Army Cavalry service, was a strong believer in military traditions, and described guidons in his stories, so it's only fitting that we represent his military and writing career with a set of these symbolic flags.

THE TEXAS-SIBERIA TRAIL
adventure stories by
Malcolm Wheeler-Nicholson
Copyright © 2014, Off-Trail Publications
ISBN: 978-1-935031-22-2

OFF-TRAIL PUBLICATIONS
Elkhorn, California
offtrailpublications.com

Printed in the United States of America
First printing: January 2014
Second printing: June 2018

Copyrights

MAJOR MALCOLM WHEELER-NICHOLSON
(1890-1965)
Portrait by Howard Cruse

CONTENTS

Getting to Know the Major
by Nicky Wheeler-Nicholson

ALTHOUGH I NEVER MET MY GRANDFATHER, Major Malcolm Wheeler-Nicholson, I heard the tales of his exploits from my mother. Before she and my father divorced, she lived with my grandparents, her in-laws, in Great Neck, New York, as a young woman working for the United Nations. As a child, I understood that my grandfather was a writer and had something to do with Superman but that he somehow "lost" the comic book company he founded. As an adult, I heard more detailed stories about his adventurous life from my father and his siblings, my three aunts and uncle.

I learned from my family that my grandfather wrote popular fiction *and* serious books on military strategy. Most everyone in the family had copies of his nonfiction work but no one seemed to know the titles of his fiction, and they were dismissed as being somewhat inferior. The references to him in comic book histories also dismissed his contributions to that medium and were contrary to the family stories of his involvement with Superman. I became intrigued and set forth on what has become a fifteen-year odyssey to discover the true facts of Malcolm Wheeler-Nicholson's life.

During my odyssey, I've searched through library archives, scrolled through old newspapers on microfilm, and studied old legal documents. After reading books of comic book history and meeting with scholars of topics from comics to military history, I have a pretty good grasp of the scope of my grandfather's life. The best part of the search has been traveling to many of the places that figured in his life in the US, as well as England and France, and hearing the stories from people who knew him well. It turns out that much of my grandfather's life story—what some historians and colleagues have dismissed as bravado or fiction—is not only true but even more adventurous and compelling than anyone knew!

However, facts, photographs, letters and even the personal reminiscences of my family did not quite give me a sense of the man. It was only when I discovered my grandfather's adventure fiction that I felt I was becoming acquainted with him. Like any good writer his "voice" comes through.

The first story I read was "The Aristocrat of the Badlands," a novelette published in the December 1948 issue of *Popular Western*, a pulp magazine with a colorful, eye-catching cover. I promptly became obsessed with the pulps, where the vast majority of Malcolm Wheeler-Nicholson's stories appeared. I joined fellow collectors in the thrill of the hunt for the now-scarce magazines, discovering more of my grandfather's stories, picking up glimpses into his amazing life.

These popular magazines were called pulps because of the cheap pulpwood paper upon which they were printed. In their era, the first half of the twentieth century, they drew potential readers to the newsstands with striking, even beautiful, covers. They published popular fiction and nothing else. It was an incredible time for a writer, and readers. I love the amazing variety of genres found in the pulps—westerns, detective stories, science fiction, and all kinds of adventure stories set in far-flung locations around the globe. The cheap paper has often been equated with a lesser form of literature, but many highly successful writers, like Dashiell Hammett and Edgar Rice Burroughs, flourished in the pulps. It is true that a lot of mediocre writing made it into the pulps—there were *a lot* of pages to fill—but the magazines had no rule against great storytelling. The pulps published all they could get their hands on, and the best stories in the best pulps were pretty great.

The Major, as he's commonly called, and the reasons why will be duly noted, published most of his best material in the late Twenties and early Thirties. During those years, he was a top name in the adventure pulps, appearing many times in *the* adventure pulp, aptly titled *Adventure*. Readers loved his realistic characters, his edgy, adult themes, and his exotic settings. Before he could write those convincing stories of adventure, though, he had to live a life of adventure. When he began to write fiction, he borrowed the settings from his own life. For this collection, we've organized his stories by setting, so that we follow the timeline of his real-life adventures through his stories.

Malcolm Wheeler-Nicholson was born in the mountains of East Tennessee on January 7, 1890, to a family of journalists and medical practitioners. His parents were Antoinette Wheeler and Lola Orlando Strahan. Although from a respected family of proud Scottish ancestors, Lola proved to be a disappointing husband and in 1900 the couple divorced in Portland, Oregon. In 1902, Antoinette married Englishman Thomas J.B. Nicholson. She was a suffragette, and out of those staunch principles, retained her maiden name, thus the family surname became Wheeler-Nicholson. Malcolm appreciated his Scottish heritage but considered Nicholson his true father.

The young Wheeler-Nicholson spent his teenage years in Portland, and on the family ranch in nearby Washington. Horsemanship ran in the family. His grandfather, Christopher Wheeler, a physician whom Malcolm revered, rode on horseback in the hills of Tennessee to make house calls. His mother Antoinette loved horses and rode well. So it was only natural that Malcolm became an excellent horseman himself.

Antoinette, a writer and journalist, was a strong influence upon his life and encouraged a military career. Malcolm attended Manlius Military Academy, near Syracuse, New York, where he demonstrated both his creative and adventurous sides. He was editor of the school paper, illustrated the yearbook and won awards for polo. He was called "Nick" and his fellow cadets remarked upon his adept social graces. After graduating with honors in 1911, he entered the US Army Cavalry, as a 2nd Lieutenant. He was stationed at Fort Meade, South Dakota, in 1912, and later at Fort Bliss, El Paso, Texas. The young officer served under "Black Jack" Pershing on the Texas-Mexico border chasing bandits and insurgents, not the least of which was Pancho Villa. He commanded Troop K of the famed African-American Buffalo Soldiers. The Texas-Mexico border became the first of his major settings, and forms the first part of this collection.

"Beelzebub the Bane" (*Adventure*, July 15, 1927) features protagonist Major Davies, who appears in many Wheeler-Nicholson stories and may be considered an alter ego. So far, I've found him in fifteen stories that cover the spectrum of Wheeler-Nicholson's army career. The story opens with a cinematic image of Fort Bliss, and a suggestion of the oppressive conditions, which we can take to be a specific memory of Nick's: "His eye roved over the bare mesa and out to where quivering heat waves distorted the outline of the distant hills, huge, angular masses of scarified rock, the slag and clinkers of some ancient volcanic blaze uprearing tortured pinnacles and twisted turrets to the pitiless sky." The Major often featured a horse or some feat of riding as an important element in his stories. Thus, Beelzebub turns out to be a horse, a particularly difficult horse. What comes through in the story is the Major's conviction for the high spiritual standards of military life, often taking the form of a criticism of leadership: "As a regiment they lacked that crackling ripple and vibrancy, that intangible whip and snap, which only comes from the hearts of the men. It can not be hammered into an organization; it has to come from within."

"Shavetail" (*Adventure*, September 15, 1930) borrows its title from the term given to newly commissioned army officers. The Major discussed the term in detail in a letter to *The Camp-Fire*, the column in *Adventure* where authors frequently discussed the facts and personal experiences motivating their stories. We include his remarks with the story.

"Shavetail" includes more of the Major's conviction for the customs of the military and his ideal of an officer and a gentleman: "In civil life you can get away with crude stuff: you can remain seated while you are talking with an older man or a woman standing; you can sit on your horse and talk to a woman or an older man standing on the ground; you can address an older man by his surname as one addresses a waiter or servant, omitting any title. You can do all those things and, in addition, pick your teeth in public, and no harm will be done except that you will be avoided by certain types of people all over the world. But when you are in Military or Naval service, or in the Merchant Marine, you can't show disrespect to your superior, because disrespect and discipline don't travel together." The Major also depicts the customs of the particular regiment in the story, which traces its roots to Scotland. Since Nick was a great lover of author Sir Walter Scott and his own Scottish heritage, it is not surprising to encounter these details. His descriptions of army and cavalry traditions, and clear details of how a large group of men and equipment is moved efficiently, add much to the reality of the story.

The action takes place on the Texas-Mexico border and dramatizes the troubles the Cavalry had with the Mexican bandit Orozco, a historical figure. During the Mexican Revolution men such as Orozco rose in influence, switching their allegiances depending upon who was in power. The real Orozco was killed in 1915 in a shootout with the Cavalry. Since Nick was stationed on the border at the time, it's likely this story was rooted in personal experience or knowledge.

Of note is this description: "He had, it seemed, all the contempt that a certain type of southwesterner has for the Mexican—a contempt very much undeserved, as the Mexican is a brave fighter; even the bandit type which infests the border is a hardy and courageous individual." This is an unusual passage for the pulps, which were themselves infested, with all manner of condescension to non-whites. Indeed, the Major was bucking the trend of the highly prejudiced American society of the time. It's a mark of his humanitarian instincts and further evidence of his thorough commitment to enlightened character.

In November 1915, Lieutenant Wheeler-Nicholson was sent to the Philippines to help quell the Moro uprising. While there, he excelled at polo. He also set records for machine-gun readiness with a group of men that he recruited from the worst of the Army's assemblage. He was promoted to 1st Lieutenant. The Philippines experience, though brief, was memorable enough to Nick that it became the second of his favorite fictional settings. The oppressive tropical heat and how officers handle their men under difficult conditions is a continuing theme in these stories. There is a hint of real-life events that may have been the catalyst for the problems that arose for Nick later in his Army career.

In the one Philippines story we've chosen, "The Colonel Who Drank Alone" (*The Popular Magazine*, June 30, 1930), the Major refers to the Muslim Moros as "Mohammedans"; in many respects, they bear an uncanny resemblance to today's suicidal Islamist fundamentalists: "These road builders of ours were at the mercy of countless *juramentados*, fanatic Mohammedan Moros who decide to perish in administering death to as many infidels as possible. They went to their fate deliberately, assured of an eternity in paradise, an eternity made doubly attractive by the delights of the Mohammedan heaven, which include a huge shade tree, a milk-white horse and a group of beautiful houris." A century later, conflict with the Moros continues to be an issue in the southern Philippines, giving this story a "some things never change" flavor.

"The Colonel Who Drank Alone" returns to an oft-repeated theme in the Major's military fiction, that of the man who has been wronged by his fellow officers and, like a true gentleman, responds with grace. The theme derives from a painful period in the Major's military career. In 1921, while back in the US, he complained bitterly against a promotion process that was forcing him out of the service; he claimed that it was principally based on a personal debt rather than his performance as an officer. He won that battle in August, under an order from President Warren G. Harding. On February 5, 1922, he wrote an open letter to Harding that appeared in the *New York Times*, which expanded his argument to a sweeping criticism of Army practices. The result was a court-martial, with the letter and other actions at issue. The highly-publicized trial was covered in newspapers from coast to coast. He was eventually cleared of all charges with the exception of the letter, which was deemed to have circumvented the chain of command. He resigned from the Army and by Christmas 1922, the Major was a civilian again. His discharge was ambiguous, neither honorable nor dishonorable, but it left him with no military benefits to care for a wife and two small children. These events, with their sour conclusion, left him searching for his next career, ultimately leading him to a life as a writer.

Prior to this momentous incident, his military career continued along its promising path. He was promoted to Captain in May 1917, shortly thereafter assigned to Military Intelligence, and sent to Asia as the US entered the World War. He visited China and Japan and subsequently went to Vladivostok as part of the American Expeditionary Force in Siberia. He was the liaison to the Japanese General Staff in Siberia. The Russian Revolution was underway, giving Nick firsthand experience in the ever-shifting alliances between the Cossacks, Bolsheviks and their foreign allies from China, Japan, England and elsewhere. He found himself up to his eyebrows in a very alien environment. Not surprisingly, it became the scene of many of his most vivid stories.

"The Tiger of the Ussuri" (*Adventure*, April 15, 1928) once again features Major Davies. He is at the mercy of the fragile balance of power between Cossacks, Bolsheviks and the supposed American allies, the Japanese and Chinese, a situation that made it hard to tell friend from foe. Siberia is an exceptionally exotic locale and the Major brings it to life with numerous colorful descriptions of the scenery, and the variety of humanity: "Russian peasants with shapeless bundles holding all their worldly goods; white clad

Koreans wearing their odd little hats, looking like miniatures of a silk top hat but woven of horsehair and showing the top knot wound up inside like some small caged animal. Chinese there were and Cossacks, fur hatted, blue and gold uniformed Cossacks of the Ussuri, Kalmikoff's men, each wearing a golden 'K' on his sleeve; one or two tall Cossacks of the Don, a Buddhist priest with his head shaven and wearing some sort of dull orange robe . . ." There is no doubt that passages like these were burned into Nick's memory before he revived them for the page.

The Cossack, Ataman Kalmikoff, who appears in the story was a historical figure, which raises the question, as with "Shavetail," of how much of the story was based on actual events and which of the characters were based on people Nick knew or had heard of.

Besides recurring human characters in his stories, Nick featured a horse named Peggy, often under the mastery of other heroes. She appears as Major Davies' steed here. "The Tiger of the Ussuri," in Wheeler-Nicholson fashion, highlights the critical role of horsemanship in military maneuvers of the era.

It is also worth noting that through all the characterizations and subplots, the Major conveys the complicated political situation in Siberia, contrasting the various political entities and their interests. And although Nick was quite taken with the horsemanship and battle strategy of the Cossacks, there are more than a few passages in his stories of Siberia in which he makes it clear that it is the peasant class who suffered under whoever was in power, the Czarist regime, the Cossacks or the Bolsheviks.

The Major's Siberia stories, with their colorful and unexpected detail, suggest a writer recalling vivid personal memories of a world he witnessed. In contrast, "The Czarina's Pearls" (a two-part serial in *Argosy*, July 19 & 26, 1930), stays in Russia but takes us outside the Major's experience and into the rarefied world of the Czar's palace in St. Petersburg, with a story featuring another historical character, the villainous Rasputin. Still, the Major managed to hook the story into his own experience, making the protagonist, the Lieutenant Prince Michael Doblestni, the nephew of an American cavalryman. With his uncle, the prince "spent many happy vacations, riding and marching along the Mexican border."

This is one of my favorites of the Major's tales; it has great characters, romance, mystery and intrigue, and a setting worthy of a Hollywood costume drama. In passages like this description of the beautiful Natalia and her jewelry, the Major reveals his romantic streak and appreciation for women: "The sheen of each pearl tinged with a faint glow of pink, like a lucent globe of solidified mist bathed in the warm rays of the setting sun. It seemed fitting that the beautiful rope of pearls should so sinuously adapt itself to the curves of her slender figure, glowing against the satin whiteness of neck and bosom, following the curved loveliness of her breast and dropping almost halfway to the tapering gracefulness of her dainty feet and ankles." It's obvious why this story ended up in the family-favorite pulp *Argosy*, rather than the all he-man pages of *Adventure*. The story combines action and romance, appealing to both genders. Prince Michael and Princess Natalia seem to me to be refined versions of the archetypal couples Nick and Nora Charles, of Hammett's Thin Man series, and the film couples played by Bogie and Bacall.

"The Dumb Bunny" (*Thrilling Adventures*, December 1932) is a short story with another view of the Siberian experience. There is no handsome hero, only a small, seemingly insignificant older man who is not even part of the official army. He merely represents the YMCA at a far post in Siberia. The Major used a favorite device in this story. Two soldiers of lower rank, who correspond to Rosencrantz and Guildenstern in Shakespeare's *Hamlet*, provide an important point of view; as they converse in the midst of menial duties, we see the problems that the officer in charge is blind to.

In June 1918, during the closing months of the war, Nick received his last commission, finally becoming the official Major we remember him as. In 1920, Major Wheeler-Nicholson was stationed in Western Europe. He rode with the US Cavalry on the Rhine, was attached to the American Embassy in London, and later continued his education at the *École Superieure de Guerre* at the Sorbonne, in Paris. While there, he fell in love with Elsa Bjorkbom, a beautiful, aristocratic Swede and a match for all his romantic ideals. He proposed to her at the top of the Eiffel Tower and they were married under the crossed swords of fellow officers at the Chapel of the Kaiser, Church of the Palace, Koblentz, Germany.

The Major was still attached to Military Intelligence in Europe. This led to the fourth of his favorite genres, the World War spy story. The pulps underwent a broad expansion into World War fiction following the popularity of Dell's *War Stories* in late 1926, thus giving the Major a home for stories that may not have qualified for *Adventure*. The compelling "Treason for Glory" (*War Stories*, April 1932) is a fine example of this phase of his career. It opens with a classic Wheeler-Nicholson signature moment which draws the reader into the setting: "To be sitting at the *Rat Morte* drinking champagne and listening to the throb and hum of violins was my lot that night. It doesn't seem a very noble lot when you figure that men were dying like flies in the trenches just a few hours' journey from Paris. But I was on duty nevertheless. As a matter of fact I had just come off a big case."

The final entry in our collection, "The Road Without Turning" (*Adventure*, May 1932), is one of the Major's finest stories, a second runner-up in the prestigious O'Henry Short Story Awards of 1932, and a favorite of mine. Another exciting spy story, it weighs the costs of war in surprising ways.

One of the central settings is the château of Sevrey-sur-Aisne, the home of Odette de Sevrey, the newlywed French wife of the German protagonist. The château was based upon the château at Vic sur Aisne in the French champagne region northeast of Paris, where Nick and Elsa lived for several years in the late 1920s. The setting would turn up in a number of the Major's stories.

In 1921, on the heels of fighting his potential discharge, the Major turned his experience into a military science text, *Modern Cavalry: Studies on Its Role in the Warfare of To-day with Notes on Training for War Service* (1922). His writing career had begun. Then proceeded the court-martial year of 1922. By the end of the year, the Major was left exploring his options. His forays into creative writing were tentative at first. His first known published fiction was a short, "The Wolves," that appeared in the slick *McClure's* (August 1924). The so-called slicks, printed on quality paper, paid more than the pulps and were more prestigious.

In 1926, the Major started a syndication service, selling comic-strip versions of classic literature to newspapers. The graphic depiction of works like *Treasure Island*, *The Three Musketeers* and *Ivanhoe* indicate the brewing ideas that would later appear in his comic books. The Major's new company fared poorly, and he was back at the drawing board. It was undoubtedly disappointing at the time, but the failure of the company led directly to the start of his pulp-writing career.

From 1927-34, he was a productive and popular author. And this is probably the period when he went from Major Nicholson to the sobriquet, "the Major." According to my family, he indeed carried himself with military bearing throughout his life. From all accounts he was very handsome and the epitome of a gentleman.

The Major entered the field at a great time. The pulps boomed—like a lot of other things—during the madcap Twenties. As the decade progressed, new titles came onto the market at an accelerating rate. The publishers needed writers and the money was great, well above what the average workingman was making. The Major was one of many attracted to the opportunities. He tends to be found in quality titles, *Adventure*, *Argosy* and *Battle Stories*. When the stock market crashed in 1929, however, the fortunes of pulp writers crashed with it. There were still dozens of pulps begging for copy, but the big bucks had fled the field. A writer could still make a living, but only if he or she was highly productive. And the Major wasn't one to crank out mediocre work; it's obvious from the stories collected here that he took pride in crafting quality work, the kind of prose you don't bang out of a smoking typewriter like the fabled million-word-a-year men of the Thirties. Still, as the Depression lingered, the Major found his work sinking into the lowest-paying commodity pulps like *Thrilling Adventures*. It had to be a blow to his pride—as well as his pocketbook. But, as with the failed syndicate, it laid the foundation for his next success, the one he is most remembered for.

In 1934, the Major founded a company to publish comics. With titles like *New Fun*, *Adventure Comics* and *Detective Comics*, the company was the first to publish comic books with new material, rather than newspaper strip reprints. He hired a young Walt Kelly, of "Pogo" fame; Bob Kane, creator of Batman; and, most significantly, Jerry Siegel and Joe Shuster, whose Superman would rule the world. Siegel said the pair never would have made it into comics without the Major's help. The Major's pulp roots were evident in the title of *Adventure Comics*; one of his editors, Lloyd Jacquet, recalled how the Major brought pulps like *Adventure* and *Argosy* into the offices as a formula for his young writers. In 1937, alas, financial difficulties led to Nick losing the company to two men of somewhat shady backgrounds. The company became known as DC Comics and, immediately after the Major was pushed out, Superman was launched. How this all went down is a tale for another day. . . . But it is fair to say that the Major invented the modern comic book.

In 1939, Nick returned to the pulps in earnest, publishing numerous stories through the Forties and early Fifties. Many of them were Westerns, a genre that it seemed readers could never get enough of, while the market for exotic adventure stories waned. Many of the Major's later stories were for the Thrilling group, who treated their writers with great loyalty—but didn't pay very well. His last known pulp story is "Rifles for the Apaches" (*Triple Western*, January 1956). He ended his career having made about 170 appearances in the pulps, a relatively modest count for the three-decade span from his first to last story.

During World War II, he returned to his military roots, expressing strong opinions on military matters in books like *Battle Shield of the Republic* (1940), *America Can Win* (1941) and *Are We Winning the Hard Way?* (1943), and articles that appeared in leading magazines like *Scribner's*, *Harper's* and *Look*.

He had one final interesting chapter to his adventurous life. In the early 1950s he taught himself chemistry and developed several industrial patents.

In 1965, Major Malcolm Wheeler-Nicholson died at the age of 75.

Searching for my grandfather through his stories has been a joy. So much of his true nature is revealed in the themes pursued, as well as the heroes and even minor characters he created. His voice shines forth especially through the words of his heroes, the challenges they face and how each meets danger and difficulty with courage and the desire to do what is right and good for a higher cause. They are not the superheroes of comic books but men who make mistakes and seek to redress wrongs.

The stories collected here are personal favorites of mine that my grandfather, the Major, wrote, representing some of his best work. I hope that you, the reader, will also get to know a little about the Major through these stories. It also is my desire that these stories will encourage readers to learn more about the pulps and, further, focus additional scholarly research into Malcolm Wheeler-Nicholson's life and creative work.

I'd like to thank Rob Preston for his help in obtaining scarce material used herein, and Howard Cruse for use of his beautiful drawing of the Major. I am especially grateful to John Locke for putting this volume together and for his knowledge of the pulp field.

For more information about the Major:
malcolmwheelernicholson.com
Facebook: Major Malcolm Wheeler-Nicholson

Authenticity and the Pulps
by John Locke

"THE PRINCIPAL AWARENESS INSTRUMENT that [film] publicists have at their disposal, obviously, is the public reputation of the film's stars. As part of their arrangement with the studios, the stars effectively allow the studios to use their reputations to publicize their films. To this end, the studios script 'back stories' that merge the stars' activities . . . with those of the characters they play in the films." Edward Jay Epstein made this observation in his 2005 analysis of the film business, *The Big Picture: Money and Power in Hollywood*, citing *Mission: Impossible II* (2000) as an example. "The strategy of Paramount's marketing campaign was to ineluctably link the star [Tom Cruise] to the title so that all the publicity [he] received in the months leading up to the release would remind people of the film. A back story was then scripted in which Cruise was seen to be indistinguishable from Ethan Hunt, the acrobatic hero he played, via the claim that he, and not a stunt double, had done the free falls, fire walks, motorcycle leaps, and other perilous stunts that Hunt did in the movie."

If one were to watch too many late-night interview shows, or let the remcon stop on *Entertainment Tonight*, or the E! channel, one might witness this phenomenon played out in many subtle ways. The gorgeous actress spent three weeks living in a filthy cardboard box to rehearse her role as a homeless person. The actor was never so sore and exhausted in his life as he was from bull-riding school.

We might speculate that it's the realism of film that makes this merging of actor with role so important. It contributes to the audience's ability to believe what's on the screen; it helps them forget that the world in the film is an illusion. We might therefore suppose that Hollywood invented this particular marketing technique which seems so modern in its craftiness.

But decades before, the pulp magazines had tread the same ground, by establishing a large fraternity of authors whose colorful and adventurous backgrounds lent their fiction credibility. The readers could imagine that the fictional heroes of the stories were these authors in thin disguise. This was in the Teens, Twenties and Thirties, the great era of pulp adventure. Perhaps the marketing men of the pulps had been inspired by that class of nineteenth century adventure writer who had walked the walk—or, in many cases, sailed the sail—seamen-turned-authors like Melville and Conrad. If there's a link connecting those authors to the adventure pulps, surely it's Jack London, America's bestselling author in the early years of the twentieth century. London had risked his life in waterfront bars, at sea, in the Klondike.

Adventure authors don't come any more authentic, or famous, and his readers knew he was the real deal. London seldom appeared in the pulps. By 1910, when *Adventure* came on the market, he was too expensive. He was getting big bucks for publishing his latest works in top magazines like *The Saturday Evening Post*. But his adventure stories would have been right at home in the pulps.

Adventure's editor, Arthur Sullivant Hoffman, is probably the person most responsible for establishing the standard of the authentic-adventurer-writer in the pulps. This status derives from the convincing nature of the fiction published by *Adventure*, and Hoffman's creation of *The Camp-Fire*, a column in which new members of "the writers' brigade" introduced themselves with brief autobiographies, with an emphasis on the experiences undergirding their stories. Contributors weren't required to have adventurous backgrounds—indeed, many fine storytellers built their fiction on a foundation of research—but readers appreciated that many of their favorite authors had been places and done things.

Returning to *Mission: Impossible II*, Epstein noted that Cruise had "at least six stunt doubles," and in fact did no stunts himself. Which only makes sense. The star is the linchpin of a multimillion-dollar production. The producers, and the production's insurers, can't afford to have the star playing basketball on his weekends, much less running across the top of a moving train. The illusion of the star's courage is enough.

This reminds us that authenticity is measured by degree, which turns out to be just as true for "the writers' brigade." For every *Adventure* author with real-life credentials, there were two or three others with questionable qualifications. One of magazine's most popular contributors was Arthur O. Friel, who wrote extremely evocative tales of the Amazon jungle. He'd never been there, though he had been the South American editor for the Associated Press. Readers assumed he was a jungle explorer, and neither he nor Hoffman disabused them of the notion. Other *Adventure* contributors were outright frauds, like Patrick and Terence Casey. Two young brothers, they passed themselves off as "Patrick Casey," a disarmingly modest man of the world. Hoffman described "him" in the September 1913 issue: "Seven years ago he shipped out of San Francisco, his native place, as a cabin-boy on 'a liner which shall be nameless, as I jumped the ship at Hongkong.' Then he traveled the South Seas and the Far East in general with a theatrical troupe. Then served under the Government at Manila. Then a year as quartermaster on the Borneo Limited Company's steamships that run between Kuching, Sarawak and Singapore." Wonderful, wonderful, but unfortunately all untrue—except for the San Francisco address. But the brothers could write. That was important. There were others who could write, too, and who were also less than they claimed to be, to one degree or another.

So far as we know, none of these authors were called out publicly for their variances with the truth. Like Tom Cruise's producers and directors, the publishers and editors of the pulps knew that the association of the creator with the romantic elements of the fiction was a big inducement to the customers. In Hoffman's case, he probably knew better than to ask questions.

By the late Twenties, when Major Malcolm Wheeler-Nicholson made his name as a writer, authentics and pseudo-authentics filled the pages of the action pulps. World War fiction exploded in popularity, spawning dozens of magazines devoted to the Western Front. A corresponding fascination with aviation, inspired by Lindbergh's 1927 Atlantic crossing, inspired a slew of aviation fiction pulps, most with World War settings. There were so many Lieutenants, Captains, and Majors writing for the pulps that, all combined, they could have formed a real "writers' brigade." Perhaps they all served in the war—millions of American men did. But they weren't all armed. An interesting case is prolific aviation pulpster, Eustace L. Adams. He served in the early years of the war, before US entry, as a volunteer ambulance driver on the Front. Back stateside, he joined the famed Lafayette Escadrille, American flyers serving under French command. However, he never returned to France. Instead he patrolled the Eastern seaboard from the air. When he became a writer he was forced into circumspection about his actual service, while his publishers gleefully promoted him as a combat aviator.

The question of authenticity did eventually come up for debate, but in regards to western writers. In the early Forties, the well-worn genre was in bad need of new inspiration, after thousands of generic stories had been published, written by hundreds of alleged westerners. In a letter to *The Author & Journalist* (May 1942), western author Nelson Nye wrote from his Double N Ranch in Tucson: "There are two kinds of Western stories. The authentic kind, written by men who have spent a great deal of time and energy absorbing the background, language, customs, peculiarities, appearance and traditions of a particular region. And the sort of tripe turned out in great profusion, speed and regularity by the New York school of blood and thunder pulpsters." These New Yorkers came to be known by several derisive names, "Manhattan Cowboys" and "Hudson Riverites," for instance—writers who had rarely ventured west of New Jersey. In the June 1942 *A&J*, another prolific western pulp writer, S. Omar Barker, claimed that Out West the term "cowboy" was fading from use because so many inauthentic stories and movies had robbed the word of its real meaning.

The implication of all this is that once we strip away all the fictional biographies—the half-truths, pretends, and maybes—we're left with a relatively small and elite group of adventure writers who had authentic and compelling experiences on which to ground their vivid fiction. Major Malcolm Wheeler-Nicholson was a member of this exclusive club. We won't recount the relationship of his life to his fiction, since Nicky Wheeler-Nicholson has done a terrific job of that in the previous introduction. We will say, however, that it's easy to imagine why the Major's personal tales might have been doubted later on—perhaps decades of marketing fakery had put every adventure pulp writer under a cloud. But now it's time to restore his status, as one of the genuine larger-than-life men of the pulps.

The Southwest Border

Beelzebub the Bane

THE SAD-FACED DRIVER BROUGHT THE CAR TO A STOP while still some distance from the group of buildings. He shifted his quid of tobacco.

" 'S's far as I kin take yeh." He indicated the boundary fence. "This here red-whiskered ol' colonel won't allow no ottermobiles in camp." He grunted disparagingly. "Says mules are good enough for him; that's rich, ain't it?" and he frowned, shaking his head at the idiosyncrasies of army colonels.

His one passenger climbed out wearily and brushed the white alkali dust from a blue suit that had all the dejected appearance of having been several days in a Pullman car. He looked a little disconsolately at the scene before him.

His eye roved over the bare mesa and out to where quivering heat waves distorted the outline of the distant hills, huge, angular masses of scarified rock, the slag and clinkers of some ancient volcanic blaze uprearing tortured pinnacles and twisted turrets to the pitiless sky.

A remorseless sun that must assuredly have melted the wax from the wings of Daedalus, hurled lances of searing heat at the cavalry cantonment before him, white-hot spears that pierced torn khaki canvas, dry pine boards and seething, stinking tar paper.

He could see men cowered in the half-open brown tents which stretched away in somnolent rows on the hard-baked soil. Farther out, drooping ranks of horses dozed despondently in the white alkali dust. Near at hand stood the slatternly cook-shacks like a procession of gaunt trollops, elbows akimbo. The only signs of life were visible outside the cook-shack doors where black, weaving swarms of flies, ceaselessly rising and falling, buzzed monotonously in constant motion, as if in some endless dance of death.

His eye rested curiously on these, then he reached down with a sigh and picked up his suitcases.

"I wonder what humorist named this place Fort Bliss?" he inquired gravely of the driver, whose dour features broke into an appreciative grin.

"You said it!" averred the man at the wheel. "You said a heap. Fort Bliss,

Illustration by Rockwell Kent

I never thought o' that before, Fort Bliss! What'd ya' know about that? That's a good one, that is, that's rich," and he disappeared, chuckling, in a cloud of dust.

"I seemed to have brought some sunshine into his drab life," the new arrival reflected gazing after the car, "but he's welcome to my share of all the sun in Texas," and he put down the heavy suitcases to mop the sweat off his face before resuming his progress toward the center of the cantonment.

One building stood out importantly from the row of nondescript huts. It was not only larger, but it boasted a tin megaphone which balanced precariously from a badly chewed post at its front.

The door hung askew on one hinge. He opened it by lifting it with both hands on the knob and carrying it inward. The room was curtained to keep out the heat, and in the semi-obscurity he made out several figures, all, strangely enough, squatted on the floor.

His eyes growing more accustomed to the dusk, he saw that they were soldiers, grouped in a tensely interested circle. There was a familiar flash and click and the clink of silver. Some one was chanting a refrain, steadily and intently.

"Eighter from Decatur, eighter from Decatur," the absorbed voice was repeating, "eighter from Decatur she is!" The voice rose exultantly and then the refrain changed. "Little bones so fine and true, you lak me and I lak you, and nobody ain't goin' to part us two—saying which I slides a long, slim, slimy, green dollar on the floor, and who fades me?"

Then the voice started its chant again, something this time about "little Jo" who figured in some manner with a nickel and a buffalo.

The newcomer watched for a space and then leaning forward tapped the nearest shoulder.

"Where can I find the commanding officer?"

An exceedingly annoyed face turned around, regarded him with hostility for a second, then became more kindly, said, "Right through that doorway, friend," and resumed the absorbed watching of the ivory cubes.

He grinned a little as he went toward the designated door.

"If this is headquarters, I'd hate to see hindquarters," he reflected.

Through the haze of tobacco smoke he made out the forms of many people filling the small office. His eyes sought and found the broad desk set four square with the room. Behind it was an exceedingly fat officer, his round face rising moonlike from an unbuttoned coat collar. The double silver bars of a captain twinkled from his fleshy shoulders and a long black cigar hung from his mouth. Other young officers and some sergeants were seated on chairs, lounging against the desk and leaning against the wall.

Every one looked comfortably at ease, blouses were unbuttoned, cigars, pipes and cigarets were sending up clouds of smoke. The gathering of officers and sergeants was marked by a pleasant informality, unusual in military circles. The man, standing unnoticed in the doorway, took in the scene, deeply interested.

"You're wrong there." One of the sergeants had taken his pipe from his mouth and was pointing it at the round-faced captain behind the desk. "You're all wrong there. You say the outfit ain't hoodooed; I say it don't make no difference whether it's hoodooed or not. The men all thinks it is—which is just as bad."

The sergeant's tone was a little impatient.

The man in the doorway regarded him curiously.

There was a chorus of assent as the sergeant finished speaking. The stout young captain at the desk cleared his throat importantly.

"Yep, I guess you're right at that. If a man thinks he's hoodooed he might as well be hoodooed and you can bet your bottom dollar on that"—his eyes grew troubled—"but it's sure funny how things have been pilin' up on this regiment."

Other voices broke in like a Greek chorus.

"What about the colonel getting kicked?"

"How about the general makin' us fire our whole record course over again?"

"Remember Montgomery's horse running away and breaking up regimental inspection and the crawling we got—"

"And the general telling us we don't look after our animals properly—"

"And Sergeant Anderson getting kicked just before brigade athletics and losing us the field meet?"

"On top of it all, we get this order to drill against the other regiment in a brigade competition. Fat chance we got o' winnin' any brigade competition and you can bet your last dollar on that," the voice of the heavy captain summed up.

Every one grew silent and thoughtful.

The man in the doorway took a step forward, thinking the argument was finished. But the sergeant took his pipe out of his mouth and used it to lend emphasis to his words.

"Colonel Jimmy gets kicked, don't he, and laid up just before regimental inspection? How does he get kicked? By that crazy sorrel mare. Why do we have to fire our whole record rifle course over again? That crazy sorrel mare runs amuck down the firing line and breaks up all the score-keepin' for the rapid fire, and they never do get 'em straight again—"

Other voices broke in—

"And she runs away with Montgomery and busts up regimental inspection and the general gives us ——"

"It's that blamed mare, that nobody can groom, that the general finds on the picket line and then we get —— about the terrible condition of our animals."

"That loco, sorrel mare kicked Sergeant Anderson the day before the games."

The sergeant waved his pipe emphatically.

"Take it from me, if that —— of a mare ain't a hoodoo, I'll take a back seat and shut up—and I don't mean maybe!"

"It sure looks queer," agreed the round-faced captain, "queer as ——!" He shook his head doubtfully. "But that won't help us any on this brigade competition. Anything I can do for you, fellow?" His voice barked in sudden unfriendly question and the stranger in the doorway saw the eyes of the room turned upon himself.

The sergeant, pipe in mouth, gazed at him incuriously for a fleeting second, then quietly knocking the ashes out of his pipe, rose quickly and buttoned up his blouse collar.

"Why, yes"—the man in the doorway stepped forward—"I'm looking for the commanding officer," he announced mildly.

There was something in his voice and in the set of his shoulders under the civilian coat that vaguely worried the second sergeant. He glanced questioningly at his friend with the pipe, saw the latter quietly effacing himself toward the door, and quickly followed suit.

"That's me, fellow, that's me," the fat officer shook in heavy jocularity. "I'm the senior officer around here and the commandingest commanding officer that ever was, and you can bet your bottom dollar on that. Anything I can do you for?" His small eyes twinkled around at the rest of the group, as if for approbation.

The two sergeants had now foregathered at the back of the room in rear of the stranger. They waited, curious, for the next word.

"I'm glad to know you, I'm sure," responded the mild-mannered man in the blue serge suit. "I'm Major Davies just reporting for duty—I seem to be assigned to this regiment."

There was a silence after these words, a silence broken only by the creaking of the door as it slowly opened and closed.

The fat, young captain puffed to his feet, his jocularity vanished, his face a blend of chagrin and amiability. The stranger, eyeing the broad bulk of the man remembered dimly some old saying about the heart of a cavalryman and the hips of a dairy-maid. Every one in the room had risen uncomfortably; collars were being buttoned.

"Well, well," beamed the heavy, young officer heartily, "well, well, Major, I'm right glad to welcome you to the good old 'Steenth." He pointed expansively to the other officers— "Meet some of the gang. This is Captain Montgomery, the regimental adjutant."

The major shook hands with a tall, lean-faced youngster who met his glance with a pair of gravely appraising eyes. The remainder of the officers left him with a confused impression of ill-at-ease, rather worried looking faces and awkward greetings. One by one they gradually withdrew, until only the fat young captain and the new arrival remained.

The captain looked a little red and warm; he wiped his forehead with a large bandanna that he drew from the capacious pocket of his gargantuan breeches, his bearing rather uneasy.

"I was jest holdin' a little meeting of some of the officers, Major, on account that the regiment is in wrong with brigade headquarters and—" The fat captain stopped uneasily, and then finding the newcomer's eyes boring gravely into his, he was forced to continue.

"Only this morning we got an order confining the whole regiment to camp—that's just a sample of the way they pick on us." The stout captain's face grew indignant.

"Yes?" queried the stranger politely. "What was the trouble?"

"No trouble at all." His words came with a rush. "Some busybody from the general's staff came snooping around the kitchens and turned in a rotten report."

There flashed through the stranger's memory a vision of weaving, black swarms of flies, ceaselessly rising and falling, outside the cook-shack doors, as if in some endless dance of death.

"I thought Colonel Jameson was in command here?" queried the newcomer.

"He's away for a few days." The bulky youth waved a sweeping hand, spoke smoothly enough, but his eyes flickered as he spoke. "He's out inspecting the border patrols, down towards Ysleta, and won't be back for two or three days, I think."

The new major regarded him, gravely wondering just why he should go to such elaborate pains to lie about the colonel's absence.

The fat captain was distinctly uncomfortable. If only the new arrival would say something, instead of looking through him so calmly.

He went on rather desperately, wiping his forehead with the big bandanna, feeling that he had to make conversation.

"Things ain't so good around here," he confided. "Everything's been goin' wrong lately—the regiment thinks it's been hoodooed." He laughed deprecatingly, but not very convincingly, his eyes watchful.

"You know, Major, we drew a wild sorrel mare from the Remount, and ever since she's been with the regiment——'s been bustin' loose. The soldiers call her Beelzebub." He chuckled again, his eyes still uneasy. "Everybody hates her because she kicked Colonel Jimmy—we call him that, you know—Colonel Jameson—the boys are all crazy about him—" he volunteered, and stopped, his small eyes searching the major's face.

"The boys?" The major looked slightly puzzled. "You mean the men or the officers?"

"I mean both. This outfit's like one big family, that's what Colonel Jim—Colonel Jameson always says, just like one big family," and the major noticed a faint flare of belligerency in his small, close-set eyes.

"Very nice, I'm sure," commented the new arrival, politely. "Are there any other field officers with the regiment?"

"No, sir, you are the first in a long time. We've only had one major before," the stout youth volunteered, "and he didn't last long, somehow. I don't think he got along with the regiment very well and the colonel had him transferred."

The stout officer looked very placid, his eyes fixed somewhere at a point above the major's head.

"Yes?" The newcomer's voice was expressionless. "You must have a highly individualistic organization here."

The round face of the captain looked faintly puzzled.

"Y-es," he agreed, uncertainly, then with an air of friendly confidence, "You know the colonel is awfully particular about the old 'Steenth Cavalry. He was born and raised in it. He won't let anybody monkey with it. He told me before he left the other day not to make any changes and he swore he'd eternally hamstring any one that tried to meddle with the regiment—he's funny that way—I'm just passin' this on to you so's you won't get in Dutch." The captain fairly oozed good will.

"Very kind of you, I'm sure. How about this brigade competition I heard you talking about? When does it come off?"

The face of the young man fell despondently.

"We jest got a couple o' weeks to get ready for it. Not a chance in the world gettin' ready in that time, and you can bet your last bottom dollar on that!"

A few minutes later the newly joined major was straightening out his one-room shack, unpacking boots and uniforms, when Montgomery, the lean-faced regimental adjutant, dropped in to pay his respects.

After some polite nothings he cleared his throat rather nervously.

"Major"—his eyes were quite serious—"this brigade competition is kind of a special benefit performance for the 'Steenth."

"Yes?" He raised his eyebrows. "I gathered as much from the portly captain's words."

"Oh, him!" And Montgomery looked disgusted. "But the fact is that

Colonel Jameson is in wrong with brigade headquarters. I've heard on pretty good authority that if the regiment falls down on this competition they'll take the 'Steenth away from him."

"What's the big idea?"

"New brigadier-general anxious to make a reputation." Montgomery shrugged his shoulders.

"What have they against the colonel, particularly?"

Montgomery looked moodily at his boot tips—

"Well, he's getting old and"—he dragged the words out unwillingly—"I'm afraid he's losing his grip a little. You see he's only got another two months before he retires for age. And it would break his heart to lose his regiment before he retires."

The major said nothing for a space, busied himself taking out the boot-trees and flexing the supple leather of the new boots. Raising his head finally, he remarked—

"Seems kind of a pity they can't let him alone for that short time."

Montgomery looked up suddenly, studying the face of the new major, then his eyes lighted up.

"It does sort of seem so, doesn't it?" he offered and thereafter departed.

The major resumed his unpacking, whistling thoughtfully to himself as he worked.

Down on B Troop picket lines, that afternoon, old First Sergeant Henderson marched slowly around his men and horses, listening to the dull knock of currycombs against brushes as the troop sweated through stables.

"Miller!" He turned to the stable sergeant. "That young fellow will have to be some pumpkins to pull this outfit outa the mud before brigade competition." The battle-scarred old top sergeant was no optimist at the best and he looked especially pessimistic under the flare of the afternoon sun.

"Ye-ah, but this baby's sure cast his milk teeth. He don't say much. You ought to seen his face when that fat young misfit was tryin' to throw the bull into him." Miller chuckled. Then, after peering off to the end of the row of men and horses, he said, "but here he comes now; he ain't losin' much time gettin' on the job. Betcha a dollar to a hole in the doughnut he roars about no officers bein' at stables—"

Sergeant Miller carefully knocked the ashes out of his pipe, put it in his pocket and straightened up to attention.

The grizzled first sergeant received a quick impression of trim neatness, of a blouse that flared to the right degree, of breeches that fitted snugly below the knee, of good leather well polished, and the little flicker of color from a row of ribbons.

"I'm Major Davies," announced the newcomer, returning the salutes, then quietly putting out his hand to Sergeant Henderson who shook hands with much dignity. "Any officers on duty with your troop, Sergeant?"

"Yes, sir, Captain Stone and Lieutenant Smithers."

"Do officers in this regiment attend stables?"

The old sergeant stared straight to the front.

"Well, sir, sometimes they do and sometimes they don't," he answered judiciously.

"I see," and he turned to the stable sergeant. "Seems to me I've seen you somewhere before—oh, yes, at headquarters. You smoke a pipe, don't you?"

Sergeant Miller looked a little uncomfortable.

Then back to the grizzled first sergeant.

"Glad to have met you, Sergeant; it's good to see an old-timer again." And with a nod and a smile he was gone.

He was barely out of earshot before Sergeant Henderson raised a raucous voice that boomed to the length of the picket line and brought the heads of both men and horses up with a jerk.

"Snap into it, you triple-dashed Siwashes, you been gettin' away with murder around here long enough. Get some elbow grease into that groomin'!" There was something almost joyous in the ring of his voice.

Up in the one-room adobe building, the only cool spot in camp, that acted as mess and club for the officers, the fat young captain was holding forth to a listening group.

"And believe me, I think I gave him the right steer. No sense lettin' a fellow like that come in here with his trick uniform and a chestful of ribbons and run hog wild. Might as well let him see where he gets off at the start. First thing you know he'll be rampagin' around here like he owned the regiment. If he starts any funny business like that I'll spill a flea in Colonel Jimmy's ear and you can bet your bottom dollar on that!"

Montgomery's lean face appeared in the doorway.

"The major directs all officers to report to their troops immediately and remain with the men until recall from stables," he announced and, swinging on his heel, he departed, leaving behind him a crowd of surprised and sullen young officers who nevertheless prepared to obey.

The sentiments of most of them were well echoed by the young captain with the chubby figure.

"He's got one —— of a nerve, blowing in here all dressed up like a Christmas tree with decorations from France, and riding —— out of a bunch that have sweated down here on the border through the whole of the war. Wait till Colonel Jimmy hears of this," he threatened.

• • •

The tall spare figure of Montgomery rejoined the major and they watched the grooming of the headquarters troop animals.

"It does my heart good to see these birds made to snap into it," grinned the adjutant; then his face grew serious. "They're not a bad bunch at heart, they've just run wild and put it all over Colonel Jameson. The colonel forgets that most of them are kids and he treats them like they're grown up, trained, professional officers."

Montgomery suddenly stiffened. He was looking off towards the road where a cloud of dust was growing rapidly nearer.

"Here comes trouble. Colonel Jameson has been on a little party. Don't mind anything he says to you," Montgomery spoke swiftly, and then snapped up to salute as a buckboard drove up and stopped with a flourish in a slowly settling cloud of white dust.

Out of the murk appeared the head and shoulders of a towering figure, a form proportioned like some ancient Viking, a huge red-bearded, rosy-cheeked, old man, his hairy chest showing through a half buttoned, olive drab shirt. Beside him sat the fat young captain, a look of unctuous satisfaction on his face.

Major Davies felt a stare from hard and hostile eyes, as the old man peered at him from under bushy, red eyebrows.

"What the —— do you mean, Major?" the old man suddenly roared at him. "What the —— do you mean by giving orders around my regiment?"

The major saluted and stood stiffly at attention.

"I seemed to be the only field officer present, Colonel, and I naturally thought the officers were neglecting their plain duty to be with their men, sweating out here in the sun."

The old man glared at him suspiciously, pulling at his red beard.

"You sure you haven't been sent down here by brigade headquarters to make trouble?" he asked, and there was a hunted look in the old fellow's eyes that was rather pathetic.

"No, Colonel, I haven't even reported my arrival to brigade headquarters yet—and I haven't any desire to be a troublemaker."

The old man grumbled in his beard for a little; then, frowning deeply, he rumbled out—

"You're right, Major, these young fellows ought to be at stables with their men, glad you checked up on them."

He signalled to the driver to move on. The buckboard disappeared in a cloud of dust. The cloud halted in a short space and then returned, the old man leaning from the seat.

"Major," he growled, "you'll have to accept the apologies of an old man who's been so bedeviled that he's afraid of every new face he sees around camp." And he drove away again, leaving a faint odor of whisky in the air.

The major returned thoughtfully to his watch of the headquarters troop. Montgomery said nothing for the space of five minutes, then—

"He's really an old prince, Major, but —— that fat chunk of mud with him!"

"Where does the fat boy get his drag?"

"Fat boy has a sister, good cook, comfortable little house near the post. Colonel lives with them and gets all his dope at the dinner table—bad combination," Montgomery grunted.

"I see." There was a silence for a time; then the major said thoughtfully, "But we've got to win the brigade competition and we haven't much time to get ready for it."

"Yes, and the regiment is firmly convinced that they can't win anything because they think they're hoodooed by a wild-eyed sorrel mare," Montgomery grumbled.

"Where is this destroying angel? Let's have a look at her." They quickened their pace until they reached the B Troop picket line again.

The stable sergeant saluted.

"Yes, sir, she's down here at the end of the line—she's sure a bad one—kicked the colonel, busted up regimental formations, got us in wrong with the general. She's a sure enough hoodoo if there ever was one. The men calls her Beelzebub, sir."

He pointed out a golden sorrel mare who snorted at them as she leaped to the end of her halter rope. The major swept his glance over her silken muzzle, her flat, slim legs and dainty hoofs, her depth of chest and the perfect curve of croup and flank, and turned an appreciative eye to find Sergeant Henderson watching him.

"She's all horse."

His eyes gleamed with the beauty of her and Sergeant Henderson nodded slow approval, but the stable sergeant looked doubtful.

"Ye-es, sir," he agreed dubiously, scratching his head, then added, "What ain't nine-tenths ——. Nobody will ride her any more. She's put about six people in the hospital, already. Yes, sir, she's a first class, A Number One hoodoo, if there ever was one!"

Sergeant Henderson looked at him, frowning, and grunted. The major caught the look.

"She's either a first class hoodoo or she has an A Number One bluff on everybody— What do you think, Sergeant Henderson? Hasn't any one in the regiment ridden her?"

The old sergeant looked a little uncomfortable.

"Why, sir, Captain Montgomery here tried but she got him."

"She put me on dismounted duty for three weeks," Montgomery admitted, a little shamefaced.

"And no other officer has even tried to ride her?" the major questioned remorselessly.

Sergeant Henderson gazed straight ahead, his eyes quite expressionless. Montgomery shook his head.

"Hum," commented the major, and studied the mare again. "I wonder if a little harsh treatment and some good, hard work wouldn't make a first class cavalry charger of her?" he queried half to himself, then looking straight into Sergeant Henderson's eyes, he remarked, "Lots of things would be better for a little harsh treatment and some hard work, eh, Sergeant?"

Sergeant Henderson gazed at him soberly, then with a nod—

"Yes, sir," he answered slowly. "Most anything needs some harsh treatment and some hard work once in a while."

The two officers had disappeared behind the next picket line.

"That new major must think he's —— on wheels if he thinks he can make anything outa that she ——," said the stable sergeant, while he shook his head and refilled his pipe.

Sergeant Henderson looked thoughtful a moment, then—

"—— on wheels is goin' to bust loose around this place or I miss my guess—and I hope he can put it over," he growled to himself, paying no attention to the stable sergeant's puzzled look.

Montgomery strode along silently beside the major until they came to the end of the squadron.

"Are you going to tackle that mare, Major?" he inquired hopefully, at last.

"It sort of looks like I'm elected, doesn't it?"—and he looked sidewise at Montgomery. "The mare doesn't look so difficult, because on that job I won't have to fight off interference."

Montgomery looked up quickly and saw the major's eyes.

"I get you," he nodded, then grew thoughtful. "It might be easier to ride off interference than you think, Major," he announced after a moment. "It's only a short while until the brigade competition comes off—yes, sir, I may be able to keep interference away for that time—if my constitution will stand the strain."

Again there was silence for a space then the major cleared his throat.

"If it—ah—should be necessary to, ah—use up any stimulants I think I could lay hands on several bottles of old bourbon."

Montgomery chuckled and said nothing.

"And you can bet your last dollar on that," continued the major gravely.

That evening the old colonel came in to dinner at the officers' mess.

"Major," he growled, staring belligerently from under bushy eyebrows, "Captain Montgomery tells me that our outpost at Fort Hancock is in bad shape and needs inspection. I'll be gone a few days. I'm taking Montgomery with me. Keep things going until I get back and don't let that —— brigade headquarters bunch walk off with the whole regiment while I'm gone, understand?"

The old man glared at him while he pulled at the two ends of his great, red beard; then, leaning closer, in a voice meant to be a whisper although it rumbled all over the room:

"I think those hounds at brigade headquarters are trying to make trouble for me and the good old 'Steenth; don't let 'em put anything over on you, Major. I trust you, young fellow." And in the old fellow's eyes was a hunted, worried look that went through the younger man like a knife.

"You can count on me to do my best, Colonel," he said soberly.

The old man, after studying him for a moment, looked relieved and, raising his head, roared out to the others—

"I want you young fellows to remember that first, last and all the time you belong to the old 'Steenth, the finest regiment in the army, and I want you to work just as hard for Major Davies here while I'm gone as you would for me," whereat they all cheered lustily and Montgomery suddenly buried his face in a paper napkin and the major forbore to look at him.

That night the harsh outlines of the camp were softened in the molten silver of the Texas moon. Sergeant Henderson, as was his custom, walked down to have a look at his horses before turning in. He stepped out of the shadow of the feed shack, then paused, and as quickly stepped back again unseen. He stared curiously at an erect figure walking down the picket line, a light Saumur saddle on its shoulder, a bridle and quirt in its hand.

Watching carefully he nodded to himself as the figure approached the sorrel mare, snorting there in the moonlight. Sergeant Henderson looked anxious as the mare reared and plunged, then nodded approval as the man steadily approached her and grasped her halter.

The mare quieted down. He heard a soothing voice and then saw the man stroking her gently. She snorted at intervals, but stood quietly while the man's hand stole up to her head and stroked her ears and continued on down, patting her neck and withers.

"It's a gift," Sergeant Henderson said to himself. "It's a gift, also it's guts, and a horse knows it."

The sergeant leaned forward as the man reached quietly for the saddle, and the old man smiled as the saddle was skillfully slid up on to the mare's back, after letting her smell of it. It took ten minutes before the cinch buckles were fastened, and the sergeant found himself sighing with relief when the mare was at last saddled.

Again he nodded approval as he observed the workmanlike way the man carried his bridle, its reins looped over his shoulder, the crown of the headstall in his right hand.

Then the old sergeant gasped. The mare had risen swiftly and lashed out her forefeet. He breathed a sigh of relief as the figure dodged nimbly and returned again, to soothe and stroke the excited animal. Minutes passed before the bit and bridoon were in place, the headstall was on, and the throat latch buckled.

"This is where the excitement begins."

The old sergeant found himself breathing hard as he saw the man unsnap the halter strap and back the mare away from the picket line. Then Sergeant Henderson straightened out; an admiring gasp escaped his lips. For the man had swiftly grasped the mare's nose in his left hand, had pulled her head around toward him with a powerful grip, and then, as she stood there, bent in a half-circle, he had leaped nimbly into the saddle.

The startled mare found her head released. In the second that she spent in shaking her irritated nose the rider had settled firmly into the saddle, knees and thighs and calves gripped firmly ready for her next move.

It was not long in coming. She stood trembling and immovable for a space.

"If she starts buck jumping in that light saddle," the sergeant breathed to himself, "he's a goner."

But she reared swiftly, instead, so that she stood high on her hind legs, trying to throw her rider over backward. The sergeant found himself suddenly breathing a sigh of relief, for the man had leaned forward from his perilous seat, had grasped the mare's nose again in a powerful grip and had twisted her head around so that she must perforce come to the ground again to retain her balance.

"Now look out!" The sergeant found himself getting excited. But before the mare had time to start any plunging the rider had brought his quirt down with one cracking blow across her flanks. With one idea and one only, to get away from that smarting pain, she leaped forward, and when she alighted she was running with the speed of the wind.

"The boy knows his stuff!" whispered the old man to himself, as horse and rider grew smaller in the distance. "He's puttin' out through the heavy sand." The sergeant sat himself down on a convenient bale of timothy hay and waited.

It must have been half an hour before his patience was rewarded, and he saw horse and rider return slowly, the mare breathing hard. Then he saw the rider dismount and mount, carelessly and easily, saw him stroke her sides and flanks, saw him lift up her feet while the mare took it all patiently and with an attitude of complete resignation. The sergeant waited until the lone figure had unsaddled and unbridled the mare and had walked away toward the officers' row, before he approached the still panting animal. She greeted him by coming suddenly to life and lashing out with both heels with all of her accustomed deviltry.

"Oho," said Sergeant Henderson, "you've still got a kick left have you? But wait till that young fellow gets through with you and you'll be waitin' on table and likin' it." And he departed, grinning cheerfully and confidently to himself.

Up in the officers' mess, the fat young captain, who had preempted the choicest chair by virtue of his seniority, was again holding forth.

"What's his idea anyway?" he was asking in an aggrieved tone. "Askin' everybody whether they tried to ride that wild-eyed mare. I says to him how the doctor had told me to stay on dismounted duty on account o' that operation I had last year and he says to me, 'you're to be congratulated that your misfortunes have not succeeded in crushing you yet,' raisin' his eyebrows as he talks—an' he asked you too, and you?" He received confirming nods from every one present. "Why, if he's so curious about our ridin' that mare, why don't he ride her himself? He's afraid to—and you can bet your last bottom dollar on that!"

"Some day, Captain, somebody's going to make you raise that dollar you're always anteing so recklessly."

The stout young captain heaved his bulk out of the chair, red-faced and embarrassed, with the major smiling at him from the doorway.

But there was no time for apologies.

For there was a loud blare of a trumpet from near headquarters, a continuing high, keen, shrill, alarming note, repeated over and over again, that brought every one up, all standing, wild surmise written on every face. From all over the camp other trumpets took up the clamor and there was a sudden sound of running and shouting.

"Fire call?" queried the fat young captain nervously.

"Fire call, ——!" snorted a lieutenant, breaking for the door, a lieutenant who as sergeant had spent many weary months in Jolo. "That's call to arms!"

Men were tumbling out of tents, buckling on belts and pistols, dragging their rifles after them. The air was full of a confused babble of shouts and commands. The young officers were running around busily interfering with the sergeants, and the sergeants, as is the habit of irritated sergeants, were taking it out on the privates. At last, after what seemed an interminable time, the wavering lines of men were standing in rank in the troop streets.

The major stood quietly by headquarters, a stop watch in his hand, an extremely bored look on his face.

After calling for reports he made a hasty inspection, then ordered the men dismissed, and sent for all officers.

"Very creditable performance," he greeted, his voice quite pleasant. "It took thirty-five minutes for the regiment to get ready to repel an attack. It took only ten minutes for Villa to ride through and shoot up that American army camp at Columbus, New Mexico. It is unnecessary to state that this leaves rather long odds in favor of Villa. The crowning touch to your smooth, orderly and silent mobilization I have yet to compliment you upon. It seems that only one troop in the regiment thought of breaking out ammunition and issuing it—I suppose the rest of you mean to throw rocks at the enemy? The next time you hear the trumpets play that little tune you heard a while back, kindly forget the cave-man stuff and remember that rocks as weapons have been out for some time. That's all, gentlemen. Good night."

He turned away.

There was something in the way he pronounced, "Good night," that made them quite uncomfortable.

It was rather a subdued group of officers who assembled for breakfast next morning. Even the fat captain, who blew in for a morning cigar, had nothing to say.

But they were to have no peace. Officers' call blew after breakfast.

"Gentlemen," greeted the major, and they noticed with sinking hearts that he had a stop watch in his hand, "we are assuming that a large band of Mexican bandits have attacked El Paso, and are withdrawing. We are ordered to pursue them into Mexico and capture or kill them. The regiment will march as quickly as possible, fully equipped, to keep the field for five days. You will report when your organizations are ready for inspection. My stop watch starts now."

But, as some one remarked later, what was needed was not a stop watch, but an alarm clock. It took that regiment of cavalry nearly six hours before the last troop moved up on line, saddles packed, men equipped and trains loaded.

Then the major made a quick but very thorough inspection of the massed squadrons, after ordering tents pitched. The inspection showed that the regiment could not have kept the field for a single day as a whole. It was short of everything from rations to ammunition, from spare horseshoes to range finders.

And the major went to great pains to point out, to a very sheepish group of officers, just what sort of a half-ready mob the regiment was. He intimated that a self-respecting Boy Scout troop would laugh them to scorn.

"And," he concluded, "it isn't as though there weren't any good sergeants in the regiment; the outfit is full of old-timers who'd show you how to hold down your jobs, if you'd let them—"

A wide-eyed clerk at headquarters, who had kept one ear glued assiduously to the office door, told Sergeant Henderson of the meeting,

"Yeh?" The old man showed no surprize. "He's puttin' them through the heavy sand now a while," he said to himself, and went on to his orderly room where his rather anxious-eyed young captain was awaiting him with a lot of questions.

The following day saw them subjected to a pitiless repetition of the same program with the added hardship of a regimental drill thrown in for good measure.

The regimental drill was a heart breaking spectacle. At the walk the lines wavered like reeds in the wind. At the trot, loose hung troops and squadrons milled around despondently; at the gallop there were ragged frayed ends and tags of troops all over the drill ground and the air was filled with enough shouting and excited clamor to have maneuvered a division at war strength.

The officers looked so woebegone that the major hadn't the heart to say much to them. After comparing them unfavorably to Coxie's army at its worst, he dismissed them.

On the following evening a group of spent and weary officers gathered in the club. The fat young captain lay sprawled out in a deep wicker chair.

"Why don't that bird start drilling us by moonlight; seems a shame to waste these fine evenings," he piped up wearily. "I wish to —— that Colonel Jimmy would come back. He'd put a stop to this foolishness and you can bet—and that's the truth," he corrected hastily.

"Well," another voice admitted, "he didn't crawl our frames today, anyway. Told me today that my troop began faintly to remind him of something like a troop of cavalry. I don't think he's going to be so bad when we get going."

"And he tells me that he detects symptoms of real, honest-to-God soldierin' in my troop. 'Foster them,' he says and cocks a wise eye and grins at me. I think he's goin' to be a pretty good scout if he sees we mean business," spoke up another, and there was no dispute from any one present.

Meanwhile the major was sailing down the wings of the wind on the light, floating gallop of the sorrel mare, somewhere out on the moonlit mesa. He took her out every night, now, a thoroughly willing and anxious-to-be-good creature of infinite speed and dainty smoothness of gait. He worked her carefully, balancing her up so that she obeyed the slightest pressure of rein and heel. He had her turning on the forehand and the haunches, had her working "on two tracks" and trying her best to learn what the good cavalry charger should know. She was a beautifully sensitive creature; one could play on her, as a good violinist plays on a Stradivarius, and get the same quick, certain response.

By day she stood on the picket line, and would cheerfully lay back her ears and kick at any one else who approached. Sergeant Henderson was the only one who knew of her surrender and he kept his knowledge under his hat.

The regiment did not progress so fast. They were handicapped by the fixed conviction that they were hoodooed and that, however hard they worked, something would occur to make them lose the fruits of victory. Their work became mechanically better, they were beginning to acquire a certain rigid correctness, but as a regiment they lacked that crackling ripple and vibrancy, that intangible whip and snap, which only comes from the hearts of the men. It can not be hammered into an organization; it has to come from within.

The day of the brigade competition came. Orderlies from brigade headquarters were out early, setting up the blue flags that marked the reviewing limits. A procession of cars rolled out to the drills grounds and deposited the general and his staff. The two regiments were reviewed and inspected. The 'Steenth was directed to dismount and wait while the other cavalry regiment went through its drill.

The waiting 'Steenth watched it anxiously. The other outfit was not spectacular. It went through a variety of evolutions, in stolid correctness. It knew its work and did it with a certain machine-like precision that discouraged the 'Steenth, waiting in long lines of horses and dismounted men.

Major Davies studied the 'Steenth anxiously. They were dead on their feet, heavy, resigned, and his face grew worried.

The other regiment had completed its drill. An orderly mounted, up near the reviewing line, and started for the 'Steenth.

At that moment a man on the flank of the waiting regiment pointed out something, shielding his eyes in perplexity. Word passed swiftly down the lines, and men were craning their necks to see the strange sight.

The golden sorrel mare, her glossy skin gleaming like molten metal, was being led up, saddled and bridled, to the major.

The whole regiment watched, breathless, while he dismounted from the horse he had been riding. They grew round-eyed with wonder as he calmly approached the sorrel mare. Then a gasp went up as they saw the mare dance up to him nervously, whickering and nuzzling his arm. They scarcely believed their eyes when he leaped lightly into the saddle, while the mare stood docile.

There was no time for discussion. The major had signaled and they were standing to horse. Another signal and the thousand men swung into the saddles as one man, the scarlet guidons whipped free and the golden regimental standard flung into the breeze. The solid, massed ranks of the regiment stretched out before him, men sitting at attention and waiting, no movement disturbing the scene except the occasional tossing head of some fretful horse.

Suddenly officers' call blew. From their posts, in front of troops and squadrons and platoons, the officers came galloping, to converge on the silent figure sitting on the golden sorrel mare out in front. They drew up and saluted, their eyes amazedly watching the strangely quiet mare.

"Gentlemen," the major's voice rasped at them, "I am credibly informed that if the 'Steenth loses this competition Colonel Jameson will be immediately relieved from command. If you love the colonel as much as you say you do, you don't want to see him lose his regiment when he is so close to the end of his active service. Tell your men that they will lose the colonel if they fall down. Tell them that the hoodoo mare is no longer a hoodoo but a mascot. Tell them that we are going to win this competition in spite of —— and high water. Are you with me?"

A growl went up from the assembled officers.

"You're —— right, we're with you, Major." And they turned like one man and galloped back to their posts.

He watched them, saw each officer draw up before his men, saw the officers vehemently talking.

Sitting in front of that great mass, the major felt, rather than saw, a tremor go through the regiment. It seemed fairly to quiver, to tighten up as a fighter's muscles tighten before the final gong; it seemed to gather in on itself more compactly. From a sprawling mass of men and horses it became suddenly welded into one complete unit, a unit that suddenly was crouching and ready for action, every nerve and sinew taut.

Looking upon that quivering eagerness his heart rose within him. With a keen swish and a flicker of steel he drew his saber and a thousand sabers leaped from the scabbards, a sudden tossing wave of burnished silver. He signalled, and the trumpets blared forth a crash of music that sounded like an intolerant burst of proud laughter.

In swift obedience, the great mass of men and horses rolled forward like a wall, a sweeping wave of molten bronze, with the sun rippling and sparkling on bit and sword and spur. He signalled again, and the huge body quickened into a trot, the great line began to waver, and suddenly it divided into three squadrons, square masses of smoothly moving horsemen, each articulating easily into the regiment as a whole. Another signal, a quick beat downward of clenched hand, this signal, and men leaped swiftly to earth with their rifles, forming into long lines of footmen, who advanced, crouching and running in alternate sections, while the horses were galloped to the rear, in swaying columns.

Exultantly he waved them again, and the horses returned, the men mounted. With instant response they broke into the gallop. Then the major played on that great mass of flowing, smoothly coordinated elements as a master plays on an organ. He flicked his wrist and the long lines dissolved and reformed with bewildering rapidity; he raised his hand and they wheeled like swallows and went coursing up the field; he and the sorrel mare were everywhere while the long, heaving, shimmering lines of steel gleamed through vast clouds of dust.

The earth shook to the tread of thousands of iron-shod hoofs; there were sudden flashes of scarlet and gold through murky clouds as the great battle standards galloped into line; there was the heave and surge and thunder of vast movement. High above the shifting, hurrying mass, the trumpets, at his beck, rang out their bronze notes, calling stridently for order, commanding, exhorting, directing the sweep and flow of this vast mass, so that it moved like one great weapon, so that it was as responsive to his control as a rapier in the hands of a skilled duelist, so that it conformed to his will with all the flexibility and quick response of a Toledo blade.

And the earth-spurning little sorrel mare was everywhere at once. She floated like a cloud down the front of the regiment, brushed lightly through its galloping flanks, shot through narrow gaps between rapidly closing squadrons; tirelessly and swiftly, her gallop never faltered.

A faint dust-cloud on the horizon grew larger. It came rapidly up the road and debouched into the drill ground. As the wind carried away the white dust, one might have seen a buckboard drawn by straining mules. It drew up with a clatter behind the reviewing line where stood the general and his officers.

A sudden clamor of trumpets and the recall sounded.

Major Davies led the regiment, in line of masses, straight at the reviewing officer and brought them from a gallop to a sudden halt. The 'Steenth stood, men and horses, panting and wet with sweat. The major dismounted before the general and saluted.

"Will you please call your officers?" directed the white-mustached brigade commander. When they were all assembled he stepped forward a pace.

"Gentlemen"—he paused as if seeking words—"I want to tell you, that not only have you won the brigade competition, but that in doing it you have put up the most wonderful exhibition of cavalry drill it has been my fortune to see in thirty years of service."

There was a commotion at one side. Every one turned and saw a great red-bearded man peering proudly at the regiment, through bushy eyebrows. Then a steady, blue eye was turned on the general.

"Thank you, General." He tugged at the ends of his red beard, and cleared his throat importantly, then his voice boomed out, "Thank you, General. I appreciate your kind words. I have put in some hard work trying to make the old 'Steenth Cavalry the finest regiment in the army."

Looking beyond the old red-bearded colonel, Major Davies suddenly spied the lean face of Montgomery, his eyes bloodshot, his face pale, looking as if he had spent ten nights in a bar-room. Montgomery winked a solemn wink.

The officers pressed around the colonel; the general congratulated him; there were many felicitations. Major Davies stepped back, unnoticed, with the golden sorrel mare.

"Well, old girl"—and he rubbed her nose—"you did all the work, old lady, and the colonel gets all the credit. But you're young; it won't hurt you any. As a matter of fact you'll soon get used to it—that's just the old army game."

25c
in Canada
30 Cents

SEPTEMBER 15th

Adventure

Published Twice
A Month

SHAVETAIL

A Novelette by
Malcolm Wheeler-Nicholson

J. D. NEWSON · F. ST. MARS · CAPTAIN FREDERICK MOORE
HUGH PENDEXTER · ROBERT SIMPSON · BARRY SCOBEE

September 15, 1930
Cover art by Duncan McMillan

It was one of the most ticklish places on the border at that; nothing much but a low hill, an adobe ranch-house at the foot of it, and our camp to the east of that, facing the river. The Rio Grande was only six miles away from us and right across it was the Mexican village where Orozco was mobilizing his forces to take the field. He had plenty of men and horses, but few guns and cartridges; and that was where our trouble started.

I found out afterward that Orozco's outfit had us under observation constantly up to the time the big smash came. There was always a patrol of three or four men hidden up above us behind the crest of the hill. They would slide in at night, relieve the old outfit and stay hidden all the next day, watching us through their field-glasses. The horses that brought in the new bunch would carry the old relief away, and it was no trick at all for two or three

Shavetail

dismounted men to hide away up there among the cactus and rocks.

They laid their plans pretty carefully and, by watching us constantly, knew as much about the troop as we did. All they lacked, and the thing they waited for, was a favorable opportunity to jump us.

"A" Troop was the outfit. A Troop of the Nth—Captain Jo Merriman's troop. But he was away and I was in command, having for second this youngster Rollins. I'll tell you more about him later. . . .

Somehow there is always something to do in the cavalry, and at this time we were going through our instruction course at pistol practise, relieving the men on outpost and river guard every day to give them their required shooting.

First-Sergeant Henderson was my top kick, and ran things like clockwork. Pistol practise season is a pretty busy time in the cavalry—and especially at this time as the .45 automatics were comparatively new, and the pistol qualification course had been changed and was also new.

The pistol butts were below the camp and those Mexicans watching us

Illustration by V.E. Pyles

from the hillside must have credited us with perseverance, for we plugged away at it steadily for weeks. You remember the heavy composition board silhouette targets—olive brown, all life size, each one representing a human figure either prone, kneeling, standing or mounted on horseback. And believe me, that prone figure thing—the "baby" we called it—was a tough baby to hit, shooting from the back of a horse flashing by as hard as he could push.

From reveille to retreat there was always a bunch of troopers lined up at one end of the track. A whistle would blow and one of them would gallop down lickety split, his pistol banging away—five targets, five shots; and very often five misses when he arrived at the other end. The markers stepped across the track and called the shots:

"No. 1, a hit. No. 2, a miss. No. 3, a hit . . ."

Each man would put a small square paster over the shot hole as he called out. Then he would duck back to clear the way for the next hopeful. And every one aspired to the honor of wearing the small silvered badge with its two crossed pistols and the proud words "Pistol Expert" engraved upon it.

It went like that all day—*bang! bang! bang!* in strings of five shots, the calling of the markers, a silence and another string of shots with the sergeant keeping the tally of each man's hits in the book.

It is dangerous business and needs constant vigilance to avoid accidents. I was on the job every minute—having plenty to do with keeping my sector patrolled, watching out for Orozco's Red Flaggers and keeping the troop up to scratch. Had I known of those Mexicans up above us on the hill watching day and night, waiting to send word the instant we relaxed our vigilance, I would have been twice as worried. But I didn't find out about them until afterward—when it was too late.

As I said, there was another officer in the troop with me, this kid Rollins, but he was more of a burden than a help. He'd only joined up a short time previously while we were still at the fort, before the First Squadron was sent out on border patrol.

I can remember the first thing I ever heard him sound off.

"Sure is one tough old geezer sitting up there at headquarters," he said, his voice rasping unpleasantly—one of those flat, rather nasal voices, irritating to a sensitive ear.

It was the first remark he had made after the adjutant brought him in and introduced him. We were at dinner, all the bachelor officers of the Nth Cavalry, some twelve of us. He sat at the foot of the table, his place by right of being the newest joined shavetail. His baggage had not yet arrived and he was dressed in civilian clothes—exceedingly awful civilian clothes, reminiscent of the sartorial ideals of the pool hall and barber shop. His collar was one of those queer rubbery looking affairs, set off by an impertinent, ready made butterfly tie full of dyspeptic green and red dots.

Not only were his clothes in strong contrast to the cavalry blue and gold of the twelve lieutenants there at mess, but his face was of even greater contrast, its unhealthy pallor showing up strongly against the bronzed tan of the rest of them. There was something else it lacked, for compared to the lean strength of the others, it lacked definiteness; and while neither weak nor strong, it was like a blank page—with no lines on it.

His opening remark made every one bristle, including myself. The privilege of growling at the Old Man was not one to be taken lightly by a raw shavetail five minutes after his arrival.

Bull Manners looked up coldly.

"Whom do you mean, the colonel?" he asked, and his voice was as friendly as the whirr of a rattlesnake's tail.

"Yep," agreed the newcomer cheerfully. "He sure is a frosty old guy. I brought him a letter from my old man. Of course the old man isn't so much"—the youngster's manner became elaborately careless. "You see, my old man is governor of—" He mentioned one of the southwest states, waiting with an air of conscious self-importance to see the effect the announcement would have.

If he expected tears, cheers or loud laughter, he must have been disappointed, for the atmosphere around that table became absolutely frigid. He had pulled one of the worst bonehead plays possible for a newly joined shavetail. In the first place one did not talk about families in the Nth, that old regiment being blessed or afflicted with too many names made famous by the Revolutionary and Civil Wars, the sort of names which are indelibly treasured in the memories of all true Americans by having five-cent cigars called after them. This being the case, it naturally followed that every officer joining the Nth was accepted on his own merits, and no one gave a royal whoop whether a newcomer was the scion of a short line of generals or a long line of Kansas dirt farmers.

"Yeh?" replied Bull Manners after a moment. "Where does he work?"

"Why, in the governor's mansion, of course," the newcomer answered. "As joints go it isn't so bad—and I've seen a few joints in my time." Again the youngster was elaborately careless, as one who could tell all about living conditions in marble halls if he were so minded.

The glacial frost around the table intensified, but did this newly joined pup—Rollins, his name was—feel it? He did not.

"So your father is governor of a whole state!" It was Gramp Jackson who spoke up, his tone full of admiration and a sort of awe. "How wondehful that must be!" he breathed; then, his voice full of solicitude, "But it must be very hard for you to come to this regiment and live this—ah—simple life after all that luxury!"

"Oh, I'll get used to it, I suppose." Rollins dismissed this with a careless shrug of his shoulders. "The only thing, it's going to be hard for me to be patient when I see a bunch of soldiers trying to shoot and ride. You see where I come from," he explained tactfully, "we're brought up in the saddle and play with shootin' irons from childhood."

I could see a flash go around the table; we nodded. This was going to be good!

Sing, our old Chino butler, was bringing in coffee and liqueurs. Cigars and cigarets were being lighted up. Gramp lazily rolled a cigaret and lighted it.

"And you really ride those terrible bucking hosses?" he asked respectfully of Gramp, who was a graduate of the Mounted Service School where they sit outlaws in flat saddles, and where one of the milder daily stunts is to ride horses over four-foot jumps without reins or stirrups.

"Oh, sure," returned the youngster easily. "That's child's play. Sometimes you get a mean one. Down to my father's ranch the cowpunchers used to save the worst ones up for me when I came home from school."

Every one looked deeply impressed. Bull Manners cleared his throat and spoke up—

"Are you one of those quick draw artists with the six-gun?" he asked guilelessly.

"Never failed to get my man yet!"

Rollins announced this calmly. No one smiled. Chairs were hitched closer to the table. The pack was in full cry.

"Do you find the revolver better than the pistol?" asked Bull respectfully.

Every one of us at that table could wear the little silvered badge with its crossed pistols, which meant surviving a grueling course of firing dismounted at quickly disappearing targets, and firing from a horse's back at the halt, walk, gallop and run. Bull Manners in addition held the gold medal for the National Shoot at Camp Perry, won against the whole Army, Navy and Marine Corps.

"The automatic, you mean? It isn't worth a damn. Give me the good old .38 revolver every time," the young fellow answered without a second's hesitation.

The Nth had just come from Jolo where attempts to stop wild eyed Moros with the .38 had resulted unpleasantly for every one except the Moros concerned. Then we had changed to the automatic pistol and it was the Moros' turn to be disgusted. The Nth was pretty strong for the heavy automatic, and had learned to do good execution with it.

"It's too bad the regulations forbid our using the .38," commiserated Bull. "Otherwise you might be detailed to show the regiment something about quick shooting with the revolver."

Rollins missed the irony completely.

"Yep, I could show 'em a thing or two," he admitted without any false modesty.

"Well, anyway, your horse experience will come in handy," suggested Gramp Jackson seriously. "We all think we're pretty good, but we can always learn more."

"Yes, the old Nth is always willing to learn," agreed Bull Manners.

"Believe me I'll be glad to show 'em anything I know," stated Rollins generously.

Chairs were hunched up nearer. On every face was an expression of deep and guileless interest.

"Methods of treating horses vary in the Army and with cowpunchers," Gramp Jackson said. "I've always been curious to know, for example, how cowpunchers go about curing a horse from slobbering."

"Slobbering—slobbering? I don't know—I don't think we bother much with it. My old man runs eighty, ninety head. If one goat isn't up to scratch we throw a saddle on another."

"That sure is disappointing. I'd hoped to hear if our method is right. It cures it all right, but I was sort of hoping you had a better one."

"Maybe," conceded Rollins. "How do you go about it? Perhaps I'll remember once I hear."

"Our way is sort of clumsy, but it works sometimes."

"How is it? How do you cure a horse of slobbering?"

There was an almost oppressive silence in the dining room.

Gramp rolled and lighted another cigaret, taking a long pull at it before he answered. Then he said, his voice very mild—

"We most generally teach them to spit!"

In the silence that followed we rose and departed, all of us, leaving Rollins sitting there, puzzled.

The next day the Old Man, who had sized the boy up pretty well, assigned him to Captain Bullen's Troop B, in the first squadron. Captain Bullen had a tongue that cracked like a whip and was reputed the strictest disciplinarian in the regiment, although his men were crazy about him. But I knew that he had a deep and abiding hatred for all green second lieutenants raw from civil life, especially if they were commissioned through political influence as this kid was.

The first thing Dorsey Bullen did was to put Rollins in the ranks under a corporal to learn his drill. He didn't even know the "School of the Soldier," let alone anything about being an officer.

The next night at mess he seemed to have forgotten the grind we had pulled on him for he babbled away cheerfully, giving us his weighty opinion on Army horsemanship, not a flattering one by any means. To him the cowboy saddle and Western style of riding were the sum and total of horsemanship. The three of us at the mess who had been raised on Western ranches harked back to the days when we had held the same ideas. As it happened there probably was not an officer in that mess who did not possess at least one thoroughbred and a couple of polo ponies, not to mention a select assortment of silver cups gained at polo, steeplechasing and horse shows.

We were also the joint owners of a promising horse maintained in luxury at the Juarez track, who had already honored the regimental colors and enriched our scanty purses by placing in three races and showing in two others.

As he prattled on I thought of my mare, Golden Dawn, slim legged and quick as a cat. I thought of the months I had put in at patient work, suppling and balancing her, working her on two tracks, making her obey the aids, until now she was as responsive as a violin in the hands of a virtuoso. What a joy she was to ride—leaping smoothly into full gallop from the halt, shifting to right or left lead at the slightest pressure, moving in any direction with so little conscious control that it seemed as though she obeyed one's slightest thought, skimming over the jump like a bird and threading in and out of the squadron at full gallop with the effortless effect of a swallow coasting down the wind.

Thinking of her and listening to Rollins' chatter, I grew a little impatient and figured that it was about time some one sat on him hard for his soul's good.

After that first evening the mess gave him almost complete silence, which is far worse than being hazed—if he only had known it. He couldn't help noticing it after awhile, and he too grew silent at last. But glancing at him occasionally, I could see that he had not put the unsociability of the mess down to any fault of his, but had, on the contrary, figured us out as a tight corporation of unfriendly snobs, high hat to newcomers.

Even Captain Bullen gave him up—told him to get the hell out of the orderly room and stay out—which was pretty bad, too. When a troop commander doesn't think his particular shavetail is worth rescuing as a brand from the burning, uncomfortable things are likely to happen to that particular shavetail.

I noticed him during a pause in squadron drill a day or two later and observed that he was carrying one of those fancy embossed revolver holsters, the kind sold by Chicago mail order houses, and instead of the blued steel .45 Colt automatic, he was carrying a nickel plated, pearl handled revolver, probably acquired from the same source. Evidently Captain Bullen hadn't been interested enough to notice it, or there would have been some sulphurous language in that vicinity.

Aside from the formal calls, cards laid on his trunk locker by the officers in the regiment, most of them dutifully placed there during his absence from his quarters, he must have realized that he was as welcome as a skunk at a lawn party. He mooned around by himself, saying little. I began to feel a little sorry for him and spoke to him once or twice. Thereafter he addressed me by my nickname, "Collie," and infested my quarters, giving me much unsought advice on how to break horses.

I could have stood the too easy familiarity of the nickname in spite of the fact that I was handling a troop when he was wearing safety pins instead of buttons, but the long winded dissertation on horses proved too boresome and I regretfully but firmly kicked him out.

The regimental hop occurred with unvarying frequency every Saturday night at the country club nearby. Some of us went to drink and dance, some of us went to dance, and some of us went to drink. I was doing a little of both, engaged in sliding around the floor to the tunes of the regimental band with an occasional visit to have a drink with the Old Guard which died every Saturday night but never surrendered—Gramp Jackson, Bull Manners, et al.—who invariably took up a position close to the base of supplies and refused to move therefrom until the last strains of "Army Blue" finished the evening.

In each of my visits to the Old Guard trenches I saw the same sight, young Rollins at the far end of the bar all alone, getting himself quietly and wholeheartedly plastered.

Back to the floor I went again, to do a couple of "duty" dances, one with the colonel's wife and one with a lanky sister-in-law of the doctor—the sort of visiting girl at an Army post whom the irreverent bachelors immediately dub an F.I.C.L., otherwise a Failure In Civil Life.

The Nth Horse put on a lot of dog at a regimental hop: the silken fringed battle standards, the national with its defiant eagle atop the staff, and the regimental golden yellow one gracing one end of the ball room while all the troop guidons, scarlet and white silk bannerets, were massed at the other.

Below the battle standards were placed the silver trophies won by the regiment. Two fine looking sergeants, their full dress uniforms bemedaled and sporting the yellow cavalry full dress cords, stood on guard with drawn sabers.

Just outside on the porch was the regimental band—all in full dress—and how those babies could play! When the evening was well advanced they invariably sounded off the quick and lively notes of "Blue Bonnets Over the Border" which was a signal for every one to cheer wildly as it was the regimental galloping song.

It was also a signal for the bachelor officers to send out large quantities of beer to the faithful musicians, and to relieve and refresh the color guard in the same manner, a duty taken very seriously by the bachelor officers aforesaid.

My dance with the F.I.C.L. ended at last and people applauded. The band leader started to raise his baton for an encore, but caught the dirty look I shot at him and blew his nose instead. Just as I was telling the girl how disappointing it was not to have had an encore, I heard a shout from the direction of the bar, which opened off the ballroom through a corridor. The barroom door was quickly closed. I think I was the only one who noticed it. At any rate I moved by the right flank and entered the bar in line of columns at the gallop, sensing that something was astir and having a hunch as to what it was.

Well, it was. Our fair haired boy lieutenant was standing in the center of the barroom, waving his nickel plated revolver at the Old Guard and calling them every variety of name on the calendar.

"You think you're pretty hot—you blankety-blank supercilious snobs! Why, my old man could buy and sell the lot of you!" he was saying. "With the pull he's got in Washington he could have you out in the streets looking for jobs inside of a week. . . ." and so on, he went, waving that ridiculous toy revolver and piling insult upon insult.

On the other side of the bar opposite him stood Jim the bartender, his face expressionless. He caught my eye and glanced significantly down at a bung starter beside him, gazing longingly at Rollins. I shook my head. Alex Rock, out of the 3rd Squadron, was standing near the door with me. We looked at each other, nodded imperceptibly and moved quietly toward Rollins.

"Why, you dressed up bunch of nincompoops, any low life cowpuncher on my dad's ranch could outshoot you and outride you—those guys could clean up on the whole regiment without half trying!" He was drunk and nasty, his flat, nasal voice grating on the ear with an unpleasant, jarring note.

The group of officers watched him curiously, paying no attention to the revolver, but examining him in the detached and impersonal manner of a group of scientists studying a strange type of savage. This made him even madder and his voice rose viciously. Then he called them the unpardonable word. . . .

Just as Bull Manners started for him, Alec and I grabbed Rollins and knocked the revolver out of his hand. Neither Alec nor I are exactly infants and he was helpless, although he kicked and squirmed.

"Come on," we said soothingly. "The bar is no place for this sort of stuff—let's go outside."

And by coercion and brute strength we somehow got him out the rear door, leaving the rest of the crowd inside the bar, all of them with the exception of Bull Manners, reflectively studying their glasses and seeming not the least perturbed.

We got him to the rear of the clubhouse and began to walk him toward our quarters. He nearly got away from us once and for a few seconds the three of us were rolling in the ditch—as messy looking a trio of officers and gentlemen as you ever saw. Somehow we got him home and into bed and snoring, and after cleaning up, we headed back for the club.

"What a complete hick!" commented Alec. "What do you suppose is next on the program for him?"

I shrugged my shoulders.

"I don't see anything but that he should be asked to resign or transfer from the regiment."

"Sure, that goes without saying—but how to get through his thick head what a complete asinine exhibition he's made of himself?"

We shook our heads. As a matter of fact we had more important matters to occupy our minds before the night was over.

We returned to the bachelor building at one or two o'clock in the morning. The telephone was jangling and ringing in nervous bursts. It was the adjutant calling. He told us that the First Squadron would move out early next day to patrol the border. Orozco was staging a raid somewhere along the line and it was up to us to protect the ranches on the American side of the Rio Grande.

The adjutant gave me another piece of information. Seeing that Captain

Bullen, by virtue of seniority, was squadron commander, Rollins, the fair haired Boy Terror of the Western Plains, was wished on me—assigned to my troop for instruction and training.

"I'll instruct and train him!" I said grimly enough as I hung up the receiver.

I was commanding A at that time, as I've said, my skipper being away attending the Army School of the Line at Fort Leavenworth. Frankly, I was none too pleased at the prospect of having Rollins wished on me. Border service settles down to lone trooping, miles from nowhere, without any companionship except the other officer in the troop—and this wet nosed kid was far from being my idea of an interesting companion.

Sunday morning breakfast before stables at a cavalry mess is never a too cheerful affair. In the middle of it, in rambles this Rollins and makes an abject and rather sickening apology, trying to explain away his actions of the night before on the plea of drunkenness, the one excuse that doesn't go down with a hard boiled cavalry outfit, used to judging men in their cups. The unwritten law in the Nth was that a man must carry his liquor like a gentleman, or never drink.

Anyway, his apology was listened to in a strained and uncomfortable silence; no one said a word. Rollins turned a shade paler and sat down to his eggs and coffee as we rose to go to duty.

Golden Dawn was tethered to the hitching rack as I came out, and she threw up her head and whinnied at me as Murphy came downstairs with my field equipment and saber. He snapped the French blade I always carried to the off cantle rings, slipped on cantle bags, pommel bags, slicker and canteen and strapped the whole works down tight and shipshape, Golden Dawn nosing him impatiently from time to time as though anxious to be off.

In the meantime I had strapped my pistol holster to my thigh, slipped the leather straps of field glasses and dispatch case under my saber belt so they couldn't flop about at the trot, felt for cigarets and matches, notebook and pencil, whistle and luminous compass, and clambered aboard while Murphy held the stirrup.

Just then Rollins came out, mounted the horse held for him by his striker and galloped away without waiting for the man to mount, which, of course, meant that the soldier had to climb up on the high packed saddle while his horse was dancing around madly trying to follow the other. I rode over and held the striker's horse while the man mounted. Golden Dawn danced and pirouetted around, making playful bites at my legs, sniffing the fresh morning air, exceedingly impatient to get going. Murphy was now mounted and followed as we rode toward the troop lines.

Sergeant Henderson had everything ready, troop lined up fully packed and equipped; nearly one hundred men and horses looking very fit and capable as they stood there at attention. Opening the ranks I went over them man by man and horse by horse, finding not a single thing needing attention. The wagons stood behind, all kits checked and ready.

I was busy examining the off front pastern of No. 38 horse, which seemed slightly swollen, when up rode Rollins, feet sticking out, elbows akimbo, and drew up his horse with a rattle and clatter where I stood on foot. I had to step lively to avoid being ridden on. After nearly knocking me down, the Boy Terror of the Western Plains continued to sit there in the saddle.

"The Old Man tells me I'm going out with your troop," he announced.

Sergeant Henderson gasped. The men around me grinned. I straightened up, looked at Sergeant Henderson and jerked my head toward the Boy Wonder. Henderson strode over and led the kid out of earshot, talking to him in a low tone. In a few seconds Rollins rode back and dismounted.

Turning out a ridiculous salute, he sounded off—

"Sir, Lieutenant Rollins reports for duty with Troop A by order of the regimental commander!"

It might have seemed a little martinet-like, but there wasn't a soldier in that troop who would have remained on his horse while reporting to a dismounted senior; and why should I let this kid lieutenant get away with it?

"See that Lieutenant Rollins is assigned an orderly," I said to Henderson, and glanced at my wrist watch. It was time to move out.

They moved like well oiled clockwork, that outfit; a blast on my whistle and every man grasped reins in right hand and placed left foot in stirrup. Another blast and they rose simultaneously and settled into the saddles. Giving them a minute to adjust packs, sabers, rifles and reins, I moved them out across the parade ground to where the squadron adjutant and sergeant-major faced each other on the line to be occupied by the squadron. My guidon sergeant snapped out of the troop, his scarlet and white pennant fluttering overhead, and galloped toward the line at the moment that three other guidons were borne rapidly toward the same point.

Down from headquarters rode the colonel and his adjutant; around the corner of the Post Exchange rode the band, the kettledrums on the white drum horse gleaming with polished brass in the morning sun.

In another few seconds four troops swung up into line to form the squadron. Captain Bullen faced the line and received the reports; a trumpet rang out. The colonel rode up. Captain Bullen barked a short command. There was a rasping, steely clang as four hundred sabers were drawn. Another bark and the officers' sabers flashed up; another and a glittering wall of steel rose above the squadron as the four hundred blades came up to the "present" and the guidons dipped.

The colonel saluted grumpily, sabers came back to the "carry," the trumpets of the band sounded off the traditional ruffle, and the band crashed into the haunting notes of "Zamboango" while the colonel galloped to the right flank, inspecting.

My troop was on the right of the line and I rode over to meet him, saluting and falling in on his left as he rode around my lieutenant, Rollins sitting there looking like a poor imitation of Don Quixote de la Mancha, elbows akimbo, feet stuck out, chest caved in, shoulders drooping and hat stuck on the back of his head at a what-the-hell-do-I-care angle. It was a sad sight and I could see the Old Man beginning to steam up.

He turned to me, sparks flying from his harsh old blue eyes, his white mustaches sticking up like the whiskers of an excited tomcat.

"Mr. Stewart, Mr. Stewart! What is your second lieutenant looking at his feet for? Tell him, Mr. Stewart, that I don't want to steal his boots." The high pitched querulous notes of the Old Man's voice carried all over the squadron. "Have some sergeant teach him the position of the trooper at attention, Mr. Stewart. . . . And look at his throat latch—look at it!" His voice hit a higher note. "Tight as a snake's skin! Does he want to choke his horse to death, Mr. Stewart? Disgraceful!"

The Old Man glared at me venomously. Then he rode on grumbling and growling to himself and inspected the rest of the troop.

Believe me, I was pretty sore. I'd gone over the troop with a hawk-like eye and there was nothing on which the colonel's critical glance should have rested. Of course I hadn't inspected Rollins—one expects an officer to look after himself—and I had received a calling down for it!

At that moment I would have traded Rollins for a hamstrung mule from a jackass battery, and thrown in something to boot. That's how much I thought of him. Sergeant Henderson looked like a thundercloud.

The colonel dispensed with the passing in review, returned Captain Bullen's salute; the band moved forward, their instruments sparkling, and prepared to play us off the post, an old custom in the Nth, where they always did things with a little extra touch.

Sabers were returned with a clang all down the line of horses.

"On First Troop, right forward! Fours right—ye-e-e-ow!" came Bullen's voice, clear as a trumpet.

There was a flash of scarlet as the squadron standard and its guard galloped to place, the sudden trampling of hundreds of steel shod hoofs on the hard parade ground, and the squadron swung out into column of fours.

The band broke forth into the gay and inspiring notes of "Blue Bonnets Over the Border" and we headed for the gates of the fort, following the music.

The gate guard turned out with a rattle and clatter and presented arms, the band swung out of column playing for all they were worth as we went by—and we were on our way toward the city below us.

"Route order" was given in a few minutes and Rollins ranged up beside me.

"What's that funny tune the band is wheezing out?" he asked. "Why don't they play something with a kick in it?"

Now "Blue Bonnets Over the Border" has played the old Nth into battle in the Seminole Wars, in the Mexican War; in the Civil and Spanish Wars, and is very dear to the hearts of the regiment. It has a story behind it as well, for the regiment was originally organized as a regiment of dragoons. Its facings of orange-yellow were afterward adopted for all the cavalry regiments. The first colonel was a Scotsman—one of the "Wild Geese" or descendants of "Wild Geese" who scattered from their native heather to offer their swords abroad when politics and religion went wrong at home. And this old Scottish colonel had brought "Blue Bonnets Over the Border" to the regiment. And with the song there was another custom indulged in by the old-timers. The casual observer never noticed that an officer of the Nth would wave his whisky or cocktail over the nearest glass of water before drinking it, a silent toast that had come down through the years from the old days in Scotland when it was dangerous to mention the name of Bonnie Prince Charlie, in exile "over the water."

I tried to explain this to him as we rode along, but I could see that he thought it silly—and maybe it was. But men will persist in treasuring silly things that are handed down to them through the centuries; and that intangible thing called the soul of the regiment is made up of a lot of seemingly silly things.

"Look here, Stewart," he asked, neglecting the polite "mister," "what was the big idea of making me get down off my horse to talk to you this morning?"

I was silent for a moment.

"Mr. Rollins," I answered at last, choosing my words carefully, "in civil life you can get away with crude stuff: you can remain seated while you are talking with an older man or a woman standing; you can sit on your horse and talk to a woman or an older man standing on the ground; you can address an older man by his surname as one addresses a waiter or servant, omitting any title. You can do all those things and, in addition, pick your teeth in public, and no harm will be done except that you will be avoided by certain types of people all over the world. But when you are in Military or Naval service, or in the Merchant Marine, you can't show disrespect to your superior, because disrespect and discipline don't travel together. While I am your senior officer, my title is mister. Do you get me?"

He nodded, frowning in thought. We rode along silently for a time. At last he looked up, his eyes somber.

"I guess you think I'm pretty much of a roughneck, Mr. Stewart," he said;

and then in a lower tone, half to himself, "And I guess I am at that."

Somehow he reminded me of a bewildered puppy after its first encounter with the family cat, and I felt a little pity for him. But pity wasn't what he needed at this stage of the game.

"It isn't sandpaper for your neck you need so much as a realization that you are in a new game and that it's up to you to keep your mouth shut and your ears and eyes open until you learn it," I said brutally.

The field music of the squadron assembled in front of us and burst into tongue as we were called to attention to ride through town. Our trumpeters were the pride of the Nth Horse and they could do things with a trumpet never dreamed of by the makers. They had a tricky way of resting their instruments on their hips and bringing them up to the blowing position with a snappy outward twist that swung the yellow trumpet cords into a graceful circle as they broke into the inspiring strains of the field music.

The horses knew we were on parade, for they marched very alertly, heads up, nostrils dilated, stepping high, wide and handsome. The sidewalks were lined with townspeople with whom the Nth got along famously and they clapped and cheered as we moved through the main street.

Glancing back at the troop as we rounded a corner, my eye registered some unusual movement in rear of me. Turning more in the saddle to investigate, I drew in my breath sharply and swore. For a second I saw red. Then I called Murphy up beside me.

"My compliments to Lieutenant Rollins and he will please turn over command of his platoon to his sergeant and fall in the rear of the troop," I said.

Murphy's eyes opened wide as he saluted, turned his horse on its haunches and dropped back. For Murphy knew what the order meant. It is like the adjutant rapping on an officer's door and asking him for his saber, or like a soldier being told to "get your blankets and come on."

It was drastic, but the circumstances warranted it, for the Boy Wonder of the Western Plains was waving his hand and smiling to people on the sidewalks—smiling and waving from the ranks of a cavalry regiment of the Regular Army, riding at attention! Smiling and waving from the ranks of the Nth Horse!

We rode on through the town and came out into the open mesa at last, through a welter of adobe Mexican shacks. The hike was really started. The squadron lengthened out into marching formation, column of twos. Looking back as we rode up a slight rise, I saw the whole outfit winding away behind me, a long column of sun and wind tanned men in olive drab and bronze, riding with that easy, alert sort of grace that is peculiarly the heritage of the cavalryman.

A cavalry outfit moving into the field is a beautiful sight to any one who knows its capabilities. It is business-like and efficient, able to move its rifles swiftly into battle, capable of striking hard blows at a long distance and of reforming and striking again and again.

The men laughed and sang behind us, the birds and jackrabbits scattered before us, raised up by the fringe of troop dogs, running in a semicircle thrown out in front of our advance.

After the first halt we started the trot—the steady, remorseless cavalry trot that eats up the miles hour after hour, the long columns winding along the mesa moving forward with a steady beat and cadence peculiarly its own—the musical cadence of clinking cups, sabers, curb chains and spurs, accompanied by the creak of saddle leather.

After an hour or two I began to feel that perhaps I had been a little severe with Rollins, and decided to end his punishment. I sent for him.

"Mr. Rollins, hereafter please remember that when men are required to ride at attention, heads to the front, that officers are required to set the example. You are released from arrest."

He looked at me in surprise.

"Why—was I in arrest?" he asked innocently.

Somehow, I felt at that moment that this fair haired hero of the West was going to succeed in getting badly on my nerves before the march was ended. It was pretty hot in the Texas sun, and both men and horses began to feel it before long. I saw Rollins sitting slumped in his saddle, looking pasty and all fagged out before we had made fifteen miles. Looking fagged out before his soldiers is one thing that an officer can't do, example being what it is and the leaders' influence being what it is supposed to be on the herd mind.

I landed on him pretty hard; told him that being a cavalry officer wasn't all waving at the girls, that he was supposed to be a leader and an example of strength and courage to his men. He straightened up in his saddle and, as I well knew, actually felt less tired himself. But had a lightning bolt cracked me wide open at that moment and scattered me all over the mesa, I'm quite sure Mr. Rollins would have borne the tragedy with surprising equanimity.

His eyes began to assume that injured expression of the man who feels that he is being unjustly picked on. I felt a little remorseful, then steeled myself with the reflection that after all he would have to be out alone on his own some day, entrusted with the lives of better men than he was and for their sakes he should be hazed until he knew something.

We made camp near a water tank along the railroad that night—making camp being a very pretty formation as done by the Nth. First the guidon sergeants would gallop forward, four spots of scarlet and white, and dismount. The squadron came up sedately behind them, the leading troop forming line, followed by the second, third and fourth troops, four lines of nearly a hundred men and horses each, every troop lining up on its own guidon. Then came a sharp command.

Single ranks opened out into double ranks, another command and every man hit the ground at the same instant, saddles were lined up, lariats joined into a temporary picket line, the horses tethered and men returned to their saddles. There was a second or two of flurry and then pup tents began to rise; in a few minutes the camp was made and ready, a compact square of khaki colored tents, rising up like magic without any fuss and feathers. Fires were started and not long after came the high pitched braying of the wagon mules who scented the camp from afar and knew that their day's work was nearly over.

We were allowed a small A-tent for the officers of each troop and it was my dubious privilege to share it with Rollins, our two canvas cots stretched out against either wall, saddles and saddle bags at the foot, field glasses, pistols and dispatch cases hanging on the tent poles, collapsible canvas bucket and wash basin outside.

First off I told Rollins to secure himself a regulation pistol and holster from the supply sergeant and wear it hereafter. This went down hard and he obeyed a little sullenly, thinking it was just some more of my martinet stuff. It was. For after all an officer has to be an instructor of his men with the pistol, and to be a good instructor he must be able to use it. Rollins carried it with an exaggerated sort of limp that night at retreat, as though its weight were overwhelming.

"If you're too weak to carry that gun, you had better put in for transfer to the Army Nurse Corps, with the other ladies," I said to him.

He flushed and stopped his grandstand stuff like a shot.

Now we had an informal club system in the Nth at that time before Prohibition, a system whereby each officer of the squadron provided the drinks for the crowd one night. It was my turn first and the officers assembled after water call and before supper to have an appetizer at my tent. Murphy was always an enthusiastic aid at these parties—filling glasses and pouring water with great willingness, and one eye cocked on the bottle—the last good drink in it belonging to him by unwritten law and custom of the service.

Rollins drank his drink and immediately unstoppered that infernal clacking tongue of his.

We all listened to him in silence for awhile. I could see that Captain Bullen was waiting for the opportunity to have an informal talk about the service ahead of us, but he couldn't get a word in edgewise.

It was Bull Manners who finally stopped the kid's flow of oratory.

Rollins had finished some particularly atrocious boast of his own prowess.

"I don't see," remarked Bull, "why the colonel sends out this whole expensive squadron to patrol the border. It would save the taxpayer a lot of money if he just sent the Boy Terror of the Western Plains out on his own. . . ." And he went on in this strain, finally ending up with some allusion to hound packs and hunting. "It's queer how the youngest puppy at the tail of the pack always does the most ki-yi-ing," he remarked.

Rollins got this and flushed, but it had the effect of silencing him for the time being.

And strangely enough, I felt a little irritated at the reproof. For Rollins was now my lieutenant and it upset me to have any one outside the troop take a crack at him.

Captain Bullen saw his opportunity now and began to outline to us the orders he had received from the regimental commander.

"Our main job, after protecting the border from any raids by this fellow Orozco, is to see that he doesn't get any arms and ammunition through. He's got plenty of horses and men, but blame few guns and cartridges. And he's desperate to get them. You'll have to watch like hawks. And we've got to hurry now that we've got men and horses shaken down; we'll increase the marching rate tomorrow, and the length of march.

"Stewart, you'll drop off tomorrow with your troop, taking post at Chico's ranch. Yours will be the toughest spot as Orozco's headquarters will be only six miles away across the Rio Grande. . . ."

I felt a little flush of pride that my troop was picked to guard the hottest spot, and swore to myself that they wouldn't get a needle through my territory. I had forgotten to figure on the Boy Terror of the Plains! Captain Bullen went on, giving each troop its orders in turn and we all made notes and asked questions. This lasted until supper time.

The officers' mess kits were brought up from each troop and we all had supper together, relaxing afterward around a camp-fire, for the nights are chilly on the high plateau of the southwest. Rollins still preserved his silence, although we talked and laughed and sang while a cheerful hum came up from the troop tents. I think the kid felt his loneliness that night, and again I felt myself beginning to be sorry for him. But no good was to be gained that way and I steeled myself against showing him any kindness until he got his values straightened out.

A strong camp guard was established that night, with an officer-of-the-day and an officer-of-the-guard, which latter detail Rollins drew down, being junior and first for duty.

A well guarded camp was an old Roman military tradition thoroughly believed in by the Nth. Had it been the Nth down at Columbus, New Mexico, Pancho Villa would never have ridden roughshod over an entire regiment at dead of night and escaped unscathed.

But Rollins couldn't see it. He growled about his officer-of-the-guard detail.

"My God, stay up all night and prowl around just because it was done that way in the Revolutionary War! Why, Stewart—Mr. Stewart—we're forty miles from the border and from the Mexicans!"

"Yes?" I said as I arranged my blankets. "Maybe so. All the same if you don't want to land into the hottest water you ever landed in, don't monkey with guard duty. This is an army you're in, not a public debating society. When that fact begins to impress itself upon you, you'll begin to be of almost as much value to the troop as one of the dumbest recruit buck privates in the outfit." And with that I turned in.

Before I went to sleep I thought of the weary days and nights I would have to suffer the conversation of this insufferable pest, and I cursed out the colonel for wishing him on me. But, after all, he was my lieutenant, and I registered a mental vow to make a soldier out of him or break him before I got through.

I couldn't have slept more than three or four hours when I heard some disturbance and woke up. I got up and buckled on my pistol belt.

The camp was boiling in silent movement. Hurrying out, I found Sergeant Henderson standing before the troop assembly point with the men flitting out of their tents with belts and rifles, quickly falling in. Low toned voices called down through the rank as the troopers counted fours. In the darkness I could hear the other troops forming up as rapidly.

"What's up?" I asked Henderson.

"Troop present and accounted for, sir!" he reported. "Don't know, sir. Some one says turn out—there's a Mexican outfit near the camp."

A crisp order came out of the darkness near me in Captain Bullen's voice.

In obedience to it I gave "Fours left, double time," and swung the outfit along the east flank of the camp, put them into line, commanded them to load and lock pieces—and waited.

Again Captain Bullen's voice came out of the darkness, telling me to take a patrol and go with the officer of the guard to reconnoiter.

Rollins came up. I called out three men and followed along with him. He was very excited and stumbled along, his pistol out, leading down toward where I remembered seeing a clump of cottonwood trees before dark.

Slowing up, we went forward more cautiously, Rollins and I in the lead. Then I heard something stirring in the cottonwoods and listened a moment, leaning forward.

I straightened up and swore.

"You've ruined the night's rest of a whole squadron of cavalry on account of one wandering burro!" I said scornfully.

Rollins looked at me piteously.

"My God, I'll never live that down!" he answered.

It was true; the whole regiment would learn of it; his life would be unbearable. I did some quick thinking. After all, he was my lieutenant, and my job was not to let him ruin himself utterly. The men were several paces in rear of us. Telling them to remain where they were, I pulled Rollins ahead.

"Fire in the air a couple of times and yell," I said.

He did as I directed, and it sounded like a battle. The burro leaped out and crashed away through the brush.

Returning, I found my troop moving forward at the double, the rest of the squadron behind it. Stopping them, I reported to Captain Bullen that we had driven off a prowler—which was true—and that everything was now quiet.

Rollins stuttered his thanks to me, but I growled at him and turned in.

We moved out early in the morning; a trained eye could already see the squadron settling into its stride after the first day on the field—sort of shaking down and hardening its fiber.

The halt that night was nearer the river and we camped close to Chico's ranch-house. It was our last night with the squadron, as my troop was to take station here while the others went on to more distant posts.

The ranch people—an old man and his two sons—had been very worried about Orozco, fearful that he would send raiding parties through as this place was only six or seven miles from the river, where, on the opposite bank, his forces were supposed to be concentrating. The Old Man told us that a small party of Red Flaggers, as Orozco's forces were called, had ridden through only the day before.

When Rollins heard this he was scornful. He had, it seemed, all the contempt that a certain type of southwesterner has for the Mexican—a contempt very much undeserved, as the Mexican is a brave fighter; even the bandit type which infests the border is a hardy and courageous individual. But there was no arguing with this half baked kid—he knew it all and more.

Of course none of us knew that Orozco's patrol was right up behind us on the hillside, watching every move we made, ready to send back word the second they saw a favorable opportunity to attack.

The squadron moved on next day, leaving my troop to make permanent camp. The small pup tents sheltering two men each were replaced with the larger tents holding a squad; canvas cots were issued and arm racks for the rifles.

It was a good camp, well shaded by cottonwood trees, its only disadvantage being that we had to water the horses at a stream over three-quarters of a mile away.

We had just finished rifle practise before going into the field and still had our pistol qualification course to finish. This I started immediately, commencing with the bull's-eye targets, dismounted, then working to the disappearing silhouettes. Rollins, of course, had to go through this like any recruit, and his ventures with the automatic pistol were pretty sad. He flinched at each shot and peppered the atmosphere everywhere except in the place where the target stood.

"It's this blame old cannon; nobody can shoot it," he averred.

"Yes?" I answered. "I'll tell you what I'll do—I'll shoot you the whole instruction course with your nickel plated toy and with the automatic, and beat you at both!"

"Done!" he growled, and we went forth.

Well, it was a little surprising. He out-shot me dismounted on the bull's-eye target with the revolver. I had to work like a Trojan to beat him at the mounted course, where I finally pulled away from him entirely at the gallop.

But when it came to shooting with the automatic pistol he just wasn't there. I shot rings around him. I had kept my word and beaten him with both weapons.

"Well," he admitted grudgingly at last, "you're a pretty fine shot. But I'll bet you nobody else in the regiment could do it."

"That's where you're all wrong," I retorted. "Any lieutenant in the regiment can do it, and about a third of the soldiers."

"Then I'm not so good as I thought I was," he admitted. I agreed with him.

"But when it comes to riding I can put it all over you or anybody else in the outfit," he came back.

You had to hand it to that bird. If belief in his own invincibility makes the great man, this kid certainly contained within himself the seeds of success. I patiently tried to explain the difference between riding and horsemanship. Did you ever try to explain the beauties of a Beethoven symphony to a man who thinks "Alexander's Rag Time Band" is the finest piece ever composed? It was just about as hopeless as that. I got sick of it at last and decided to demonstrate to him that he wasn't so wonderful.

At Chico's ranch they had a few horses, among which was a white eyed, mean looking bronc. The old rancher willingly brought it forth, for a private séance in his rear corral.

The bronc was snubbed against the corral fence. Rollins found a Western saddle, threw it on and mounted. That bronc carried him out to the center of the corral on the first leap. I must say the kid could ride. The brute reared and plunged and rocketed about stiff legged and Rollins sat him with an easy grace, slapping the flanks of the bucking animal with his hat and emitting an occasional high pitched yell. It lasted about five minutes. It was good. I was satisfied and the horse was roped and again snubbed to the fence.

Rollins swaggered toward me, hands on hips, very pleased with himself.

"How about that?" he asked.

"Good as far as it goes," I admitted.

"What do you mean?"

"I mean this"—and I pointed down to my Saumur flat saddle, an inconspicuous looking postage stamp affair compared to the great heavy Western saddle with its high cantle and pommel and its bucking rolls holding the rider in. "Can you ride that bronco with this?"

He laughed and shook his head.

"Nobody can ride a bucking horse with a thing like that," he stated.

"You mean you wouldn't try?" I asked as I loosened the cinch of the Western saddle and flung it off, replacing it with the flat saddle.

He didn't reply, but watched me curiously as I swung on to the horse's back.

In another second there was a rush of air in my face as the bronco leaped straight out away from the fence. I settled deeply down into the saddle, gripping with calf and thigh for all I was worth, my legs clamped like iron and my waist and shoulders bending like rubber to the horse's wild leaps and stiff legged jumps. Then he started a sort of corkscrew motion as he landed, jarring every bone in my body again and again, but he couldn't shake me loose, long legged as I am. After five minutes I worked him back toward the fence. He was caught up and I dismounted.

"Want to try it?" I panted.

I'll give the kid credit. He didn't bat an eye, but swung right up. I knew instantly what would happen—I could see daylight between his knees and the saddle on the first leap of the cayuse. On the second leap Rollins was high out of the saddle, and on the third he flew clear and rolled several yards away, jumping to his feet again. He came toward me ruefully, brushing the dirt off his uniform and shaking his head.

He studied the horse and the flat saddle. I could see a resolution forming itself, and inwardly rejoiced. There must be some good in a pup who could take a licking and own up to it handsomely.

Thereafter he listened when I talked horsemanship, and he spent every spare minute shooting with the pistol. I found him after hours one day going out to practise, his face very grim.

"Why don't you take out some of those *other* rotten pistol shots of the troop," I suggested, "and let them have some practise as well?"

This suited him and he began to work with the backward men. It was a good way to bring up the average of the troop shooting. Then we progressed to the mounted pistol course—flashing by five silhouettes at the gallop and firing at them as the horse swept by. It takes good shooting to hit anything from a horse's back at a gallop. So poor was Rollins' showing that his face grew grim again. Then I taught him the trick of shooting as the horse hit the bottom of his stride, and pulling his trigger as the gun swept into the left edge of the target. He began to make a few hits and grew wild with enthusiasm.

Now the ammunition allowance per soldier and officer is limited to just enough to qualify an ordinarily good shot. Rollins, learning of this, asked if he might buy extra ammunition from the Ordnance for the troop. This was beginning to look hopeful, and I agreed. As a consequence, the shooting picked up wonderfully and when qualification course was held we made nearly three times the average number of Pistol Experts. Rollins himself only made Pistol Marksman, but I could see that the kid had taken a new lease on life because of his improvement. The only trouble was that he was in danger of becoming a pistol crank, believing in no other weapon.

When he became a little fulsome about his prowess with the pistol, I reminded him that he still had to qualify as a rifleman, a swordsman and a horseman.

He snorted at this but forbore any remark. I went on a scouting trip one day riding my second mount and leaving Golden Dawn in the picket line.

I returned about dusk and, riding up to the camp, saw a group of men watching something on our exercise ground. Following their glances I looked, then made a break for the place, as mad as I have ever been in my life.

For there in the middle of the exercise ground was Rollins mounted on Golden Dawn—jabbing her with the spurs and jerking at her velvety mouth with the reins. Golden Dawn, who had never known such treatment, was fighting him, her eyes wild and her flanks heaving. I shouted at him, but he didn't hear me. As I ran toward him Golden Dawn decided that she had stood enough of this sort of treatment. Suddenly she reared and plunged, and went rocketing across the field like an outlaw. The first rear unseated Rollins and he clutched leather madly. The second leap shook him still more and about halfway across the field he tumbled out of the saddle and rolled on the ground.

Golden Dawn came running toward the picket line, whickering with indignation. I stopped her and began to soothe her. She nuzzled me with her velvety nose and stamped around, looking back occasionally at Rollins who had picked himself up and was coming toward us. I turned her over to my striker and met him halfway.

What I said to him I don't know. Evidently it was the first time in his life that he had been subjected to a thorough dressing down, and his eyes opened wide and he turned pale as I went on, telling him just how many kinds of an impossible cad he was to take another officer's horse without permission, telling him just what a clumsy handed, bragging nonentity he was, generally giving him a tongue lashing that he would never forget.

He was white faced and shaking when I got through. Thereafter I didn't speak to him except officially for three days. By the time I recognized him again he had grown quite humble and apologetic. But he had learned that horses weren't common property, and had also re-learned the fact that he was no horseman, and set about correcting that deficiency.

I maintained a strict guard system, two men on picket line guard and two on camp guard. It was my custom to rise any time after midnight and before dawn and inspect the camp. I could see that he thought this another evidence of pedantic queerness; but without a word from me he began to do the same thing, and we inspected alternate nights thereafter. Guard duty was one thing he couldn't grasp, despising the Mexican as he did; he didn't think they were worth losing sleep over.

Rumors about Orozco and his raids were flying up and down the border. The old man at the ranch warned me once or twice that a raid was due, but we were always ready and I took the situation calmly—simply designating an assembly point for the troop in case of a night attack, and watching the roads and fords.

Word came one day from Captain Bullen directing me to report to squadron headquarters for a conference of troop commanders. I wasn't so keen on leaving that untried kid in command, but I figured I could get back late that night, and took the chance.

Warning him to keep his eyes open and maintain a careful guard at all times, I mounted Golden Dawn, and Murphy and I set off to cover the twelve miles to squadron headquarters.

It was about noon when I arrived—just in time for chow. Bull Manners was there and Gramp Jackson and the others, and we foregathered joyfully. With great pride they showed me a galvanized iron wash tub filled with lumps of ice and water in which rested many dark bottles of beer, cool stuff which cut the alkali. After getting two bottles of it down to Murphy, I returned and listened to the news and border gossip.

"How's the Boy Terror of the Western Plains?" asked Bull Manners, and they all stopped drinking their beer to listen.

"He's learning," I answered warily.

A grunt of disbelief went up.

"He'd better learn while the learning is good," said Bull. "He's not due to last very long in this outfit."

"What do you mean?" I shot back.

"Hell, after the stunt he pulled at the club, do you suppose we're going to stand for that pup in this outfit? Not on your tin type, Collie. It's up to him whether he wants to resign or transfer, but it'll have to be one or the other."

Every one nodded. I could see that Rollins had signally failed to win himself a niche in the affections of the Nth, and that they had decided on a course of action in my absence.

"Is that so?" I asked sarcastically. "I suppose all of you paragons of perfection were born capable cavalry officers?"

In a second the whole gang had turned on me, all talking at once, telling me of various bonehead plays he had pulled, many of which I heard for the first time.

Bull Manner's voice rose above the rest and drowned them out.

"Twice he was late for formations in Bullen's troop—and did he report himself? He did not!" Bull was emphatic.

That wasn't so good. It was a point of honor for an officer to report himself for any dereliction of duty. I shook my head over this. It was the first time I'd heard of it. I had mentioned that custom of the service to him only last week. I remembered that he had looked a little queer. But after all, he was my lieutenant and I fought back.

"Good old Collie's maternal instincts are aroused," said Gramp placatingly when the battle waxed most fiercely.

Some one announced that chow was ready and we broke off as we moved toward the mess shack and the waiting meal. I was a little heavy hearted for I saw all too plainly that the officers of the Nth were down on Rollins, and were bitterly intent on getting rid of him.

But that particular waiting meal was destined never to be eaten. I heard a shout from the other end of the camp and the rattle of hoofs of a horse at the gallop. Captain Bullen came to his tent door and stood by the squadron standard which flaunted itself outside his tent. Up the troop street galloped a soldier; I recognized the horse before I did the man. It was that jug headed skate, No. 46, and he certainly had been pushed, for his flanks were heaving and he was drenched with sweat. Farnsworth, a man out of the Third Platoon, was riding him, and as soon as I saw Farnsworth's face I knew something had happened to my troop.

Anxiously I waited until the trooper drew up before me and leaped to the ground.

"Sir, Orozco's whole outfit has jumped the camp and stolen all the rifles and ammunition! Lieutenant Rollins is pursuing them toward the river with the hull troop!"

Captain Bullen was standing beside me. He didn't bat an eye but turned to Bull Manners, the squadron adjutant.

"B and C Troops to move out immediately, leaving guard detachment of ten men each. Word to D Troop to follow up. To horse, gentlemen!"

The camp woke to sudden life. I could see Murphy hurriedly putting the saddle on Golden Dawn.

"Captain Bullen," I said. "May I join my troop?"

"Go on!" He nodded and I flew to my horse; and Murphy and I were on our way in a few seconds, Farnsworth accompanying us on a fresh horse.

He was too excited to tell much about the riot and I rode ahead grimly,

pushing Golden Dawn for all she was worth. I thought the twelve miles
would never come to an end, but at last we came in sight of Chico's ranch
and the camp.

Some strange silence and lifelessness about the camp warned me as I
approached. There was not a horse in the picket line, or a man to be seen.
The tents stood there—deserted.

Riding in past the ranch, I heard a shout, and the old gray bearded rancher
came running toward me. Waiting for him to come up, I looked over the
camp. The place was trodden by many hoofs; the field range in the kitchen
was overturned, the guidon was gone from its position by my tent, trunk
lockers were scattered around the troop street—the whole place looked as
though it had been looted.

The graybeard came up.

"Looka here, Mr. Officer. That theah young officer done gone away from
heah ridin' hard after some greasers. Seems he took the hull army o' soldiers
down to watah the horses. While he was gone about two hundred o' Orozco's
men come ridin' in—they grabs everything they can lay hands on, includin'
all the rifles, and skeedaddles outa heah, takin' the two army wagons and
mules with 'em. The young officer comes back and goes after them!" and he
pointed toward the river.

"What time did this happen?" I asked as calmly as I could.

" 'Bout two hours ago!"

I turned to Farnsworth, telling him to remain behind to direct the squadron
which I figured could not be very far behind me.

"All right. Murphy, let's go!" I said, and set Golden Dawn into a gallop.

She'd made twenty-four miles that day, but she seemed to feel that a lot
depended upon her and settled tirelessly into her easy floating stride as we
followed up the broad trail made by the troop horses.

On we went, following the road as it led in and out of cactus growth
interspersed with outcroppings of rock. I tried to picture what had happened
as the road flowed beneath Golden Dawn's steady stride.

Evidently Rollins had taken the entire troop to water, leaving no guard in
camp. The men always wore their pistols to water, which meant that at least
they were armed to that extent. But the rifles were gone, and the rifle, after
all, is the cavalryman's chief weapon. Not only was the present situation bad,
but it was liable to grow much worse. Should the Red Flaggers turn at bay
there would be slaughter, for they could hold off the pursuing cavalry with
rifle fire—shooting them to pieces before the troop could get close enough
to use the pistol.

We must have traveled nearly halfway to the river when we came over a
hill crest and saw the valley stretching away to the Rio Grande before us.

About two-thirds of the distance to the river, rising from higher ground, was a heavy cloud of dust out of which I could catch an occasional flash of sun on metal and see the outlines of tall sombreros. Look as I might, I could see no sign of the troop. Whether they had all been killed or captured I knew not, and I feared the worst.

Hurrying down the rise, we hit level going, and galloped along, watching the cloud of dust ahead; then we dipped into a hollow and I lost sight of it for a space.

As Golden Dawn galloped up the other side I began to check her. The nose of Murphy's horse was level with Golden Dawn's tail. Anxious to see how his mount was standing the grueling pace, I glanced backward. As I looked I saw puffs of dust spring in a line on the trail behind him. It was exactly as though some one had thrown a handful of pebbles at a dry earthbank. Again the line of dust puffs rose up, this time nearer.

Then on my ears fell the unmistakable chatter of a machine gun, coming somewhere from the right rear, down the draw through which we had just ridden. The only protection against it was to be found on the far side of the hill crest just before us. Waving to Murphy, I closed my spurs in on Golden Dawn. She fairly leaped at the hill crest and we slid down the other side, not a second too soon. As I checked her in her downward progress, Murphy and I looked back in time to see the line of dust puffs graze the hill crest, and to hear bullets singing overhead.

In front of us the dust cloud had resolved itself into a large band of mounted Mexicans. They must have seen us at the same instant, for I heard the faint reports of several guns, and saw men hurriedly dismounting to fire. In about two seconds this place was going to be too hot for safety. We couldn't go back and we couldn't go forward. Glancing about for shelter, I spied a small, dry arroyo cutting the surface of the hill off to the right. We rode for this as the bullets began to sing around us.

Its high banks afforded some measure of protection and Golden Dawn and Murphy's horse slid down into it on their haunches. Once arrived at the bottom, I dismounted, throwing the reins to Murphy, and crawled up to the top of the nearest side. Bullets were whirring about the place like angry bees, but I worked my way up toward the hill crest above, over on the other side of which was that devilish machine gun.

Suddenly I paused and a cold chill ran through me. The squadron was following closely behind! They would gallop down into that draw, all unconscious of the danger, and when they were fully in view that machine gun would plow into them, tearing men and horses to pieces. It was a trap skillfully set.

With my heart going like a trip hammer, I pushed my way up the sides of the arroyo, working toward the hill crest. I must have been in plain view for a moment to the Mexican force in the valley toward the river, for a perfect swarm of bullets smacked and thudded on the rocks around me. Crouching low, I continued my progress.

Inch by inch I worked toward the hill crest, filled with fear for the safety of the squadron. At last I drew up directly below the top, getting some sort of protection toward the rear by intervening outcropping rocks which saved me as long as I remained prone. But I had to get up where I could warn the squadron before it galloped down into that treacherous valley on the far side.

Drawing a deep breath, I rushed forward, throwing myself down just as I reached the top. A perfect storm of bullets hammered the rocks around me. I could see the valley now. My eyes followed up the trail we had come—it ran across the small valley to the far side and disappeared over the knoll. Behind the knoll I could see a faint cloud of dust rising in the heat waves of the afternoon. The squadron was almost to the valley.

Staring up to the left, I sought for the machine gun, and my eyes lighted on it almost instantly. It stood in plain view from where I crouched—a squat, ugly affair on a tripod mount with four or five boxes of ammunition open behind it, a belt of ammunition in its breech and several Mexicans crouched around it; one of them sat with his hands on the firing mechanism.

The bullets still whined around me. Very quickly I made up my plan of action. I would wait until the advance troopers of the squadron rode over the crest on the opposite side of the draw, not over five hundred yards away, then rise and signal them from the hilltop, taking a chance with the Mexican's fire. Crouching, tense, with my heart hammering and my breath coming in nervous gasps, I waited, staring at the point of the trail where it disappeared over the opposite hill.

Then I noticed a sudden cessation of the fire from behind and glanced over my shoulder to see what it was all about. I caught my breath sharply at what I saw.

For there in the plain below me, not four hundred yards from the Mexican force, was my own troop issuing from a cleft in the hills.

As rapidly as they entered the plain they galloped out into a long line of foragers and began to move forward, slowly at first, then faster and faster until they were galloping full tilt at the enemy—a wave of horsemen attacking twice their number!

It was too far to make out individual men, but I could not see Rollins' horse with its three white stockings and its blaze face. The line swept onward. God, how I wished I were with them! But my job was to save the squadron if it was humanly possible. There was no time to mount up now and gallop to meet them. It was a case of staying right where I was and warning them by signal, keeping myself concealed from the machine gun crew until the last possible second.

Still, there was no sign of the approaching squadron—only that cloud of dust hanging above the road to the rear. The machine gun waited, its crew grim and silent, hands on firing mechanism ready to unloose a hail of death when the unsuspecting cavalry was completely in its field of fire.

The distant crack of pistols began to reach my ears. Turning to glimpse the scene below, I saw the line of foragers almost upon the Red Flagger force, when suddenly I heard a whistle blast and saw every trooper turn his horse to the left, forming a column of troopers—a long, flexible formation that began to circle the Mexicans like a whip lash.

As the tail of it snapped forward I could see that the pistols were doing execution, dropping men and horses among the enemy. The Red Flaggers seemed to be bewildered, and fired only desultory, wild shots at the rapidly moving target. The troop galloped steadily around their flanks, the men, fresh from weeks of pistol practise, firing as calmly as though they were shooting at cardboard silhouette targets instead of living flesh.

From them I glanced back at the valley with its silent machine gun crew. There was no sign of the squadron, yet I did not dare leave my post, as they might appear any second. Glancing to the rear again, my eye picked up another movement far to the left and rear of the Mexican force, and I made it out as the two troop wagons. My heart sank at this sight, for there went all our rifles and ammunition toward Mexico. I craned forward, anxiously studying the distance they still had to go before they reached the Rio Grande and were out of our clutches on the far side. They only had about two miles to make—and mules travel fast!

The troop was still circling the Mexican flank, drawing steadily toward its rear, the continuous crack of the pistols sounding like corn popping at this distance. Far ahead the wagons rolled along.

Then like a flash of lightning it came over me what the troop was after; they were after those wagons and their rifles and ammunition. The Mexican force must have seen it at the same instant, for I saw a sudden flurry among them and a large mounted group began to detach itself and parallel the troop as it moved in the direction of the wagons. The pressure was a little relieved on the remaining group, and they announced this fact by resuming their fire on my position. Bullets began to thud and smack around me again, and I crouched down like a man trying to avoid a burst of rain.

But there was no time for crouching. My anxious eye spied a black spot on the opposite side of the valley from whence the squadron was coming, and a trooper began to top the rise. I could make out the pink blur of his face behind his horse's ears as he rose up steadily, coming on at a trot. Behind him, other men appeared, then I saw the flash of the squadron standard. The whole outfit must be jammed up on the advance guard, I reasoned, and moved forward, ready to spring to my feet and wave them back. Giving a last glance at the machine gun, I saw that its crew were aware of the squadron and were ready to unloose their infernal clatter as quickly as the troopers were fully exposed.

Now the leading troopers of the point were in plain view, riding down the slope. Behind them came the advance party—squad—and behind them I could see the solid mass of the squadron beginning to roll over the hill crest.

It was time to warn them.

I rose to my feet, leaping to the top of the hill. The firing had died down behind me but I expected it to start afresh at any second. Just as I appeared in full view the machine gunners saw me and pointed excitedly in my direction. The stubborn firer shook his head and continued to train his gun on the larger target—which proved him not so dumb at that.

I flung up my arms and semaphored to the leading units of the squadron. No one seemed to see me. It must be my background, I thought, and went below the crest, signaling again. Still there was no response; every one in the squadron was riding to the distant sound of firing to the front. I tried shouting, but the wind was against me.

Now nearly the whole of the leading troop was in plain view of the machine gunners. I saw the guidon of the second troop mounting the crest of the opposite hill. I waved and shouted again, my heart sick with dread, my ears strained to catch the first premonitory rattle of the machine gun as it swept down living flesh and blood with its leaden hail.

Glancing in despair at the machine gunner, I saw him settle into his position and unlock a lever. Now it was coming!

I gave one last shout and glanced helplessly at the machine gun. Now the gunner was looking along his sight and swinging the barrel back and forth to test it. An officer stood above him, his hand raised. The gunner now watched this man's hand.

I watched in dread fascination for that hand to descend. Nearly the entire two troops were in plain view now. The leader nodded. His hand began to drop; I held my breath. . . .

Suddenly I saw the machine gunner look up, startled. His glance was followed by the others. The crouching men rose, tugging at their revolvers. There was a shout on the hillside above them.

Down at full gallop came a blaze faced sorrel with three white stockings. In the saddle was Rollins, twirling something about his head. The horse came down that hillside like a bat out of hell, scattering fire as it struck the rocks, slipping and sliding and leaping, but coming on like a bullet straight at the gun crew.

Frightened at this four footed apparition about to land among them, the Mexicans drew back. Rollins' horse leaped among them. There was a whirl and something coiled through the air.

The machine gun suddenly toppled over on its base and began rapidly to bound and slide along behind the lone horseman. The Mexican gun crew fired after the despoiler of their weapon, but they were too late; he was rapidly galloping toward the squadron, the blued steel gun leaping and bounding along behind him like some live thing.

I found myself shaking like a leaf and ran back down the hillside to Murphy. A hasty glance at the plain below showed the main group of Mexicans still standing fast while the detached body was hurrying toward the river to protect the wagons and their precious freight from Troop A. I saw the golden sorrels of the troop nearing the wagons, and the wagons nearing the river.

I threw myself into the saddle. Our horses scrambled up the walls of the arroyo and teetered precariously a second on the edge above. We drove them on. Just at that second I saw a horseman flash over the hill above me and speed down the slope recklessly. It was the blaze faced horse with the three white stockings.

After him, like a torrent, poured the river of men of the squadron, rolling resistlessly down the slope. Once at the bottom they formed rapidly. I galloped on their flank as sabers flashed out and the squadron swept forward like a steel set wall.

The main group of Mexicans saw the wave of horsemen rolling at them and broke, scattering in all directions. That was a wild ride. I can feel the wind rushing in my face to this day, with Golden Dawn stretched out under me and the swift earth flashing past, and a sea of waving manes and gleaming bits and glittering steel on my left as the squadron thundered forward.

Ahead of us the white stockinged sorrel scattered pebbles behind him. Still farther ahead a confused group milled about the two wagons. The white stockinged sorrel disappeared in the welter of men and horses.

When we arrived the fight was over. I saw Rollins shoot a Mexican driver out of one of the wagons; willing hands seized the frightened mules. The main group of Red Flaggers were flying toward the river.

Captain Bullen shouted an order. There was a sudden halt and the thump and creak of men dismounting. One or two rifles began to speak; more and more took up the burden until the front of the squadron was outlined by a steady crackling as the dismounted men sent storms of lead after the fleeing Mexicans, who were getting out of range as rapidly as their horses could carry them.

A trumpet sounded "cease firing." Sergeant Henderson rode up and reported the troop present and accounted for, with three men slightly wounded and one horse gone, and all arms and ammunition recovered. He went away and soberly began to reorganize the troop, designating drivers for the wagons and horse holders for the led animals.

The officers of the squadron assembled. Rollins came up as I stood there talking to Bull Manners and Gramp. I looked at the youngster curiously as he approached. A silence fell on the group.

He came to a full stop in front of me and drew himself up, saluting.

"I have to report myself, sir, for disobedience of orders in leaving the camp unguarded during your absence," he announced, and stood there silent, his face white.

Manners and Gramp tactfully withdrew out of earshot.

"Do you suppose it will be a lesson to you to obey orders hereafter?" I asked. "Or will it be necessary to try you by court-martial to impress it on you?"

"I deserve a court-martial," he answered without a tremor.

He stood there straight and silent. I gazed at him a moment searchingly. Suddenly I put my hand on his shoulder.

"We'll try to get along without the court-martial, kid," I said, and looked away so as not to see his eyes, which had suddenly filled with tears.

Strolling back to where the others stood, Captain Bullen stopped me.

"What happened?" he asked.

Briefly I told him—told him everything, almost. He nodded after I'd finished.

"Pretty gritty stunt, roping that machine gun," he commented. "He ought to be commended for that."

I shook my head. Bullen looked at me a second, then nodded understandingly.

"He's your pup," he said. "You train him." And he walked away. Bull Manners spoke up—

"What's going to happen to the Boy Wonder of the Western Plains?" he asked.

"Nothing is going to happen," I said dryly, "except that in the future, as in the past, he'll get all the objection and reproof he needs from his own troop commander." And then in a low voice I told him about the roping of the machine gun, a maneuver they had not seen or, if they had, had not understood. They said nothing, only nodded. Bull Manners reached into his saddle pockets and drew forth a silver flask. He unscrewed the small cup from its cover. Gramp Jackson took the cup.

The two of them marched solemnly over to where Rollins stared off into the distance. Gramp held the cup while Bull poured the whisky.

"Kid, how about a little drink?" they asked him.

Excerpt from The Camp-Fire

Bridgehampton, L.I.

THERE ARE PROBABLY FEW CAMP-FIRE READERS who have not heard the term "shavetail" applied to a second lieutenant, but I wonder how many of them know the origin of the term. The name was first applied in the Army to the green mules when they arrived to do their service, it being the dealer's custom to shave a mule's tail for several inches down its length, leaving a tuft of hair at the end. The transition of the name from green mules to green second lieutenants seems to have been an easy and natural process in the mind of the soldier.

The regular Army soldier, be it said to his credit, has generally regarded the shavetail officer with a certain amount of kindly tolerance, making allowances for his youth and inexperience, an attitude not always earned by the war time second lieutenant, known often as "the ninety day wonder," "the Sears Roebuck looie," and other terms not so complimentary. Some of the Camp-Fire will remember the story of the old French woman who was saving up her money, earned serving *vin rouge* to the doughboys, and contemplating a trip to America, where she hoped to meet the famous Madame B., the mother of all those second lieutenants.

But where the "shavetail" did not attempt to cover ignorance by arrogance, the soldier was more than willing to meet him halfway, realizing that the junior subaltern officer's life was a hard one. One of the verses of "Parlez-Vous," that famous battle song of the Western Front, takes cognizance of this fact:

> The second lieutenant goes over the top,
>> Parley-vous,
> The second lieutenant goes over the top,
>> Parley-vous
> The second lieutenant goes over the top
> For he's expendable, is he not?
>> Hinky dinky, parley-vous!

But while the mortality records showed that the much abused class of officers wearing the tiny gold bar certainly did their share, I can imagine a tired soldier, his arm weary from saluting, paraphrasing Lincoln by saying that "God must love the shavetails, he made so many of them!"

In this story, "Shavetail," I have tried to show the impact of a certain type of newly joined second lieutenant upon a staid old regiment of cavalry. Any of the Camp-Fire readers who have served in these old regiments will know what I mean when I say that each of those regiments has a character and soul of its own, which differs from all other regiments, as distinctly as the character and soul of an individual differs from all other individuals. In the older regiments the differentiation is even more marked because they have the force of tradition behind them. In the Second Cavalry we were very proud of the fact that the regiment had been the old Second Dragoons and had fought through practically every war in the history of the country. We were also proud of the fact that the orange yellow facings of the old Second Dragoons had been adopted as the cavalry color for all cavalry regiments and persists today.

Seeing what value men place upon comparatively small things, it has always seemed to me a pity that the staid and portly old gentlemen in the Quartermaster Corps who regulate such matters as uniforms do not allow some small differentiation in regimental facings so as to accentuate regimental individuality and increase a man's pride in his unit. The British show more wisdom in this respect, realizing that pride in the regimental name will hold many a battalion doggedly to its task when patriotism for the country at large might not do the trick.

Men who are called upon to fight and die need something tangible upon which to center their loyalties, and the regiment provides this. There was no need of fostering this instinct in the old Second Cavalry, nor in many other old regiments, but the 2nd happened to be my first regiment, and has succeeded in retaining all the glamour of first love in spite of assignment to many another regiment thereafter.

My striker, who served with me for years, has joined me in civil life, but is still a staunch Second Cavalryman in spirit, and often, when the children are asleep, the house is quiet and the dishes are finished, we foregather in the kitchen, being joined by another ex-Second man, now working as chauffeur for one of my friends, and the three of us talk of the glory of the Second Horse, forgetting the duties and claims of the present and being wafted back on wings of memory to the days when each morning was the start of a fresh adventure, when we rode with steel at our sides and steel on our heels, heard the thunder of galloping squadrons and the arrogant bronze notes of the trumpets and rejoiced exceedingly that we were part and parcel of that living, breathing, entity called the Second Cavalry.

Such hold has the old regiment upon us. I hope that, in the story, some of you Camp-Fire readers who have galloped, "left front into line" will recognize a touch or two of the old days, and that you who have not had that experience will gain a little understanding of our affection for the crossed sabres.

—MALCOLM WHEELER-NICHOLSON

The Philippines

The Colonel Who Drank Alone

"IT SEEMS A SHAME TO TURN HIM THE COLD SHOULDER when there are only three of us aboard the ship," I offered.

"To hell with him!" growled Neal and viciously punched the call bell for the steward. The latter, a portly, solemn-faced cockney Englishman, came out of the bar, looked over the bunch of British officers in one corner of the smoking room, then headed over our way.

"Why don't you like him?" I continued.

"Whiskies and sodas," Neal said to the steward, then turned to me. "Why don't I like him?" He laughed harshly. The lines around his mouth deepened. I looked over at the British officers soberly sipping their drinks. We were only the first day out from Nagasaki and so far we had neither spoken to them nor had they as much as nodded at us.

I figured that it would be a pretty lonely trip for this other American army file, a Colonel Garbner, with Neal and myself letting him strictly alone and the British sitting tight in their own little group of serious thinkers. I shrugged my shoulders a little impatiently.

"I don't know him from Adam," I said, "but before I begin to treat him like a red-headed stepchild, I'd like to know what it's all about. He's regular army, like us, and he's cavalry, like us. And if we turn him out a silence, he'll have to go fluttering around this ghastly big lonesome ship all by himself for fourteen days. Certainly the Limeys over there won't loosen up and take him in."

Neal sipped his drink and looked over at the group of British officers seated at the far side of the big smoking lounge.

"Oh, they're all right," he said absently. "It's best to be a little formal with that breed on the take-off; besides, we're guests on one of their ships and they always do the right thing eventually. And also two of them are Canadians and they're good mixers. No, he'll be looked after and have somebody to chin with. As far as I'm personally concerned, all that Garbner will get is strictly military courtesy—the—"

I looked up sharply. The short and biting term he used, a sort of a picket-line word, if you know what I mean, is very rarely applied as a term of opprobrium toward brother officers—at least in our service.

Neal sat frowning at his glass. He looked up after a while.

"I'll tell you why I don't like him," he said. "It's because of what happened to Leeds. Leeds was before your time. He was a classmate of mine, my roommate at West Point. We joined up with the old Seventh together. Then Leeds drew down a foreign-service tour and went out to the Philippines. He drew this bird Garbner for a troop commander. Leeds was one damn fine officer and one damn fine man. I loved him like a brother. Everybody loved him—men, women, children, horses, dogs. Garbner was captain, Leeds the shavetail. They went out to get that Moro outlaw, Bakiri, down in the Southern Islands. They got Bakiri. Garbner came back. There was a nasty smell raised, and a board of inquiry whitewashed Garbner. But nobody in the service has had any use for Garbner since. It was too raw a case of springing one's rank."

Neal subsided moodily. He was much older in the service than I was, although we were both majors of cavalry. I could not help but be sorry for this poor bird of a colonel who had the whole service down on him, and reflected on the exceeding cohesiveness of a tag once stuck on an officer. You'd think, what with the regular army being scattered from hell to breakfast, that an officer's reputation at one place would not bob up at another place thousands of miles away—but, boy, how she do bob! It's because there is always, in any group of regular-army officers, or their wives—especially their wives— some member of the famous "I-Knew-Him-When" club.

From West Point itself, where the corps of cadets can turn out the terrible "silence" that ends a tactical officer's usefulness to the academy, to isolated army posts, where a man can sit alone in his quarters for weary months, to this ship out on the bosom of the north Pacific, where two officers of his own branch of the service treated him with the coldly formal courtesy required by regulations, his life must have been a veritable hell on earth for years.

I found it in my heart to pity that man and to wonder if he had not sufficiently expiated, in misery and loneliness of spirit, the thing with which he had been charged.

The old north Pacific was doing her best to prove that her name was a mistake. The steward came again and renewed our drinks.

"Tastes pretty good after that vodka," I mumbled, thinking of the muddy roads of Siberia and the fiery drinks on the far Amur.

"It's the first Scotch we've had since we left Manila to go to Vladivostok," Neal remembered. And thinking of Manila we began to talk about the gang at the Pasay Polo Club and to argue about the last polo championship wherein Neal's team had lost to mine.

Engrossed in this I scarcely noticed that the outer door, leading to the promenade deck, had opened. I was kidding Neal about the aftermath of that last game and the resulting party when he'd wandered out in the night and lost himself on the polo field. He was grinning at the memory when I saw him wipe the smile from his face as he looked up at the door. Then he rose stiffly and bowed, his face suddenly engraved into a stony mask. Looking behind me I caught a glimpse of olive drab and polished leather and the glitter of silver eagles, and I rose likewise, half turning toward the newcomer.

The first impression I received of him was of strength, allied with soul weariness. Tall, well built, iron-gray haired, wearing his uniform well, looking every inch the capable colonel of cavalry, fit and able to swing a thousand horsemen through a complicated maneuver, there was yet something world weary and bitter about his eyes.

He stopped before our table and bowed formally.

"Nice day, gentlemen," he said coldly.

"Yes, sir," we replied both together, both standing like wooden images. He looked at us a second with those tired eyes and then, bowing again, went on. We relaxed and sat down as he found himself a table alone, halfway between us and the British officers. Neal's eyes were stormy looking.

"The ——," he said under his breath, again applying that picket-line term to a brother officer—a thing rare in my experience. Somehow it shocked me worse this time than it had before. The expression seemed doubly inappropriate after I had seen Colonel Garbner. The epithet seemed needless, for, after all, we had given Garbner the cut direct, it being ordinarily an unheard-of thing for two officers to turn the cold shoulder to a third officer as we had done by not asking him to join us.

I felt pretty rotten about it somehow and it took the joy out of things. My drink tasted flat and the pleasure I had felt at being once more in civilized surroundings, after those weary months in Siberia, seemed suddenly to have vanished.

The smoking room was pretty quiet. In the far corner were the British officers and the two Canadians. In the center sat Colonel Garbner. At the other side were Neal and myself, saying little. We adjourned to dinner after awhile and the big dining salon was just as sad and whispery as the smoking room. Neal and I found ourselves at a little table in a corner, Garbner sat alone some distance from us, and the British officers dined with the captain. The exceedingly small passenger list accentuated the entire loneliness of the colonel. On an ordinary voyage he would have been lost in the crowds that fill smoking room, dining room and decks, but here on this almost-deserted liner he was as conspicuous as a white horse in a troop of bays.

On the second day out the Canadians flocked with us and we punished some drinks. On the third day out the British came over and we all forgathered in state. Garbner did not come to the smoking room after that first day. I saw him sitting alone in the dining room. Once, passing by the writing room, I saw him reading alone in there, but he was conspicuous by his absence from the gatherings in the smoking room. Nor did we see him in our walks around the deck.

The British and Canadians were regular fellows, and since we were all officers, all of us having been in active service and having "fit and bled," we hit it off famously, finally deciding to mess together in the dining room.

It got to be the custom for us to forgather for cocktails in the smoking room and all repair to dinner simultaneously, thereafter returning to the smoking room for coffee and liqueurs and much chin wagging from then until bedtime.

I thought very often of the lonely figure of the colonel, and felt pretty sorry for him and the ghastly time he must be having all alone on that great ship.

No landsman on board ship, after contemplating the vastness of the heaving waters, can do anything but turn and cling to humankind, so huge is the sea and so immense the sky and so tiny a dot is the little floating bit of steel and wood venturing across its surface.

Friendships ripen quickly at sea for this reason and our little group became very chummy after a few days out. Once or twice they asked curiously about the colonel and we returned some evasive answer, but I am quite convinced that they thought the colonel took his rank too seriously and didn't wish to mix with lower orders, and they became more or less accustomed to disregarding him.

The Canadians and we Americans used to kid the British a lot and they came back in their own way, each of us, as is the way of the Anglo-Saxon, serene in the knowledge of his own perfection and mildly tolerant of the other fellow's deficiencies.

The coziness of the smoking room was accentuated by the bleak and wintry aspect of the north Pacific—a tossing waste of gray water overhung with scudding, dark clouds. We must have been about five days out when the British started some sort of a celebration. Whether it was Guy Fawkes Day, the king's birthday or the birthday of the Prince of Wales, I've forgotten now, but whatever it was we helped them celebrate it, with the consequence that things livened up around the smoking room and we all became cheerful to the point of a restrained hilarity, if you know what I mean.

Along toward midnight the more conservative members "toddled along" to bed, leaving three of the British, the two Canadians and Neal and myself, all going strong with the barroom left open after hours as a special dispensation.

Pretty soon the two Canadians began to whisper together, then disappeared, returning after a few minutes with Colonel Garbner. What they had said to him or how they had prevailed upon him to join us, I never did know, but there he was, his eyes grave and a little tired looking. We all rose as he joined the table, and he was introduced by the Canadians, thereafter seating himself as far from us two as he could get.

It may have been that the loneliness had begun to wear on him and that he welcomed an opportunity, any opportunity, to hold speech with his own kind. At any rate he sat there with the courteous tolerance of the man who comes late to a drinking party, not looking at us. I stole a side look at Neal. He was slumped back in his seat, staring at his glass and saying nothing.

It wasn't long before Garbner, of course, felt it incumbent upon him to set up a round of drinks, and he sent the steward around to each of us to take the orders. When the man came to Neal, Neal pointed to his glass, already three quarters full of whisky and soda, and shook his head ever so lightly. Garbner saw it and the smile faded from his face and the weary look came back into his eyes again. I had nearly a full glass myself but luckily the steward missed me in his rounds—for which I was heartily glad. But the drinks came and there was a chorus of "How!" and "Maskee!" and "Cheerio!" on every one's part—except Neal, who mumbled something and looked the other way. No one noticed it except Garbner and myself.

We toasted the President of the United States and the King of England, told stories and inevitably began to wax a little sentimental. It's funny what a streak of sentimentality there is in the average Britisher! At any rate they began to reminisce about various of their friends who had passed on, this one at Ypres, the other at Gallipoli and so on, and then solemnly hoisted themselves to their hind legs and drank a toast to the absent and gone.

It was in the rather uncomfortable hush that followed this that Neal spoke up. We were all standing, no one quite looking at any one else. Neal seemed steady enough on his pins, as steady as one could be with a gale on and the old ship rolling six ways for Sunday. But there was a funny flare in his eyes, a flare I'd noticed before when he was well along in the shank of the evening. His words came very clearly and slowly. He stared off at a corner of the smoking room not looking at any one as he spoke.

"I'd like you all to drink a little toast to one of the finest white men who ever lived," he said, "one of the fairest, finest, squarest men I ever knew, who passed out fighting the Moros in the far Philippines. Gentlemen, I drink to Jimmy Leeds!"

The British and Canadians started to drink the toast solemnly. Then they paused, sensing something out of the way, and stared curiously at us, the three American officers. For Garbner had turned white. Neal's face was impassive. What my own face showed I don't know, but it was patent to every one that there was more to this toast than appeared on the surface. I know that I held my glass halfway to my lips and stared at Garbner.

He certainly had iron self-control, that man. Very quietly he drank in response to the toast, then, looking directly at Neal, he spoke without a tremor.

"I echo your statement," he said. "He was one of the finest men I have ever met, in the army or out." And he emptied his glass and placed it very carefully in the leather-covered iron ring provided for rough weather. In, the silence that followed, some one sat down and we followed the example.

"Haw!" said the British major, breaking the silence. "He must have been quite a decent sort, this man Leeds. You knew him, colonel?" he asked Garbner.

"It was while under my command that he came to his end," said Garbner steadily, looking at Neal as he spoke. Neal nodded and waited. The British were a little awkward and constrained, sensing some tenseness in the atmosphere, but Garbner and Neal were calm.

"It is somewhat of an interesting story," continued Garbner. "Perhaps you would like to hear it—and pass judgment on it?" The British and Canadians nodded. Neal sat silent and aloof in the attitude of a judge listening to evidence. And it was very strange, but I felt at that moment as though the smoking room had suddenly turned into a court-martial chamber. In just a few seconds the table had lost its character as a convivial board and had assumed a sterner aspect. And we sat around it, all of us officers, all in field-service uniform, and just about the right number for a court-martial. The effect was heightened by Garbner's position; he did not sit directly at the table, it being crowded, but a little to one side, where an accused might sit during a trial.

"It's about time that you heard the story," Garbner said to Neal directly, "that you heard the real story of what actually happened. It might interest you, gentlemen"—Garbner turned courteously to the British and Canadian officers—"as showing the type of fighting we have in the Southern Islands of our Philippine group."

"Quite so," agreed the British major. "The natives there are Mohammedans, are they not?"

Garbner nodded.

"It was a pretty lonely place, away out of the world. It took us about thirty days from San Francisco by army transport, and then another week or two getting down to the Southern Islands at the extreme tip of the Philippine archipelago near Borneo. As there was active service down there, I had tried to get transferred over and finally succeeded in reporting at San Francisco to sail on the next transport. Happy as I was at the chance of active service, I was under no illusions as to the loneliness and distance of the place I was going to. There were about three days to wait for a transport and I meant to enjoy those days gaily, not knowing when I would have a chance again, if ever. You know the feeling?"

Every one nodded.

"To explain a little what followed and to show you my state of mind when I first met Leeds, I must go back a little to the period before I started for the Philippines. I was foot-loose and fancy free, but I met an exceedingly beautiful girl in San Francisco—met her very unconventionally and in two days found myself infatuated with her. We dined and danced together. The night before sailing we were at Tait's. I saw a classmate of mine there at another table—Powell of the artillery. He looked at me rather strangely and bowed, but I forgot him, being interested in the girl. Betty her name was— not that it matters—but anyway the evening was perfect, as such an evening frequently is—when a not unattractive officer meets a beautiful girl on the eve of departure to war. When I saw her the next day she appeared troubled about something and it finally came out that she was in a little temporary financial difficulty. I lent her some money—three hundred dollars I think it was. At the transport dock I met Powell. In the course of conversation he asked me about Betty, calling her by her name.

" 'Did she nick you for some cash?' he inquired casually, and before I could answer, he went on, saying that her usual request was for about three hundred. It made me pretty sick, I can assure you. I am telling all this to explain the rather bitter and disillusioned state I found myself in on arriving in the islands. But once reported for duty I found an individual who was a cure for any one's cynicism. A lieutenant was in charge of the troop—Second Lieutenant Jimmy Leeds."

Garbner stopped a moment and tapped thoughtfully on the table edge as though recalling memories out of a distant past.

"In the heart of all of us," he went on, "I suppose there exists a little envious admiration of the Chevalier Bayard type of man—the knightly officer, '*sans peur et sans reproche*,' " he said gently. "We are envious of him because he represents the lost ideals of our own youth; we admire him because of those ideals. Seldom do we love him. Yet there comes on the stage of life occasionally one who has all of these qualities and, in addition, has the faculty of winning the love of his fellow men."

I looked up and stole a glance at Neal. He was leaning back, staring at Garbner with hard, bright eyes.

"Such a man was Leeds," said Garbner. "In spite of the experience I had just gone through it was impossible to remain cynical around Leeds. We had been at Jolo a few weeks when the States mail came through. Among my letters was one from Betty. It shocked me a little, for her letter betrayed a coarseness that I had not noticed in her presence. She had ended the missive with a crimson smear of lipstick, the imprint of her lips on the paper. Leeds and I were reading our mail at the same time in the orderly room. I looked up to see his face glowing with a rare light.

" 'Good news, son?' I asked.

" 'A letter from my wife!' he said reverently. Suddenly I felt like a cynical old satyr and envied him and his perfect love and felt ashamed of the grossness of my own experience. I tore my letter into little bits and threw it away, determined to forget Betty for all time.

"Leeds was the type of officer that soldiers adore—cleanly bred, quiet voiced, capable, with a smile that would disarm the grouchiest guardhouse lawyer in the army and he had the troop eating out of his hand. You know how you can tell those things—the little extra attention from the mess sergeant, the extra hours put in by his striker, the saddler who labors over a new belt or spur straps and replaces the old ones without a word, the bedding roll that is always dragged along somehow, no matter what else is left behind, all the various little things that soldiers do quietly and on the side when they approve of an officer.

"We were cleaning up the island of Sulu, disarming the Moros gradually and affording what protection was possible to the road-building parties. These road builders of ours were at the mercy of countless *juramentados*, fanatic Mohammedan Moros who decide to perish in administering death to as many infidels as possible. They went to their fate deliberately, assured of an eternity in paradise, an eternity made doubly attractive by the delights of the Mohammedan heaven, which include a huge shade tree, a milk-white horse and a group of beautiful houris. The old priests had worked out a regular scale of rewards—so many houris for the death of each American private, a correspondingly larger number for corporals, sergeants and officers, so that the murder of an American captain would assure the true believer a harem of huge proportions.

"There were some rather amazing ceremonies attendant upon the preparation of these fanatics for their fate, ceremonies deserving of discussion themselves; but the upshot of the whole business was to make life an exceedingly precarious and risky affair for our men and officers. One could never tell when one of these opium-crazed, wild-eyed men would come leaping out of the jungle cutting and slashing at all and sundry with a heavy, razor-edged *barong*. Of course, they were always brought down eventually, but it took a lot of shooting to do it. I've known of one of those fellows with twenty-two bullets in him who still kept on going and cut down a couple of men before he was laid low with the butt of a rifle. It was mainly on account of these fanatics that the American cavalry adopted the .45 pistol in preference to the old .38.

"Jolo, the ancient walled city, had been the stronghold of the Spaniards and practically their only foothold on the island. After we had had a few nasty experiences with the *juramentados*, strict orders were issued that no armed Moros were to be permitted within the walls, and a rigorous search was made of every native entering the two gates.

"Leeds and I messed together in a *nipa* shack near headquarters, making ourselves as comfortable as possible. We spent a great deal of time in each other's company. I grew very fond of him and I think he liked me, for we were together almost constantly, reading and smoking and talking. Occasionally he would speak of his wife. If ever a man worshipped a woman it was Leeds. When he spoke of her his face lighted up with a rare beauty, a hushed note came into his voice, his whole bearing assumed the exalted manner of a devotee worshipping at a shrine. He had left her behind in the States, fearing to expose her to the hardships of life in the tropics and the dangers of savage warfare. There were few women in the regiment, one of them being the wife of Lieutenant Bradney, who had followed her husband, to Jolo, bringing their small, six-year-old daughter with her.

"Bradney was a classmate of Leeds and the two men were good friends. The small daughter worshipped Leeds. It was an attractive home and Leeds dined there two or three evenings a week—almost a member of the family.

"We had plenty of guard duty, 'Bud' North, our fiery old colonel, being a stickler for guard duty. We drew a tour one Sunday, it being my turn to go on as officer of the day, with Leeds on as officer of the guard. The guardhouse was near the west gate with about six posts around the town.

"You can imagine how quiet things are in the tropics at siesta time on a Sunday afternoon. It's sort of a slack time for the guard, for every one is engaged in getting in all the sleep possible in readiness for the long night ahead. And with Bud North it *was* a long night ahead, for the colonel required three inspections before midnight and two after midnight by the officer of the day, and two before midnight and three after midnight by the officer of the guard, in addition to a raft of special orders and requirements which had to be carried out.

"Leeds was, of course, at the post of the guard, where he sat on the porch, leaning back in a canvas camp chair. From there he could keep an eye on the west gate and on the sentries of Posts Nos. 1 and 2. The sergeant of the guard was about, as was the corporal whose relief was on post; but aside from these there was little stirring except a gecko lizard whose mournful and monotonous notes echoed from behind the guardhouse at annoying intervals.

"There was little traffic through the gate—an occasional native servant returning from a cock fight, an occasional Moro woman bringing in produce to sell, or an occasional Moro dandy, scented and oiled, mincing gingerly along, would pass in and out. Every Moro, of course, felt a little downcast at having his *barong* taken from him at the gate. After a while a two-wheeled cart, loaded with produce for the market, was stopped by the sentinel and inspected. Leeds rose and walked over, looked at the leathery-faced, red-eyed old Moro who drove it, and strolled around the cart examining its contents. Finally he nodded his permission to its driver and went back to his chair on the guardhouse porch. The cart drove on toward the market place. The heat and silence settled down with even more rigor. The gecko lizard kept up its mournful plaint. Leeds found his head nodding. But suddenly he sat bolt upright and leaped to his feet.

"A fiendish tumult of horror-stricken screams and yells had broken forth from the direction of the market place. In a second the place sounded like a bedlam. Without command men began to tumble out of their bunks. Pulling forth his pistol, Leeds ran toward the disturbance, followed by several scantily clad men of the guard. As they neared the racket they heard a long, wolflike howling dominating the lesser sounds.

"Rounding the corner Leeds saw a small group in the roadway. His eyes caught the glitter of steel as a *barong* swished through the air and descended again and again. It was wielded by a half-naked Moro *juramentado* standing over the prone figure of a khaki-clad white man. Not ten feet away Leeds saw Bradney's little daughter horrified and screaming. Leeds was first there and rushed at the Moro, firing. But the drug-crazed fanatic, paying no heed to the officer's weapon, simply swung in his tracks and came leaping toward the new victim. One of the members of the guard, nimbler witted than the rest, dropped on one knee and, from behind Leeds, cracked down on the Moro with several well-placed shots from his rifle, effectually crumpling up the savage, but not before he was almost on top of Leeds. More bullets thudded into the Moro until his twitching body was stilled.

"When I arrived on the scene, Leeds was kneeling by the body of the fallen white man. Some one had taken the little girl away, still screaming.

" 'It's Bradney!' whispered Leeds, and his eyes were staring strangely. The Moro had certainly done a thorough job on poor Bradney. An immediate investigation, held on the spot, disclosed that the *juramentado* had entered the town not ten minutes previously, slipping by the sentries and Leeds at the west gate, under the load of provisions carried by the two-wheeled cart. The fellow leaped out from under the load of stuff not six yards from where Bradney was walking along unarmed, going for a stroll with his little daughter. Seeing the leaping, yelling savage almost upon him, Bradney had no time to do anything except place himself in front of the child, before the Moro cut him down.

"This was bad enough but along came Colonel North, white haired, white mustached, with his angry-looking blue eyes blazing with wrath.

" 'How in the name of ten thousand blankety-blanks did this blankety-blank Moro get past the guards?' he shouted, shoving the dead Moro with his foot. Explanations came. It didn't take much explaining before the colonel turned like an angry bull on young Leeds.

" 'What in the name of half a dozen hells were you supposed to be doing as officer of the guard, Mr. Leeds?' yelled the Old Man, twisting his mustache. 'What in blazes do you think an officer of the guard is for—to sit up in the guardhouse and look pretty—' And so on for several chapters.

"Leeds was growing whiter and whiter, but the colonel went on:

" 'If it's any consolation to you, Mr. Leeds, you can comfort yourself with the fact that your inefficiency has cost Bradney his life. You're no better than his murderer, Mr. Leeds—d'ye understand? His murderer!' finished the Old Man and turned on his heel and went away.

"Leeds stood there, his face white and his eyes stricken. I took his arm.

" 'Come on along,' I said. 'It couldn't be helped; don't take the colonel too seriously.' I led him away.

"He followed me without protest, looking dazed.

" 'I killed him!' he whispered to himself. 'I'm his murderer; the colonel is right!' And he paid little attention to anything I said to him. Gentlemen, I tell you frankly, I felt that there had been a double tragedy that afternoon—first the killing of Bradney and second the killing of Leeds' youth by those ill-considered words of the colonel's. It was as though the freshness and resiliency of youth had passed out of him in those few minutes.

"Brooding over a fixed idea is bad for any one at any time or place, but it was especially bad for such a sensitive, high-strung chap as Leeds—and in the tropics, of all places, where a man's mind can so quickly become unhinged under the pitiless impact of the equatorial sun. It was not long until Leeds began to show unmistakable signs of going to pieces. He kept to himself, spoke seldom, and his face lost its healthy color and became grayish looking, his eyes haggard. I became desperate in my efforts to shake him out of himself and get him back to normal before it would be too late.

"It was only by accident that I found out the one thing that would take his mind off the constant preoccupation with Bradney's death and what he considered his responsibility for it. One of Bradney's hands had been severed by the Moro's *barong* and the memory of that severed hand returned to plague Leeds. I heard him moaning and tossing one night under the mosquito netting, talking about it. I turned on the lights and made him sit up and smoke with me. We chatted.

" 'You're a fool to take the thing so much to heart,' I said, deliberately brutal in an effort to shake him out of it. 'You have more than yourself to think about; remember your wife in the States and consider your responsibility to her.'

" 'My wife!' he whispered, and his eyes lit up with the glow that her name always evoked. For a second his face was transfigured. I saw my cue immediately and pressed the point, getting him to talk about her.

"It was the first time in a week or two that he forgot himself and his troubles. The dam once loosened, there was no stopping him. I sat there on the edge of my bunk, smoking and listening, while the tropical insects dashed themselves noisily against the lamp, and far down we could hear the murmur of the surf of the Sulu Sea. Never have I heard a man talk of a woman as that fine youngster talked of his wife; never have I heard such heights of devotion or such depths of reverence as Leeds poured forth, his eyes rapt, his whole being glowing. Gentlemen, it made me a little wistful, I tell you frankly, comparing the high idealism of his romance with my own muddied and bedraggled adventure, to hear this fervid youngster pour forth his soul like some knightly troubadour of ancient days—"

Colonel Garbner stopped suddenly and stared into space a moment as though recalling the scene in all its details, as though listening again to the low voice of Leeds throbbing to the murmur of the tropic sea. Neal was studying Garbner impassively, his eyes curiously alert and bright.

The colonel went on after a few seconds:

"If the lover's image of a woman is the reflection of his own soul, then I must say that Leeds had a very beautiful soul—and I count it a rare privilege to have been able to look into it for those few swift glimpses. It helped to restore a little my own lost faith and illusions. But the practical effect of these long talks in the night was to bring Leeds back again to something approaching normalcy. And then came an opportunity for active service, which I welcomed as further help.

"The Moros were getting more and more obstreperous and we punished them severely, sending out expeditions to disarm and arrest the worst of them. A short time after Leeds began to show signs of taking interest in life once more, I received orders to sally forth with my troop and capture a notorious Moro outlaw named Bakiri, who had been instrumental in chopping up several American sentries and generally defying our authority.

"He was hidden somewhere back in the hills behind Jolo where he was said to have a stronghold. It was on a Friday night that we received our orders to move out before daylight the next morning and round up this fellow and his followers. Naturally we were delighted. There was only one fly in the ointment. The monthly inter-island ship, bringing news, mail and friends from the States, was due in the next day at noon and we would miss the flurry of excitement that its arrival always caused in this out-of-the-way place. Leeds was a little glum, for he expected letters from his wife, but the bustle of departure and my promise to arrange to have mail brought to us a day or two later, cheered him up and he went hammer and tongs at the job of preparing for field service.

"We moved out between the darkness and the dawn, passing through the gates and heading out south. As we cleared the gates and walls I saw Leeds look back, a queer expression on his face. Following his glance I saw nothing but the gate. Then I remembered that it was the gate through which the Moro cart had entered with the Moro *juramentado* concealed under its load.

" 'I won't come back to that place until I've redeemed myself,' remarked Leeds quietly, his jaw tightening. I said nothing in reply but busied myself in sending out an advance guard and flankers to protect our march. Leeds asked if he might take charge of the advance and I nodded, warning him to keep a sharp eye out for sudden rushes of half-naked savages from the underbrush. I ordered every man to move with loaded rifle and hand on revolver trigger. Knowing this country, I figured well that it was no Sunday-school picnic upon which we were embarking.

"To make matters more dangerous the trail which we followed was narrow and crooked. I posted myself well at the head of the main body, following closely on the heels of the connecting files, requiring every one to keep the man ahead in sight.

"It grew devilishly hot in that heavy, moist growth as the sun mounted up, and we were soon soaked in sweat. The men began to look fagged out before the morning was half advanced, but I pushed them ahead relentlessly, allowing no more than the regular ten-minute halt every hour. Things were quiet until a short time after the third halt. Then business began to pick up.

"The trail led up a small hill, under foliage and jungle growth so thick that it seemed as though we were moving through a tunnel. After five minutes of this it opened out into a sort of meadow filled with high, coarse-bladed grass. This meadow was not much more than twenty or thirty yards wide. The connecting file ahead of me had just disappeared into the tunnel on the far side of the meadow when I heard a shot ahead. It was followed by several more in quick succession, interspersed with high-pitched Moro yells and the deeper shouts of my own men. Rushing ahead, I came up with the rearmost connecting files.

" 'Where's the lieutenant?' I yelled above the noise of the firing. The nearest man, Corporal Grigsby, pointed forward, and I went on, followed by the first sergeant and the rest of the troop. It was so narrow that not more than three or four men could move abreast. Rounding the turn I saw Leeds, resting on one knee, firing steadily, protecting by his own body the body of one of our men stretched out flat across the trail.

"Beside him were the men of the advance guard and flankers, all firing like mad into a group of some fifty Moros bunched up where the trail opened out ahead. The bars of sunlight, piercing down through the tangled jungle, glittered and snapped from spear points and *barongs*. Throwing myself down beside Leeds I opened fire with my revolver. The men of the troop went into action as they arrived, dropping down to our right and left.

"It was at that second that the Moros decided to rush. In a second the forest trail was filled with leaping brown savages coming straight at us. More and more of my men had opened up with their rifles, some prone on the ground, others kneeling behind them and the rearmost men firing from overhead. Without command every man began to work his bolt and trigger at rapid fire. It began to tell as the Moros came on; they dropped like flies until at last there was scarcely a handful left. But that handful was among us and there began a silent battle with clubbed rifles against *barongs*. In another minute they were subdued and the *coup de grâce* administered to the last of them.

"Taking stock of our losses I found that two of our men were badly cut. The first man down, the one whose body Leeds had protected, was dead, drilled neatly through the head with a slug from an old musket. Leeds was shaken over this.

" 'It's my fault,' he whispered. 'Oh, God, can't I ever do anything but bring bad luck on the people around me?'

" 'Don't be a damn fool!' I told him sharply. 'You handled the situation very well. We can't fight these savages without an occasional loss.'

"But my words had little effect. I soon found out that he held himself responsible for the loss of the man who was killed, being certain that it was all his fault because he had not seen the Moros in time. There was little use arguing with him. I busied myself in caring for the wounded. Neither one of them was in danger except from the infection that is always present in this climate, so much so that it is difficult to heal even the smallest wound. For this reason I figured that it was better to send the two back to the post where they could have better medical attention. Starting them out with a good, strong escort, I headed forward again with the troop.

"We were making for the *cotta* of a certain *panglima*—a lesser Moro chieftain named Tawassil, who was said to know a great deal concerning the activities of the outlaw Bakiri. Tawassil was a suspicious character himself, and I had been warned not to trust him much farther than I could throw a mule by the hind leg.

"Later in the afternoon we were fired upon by two Moros hidden in trees. They were brought tumbling down in short order, falling all sprawled out through the air. So sudden was the end of their activities that shooting at American soldiers from treetops must have lost its interest as a major outdoor sport in that particular vicinity.

"We approached Tawassil's place along about four in the afternoon, walking up to the gate indifferently enough; but I was watching the heads bobbing up and down along the top of the mud-and-log wall, not knowing when they might decide to cut loose with a ragged volley of rusty nails and scrap iron from their old muzzle-loaders. But we succeeded in bluffing our way in without any trouble, and I held a little *hobla* a while with the old *panglima*, as villainous a specimen of criminal-looking savage as ever escaped hanging.

"The upshot of the talk was that he confessed to knowing where the outlaw held forth and agreed to send guides with us to show us the way. The valley in which the stronghold of the outlaw was supposed to be was not over half a mile from the *panglima's cotta*, and we continued our march immediately. I took the precaution of making the old villain go along with us.

"According to the *panglima*, Bakiri had about ten men with him—not much of a force if they were not ensconced in too strong a position. I gathered, from the remarks of the old boy on the way to the valley, that he wasn't any too fond of Bakiri, for he very cheerfully gave me much information that I didn't request.

"We soon came to the opening of the valley and I made camp there, arranging things for defense, and leaving a guard over our heavier equipment and the *panglima*.

"With a final "look-see" about the camp, we headed forth to make our way up the valley. It was a steep and precipitous affair with a trail not much bigger than a goat's track clinging to its side. Ahead of us were the two Moro guides and we toiled along in rear, envying the barefooted natives who made such quick progress compared to our toiling and heavy-footed ascent. Their good behavior was assured by the fact that the *panglima* was held as hostage down below in our temporary camp.

"After about half an hour of climbing, the Moros ahead suddenly halted before an outcropping elbow of rock around which the trail twisted and lost itself. They shook their heads and grinned at us, pointing at the rock.

"The hillside went sheer up above our heads at this point and dropped away for a hundred feet straight to the floor of the valley. The only possible means of advance was by the use of this trail. It was so narrow that only one man at a time could pass by the rock. And the Moros made it very clear to us that just around the corner lurked Bakiri himself with a *barong*, ready to slice off the first head that showed itself.

"The more I studied the situation the less pleasing did it look. There was absolutely no way above, below or around that rock except the narrow trail, which led to almost certain death for any man that followed it. The cliff overhead jutted out and overhung the place, making it impossible to toss dynamite or anything else from above. Nothing without wings could approach the place by any other route than the one which lay in front of us—the dusty trail, looking innocent and inviting as it led away around the rock.

"It was clear in my mind that the first man around that point would have a nasty time of it and that the second would stand almost as good a chance of getting his as well. I hadn't any idea of sacrificing any of my men in any such cold-blooded fashion.

"But Bakiri must be captured. And young Leeds volunteered immediately for the job of going first.

" 'You'll do nothing of the kind,' I told him shortly, knowing full well that the quixotic idea of redeeming himself was still possessing his mind.

"It was growing dark. After assuring myself that Bakiri could not escape from the other end of the valley, I decided to return to the camp for the night. It's strange how things work out sometimes."

Garbner looked at us all a moment, as though he saw us not at all but saw instead a hot valley far to the southward on the island of Sulu. We waited, no one daring to speak.

"Anyway," he continued, "we returned to camp, placing a careful guard at the lower end of the valley, making sure that our prey should not escape us.

"In the morning there returned the detachment we had sent back with the wounded men, bringing with them the mail and news from home that had come in on the ship after our departure. Leeds seized his mail eagerly and, turning his back on me, devoured a letter he'd received. My own mail was rather heavy. Among the letters was one from Powell, my classmate, whom I had last seen in Frisco.

"As I opened the envelope, out of it dropped a newspaper clipping. Intrigued and wondering what this was about, I picked up the clipping and read it in puzzled fashion. It was the description of a police raid on one of the toughest and most notorious road houses in the environs of San Francisco. The article gave the names of several people, men and women who had been seized in the raid. Among them I saw a name that seemed vaguely familiar. It was the name of a woman. Then, looking up at the corner of the scrap of paper I saw something written in Powell's fine handwriting—the word 'Betty.'

"It came over me in a second why the name was so vaguely familiar. I turned faintly sickish and cold, and was surprised to find that the episode of our meeting and my disillusionment still rankled after all this time. And looking through the remainder of my mail I found that, for the first time since I had been in the islands, there was no letter from her—that familiar letter with its great, scrawling characters and with the pair of rouged lips at the bottom of the last page. The absence of her letters was ominous in itself and confirmed the news of the clipping.

"The sergeant who had brought the mail saluted and reported several matters, among them the fact that he had started back to rejoin the outfit before the distribution of the second-class mail, and therefore had not been able to bring the newspapers and magazines, but that they were coming up with a supply detachment late that evening. This was cheerful news. I was hungry for reading matter from the States and the prospect of a great bunch of newspapers to go through was pleasant indeed. Glancing up from my mail I saw Leeds' face. His eyes were shining as he read his letter and, not knowing that he was observed, he raised it swiftly to his lips and kissed it. Again I felt that tinge of wistful envy go through me, thinking of his rose-colored romance and my mud-daubed adventure which had ended so drably. With a sigh I turned toward the official mail in its long envelopes.

"Among the letters was one from the regimental commander, Colonel North. In baldly flat language that left me no discretion, it ordered me to prefer charges against Second Lieutenant James Leeds under the 'Articles of War,' for neglect of duty because of the killing of Bradney by the *juramentado*.

"This was sickening news. Not that any court would find him guilty, but it would break the kid's heart. And then you know"—here Garbner looked at Neal very directly—"that once an officer is tried before a court-martial or has to appear before a board of inquiry, he becomes sort of an outlaw and is thereafter tagged in the service, no matter whether the findings are favorable or unfavorable."

Neal nodded. Garbner went on:

"There was no use breaking the bad news to Leeds before I had to. I stuck the letter in my pocket. It was time to start operations against Bakiri again, the outlaw waiting for us up above in the valley cave, around that shoulder of rock. I asked Leeds to form up the troop and have it ready to march. He rose joyously and hurried out of the tent, placing his letter on our camp table, face downward. The wind started to scatter it. I picked up two of the sheets from the ground and placed his canteen over them to keep the letter in place until his return.

"Outside there was the clatter and racket of soldiers forming up. Slipping on belt and revolver, I took over the troops, setting it in motion up the valley again. Leeds walked along silently beside me, his eyes shining. It was a beautiful morning, as fresh and clear as a spring morning in the States. The air was like wine.

"We came at last to where the trail narrowed again before rounding the outcropping shoulder of rock around which lurked Bakiri and his murderous *barong* and the murderous *barongs* of his gang of desperate men. They would fight like cornered rats, for they knew that they could expect no mercy from us after the atrocities they had committed. Somehow we must get Bakiri.

" 'Please let me go,' begged Leeds.

"I shook my head. Three or four soldiers asked if they could have the job, among them Corporal Grigsby. Again I shook my head.

" 'It's an officer's job,' I said, and refused to listen to any argument. Taking out my revolver I examined the cartridges. But Leeds was speaking again.

" 'In a case like this, captain,' he said very gravely, 'it isn't a matter of rank. I want a chance to redeem myself. The first man in there deserves a medal of honor. Let me have my chance, captain!' he pleaded. I thought of that letter from Colonel North—and thought of other things.

" 'Maybe I'd like to have a crack at that medal of honor myself, young fellow.' I smiled and took a coin from my pocket, one of those big Spanish silver pesos. 'How about a sporting proposition? Call heads or tails—winner to go first, loser to go second supporting him.'

"It was fair enough. The men crowded around as I spun the coin into the air.

" 'Heads!' called Leeds.

"The shining silver piece fell down on the rocky trail between us. The head of Alphonso XII stared up at us.

" 'Heads it is!' cried Leeds.

"I made him take a rifle instead of the .38 revolver he carried, feeling that he could better protect himself with it. I also armed myself with a rifle. The men crowded behind me ready to rush the outlaws as quickly as we had forced the way past the entrance.

" 'Ready?' I asked Leeds.

" 'Ready,' he answered, a thrill of excitement in his voice.

" 'Go on—and God bless you!' I added under my breath.

"He plunged around the jutting corner of rock. I was behind him with my rifle over his head trying to protect him from any downward cut.

"There was a nasty flicker of silvery metal and a coughing grunt. I felt something warm and wet strike my face. I had time to feel Leeds stagger against me as I reached forward with the rifle shoving it against the stomach of one of the tallest Moros I had ever seen. I pulled the trigger and he spun sidewise, his whole back blown out. A rifle spoke over my shoulder, nearly deafening me. Leeds had dropped to the ground. I stepped over him, shooting from the hip with my rifle. The men were firing from behind me. The whole show was over in two minutes with every Moro killed."

Colonel Garbner stopped and looked about the circle of men, all bent forward, scarcely breathing as they followed his narrative. He looked into Neal's eyes as he spoke again.

"And that, gentlemen, is the story of how Leeds came to his end."

The tension of the crowd did not relax in the slightest. In the silence I heard Neal clear his throat.

"But you say yourself the court-martial would not have found him guilty," he remarked quietly.

Garbner gazed at him, his eyes very patient.

"Yes, but don't you understand?" he said wearily. "I saw the letter from his wife when it fell to the ground back at camp. It was written in sprawling characters—and had a pair of rouged lips imprinted at the bottom of the last page—and—all the Frisco papers would have been in that afternoon."

There was a long silence at that table. Outside the north Pacific howled and flung spray against the portholes.

"Gawd!" said the British colonel jerkily, staring.

Neal rose to his feet.

"Colonel Garbner," he said very quietly, "I would feel myself very honored if you would join me in a drink."

Garbner said nothing for a space, but simply gazed at him with those tired eyes. Then, glancing down at his glass, which was about three quarters filled, he shook his head.

"Thank you," he replied, "but I *have* a drink."

Russia

The Tiger
of the Ussuri

THERE IS NOTHING LIKE A VOLLEY OF RIFLE FIRE, crashing from close at hand, to bring one out of a sound slumber. And Davies had slept soundly; the long trip from Vladivostok to this town near the Ussuri River, in the swaying, jolting Trans-Siberian train, had made him drop into his bed like a log and sleep the sleep of the just and the weary.

True to training, however, his muscles had propelled him out to the center of the floor while in his ears still echoed the crash of musketry which had awakened him. The silence that succeeded was broken again by a single shot.

Now thoroughly aroused, he hurried to the window, the double paned Siberian window with its single small panel open. Looking out in the dimness of the half dawn, he could faintly descry a group of men moving like gray shadows. Peering more closely, he saw one or two of them stooping over some huddled object that lay on the ground. Suddenly there came a sharp command from one of the group. All of them moved away toward some tethered horses which he observed for the first time. As the light grew stronger he saw them mount the horses, shaking out the long lances they carried. Another sharp command and the whole group hurried away. Seen dimly, he could make out the fur caps of Cossacks and could hear, as they trotted away, the unmistakable silvery jingle of spurs and bits and sabers.

The huddled figure still lay on the ground, silent and inert.

Davies turned from the window. There was a soft double knock on his

Illustration by
A.E. Lundquist

door. Some one was trying the handle.

"Come in!" he called. The door opened and a tall sergeant entered. Sergeant Duggan was attired in little else but underwear, but strapped on his hip rode his .45 automatic.

"What's all the shooting about?" Davies inquired.

"That's what I was aimin' to find out, Major." Duggan's voice, with its sun-hurried drawl, had never in Davies' experience betrayed the slightest trace of excitement.

"Well, with a pair of breeches apiece we might go out and investigate." Davies set about dressing himself.

Duggan looked down at his own scanty attire and grinned.

"Yes, sir, we sure enough ain't burdened with too many clothes." He disappeared, to return shortly, fully dressed.

The house was silent as they made their way out of the front door. The Russian *polkovnik*, a colonel in the former Siberian Rifle Corps, in whose house they were billeted, evidently considered curiosity an unsafe failing in these troublous times, for neither he nor his family showed themselves as the two Americans made their way out the door and across the street. They had scarcely reached the opposite side when another soldier joined them, a heavy set, morose eyed man, wearing a corporal's chevrons on his blouse. Nadonsky was an Americanized Russian who had been detailed as interpreter to accompany Davies on his mission.

The three made their way quietly to where the huddled figure lay on the ground. It revealed itself as the body of a man, in the Russian peasant boots and blouse. The frame was riddled with bullets. A little trickle of blood still oozed from a powder blackened hole in the forehead.

Nadonsky bent low over the body, then rose, crossing himself in the Russian fashion.

"Old Kill-'Em-Off is at his tricks again," Sergeant Duggan commented grimly. "Do you know who that guy could 'a' been?" he asked the silent and thoughtful Nadonsky.

"Yes." He nodded. "I once knew him verree well; he was with me, one time, long ago, ago—a—what do you say?—a comrade of mine." And Nadonsky reached down, straightening out the body tenderly and crossing the hands.

"Old Kill-'Em-Off is sure on the job," Duggan snorted.

"Kill-'Em-Off" was the soldiers' name for the Cossack Ataman Kalmikoff, the leader of the Cossacks of the Ussuri. These Cossacks were, under the Japanese command, acting as a sort of gendarmerie for the Allied forces in Siberia.

"What do you suppose they shot this fellow for?" asked Davies.

Nadonsky raised his inscrutable eyes to the officer's face and shrugged his shoulders slightly.

"Who knows?" he asked. Davies, studying the enigmatic gaze of this Russian interpreter, felt somehow that the man knew more than he would tell. Damn' funny people, these Russians. Just about the time you had figured them out as being real sure enough white men, they'd suddenly pull their shirts outside of their trousers and become the blandest and most devious of Orientals.

"But this man"—Nadonsky bowed his head and crossed himself again—"I knew him long ago. We were prisoners on that island—Sakhalin," he pronounced the name hesitantly.

"Oh, you were a prisoner on Sakhalin."

Davies looked on him curiously, remembering that only the worst and most hardened criminals were sent by the former Imperial Russian Government to that drear island which stretches along the Siberian coast from the Straits of La Perouse to the mouth of the Amur River separated from the mainland by a sea passage of from twenty to eighty miles in width.

"Yes, sir," Nadonsky nodded; then as if reading the mind of the American, "But sent there from Odessa only because I had tried again and again to escape. We were put aboard a ship, the Ship with the Dark Flag. I was chained to five other men and placed in an iron cage to be sent to the *katorga*—"

"What is that?" Davies asked curiously.

"It is very hard labor, for all peoples at Sakhalin—that is, for all except the executioners."

Nadonsky grew suddenly silent; he clenched his fists as at some bitter memory.

The three were returning gravely to the shelter of the house. Davies paused on the porch, keenly interested in the experiences of this silent and morose Russian.

"What were the executioners?" he asked.

"They were convicts, verree bad convicts. It was cruel on the island. We were chained to wheelbarrows, to pumps. Our tools were chained to us. Sometimes the mines would catch fire and many would die, or sometimes the mines would cave in and many would perish. It was hard, the *katorga*. But the executioners were given good time. They had nothing to do except torture and kill their comrades. Many times there was such brutality and such suffering that the convicts would mutiny. Then they would be overpowered and whipped by the executioners. From fifteen to three hundred whippings on the back they would get, with willow rods boiled in sea water." Nadonsky shrugged his shoulders. "Very few lived to tell about it," he remarked quietly. "Most would die before they had been whipped three hundred blows."

"But these executioners, what happened to them?" asked Davies.

"They were given their freedom early and could live on the island in their own houses—but they did not dare. One tried to and he was found dead. It is an oath the convicts take. They pass sentence of death on these executioners, the convicts do, and swear that they will kill them wherever and whenever they can be found. Sometimes they kill them years afterwards.

"Now, of course, it is all finished. There is no longer prison camp on Sakhalin. But somewhere in the world there are many executioners still alive and there are many of ex-convicts who will never forget"—and Nadonsky, his eyes somber, and a frown on his face, moved away absently, disappearing around the corner of the building toward the kitchens.

"Cheerful guy," Duggan looked after him, "cheerful as a mule with a mouthful of sour grass. I wouldn't like that bozo to start on my trail with the idea o' doin' away with me eventual."

"Queer people. Sort of a tragic country underneath all the music and carelessness," Davies reflected out loud. "Always some kind of a tragedy just around the corner in Russia." Then he shook his head as if to throw off the depression caused by the huddled figure on the opposite side of the street and the gruesome story of Nadonsky. "Well, we'd better get some chow and get busy. Nothing we can do over there." He jerked his head in the direction of the dead body. A new sound fell on his ear and he turned around.

Up the street, marching with steady, clumping seriousness came a detachment of stolid Japanese soldiers in mustard colored uniforms, their hair covered knapsacks glinting with the drops of dew in the first rays of the morning sun.

They approached steadily, finally coming up to where the body lay across the street. Their officer, standing on his toes like a bantam rooster crowing, gave a shrill command. The detachment halted. Another shrill command and they broke ranks. Several men formed around the body.

Duggan growled deep in his chest. Davies swore. For one of the Japanese soldiers had stuck his bayonet into the prone figure. His comrades laughed as they picked up the body and moved off down the street with it.

"What do you suppose they stuck a bayonet into that poor stiff for?" Duggan's usually cheery face was dark.

"Search me." Davies shook his head. "I must say I don't like all this rough stuff before breakfast."

"You said it, Major, things sure do happen around here, as the hound dog said when he sat on the hornet's nest."

"Hornet's nest is good. I wish we could get the gang of hornets straightened out that brought us up here."

"What are we headed out for anyways, Major?" asked Duggan curiously.

"Nothing much except to get all the Russian military maps and keep them from falling in the hands of some of our Allies."

Duggan looked puzzled. Davies, noticing this, went on more fully.

"You see, there are quite a bunch of Allies in Siberia—Japanese, British, French, Checko-Slovacks, Belgians, Chinese, Italians and Americans—"

"With the Japs kinda rulin' the roost," Duggan interpolated.

"Yes, they were supposed to put in seven thousand troops and they've put in seventy-seven thousand and are running things with a free hand."

"What's the maps got to do with it, sir?"

"Well, the Russian topographic maps are very fine. They show everything, *including* a whale of a lot of information about mines, and valuable deposits of iron, coal, zinc and other stuff. Japan wants all that she can get, being short on minerals at home. They are trying to hold on to the rich deposits up around St. Olga and St. Vladimir bays on the coast. There's some high grade stuff there—iron, copper, coal, zinc and everything else, almost inexhaustible beds of it."

"Where are these maps?"

"They're supposed to be out here somewhere. They used to be kept at Khabarovsk but some of the Russian officers loyal to the old government have hidden them away along the line of the Trans-Siberian. It's our job to find them. The Japs are hunting for them too. We're liable to run into them."

"What good'll the maps do us after we get 'em?"

Davies shrugged his shoulders.

"Not much, except keep them from the Japanese and save them for the Russians themselves."

Duggan nodded soberly.

"That's why we're staying here; this old Russian colonel knows more than he'll tell about the maps and the secret archives of the old government."

It was a thoughtful Duggan that went back to the kitchen where the other men were waiting their breakfast.

The kitchen was a comfortable place, with its great Russian stove filling one side, its carefully scrubbed floors and its broad table. Above on the wall hung the ubiquitous *ikon*, the enameled likeness of some saint, with the taper burning constantly in front of it.

Busy cleaning and oiling the major's pistol was Schneider, his fat, chubby form bent over his task. Next to him sat the maid of the house, peeling some vegetables. Corporal Nadonsky sat alone, staring abstractedly into space, his eyes still brooding.

"Well, well, everything all quiet and happy," Duggan's voice broke in as he watched the peaceful scene from the doorway. "Everybody takin' things easy and graceful like. Schnitzer here cuddlin' up to the only woman in sight as usual."

Schneider blushed but made no effort to remove himself any farther away. The back door opened with a bang and Daniels poked his flaming head in.

"When do we eat?" he inquired briefly.

Duggan looked at him in wonder.

"Boy, if you was ever to get as far as St. Peter's gate, first question you'd ask the old boy would be, 'When do we eat?' Get your mind above your waistline for about two minutes and I'll tell you some dope: We're headin' outa here *muy pronto*."

"What t'hell are we headin' for anyways?" growled Red with his usual before breakfast grouch.

"I know," informed Duggan, "but I ain't tellin', not around here, leastways"—and he looked significantly toward Corporal Nadonsky, who still continued to gaze somberly at nothing. Daniels gave the merest flicker of a nod.

Just then the soft voiced maid called them to the table, and they wasted no time seating themselves and starting in on the rich bowl of *borscht* flanked by great stacks of dark bread and fresh butter, with jars of preserved fruit to top off with.

"I sure hate to leave this billet," Schneider remarked feelingly, with a languishing glance at the buxom serving maid, a languishing glance which was marred somewhat by the oversize chunk of bread filling his cheeks to huge proportions.

"We sure hate to have you leave it," agreed Duggan. "Bein' as you've got your mind on nothin' but women, you ain't so powerful much use to us. Not that this here girl ain't kinda nice at that," he admitted generously, cutting off another slice of the bread and putting his coffee cup forward for a second helping. The girl couldn't understand the words but, womanlike, knew that she was being favorably commented upon and bridled up. Unfortunately, in bridling, she forgot the coffee pot and succeeded in spilling a scalding stream on Corporal Nadonsky before she caught herself.

Nadonsky rose in a towering rage and shouted a flame of Russian invective at her, a vituperative blast that sent her cowering to the far side of the kitchen.

"You hadn't ought to speak to the girl so rough," suggested Duggan mildly.

"Faugh, a woman's hair is long, but her wit is short!" growled the Russian and sat himself down again sullenly to finish his meal.

Davies, eating with his host, had seen the old Russian colonel called out by two husky looking peasants with whom he held a long and exciting colloquy. The colonel returned from this in great excitement and started to talk to the American officer as he rose from his breakfast.

By dint of much gesticulation, and a weird mixture of Russian, French, and German interspersed with a few words of English, he made it clear that there was a tiger in the neighborhood.

Davies grew interested immediately; he had always wanted to get a Siberian tiger, sometimes known as the Amur tiger, a cousin of the Royal Bengal beast farther south. It is a strange thing that the Ussuri country in Siberia is a blending of the Arctics and the tropics, being one of the few places in the world where the flora and fauna of both places mingle. Near Vladivostok can be found not only the reindeer, brown bear and sable of the North, but with them can be found the tiger and boa constrictor of the South. Both varieties thrive in a country covered not only with pines, firs and cedars but lime trees, a species of palm tree and vines of more tropical countries.

Under the guidance of the Russian colonel the party set forth to hunt down the tiger, Davies armed with a Springfield rifle, Sergeant Duggan likewise outfitted, and the Russian carrying a sporting rifle. With them they had two dogs. They had not left town very far behind when their way led them up a small valley where the dogs immediately grew excited.

The Russian fell behind. Davies and Duggan grinned a little as they noticed the consistent and careful way the old fellow kept in the rear. They went ahead quite blithely.

The dogs were whimpering and whining with eagerness. Davies felt his heart beat high with excitement as he scanned each bush and tree for a sign of the powerful animal. Even Duggan was breathing hard, joyously excited.

Suddenly they heard a roar and a shot behind them. They turned swiftly and ran back a few yards on the trail.

Rounding a turn on the path, they found their host, the old Russian colonel, calmly reloading his rifle. Near him, sprawled on the ground, lay the splendid dark body of a fine Amur tiger.

"What the blazes!" Davies looked puzzled.

The old Russian nodded.

"It is the *tigre de Siberie*," he informed them. "When followed, he always attacks from behind. He thinks always to hunt his hunter."

Two rather crestfallen Americans waited while the Russian servants came up and skinned the animal. Davies noticed that they carefully cut out its heart and liver. Questioning brought out the fact that these were sold for big prices to the Chinese, who esteem them highly in their medicinal lore.

"Well, my brave lad," Daniels met Duggan as he returned, "where is the mighty animal you slaughtered?"

"Slaughtered, hell!" grunted Duggan. "This here Siberian tiger don't fight fair. Whilst we're chasin' him, he takes it into his head to go chasin' us and comes up sudden like, makin' a sortie against our rear. That ain't no way for a tiger to act at all," he grieved.

"Ho, some tiger hunter you are," jibed Daniels. "Huntin' vodka is about your speed."

"Yeh?"—Duggan's eye was frosty. "You better hunt a nice soft place to drop if you aim to keep up that line of chin music." And Daniels, having had experience aforetime of that peculiarly frosty eye, wisely forebore any further remark, simply contenting himself with reaching down to pet the cat that purred against his puttees.

"Don't you go runnin' around the woods alone, kitty," he counseled the friendly little animal, "or somebody's liable to mistake you for a tiger and blow you sky high. Can't be too careful with all these bold bad hunters around, kitty." But Duggan snorted and betook himself away.

The old Russian colonel found himself in a high state of good nature after his successful killing of the tiger. Davies judged the time was ripe to broach anew the subject of the military maps and the secret papers of the Siberian headquarters.

And he hit at the right time. The colonel mellowed up and volunteered the information that the stuff might be in a small town farther up the line, in the hands of an old priest at the church. He was further prevailed upon to give Davies a note to the old priest.

Of course no one at the station knew when a train might come through. The system was simply to take one's bags and baggage to the place and wait, in company with the fatalistic group of Russian travelers, who accepted a week or two in waiting for a train as part of the scheme of things.

The farewell scene between Schneider and the serving maid once finished, the little group of Americans made for the station, passing down the town's one street, past the church with its gilded cupola, to the rather large and well built station. The floor was filled with all sorts and conditions of travelers—Russian peasants with shapeless bundles holding all their worldly goods; white clad Koreans wearing their odd little hats, looking like miniatures of a silk top hat but woven of horsehair and showing the top knot wound up inside like some small caged animal. Chinese there were and Cossacks, fur hatted, blue and gold uniformed Cossacks of the Ussuri, Kalmikoff's men, each wearing a golden "K" on his sleeve; one or two tall Cossacks of the Don, a Buddhist priest with his head shaven and wearing some sort of dull orange robe; muchly medaled *tchinovnik* or minor government official, extremely haughty and self-important; two or three full skirted, gold belted Russian officers in shiny patent leather boots and jingling spurs; and a lone Serbian officer in gray, wearing a high crowned creased red cap. Here and there about the station were the inevitable Japanese soldiers guarding the railway.

Finding some place to sit, the Americans waited with what grace they could muster. Corporal Nadonsky loosened up his tongue at last and contributed some information about Siberian tigers.

"Strangely enough," he announced, "they will not eat a white man, much preferring a native and especially liking Chinese. They will leave the body of a white man, and will pick the body of a Chinese as one picks a chicken's bones."

Sergeant Duggan grunted and walked away. Davies had started a conversation with the Serb officer when a shout from Duggan heralded the approach of the train.

It drew into the station with immense whistling and much important ringing of bells. Passengers swarmed from it, each person—man, woman and child—carrying the inevitable Russian teapot, seeking the hot water kept on tap at each station for the use of passengers.

Davies demanded and received from the train master a full compartment for himself and his men. Broad and roomy, the compartments on the Trans-Siberian trains were like small rooms. The hard benches left something to be desired, but then, as a Russian might say, it was much better than walking.

A few minutes after they had left the house of the old colonel, an officer of the Ussuri Cossacks had ridden up and called him to the door. The young officer was brilliant in blue and gold, his jeweled dagger and saber glinting in the sun, his restive horse dancing with the pain of the heavy bit.

He held a few minutes' quick conversation with the colonel, who seemed frightened. They both pointed toward the station; the officer put spurs to his horse and galloped to the station, arriving just before the train pulled in. Turning over his horse to some Cossack orderly, he went aboard the train after speaking to the Japanese officer on duty on the platform. He was on the train when, with much ringing of bells and blowing of large and small whistles, it pulled out of the station.

The Cossack officer found himself a compartment near the Americans and drove every one out of it. The passengers were only too glad to please this tall, broad shouldered officer.

They had not made many versts before a Japanese officer came from somewhere on the train and closeted himself in long and serious conversation with the Cossack. The Japanese officer, a bespectacled, sturdy little man in mustard colored field uniform, wearing soft brown riding boots and a curved Samurai blade, finally bowed himself out, hissing politely, and went by the open door of the compartment which held the Americans. Halting before this door, he stared long and carefully at the white men who were engrossed in their own conversation. It was as if the Japanese tried hard to fix each face in his mind's eye. Finally he left.

Duggan, who had been watching the man's reflection in the window glass, turned quickly to Davies.

"The Jap officer has been givin' us the once over pretty careful like, Major. What d'you suppose is on his mind?"

Davies looked thoughtful.

"Don't know, except that they know what we are up to, I suppose."

"He's been in the next compartment chewin' the fat with a tall Cossack fellow who got on the train about the same time we did, comin' from nowhere all of a sudden."

"Was he one of Kalmikoff's men?"

"Yes, sir, got one o' them yellow K's on his sleeve. He's an officer too; wears them funny little boards on his shoulders with gold lines on 'em."

"It might be just as well to look him over," said Davies thoughtfully, and rising, went out into the corridor and into the next compartment.

The tall Cossack officer, a captain by his rank markings, drew himself up smartly as the American appeared in the doorway. Both bowed and saluted. The two men were strangely contrasting types, the American officer, tall, easy going, his eyes smiling, his chin and lips grave and strong; the Russian, equally as tall, his broad features showing traces of Tartar, his eyes brown, with queer golden lights in them, with something sleepy in their depths.

The Cossack introduced himself as Captain Grineff, Boris Alexandrovich Grineff, or in the Russian fashion, Boris, the son of Alexander Grineff. No, he did not speak English, answering the query with a shake of his head and a decided "*Nyet*." "*Ah, oui,*" he spoke French, and it was in French that they carried on.

Davies felt the eyes of the Russian studying him intently, those strange, tawny yellow, sleepy lidded eyes, with a faint almond shape to them. Grineff was white and blond, but, the Tartar slant to the eyes belied all that was Nordic in his appearance.

The courtesy of the Russian was perfect. He had risen and bowed, clicking his heels politely at the entrance of the American officer. Something Davies had noticed so many times before in his contact with European officers occurred to him—the extremely easy way these people could mask their sentiments under a blanket of cold courtesy so that they would bow and smile politely to the man whose death they might be plotting.

"A beautiful country you have here in Siberia," he remarked to the Russian, glancing out of the window where there flowed by a succession of green fields and pleasant meadows, comfortable looking villages, followed by wooded valleys; the whole countryside was well watered and exceedingly rich.

"A good country," echoed the Russian, "a birthplace of warriors; world conquerors have been born in this land." He spoke with the faintest trace of arrogance.

"Yes," agreed Davies quietly, "it seems to be quite a graveyard of world conquerors," thinking as he spoke of the tomb of Genghis Khan, the great mound of Goondjun Khan at Erdeni Djir and the grave of Tamerlane.

"You know of the graves?" asked the Russian slightly surprised.

"Who does not?" countered Davies.

There was a silence for a space. The Russian cleared his throat.

"And you, you young Americans, what are you doing in this ancient cradle of the world?" he asked.

"It *is* strange, isn't it?"—Davies' tone was thoughtful—"to think of Mongolia and Siberia and Central Asia pushing so relentlessly against Europe that they forced Europe to seek out the New World. And now the New World comes knocking at the back door of Siberia and Central Asia. The circle is complete. What it can lead to no man knows. But here we are at any rate"—and he shook himself from his temporary abstraction.

Noticing the green ribbon of the Cross of St. Vladimir on the Russian's chest, Davies inquired about it.

"Oh, it is nothing; I fought through the war with the Ismailovsky Guard Regiment," he explained.

"And afterward?"

"My soldiers bound me and threw me into prison when the Revolution came. I was in the fortress of St. Peter and St. Paul for months. It was very bad. Three of us were condemned to be shot one morning. One, a young fellow from Kiev, had been arrested for buying white flour from a speculator. He wanted it for his wedding cake. But afterward there was no need of a wedding cake. The Bolsheviki killed his sweetheart. The other man was an engineer. Him they had forced to take charge of a factory. When he notified the Bolsheviki that expenses exceeded income, his workers threw him into jail. He was very angry," commented the Russian.

"How did you escape being shot?" asked Davies curiously.

"Oh, they took us out in a truck. It was very unpleasant, as the floor of the truck was slippery with blood from the bodies of the ones already executed that morning. The truck had already made three trips and the driver and the firing squad were tired and wanted some tea. So I told them, 'Never mind about shooting us just now; we are in no hurry. Let's all have some tea.' 'Fine,' they shouted.

"So while they were having tea we all walked away. But the young man, when he found his sweetheart was dead, was very sad. He went back and tried to have himself shot. But they would not. They suspected some bourgeoisie plot and chased him away."

The train began to slow down with much jerking and jolting. Sergeant Duggan suddenly appeared in the doorway.

"Looks like these Roosians is goin' to try to pull something, Major," he announced calmly.

Davies, listening, heard shouts coming from somewhere forward. Looking out the window, he saw many Cossack horses held in groups of eight or ten near the track. Lances were stuck into the earth here and there, showing that the men were temporarily absent on dismounted duty. The excited voices and the tramp of footsteps came nearer, approaching the compartment along the corridor that ran the full length of the car.

"Bring the rest of the men in here," Davies ordered swiftly.

Duggan disappeared, to return almost immediately with Schneider, Daniels and the Russian American, Corporal Nadonsky.

The Cossack officer looked his astonishment.

"*Je suis desolé*," Davies addressed the man, "but we are forced to use your good offices to see that no unpleasantness occurs."

And he drew his pistol quietly, slipping in a loaded magazine and snapping a shell into the breech. The rest of the Americans followed suit without a word. The Russian eyed them, puzzled and half admiringly.

Voices and footsteps had approached the door of the compartment. The Americans were calmly examining their loaded pistols, each man negligently occupied, as, past the open doorway, strode the serious, bespectacled little Japanese officer, followed by a group of Cossack soldiers carrying their carbines at the trail. They were wild looking fellows in their soft boots, dirty blue uniforms and shaggy fur hats.

A sudden commotion outside of the compartment which the Americans had so recently vacated showed that their absence had been discovered.

One of the Cossacks, turning, suddenly saw Davies and his men close at hand. He shouted something. The Japanese officer appeared, bowing and hissing politely. His impassive face showed no surprise as he took in the scene before him.

Five Americans were sitting quite calmly, indifferently toying with their rather large and exceedingly vicious looking automatic pistols. The American officer, without seeming to be aware of it, held his pistol pointing somewhere in the general vicinity of the Russian officer's stomach.

The Japanese hissed again politely and bowed very low. Behind him the Cossack soldiers crowded and growled angrily.

"Verree sorree," he spoke sibilantly, "but I have to ask that you leave the train here and await the next one coming from Vladivostock."

Davies gazed at him curiously, inclining his head as if in apology.

"I am just as sorry," he returned, "but I must insist upon staying just where I am with my good friend here," and he pointed at the Russian officer with the muzzle of his pistol. Very quietly, as if by prearranged signal, the pistols of the Americans swung themselves around so that they all pointed at the open doorway, four blued steel muzzles which promised all sorts of things to any one who should arouse them.

The Japanese spoke in a low tone to one of the Cossacks behind him. There was an angry demur. The Japanese shrugged his shoulders and stepped aside so as to allow the Cossacks behind him to get the whole view. The Cossack murmur of protest died down instantly.

Again the Japanese started bowing and hissing.

"Yes, indeed," he agreed politely, "I am verree sorree to have disturbed you—"

So saying, he bowed himself out. The Cossacks cleared away from that silent and none too pleasing doorway, the tramp of feet lessened in the distance. With much blowing of whistles and ringing of bells the train started again.

As it pulled slowly ahead, Davies, glancing out of the window saw the discomfited Cossacks gathered in puzzled groups alongside the track. As he drew past they gazed at him curiously. One of the Cossacks, a tall fellow in a full beard grinned at him, then drew his hand suggestively across his throat, pointing ahead in the direction which the train was taking. It was a plain promise of trouble ahead. Davies bowed to him ironically and turning, continued his conversation as if nothing had occurred.

"Yes," he broke the silence, "the New World is knocking at the back door of the Old. The circle is complete."

• • •

Throughout the entry of the Japanese and the Cossacks, the Cossack officer had watched Davies with anger in his eyes, keeping however a respectful glance upon the pistol.

"Yes, the New World is knocking at the back door of the Old," he commented, then, with a grim smile, "but it would be wise not to step too quickly inside."

Davies glanced at him as if not understanding.

"Siberia is a very rich country," he commented.

"Yes," growled the Cossack, "it is rich, too rich unfortunately. We have a proverb in Russia which says, 'Where there is a trough there will pigs be also.' "

Davies looked at him gravely.

"Yes? The Chinese have a proverb which says, 'The pork butcher always likes to talk of swine.' "

The Cossack officer flushed in anger. Davies went on as though not noticing, his voice even and unhurried.

"It is perhaps the misfortune of Siberia that she is so wealthy and is such a good trough and that so many pigs insist upon getting their feet into it. But it strikes me that the Russians are more than foolish to call in the Japanese to aid them. Does the wise man call in the tiger to drive away the pigs?"

The Cossack looked at him sharply, with eyes narrowed. Plainly he was nonplussed. He sat in silence for a space. Finally he nodded his head thoughtfully. Then suddenly, in that quick change of viewpoint so typical of Russians, he seized both of Davies' hands in his and shook them warmly.

"Why should I carry out the orders of those cursed yellow devils?" he asked, his eyes gleaming. "You are right. I spit upon them. I must have been mad to have allowed myself to consider arresting you and seeing that you were done away with. A white man carrying out the filthy orders of another race!" The Russian had tears in his eyes. "Can you ever forgive me?" he pleaded.

Duggan, watching the rapid interchange of words between the two, looked startled when the Russian reached forward and threw his arms impulsively around the American. Then he saw the two enter into deep voiced and friendly conversation. He shook his head in amazement and turning, whispered to Red Daniels.

"Didja ever see anything to beat it, the way the major makes 'em eat outa his hand?"

Daniels nodded.

"That guy could talk a bill collector into settin' up the drinks, and make him like it. He sure ought to run for alderman or somethin'."

"He'll need it on this trip or I miss my guess," Duggan commented. "These babies are out to get him and they don't mean maybe."

"They'll have to lay awake nights doin' it," Daniels yawned comfortably. "This guy is not lettin' the grass grow green under his feet, not so's you could notice it, he ain't."

Davies leaned forward, and caught Duggan's eye.

"Our friend here tells me that the Japanese have sent out word to stop us at any cost. He's got a colonel who sent him on the job to get us. They'll be waiting for us at the town we're heading for, the whole kit and caboodle—horse, foot and guns. It seems that this colonel of his is by way of being a most unpleasant character. Our friend here is scared to death of him, won't even call him by name. Just calls him 'That One.' Find out from Nadonsky if he knows anything about the Cossack colonel."

Duggan nodded and was soon in deep conversation with Nadonsky while Davies resumed talking with the Cossack officer.

"Yes, my friend," went on the captain, "I am very happy that you prevented me from carrying out the orders of those cursed Japanese. But they will not be content with this failure. They have put a most terrible one on the task of running you down." The eyes of the Russian grew somber and something like fear showed again in their depths. "And I am afraid that he will succeed. Few have ever escaped That One—almost none. He would torture and kill his own mother—" The man looked around him swiftly, then lowered his voice. "Say nothing of what I have told you. Even now my life will be in danger because you have escaped. But I, what do I care?"

He straightened out recklessly.

"What is life anyway? A puff of driven snow rising like smoke against the ground and as quickly vanished. A fallen leaf on the bosom of the black stream floating from whence and whither no one knows. *Nitchevo!*" He shrugged his shoulders, and his tragic mood passed as it always passes with these mercurial Russians. Leaning forward seriously, "What we need, my friend, is a drop or two of vodka before we arrive at the town and are taken out and shot."

Without saying a word, Davies reached into his musette bag and brought forth a silver flask surmounted with a cup which screwed over its top. Pouring out a good stiff drink of the excellent brandy which it contained, he handed it to the Russian, who accepted it ceremoniously, raised it high, then downed it with a deep toned, "*Vashi darovia!*" "Wishing good health."

As the drink coursed through and farmed up the Russian's veins it was plain to be seen that his opinion of all Americans had risen enormously and that he now looked upon them as brothers. Another drink from the same flask and he was willing, nay anxious, to lay down his life for his new found friends.

Duggan, Schneider and Daniels watched this scene with their tongues hanging out. It was Duggan who noticed that, while Davies seemed to be pouring himself a drink, in reality he was only going through the motions of drinking. He spread the word of this to the others and they nodded understandingly and were more content.

The eyes of the Russian suddenly suffused with tears.

"I am so sorry that you are to die so soon," he commiserated, wiping his eyes. "That dog"—he jerked his finger, pointing ahead—"will surely have you killed. He is relentless as the very devil, That One."

"I'll try to avoid this unpleasant individual," suggested Davies. "What sort of a looking person is he?"

The Russian threw his arms wide in an extravagant gesture.

"Terrible. Not big, ah, no, small, but with the eyes of hell and a voice like a snarling, fighting tiger. Not for nothing is he known as the Tiger of the Ussuri." He leaned forward and spoke in a low tone, his voice tense and grave, "Be sure you look behind you when you talk to him," and resumed his sorrowful pose again, refusing to explain this mysterious admonition.

The train was slowing down at some small station.

"Why are all the stations so far from the town on this Trans-Siberian Railway?" asked Davies.

The Russian laughed cynically.

"It was the engineers who laid out the line. They would come to each town in advance of their parties. 'How much will you pay us to have the station at your town?' they would ask. If the town would not pay enough they would run the railroad far away."

The station platform was filled with the usual polyglot crowd of peasants, most of them wearing thick woolen homespuns, their feet wrapped in sacking in lieu of boots. Old women, shapeless bundles of clothes with broad flat faces, were sitting behind the inevitable samovars or behind tables piled high with black bread and cucumbers and tomatoes and sunflower seeds. Some served hot meat balls wrapped in pastry, some the sweetish, sourish drink known as *kvas*.

"Picturesque types," commented Davies.

The Cossack looked at them scornfully and shrugged his shoulders.

"Loathsome dogs," he snorted, "ignorant and superstitious. Dark people—all, all dark people." He used the Russian peasant's expression for describing his own childish ignorance.

There was something about this Russian officer's careless dismissal of the lower strata of his own race that grated on Davies. The peasants, as he had seen them, were kindly and courteous, undoubtedly uneducated but possessing a droll shrewdness of their own.

Superstitious they were as well. What could be more delightful than the peasants' specific against lightning? For Ivan, when frightened by its glare, simply recalls the names of all his bald headed friends, which immediately lessens his worries if not the flashes of the lightning. And after all, why not?

From down the passageway came the strum of *balalaikas* and voices raised in song. The traveling Russians were amusing themselves, their voices melodiously blending with the click and rattle of the rails, all of their songs starting sadly and ending with a wild burst of dance music so that in one moment the listener was thinking of all the sorrows of life and in the next trying hard to keep his feet from beating time to the gay melody.

A fat conductor came through, uniformed like a major general and accompanied by two aides.

"When do we arrive at our destination?" asked Davies.

"*Cechas*," was the reply with a polite shrug, and Davies cursed, the word "*cechas*" meaning literally "within the hour" but actually "wait awhile." It is the Russian equivalent for the Spanish "*mañana*."

"You should not worry about getting to town," said the Cossack officer after the conductor took his departure. "Enjoy life while you still have it," went on this somber Job's comforter. "The longer you can stay away from that place, the better for you."

The *balalaikas* and the voices rose in some crashing war song. The Americans unconsciously beat time to it. The Russian's eyes flashed, he hammered on his chest with clenched fists and joined in the words.

"It is the song of Yermak, the Cossack conqueror of Siberia," he explained when the song ended with a shout.

"Whom did he conquer it from?" asked Davies.

"Oh, the ancestors of these"—and he pointed out the window to where, on a distant prairie, some dome-like structures arose from the sod, looking like large beehives—"from the Yakuts, the Ostiaks, the Golds and many more, now dying out with too much vodka."

The music rose and fell from down the corridor. The train was passing through beautiful groves of beeches and fir and larch, with pleasant vistas of shaded valleys and wooded knolls and streams of clear water running between grassy banks.

The gay music of the travelers down the corridor suddenly turned to a dirge, something ineffably sad and haunting and hopelessly morose. The train had entered a blackened and burned tract of land. In the center of it was a destroyed village. There suddenly flashed by the car window a gruesome sight, the body of a man hanging to the telegraph poles swinging loosely in the breeze. Jerking rapidly by, more and more bodies were seen, from which rose clouds of vulture-like birds in a flapping, squawking chorus.

"God, what happened here?" asked Davies.

The Cossack crossed himself, Russian fashion.

"That One punished the village for harboring Bolsheviki," he explained. "Pretty harsh treatment."

The Russian shrugged his shoulders.

"The dogs, hanging is too good for them!" he snorted.

It made Davies pity the peasant exploited and abused by Bolsheviki and White Armies alike, so that the very sight of an armed man spelled oppression to the poor *moujik*.

A burst of song from down the corridor set the Russian to singing again, a song the chorus of which went something like "*Perochicky, chicky, perochicky*," and which he sang with great gusto.

"That," he explained, when the song ended with a burst of laughter down the length of the car, "is a song about a second lieutenant, a *peroochek*. Like a second lieutenant, it is very gay."

The Russian looked curiously at the American officer and then from him to the soldiers. Finally he turned toward Davies.

"Your soldiers look clean and well fed. How much squeeze do you get from their pay and food?" he asked simply, as one desiring professional information from another.

Davies looked puzzled. The Russian proceeded to make his meaning clearer.

"Why, nothing." Davies looked shocked.

The Cossack smiled incredulously.

"Nothing?" He shook his head in polite disbelief.

"Not a cent," insisted Davies.

Plainly the Cossack was unconvinced.

"Come, I'll tell you how many rubles a month I make from my command; be frank." He shook a reproachful finger at the American.

And there the matter rested in mutual miscomprehension, but Davies reflected that the stories he had heard of Russian soldiers going into battle clad in shoddy uniforms, paper soled shoes and carrying wooden guns and ammunition loaded with sand had their foundation on fact. He also reasoned that any Russian officer who exploited the soldiers entrusted to his care got exactly what was coming to him when the Bolsheviki finally ran wild.

Another drink or two had reddened the Russian's eyes and made him garrulous.

"America and Russia, the two great nations of the world," he announced suddenly.

"Americans and Russians are *ochinn simpatiska*," he added, throwing an affectionate arm around Davies' shoulders. Sergeant Duggan grinned at his officer's obvious embarrassment.

But the Russian was not to be halted in his enthusiasm.

"You have befriended me. I will befriend you in turn," he declared.

"Never will I desert you!" he swore, and then wept softly.

"Why are you weeping?" asked Davies.

"It is my youth that is passing," he moaned, full of Russian woe. "Old age, old age on my gray head, like a raven hast thou alighted today; and youth, my youth like a falcon over the plain hast thou sped away."

It was all very sad. He must have been all of twenty-five years old as he intoned the song of the Old Kazak, Ilya of Morum, and mourned over the years that had passed. A man of most surprising moods was this Russian, Captain Boris Alexandrovich Grineff.

Had Davies known what was in store for the poor fellow in the next twenty-four hours he would have found plenty of justification for his tears.

They were now entering the outskirts of the town. Grineff braced up and began to look worried, staring apprehensively out of the window as the train began to slow down preparatory to entering the station.

"Remember what I have told you, my friend," he whispered anxiously, "beware of That One. And if you are taken to Room Forty-two especially be careful and on your guard. Don't forget to look behind you!" And Grineff pressed his hand as one might clasp the hand of a man condemned to death.

It was therefore in no very cheerful mood that they drew into the station. Davies did not really believe that any Cossack would have the nerve to harm Americans. At the same time he was worried by the insistent warnings of the Cossack officer, who certainly ought to know his own people best. And this mysterious individual whom Grineff referred to as That One—who and what was he?

Leaning over to Duggan, he asked, "What did you find out about the Cossack colonel?"

"Nadonsky says he's heard of him, that he's a guy named Nagoi, a ten minute egg if there ever was one. He calls hisself the Tiger and he ain't so particular who he kills nor how he kills 'em—"

They were drawing into the station. The platform seemed to be filled with Cossacks. Davies, after looking out the window turned again to Duggan.

"They're not liable to bother anybody but me. I'll face the music while you chase after the maps. They're in the hands of an old priest at the big church. His name is Aksakoff. Give him this." Davies handed over the slip of paper which he had received from the old *polkovnik*. "Get the stuff, get it to Vladivostock and get word to headquarters about me. You all wait here in the train, then slide out the other end of the car while every one is interested in me."

Sergeant Duggan nodded, very ill content.

"Can't we stick together, Major? Kinda hate to pull out leavin' you to hold the sack; them bozos may pull some rough stuff on you."

Davies shook his head.

"I don't think so—at any rate I'll take a chance on it."

The train came to a stop.

Davies, followed by Grineff, walked calmly down the corridor.

Duggan waited with the rest of the men, in the compartment.

"He's liable to walk into a peck of trouble facin' that gang all by hisself," growled Daniels.

"You said it," agreed Duggan, "but orders is orders."

"Yeh, but plain suicide is damn' foolishness," snorted Daniels.

"All the same, he might fool 'em at that. First time you meet him you think he was raised a pet and wouldn't kick if you was to tickle his heels with a feather duster, he's that easy spoken. Then try and get funny with him and you find you can't harness him with a pitchfork. But look at the hard lookin' baby who's sashayin' up to him now." Duggan pointed out on the platform where a tall Cossack officer had approached Davies and saluted politely.

The Cossack officer wore a white Astrakhan hat set at a jaunty angle on his head. The breast of his sweeping, wine colored coat was covered with a double row of silver cartridge cases. Broad shouldered and wasp waisted, he walked like a cat in his soft, red Morocco boots. His eyes were slanted like the eyes of a Tartar, and were cold in their glance. His face was broad and his cheek bones high, still further showing his Tartar ancestry. Here plainly was one of the descendants of the old Zaporogians, the "men beyond the river rapids," who terrorized sultan and king and tsar alike.

"Major Davies?" he asked politely in excellent English.

Davies nodded and returned his salute.

"My commander, Colonel Nagoi, wishes that you might honor him by calling on him immediately," the Cossack spoke smoothly, but there was a strange flicker to his eyes as he spoke the name.

Looking up and down the platform, Davies saw that he was surrounded with Cossacks, shaggy hatted and clad in the blue and yellow of the Ussuri Cossack.

Davies, turning, saw Captain Grineff behind him and was surprised to see him pale and trembling, looking at the white hatted young Cossack with eyes full of a nameless dread.

His eyes flashed some warning; what it was Davies could not tell. He reached out his hand to say goodbye to his train companion. Grineff took it convulsively.

"Goodbye!" he whispered forebodingly and gazed sadly at Davies as if looking at him for the last time.

"Confound the fellow!" thought Davies. "He's as cheerful as an undertaker." He turned to follow his guide.

There was something cold and impersonal about the tall young Cossack who accompanied him to the waiting *droshky*. Four mounted Cossacks acted as escort. They looked curiously at Davies as he stepped into the carriage. Their gaze was remote and detached. They stared at him but avoided his eyes, as the sheriff who was to pull the trap might avoid looking into the eyes of the condemned.

The horses were put into the gallop. The Cossack officer sat beside him, leaning on the handle of his curved saber. They went rapidly through the main street of the town and up a small hill, finally bringing up with a flourish before a large barracks, above whose great door there looked down arrogantly the great black, double headed eagle of the old Empire.

Sentinels at the door drew up in a sharp salute as the two entered. Passing up a broad staircase, they came to a narrow door. Above it Davies noticed the number. It was Room Forty-two. This was the room that Grineff had warned him against.

"Doesn't make this whole party any more cheerful," reflected Davies, and hitched his pistol holster around.

The door opened noiselessly from within. Entering, Davies found himself in a narrow anteroom screened at the farther end by two long red curtains, which evidently concealed the entrance to a larger chamber. The anteroom was sparely furnished, with one or two chairs, and a long bench. Seated on this long bench was a huge Chinese, his face bland and gentle, his arms folded in his sleeves, his gaze bent upon the floor as if in meditation. He did not look up as the officers entered.

The Cossack officer remained standing near the entrance door, his arms folded. Turning to look upon him, Davies found his eyes raised staring indifferently into space. Turning quickly he discovered the Chinese in the act of studying him furtively.

From behind the curtains voices were raised. There were several of these voices talking and arguing about something at great length, all of them busy at once. It made a lot of noise and confusion. Suddenly the racket was stilled as if by magic. Another voice had growled some word. All was silent.

As the new voice went on, Davies listened curiously. The timbre of it was faintly disturbing; it was high pitched and catlike; it had a sort of snarling, whining note about it that made one a little chilled, made one think, in fact, of the great tiger cats at feeding time.

There was a sound of departing footsteps and the closing of a door behind the curtains. The tall Chinese still continued to sit in his long padded robes, seemingly sunk in calm reflection. Again Davies caught the man's eyes and found them gazing upon him with a disinterested, speculative sort of look that the American found uncomfortably creepy. Seeing himself observed, the Chinese quietly veiled his glance, his eyes seeming to sheath themselves behind a film. The sleeves of his jacket were long and capacious. His hands were lost in their immensity. Something faintly sinister about this Chinese made Davies observe him with more than usual attention. The sleepy, heavy lidded eyes of the Celestial had something almost serpent-like about them.

Behind him, at the door, stood the Cossack officer, his arms still folded. All was silent in the room. Davies had the feeling of being trapped. The sensation suddenly made him very angry. It was not fitting that an American officer should be placed in such a situation by such people. It was just such pride as this which makes for audacity. And it was his pride that drove him to do the unexpected and therefore the most strategic thing.

For suddenly, to the amazement of the Cossack officer behind him, the American officer strode forward to the curtains.

Out of the corner of his eye Davies felt, rather than saw, the Chinese raising his bulk like some serpent uncoiling its fat length. As the man rose there gleamed somewhere about him the flash and angry glitter of steel. Behind him Davies felt the Cossack officer spring to action—of what nature he neither knew nor cared. A shout rose from the rear. He paid no heed.

Flinging aside the curtains, he saw before him a large desk behind which a form rose up, startled. Remembering the warning about looking behind him, Davies wasted no time in getting away from those curtains in his rear. He stepped swiftly away from them to the left, where he had good solid wall behind his back.

He stepped not a second too soon, for the curtains bulged crazily into the room. There was a grunt, as if some one had lunged. The man at the desk stared at him, white faced, looking from Davies to where the bulge in the curtain had straightened itself out.

The figure behind the deck was short and almost dwarf-like, with a large head set upon a small body. It was dressed in the black and silver of a famous old Hussar regiment. But what the figure lacked in size it made up in intensity. The face was handsome, handsome with the unhealthy, decadent beauty of the face of some Roman emperor. It was unusually white, of the dead white of the belly of a fish. The arresting pallor was set off by the brilliantly colored lips, so brilliantly colored that they had the look of being painted. They were beautifully formed lips, almost girlish in their soft curves. The eyes were the most arresting thing about the man, large and icicle cold, cold with a depth of ferocity that spelled the madman, the sadist.

Davies conceived an instant dislike for this Cossack officer.

"Colonel Nagoi?" he inquired bruskly.

The man nodded.

"Sorry to break in upon you unannounced"—Davies' voice was dry and matter of fact—"but I must confess that I am unaccustomed to waiting in people's anterooms. I hurried here immediately upon my arrival, knowing full well that a Russian officer would not keep an Allied American officer awaiting his pleasure without some excellent reason."

The Russian replied nothing to this, but continued to stare at the American before him. Davies, looking calmly into his eyes, caught a flicker of something that he did not like. He saw the Russian's finger crook slightly, signaling to some one through the curtain.

The Russian, Nagoi, suddenly found himself gazing into the blued steel muzzle of a .45 automatic. Where it had come from he was at a loss to discover. The American had simply dropped his hand at his side and the gun had seemed fairly to leap into his hand.

And Davies was in a towering rage. His face was white with anger, that deadly cold anger which concentrates a man's energies and gives him the strength of ten men.

"Damn your miserable impudence!" his voice rang, as if he were dressing down a battalion. "What in hell do you mean by running me up to your filthy barracks and standing there like a wooden image signaling to your people. For two cents I'd put a bullet through you. If you try any more funny stuff I'll kill you so quickly you'll never know what hit you."

The unmistakable note of command in the American's voice, the unhurried and businesslike manner in which he carried off the proceedings, had its effect on the Cossack. He made some quick motion with his hand, as if pushing some one away, as if ordering his people to remain out of it, and suddenly became all graciousness. His lips wreathed themselves in a smile.

"I am sorry to have kept you waiting." His voice was harsh and snarling and full of that whining note that Davies had heard from the anteroom. It certainly was tiger-like in its queer, purring, singing note.

"You will accept my apologies?" he said, and waved Davies to a chair.

Davies, relaxing no whit of his vigilance, and keeping the corner of his eye on the doorway and the curtains, sat down easily, his pistol in his lap.

"Just why did you ask me to come to see you?" he asked Colonel Nagoi.

The Cossack bowed, his voice purring and sugary. Beneath its notes there was the repressed note of that angry snarl.

"I wished to extend the courtesies of the town to you." He threw his hands wide open as if showing the purity of his intentions.

"Very kind of you, I'm sure," Davies disposed of this briefly. "You will pardon me for not knowing exactly what you meant by courtesies. It had all the air of an arrest to me, and it did not strike me as *comme il faut* for an American officer to be arrested by Cossacks."

The colonel's voice broke in again, that same silky whining purr.

"I am indeed sorry," he said. "I would not have had you misinterpret my actions for a moment. I certainly would not have attempted to put a representative of the great American nation in arrest."

Davies rose quickly.

"Good," he returned. "Now that's settled, I must be about my duties."

Colonel Nagoi's eye lighted for a second. He betrayed himself by a furtive glance at the curtains. Davies, having sat through too many poker games, was keenly alert to the bearing of a man who conceals an ace in the hole.

"I'd consider it a great proof of the honesty of your intentions," he said sharply, "if you would kindly accompany me to the street." The words were reinforced by the careless wave of the pistol he still carried in his hand.

The Cossack looked rebellious for a second, then thought better of it and led the way to the curtains. Before stepping through them, he called something in Chinese to the other side.

Davies followed him closely, his eye quite bleak and frosty. He didn't like this queer man in front of him; he didn't like the idea of going out alone into that anteroom. Therefore he gently poked the Cossack in the ribs with the muzzle of his pistol, just to remind the fellow to play the game straight.

"Just a moment, Colonel," Davies halted him, "I've got a soft nosed bullet here reserved especially for you if any of your subordinates do anything hasty."

The Cossack glanced down at the pistol and nodded.

"Swing the curtains wide!" ordered Davies.

Colonel Nagoi swung them wide. Davies followed him closely, stepping into the anteroom at the Russian's heels.

He was just in time to see the Chinese hurriedly seat himself again on the bench, so hurriedly that the blade of a heavy knife showed for a second before he concealed it under his flowing robes. The tall young Cossack officer stood fingering his belt and glaring at the two as they made their way out of the anteroom and down the stairs, Davies walking arm in arm with the colonel, on Nagoi's right side.

Near the entrance of the building stood a *troika*, a three horse carriage, its huge driver wearing an immense blue cloak from which his arms stuck out like sausages.

The sentinels at the gate did not see anything out of the way in the passage of the two officers. They saluted snappily and remained at the salute while their colonel preceded the American officer to the curb.

"I am sorry to have to ask you to accompany me, Colonel Nagoi." Davies' voice was polite but exceedingly firm. "I can not risk having my duties interrupted by any accidents."

The Russian obediently climbed into the *troika*, seating himself quietly enough. He turned to Davies, his eyes smoldering.

"I can promise you that no *accident* will happen to you, my friend," he snarled in his sing-song voice.

Davies laughed, immensely tickled.

"Good for you, old sport," he complimented. "Go as far as you like."

Nagoi trembled with rage; he seemed about to spring at the American.

"Now, now," reproved Davies, "keep your shirt on. You mustn't be rude to Americans, little man; they are your friends, you know."

"Bah!" snorted Nagoi contemptuously. "I would like to cut all their throats with one stroke of my dagger."

"So?" commented Davies mildly. "My goodness, you *are* a regular little fire eater"—and he leaned forward, directing the *isvostchek* toward the general direction of the church, whose great bulb of a dome he saw rising above the roofs midway in the city.

He hoped against hope that he would find Duggan and the rest of the men there. The thing to do was to carry this little rattlesnake of a colonel far enough away from the barracks to prevent him calling out his men in pursuit too soon. Davies scanned the street anxiously, worried that he might run into some wandering detachment of Cossacks, who could surround them and rescue the colonel.

Davies, in spite of his jocular tone with the little Cossack, realized only too well what would happen should the colonel get the upper hand. It probably would not be a short shrift that he would donate but something long and lingering, with a refinement of Oriental torture incomprehensible to the mind of an American.

Far down the street, Davies caught the glint of sun on Cossack lanceheads. A detachment was advancing toward them. Colonel Nagoi sat up eagerly. About midway between the approaching Cossacks and the *troika* a side street turned off.

Davies leaned forward and signaled the *isvostchek* to speed up. The driver whipped up his horses. Nearer and nearer they came to the Cossack detachment. Grasping the colonel's arm firmly, Davies pressed the pistol into his side.

"You let a single yap out of you and there'll be a new face in Cossack Heaven!" he growled.

But it was going to be nip and tuck. They seemed to be running square into the approaching horsemen when suddenly they reached the corner of the side street and turned into it on one wheel.

Nagoi, fearful of the pistol pressed into his side, made not a sign. The Cossacks clattered past the mouth of the street behind them. Without pointing directly at the church, the golden dome of which was nearer now, Davies kept the coachman going in that general direction by judiciously prodding him at the turns. Coming at last within quick walking distance of the ornate building, which could now be seen in all its glory of spires and domelike towers, Davies stopped the *troika*.

"Here's where you have to get out and walk," Davies told Nagoi. The colonel lost no time in getting on the ground. "Goodbye, my dear sir," Davies said pleasantly.

Nagoi, looking up at him from the ground, smiled very bleakly. His harsh, whining, snarling, cat-like voice broke out—

"Not goodbye, my friend, but *au revoir*"—and saluting very formally, he turned and hurried away in the direction of his barracks.

Davies speeded up the coach, turning around the next corner and down a street until the colonel was out of sight. Here he dismounted and paid the coachman.

Waiting until the fellow was out of sight, Davies walked quickly toward the church.

Three minutes of swift progress brought him to the doors, surrounded as usual by a crowd of ragged beggars who select the place to display their infirmities for the charity of passers by. Luckily the beggars were all occupied in dividing up the gifts from the worshippers who had already entered the church and did not see Davies as he went in quietly.

As he pushed open the doors a heavy odor of incense filled his nostrils. The interior of the place was in semi-darkness, faintly relieved by the dim light of hundreds of tapers. Above him stretched the dome of the building, painted blue and sprinkled with silvery stars.

There were no seats nor benches; the floor was crowded with kneeling worshippers.

At the far end a golden screen gleamed and glowed in the candlelight. Around the walls were innumerable *ikons*, pictures of the saints, lighted by the tapers from heavy candelabra, tapers that were presented as gifts of the devout.

The rise and fall of men's voices filled the air, deeply rich voices raised in a glorious chant, as beautiful as the Gregorian chants but possessing some Slav quality of its own, a deep and passionate strain, like the moaning of wind over immense pine forests.

In the middle of the screen a small door opened noiselessly. Priests appeared, long haired and long bearded men, not unlike the pictures of the apostles of old. They were gorgeous in purple vestments, stiff with gold and silver embroidery which created an effect of magnificence in the flickering light of the candles.

The leader stepped forward on the steps, swinging a censer. His voice rang out very melodiously.

"*Gospodi pomiliu*," he intoned. "Lord have mercy!"

"*Gospodi pomiliu*," moaned the congregation after him, a rising, throbbing chorus that beat against the dome, like waves of the sea, and suddenly they all touched the ground with their foreheads, the old Eastern form of obeisance, just as the subjects of some ancient Assyrian king performed it thousands of years ago.

Lights gleamed on a golden cross behind the screen in the Holy of Holies, where an old priest elevated his arms in prayer.

Like another wave of passionate melody the voice of the immense male choir surged up, following his words with their responses. The cry of "*Gospodi pomiliu*" broke again and again from the throats of the congregation, in passionate supplication. Music and incense, glimmering tapers and gold incrusted pictures of saints, a half delirious and wholly beautiful harmony of voices, and Davies found himself drinking in the rich riot of sound and color, almost forgetting the danger that pressed even as he waited, forgetting that Colonel Nagoi might be even now stirring up the Cossacks to set forth and seek and capture him, dead or alive.

It was a husky whisper in the darkness beside him that brought him back. Sergeant Duggan's voice breathed in his ears.

"We got the stuff, Major, a whole roll of it," came the reassuring accents.

"Is everybody all right?" asked Davies anxiously.

"All here with me."

"Fine. We've got to get out of here in a hurry."

Briefly he told Duggan of the encounter with the Cossack colonel and heard the sergeant chuckle quietly.

"Is there a back way out of this place?" he asked when he had finished his recital.

"Yes, sir, if the Major'll follow me I'll show the way."

Concealed by the darkness, Davies saw the forms of Daniels and the other two men. Slipping quietly among the kneeling worshippers, they filed along the walls unnoticed, coming at last to a passageway that led out into the fresh air and light. They found themselves in a small courtyard to which a gate gave on an alleyway.

They had no sooner stepped into the courtyard than they heard a commotion in the church behind them. The singing of the choir had ceased in the middle of a note. There was a hurried step in the passageway behind them.

Davies drew his pistol and waited. The door was flung open and an old, white haired priest stood in the opening, his eyes blinking from the strong light and his vestments gleaming and sparkling with many jewels. He pointed behind him and said something rapidly in Russian. Nadonsky translated—

"He says that they are coming in the church and seeking among the congregation for the American officer."

Davies looked toward the gate in the wall. From afar he heard a new sound, the trample and clatter of mounted men. The rattle of many horses' hoofs and the shouting of many voices came up the alley.

The sound came nearer and nearer. The old priest crossed himself and began to pray. The Americans fingered their pistols. It looked as if they were trapped. Davies waved his men back from the doorway into the shadow of the wall.

The sounds from the alleyway were almost upon them. They could plainly hear the clatter and rattle of spur and saber. Suddenly over the top of the wall appeared a clump of lances held slantingly, their steel tipped heads gleaming viciously, their black and red pennons snapping in the breeze as they moved hurriedly across the entire length of the wall and disappeared with a lessening rattle of hoofs in the distance. The alley was silent again.

Far away they could hear the noise of shouts and excitement. From the passageway inside the church they heard the tramp of armed men.

Davies crossed the yard quickly, swung open the gate and peered down the alleyway.

"Come on!" he whispered and the men piled after him.

Across the alleyway was another gate. It was unlocked. They opened this and found themselves in a small garden with a rustic summer house in its center. Swinging the gate shut behind them, they locked it from the inside.

The house was silent, the windows were curtained.

Evidently it was deserted. The men went to the rustic summer house and flung themselves on the benches. Davies examined the house narrowly. The windows stared at him with all the eerie, blank effect of the sightless eyes of a blind man. Something about the house vaguely troubled him. He sat down on a bench to plan the next move.

"They are sure combin' the town for us," Duggan spoke up after lighting a cigaret.

"They sure are, the blankety blanks," swore Daniels.

"Yep, they sure are," agreed Schneider.

"Don't that beat the Dutch!" ejaculated Duggan plaintively. "The way them guys act is sure disgustin'. Looks like we'd have to do some tall figgerin' to get home without havin' our skins punctured."

"You said it," averred Daniels, "we sure are a long way from home."

Duggan grinned.

"Like Schneider here," he reminisced, "the first time he sees a Salvation Army man. Schneider is hustlin' for barracks, tryin' to make roll call before taps and bumps into this guy and knocks him appetite over tin cup. The Salvation Army man picks hisself from the mud and helps Schneider up.

" 'What outfit d'you belong to?' asks Schneider.

" 'I'm a soldier of Heaven,' says the Salvation guy.

"Schneider looks at him and shakes his head.

" 'You sure got a long way to get to barracks,' he says finally and digs out for his squad room."

Davies, overhearing this, grinned in spite of the worries that possessed him. After seeing Colonel Nagoi's cruel eyes and beastly face, he had no desire to let his men or himself get into his toils. That One certainly was entitled to all the notoriety he had managed to make for himself. He thought of Captain Grineff, his companion of the train trip, and wondered idly what had come of him.

"Did you see anything of that Russian officer who rode with me on the train?" he asked Duggan. The sergeant shook his head.

Poor Grineff! Davies hoped that he wouldn't be punished for his friendly attitude toward the Americans. Well, life was uncertain in Siberia, and Grineff could probably take care of himself. Davies had his own troubles to worry over.

Again he looked at the house behind him. He hoped that it was vacant but somehow he had the feeling that it was not.

It was late afternoon and the sun would soon be down. Best thing to do would be to wait for darkness and then make a break for it, hoping to get through town under the cover of night and to the railroad at some point outside the place.

Evidently the hue and cry was still going on in the town. They could hear occasional shouts and commands. Once another detachment of Cossacks came down the alleyway. They could hear them stop behind the church and hold a discussion before going on.

Duggan carried the maps in a roll, wrapped in cloth, slung over his shoulder. It was one thing to get the maps; it was another thing to get them back to headquarters and save them from their enemies.

Corporal Nadonsky came up quietly while Davies sat in thought.

"I beg your pardon, Major, but what did you say this Colonel Nagoi looked like?"

Davies described him as well as he could. Nadonsky listened intently, a faintly puzzled look on his face.

"Do you know him?" asked Davies.

"I don't know, sir," Nadonsky replied gravely. "If he is the one I think he is, then he is a devil, that man. It will go hard with us if he catches us. He will not be content with simply killing us—oh no," he comforted. "He will use Chinese tortures."

And Nadonsky went on to describe some of the Chinese tortures. The least cruel of these was one known as the Benignity of the Vermilion Flower Pot. In this pleasant little arrangement, a man is tied, seated, over the top of a flower pot in which a live rat is imprisoned. A red-hot iron introduced through the bottom of the pot incites the rat to gnaw his way through the only yielding substance.

The Americans grew grimly angry when they heard of these things. They patted their automatics and swore softly.

"Believe me, there'll be a few o' these here bullets thud home before they get this baby," promised Duggan.

The group was silent for the most part while they waited for darkness to come. Davies sat smoking, deep in thought. Some one touched him on the elbow.

"Don't look around too sudden," Duggan whispered. "There's some one staring at us outa one o' the windows of the house. It's enough to give you the creeps just to look at the face of it."

Turning slowly and as casually as possible, Davies glanced up at the silent house behind them.

Involuntarily he started at what he saw.

For high in the second story window, gazing down at them, was such a face as one might see in a nightmare.

Whether it was a man or woman could not be told. The hair was long and dank. The face was almost skeleton-like in its boniness. Great tragic eyes stared out from under the thatch of hair, stared with so much of agony and suffering and so much of half maniacal woe that it sent a shiver through one just to look at it.

"My God!" whispered Davies. "Who can it be?"

Dusk was coming on rapidly. Somehow no one wanted to go into that sinister looking house to investigate the strange apparition at the window. As it grew darker they could still see it there, staring, staring, staring, its wild eyes seeming to hold all of the tragedy and horror of life in their depths.

"Who ever it is, is too cuckoo to warn anybody about us," reflected Duggan.

Every one was anxious for it to get dark enough for them to leave that eerie place. A few more minutes and it would be completely dark. As they sat there silent they heard the door of the house open softly behind them.

Footsteps dragged along the walk, coming remorselessly toward them. Davies felt a shiver of horror go through him. He saw Nadonsky crossing himself. The other men had brought their pistols out ready for they knew not what.

The bent figure of a woman finally loomed up out of the dusk. She mumbled unintelligibly, her eyes wild in the dusk. She was a terrible creature to look upon, emaciated and in rags. She kept pointing to her mouth. Finally Duggan exclaimed in horror.

"God! she ain't got no tongue—it's been cut out!"

Nadonsky stared at the woman. He said something to her in Russian. She nodded wildly. He reached in his pocket, bringing out pencil and paper and struck a match holding it for her to write by. She seized the writing materials eagerly and wrote. Nadonsky took the paper when she had finished and read it, frowning.

The others waited curious to see what all this might portend.

Nadonsky studied the writing for a long time before he spoke, then asked some questions in Russian. She nodded to some; to others she shook her head violently.

Finally Nadonsky spoke in English.

"She has been injured by Nagoi. He has killed her sweetheart before her eyes. She called him a butcher and he had her tongue cut out. She wants to know if we will kill Nagoi for her?"

"Tell her we'll do our best," growled Duggan. The others nodded grimly. As wraithlike as she had come, she disappeared in the darkness to take up her vigil in the lonely house.

It was dark enough to make their escape under cover by now. Davies led the way out of the yard into the alleyway. It seemed deserted. The town had quieted down. Evidently search for the Americans had been abandoned; at any rate it had lessened in eagerness.

Making their way silently down the alleyway they approached the street. Here Davies waved to the rest of them to remain while he and Sergeant Duggan reconnoitered.

The old man passed on into the gloom. From far down the street they could hear the reiterated clatter of his wooden badge of office lessening in the distance.

They were about to pass out into the street when Davies suddenly grabbed Sergeant Duggan by the elbow and held him. They both listened intently. Yes, there it was, the unmistakable stamp of a horse's foot. It was followed by a man's voice muttering some imprecation. The sound came from down the street about a hundred and fifty feet distant.

Watching the spot, they saw the flare of a match. Its tiny circle of light showed the shaggy fur hat and bearded features of a Cossack who was lighting his pipe. Dimly behind him they could see horses tethered and the shadowy forms of men, some standing and some prone. Davies figured that there must be about ten men in the group. The match went out.

Plainly the town was thoroughly guarded against their escape. Duggan disappeared quietly into the darkness in the other direction. In a minute he returned, shaking his head.

"Another lot of 'em 'bout a hundred yards down the other way," he whispered. "About six horses bein' held by one guy and the rest of them layin' around on the ground except one who's on guard."

Davies listened, nodding.

"Probably the other end of the alley is guarded as well," he commented. "Six men you say and six horses? That's just one more horse than we need!"

Duggan nodded grunting his approval. He went back to get the other three men. They came up silently in the darkness. Davies explained the situation.

"We've got to grab those horses," he whispered. "I'll take the man on guard and one more. Each of you pick out your man and land on him when I slap my hand against my boot. That will be the signal to attack. Above all, try to do it silently. Duggan will grab the man with the horses and knock him out and hold the horses ready for us to mount. Use your pistol butts or your fists or anything else. Be sure to take a fur hat and a lance as we want to look like Cossacks when we pull out."

They nodded. Creeping down the street behind Davies, they soon closed in on the Cossacks. The horses were gathered in a half-circle at the street curb, their reins held by one man who sat on the curb, half asleep. The glow of a cigaret or two and some low toned conversation showed that some of the men were awake. Standing above them, looking in the opposite direction, was the sentinel, leaning on his carbine.

Davies, holding his pistol by the muzzle, silently motioned each one to his position, then slapping his boot loudly, ran swiftly forward and leaped at the sentinel, bringing down his pistol butt on the fellow's head with all his strength. The man fell forward with a grunt, dropping like a sack of meal, and remained quiet and motionless on the ground.

Simultaneously the others attacked the Cossacks on the ground. Davies ran swiftly to their assistance, attacking the nearest, a burly Cossack who had risen, calling something that sounded like "*Kok eta?*"

Davies closed with him, sending a vicious left and following this up with a right, giving the fellow all he had of six feet of bone and muscle and brawn squarely on the point of the jaw. The Cossack went down like a man of straw, completely knocked out.

To Davies' dismay, a shout went up from beside him. Two figures were threshing on the ground near by. Stooping, Davies saw that it was Schneider, fast in the grip of a big Cossack. Davies quieted the Russian with an emphatic tap of the pistol on his head. But the damage was done.

Down the street came an answering shout. Hastily looking over the battlefield, Davies saw that every man was accounted for, including the horse holder.

"Don't forget the hats," he called to his men. He ran to the clump of lances and picked them up, distributing one to each man and keeping one for himself. Every one was busy scrambling into the saddles. From down the street came another inquiring shout and the sound of running feet.

The horses were frightened and plunging. Davies pushed and hauled, helping Schneider into the saddle and handing him his lance. Seizing the nearest horse he vaulted on to its back.

The sound of running and shouting was upon them.

Spurring up his horse, he set out at a gallop followed by the rest of his men, just as the alarmed Cossacks from the other patrol reached the spot. Luckily they had come on foot. They shouted again. There was a sudden spurt of flame and a shot followed by the *ping* of a bullet overhead. The Americans by now were well out and making good speed down the street. Shouts and yells and the sound of running feet came from all sides.

Davies drew an exultant breath as he felt the surging muscles of the small Cossack horse under him, in spite of the queer feeling of the high padded Cossack saddle with its round bolsters.

More shots came from behind them. Ahead lights flashed and moved about in the darkness.

"We've got to ride for it." Davies turned in the saddle. "Keep those lances up and slanting to the rear like the Cossacks carry them!" he ordered.

Schneider was rolling around in the saddle like a loose gun on a ship's deck. His lance was pointing in all directions at once. Duggan rode beside him, with one arm ready to rescue him should he fall.

Dim figures loomed out of the darkness ahead, mounted men barring the way.

Davies dropped his lance in rest and rode straight at the nearest antagonist.

The lance head hit the Cossack square in the shoulder, sweeping him backward and out of the saddle. Davies, blessing the curiosity which led him to study the use of this weapon, let the lance turn under his wrist and loosened the point as he rode past the fallen man, pulling it out from the rear and returning it in a sweeping circle to the position of charge.

It was a small group which had barred their way, and they had succeeded in scattering it completely.

"I stuck one of the skunks with my sticker," he heard Daniels' voice, exultant, "but the darn thing jerked out of my hand. Kin I go back and get it, Major?"

"No, take Schneider's—he's got all he can do to stay on the horse."

The drumming of their horses' hoofs did not drown the noise and confusion surrounding them on all sides. An occasional bullet went whining overhead. They could hear a fusillade of shots in the darkness. Above this, Davies picked out the shrill clamor of a bugle trumpeting out the alarm for all to hear. Lights were flashing ahead of them and people were swarming out on the sidewalks.

It was high time to turn off this main street. The next side street they came to Davies turned in, slowing down to a walk as he left the main way.

"Anybody hit?" he asked.

"Everybody all safe and sound," reported Duggan, " 'ceptin' Schneider's lost a little o' his aplomb." And Davies heard Duggan's chuckle behind him in the darkness.

"Corporal Nadonsky, you ride up here with me. Answer anybody that challenges us. Tell them we are a patrol sent out to hunt the Americans or tell them anything you want that will get us by."

"Yes, sir," came Nadonsky's voice from the darkness and Davies felt, rather than saw, him ride up alongside.

Behind them, the main street was boiling with activity. A bell started ringing in an excitable sort of way, with rapid short jerks booming a warning to the countryside.

A voice shouted at them from the side of the road.

Nadonsky yelled something in reply. The voice made answer, evidently reassured. Certainly in the darkness the Americans, wearing shaggy fur hats, carrying lances and riding the stocky Siberian ponies, could easily pass for Cossacks.

Davies found at the saddle bow the terrible Cossack whip, the *nagaika* which, weighted with lead, is a weapon in itself, as it cuts like a sword. He did not wonder at the fear of the Russian crowds when the shouts of the Cossacks broke on their ears.

They were approaching the edge of town. The last few houses were just ahead of them. Beyond these houses, casting flickering shadows and lights across the road, was a large fire around which many figures moved. The fire was suddenly obscured by some large body moving between it and the Americans.

Davies, studying this, discovered it to be a large group of horsemen evidently moving in their direction.

"Not so good," he muttered to himself.

Behind him he could hear the rattle of hoofs and the jingle of accoutrements. He felt a stir and pulsation, as of the movement of many people in the surrounding darkness. He had the feeling of being helpless in the center of a net which was slowly being tightened around him and his men.

Ahead of him he could see the lance pennons of the approaching body of horsemen fluttering against the stars. From one of the houses ahead a lantern appeared, dancing and bobbing around as it came, casting long grotesque shadows of the Cossack soldier who was carrying it out to the road.

It shone on the leading files of a long column of Cossacks, at least a *sotnia* of them, their horses' heads tossing in the light, the shaggy riders looming above them in the gloom.

For one swift second the light shone full in the face of the officer leading the column. In that second Davies saw, clearly etched against the background of the night, the white face, the delicately formed, almost girlish, lips and the cruel eyes of Colonel Nagoi. The lantern was lowered, blotting out the picture. Davies heard a low growl from his left where rode Corporal Nadonsky.

Turning to his men, Davies called, "It's time to get out of here," and setting spurs to his horse, he turned to the right, galloping out between two houses. He swept through to the rear of them, keeping a straight line as far as possible for several hundred yards, then swinging again to the left and toward the open country.

He did not run into any more Cossacks. Guiding himself as well as he could, he kept at a steady gallop across the open fields for some ten minutes.

Finally missing Nadonsky at his side, he turned.

"Where's Corporal Nadonsky?" he asked the nearest figure behind him.

"Dunno, sir; he lit out before we left the houses, and Sergeant Duggan right after him. I think they're followin' behind us." It was Daniels' voice that replied.

Frowning in worry, Davies halted and listened. He could hear the town behind him bustling with activity. The bell was still sending out its strident note of alarm. An occasional shot broke on the night air.

He certainly couldn't leave Sergeant Duggan and Nadonsky alone back there. Nadonsky he didn't know so well, but Duggan—an old-timer, a cavalry soldier, a resourceful, cheerful, steady sort whom any man would be proud to have as friend. It came over him suddenly how genuinely fond he was of Duggan. No, he couldn't let him be taken by any sadistic beast of a half crazy Cossack colonel.

There was a clump of woods off to the right and a stack of hay near at hand. He could find his way back again.

"Listen," he addressed the two, "I'm going back to find Duggan. You two stay here and wait for me. If I don't get back by daylight, bust out and find the railroad. It's over that way—you can't miss it—and get to headquarters some way and report that we are in the hands of these people."

Schneider nodded. Daniels said nothing for a second or two, then:

"Major, can't I go along? Two are better than one among that pack o' coyotes back there. And Schneider here can beat it back and make the report to headquarters. I'm just asking it as a favor, Major."

Davies shook his head.

"No use all of us getting in hot water, Daniels. I'll mosey along and try to find them. You bring a rescue party if we get caught up. Stick around the edge of the woods back there where nobody can see you. I'll whistle if I get back." And Davies turned his horse around.

"Well, so long," Daniels mumbled.

"So long." Davies put out his hand. Daniels took it awkwardly.

"Well, so long," Daniels said again, and Davies was gone, into the dark, the faint padding of his horse's hoofs on the sod lost to hearing after a minute.

"Well, that's three of 'em gone," remarked Daniels bitterly as he and Schneider dismounted by the haystack. Their horses started to graze, munching away busily as the two soldiers stood silent and thoughtful in the darkness.

"Yeh, they're sure enough gone," echoed Schneider.

"Looks like we're the last of the Mohicans," added Daniels after a space in which they could hear the distant tolling of the bell from the town and the sound of the contented *munch-munch* of the horses pulling at the succulent grasses near by.

"It sure looks like it," agreed Schneider, wondering what Mohicans were anyway.

"Well, if they get Duggan and the Major, it'll be open season on Cossacks as far as American soldiers are concerned," growled Daniels vengefully. "Believe me, I'll put a bullet through every fur hatted son of a vodka drinker I can find."

"Me, too," echoed Schneider, swelling his chest.

"Ah, you!" Daniels growled in disgust. "You couldn't hit a flock of barns standing on the inside."

He threw himself down morosely, his head against the stack of hay.

Schneider philosophically rolled and smoked a cigaret; then, to amuse himself, he played with Daniels' lance, lunging at the stack of hay with it until he succeeded in ripping off the red and black pennon.

Meanwhile Davies gave his horse its reins. The tireless Cossack pony, headed toward its comrades and its stables, pricked up its ears and fairly flew over the ground. The fur hat that Davies had picked up from one of the Cossacks becoming too warm, he carried it in his hand. The lance held by a leather loop passing around his elbow, hung slanting to the rear, its butt contained in a small bucket on the stirrup leather.

As his horse coursed over the ground, he mused on the Cossacks and their ways, and reflected on the strangeness of his present situation—an American officer, riding alone through the Siberian night in far off Asiatic Russia, with lance at his side and Cossack horse and saddle under him.

He was becoming accustomed to the Cossack saddle by now, and rather liked the seat. The stirrups were a little short, and he let his feet out of them to rest his legs, riding along balanced in the saddle and giving easily to the horse's motion. Hanging from the near side of the pommel was a length of coiled rope. Running his hands over it, he found that it was knotted quite like an American cowboy's lariat, with a running noose spliced on to it. He wondered whether the Cossacks were adept in throwing the noose and remembered reading an old story of some Cossack hero who dragged his foe out of the saddle and over the ground in triumph by means of the lariat. It was a Cossack method of showing contempt for a fallen foe, quite like the old Greeks who used to drag their dead enemies behind their chariots. Who was it—Hector?—whose body was dragged around the Trojan walls? By Achilles? He could not remember.

Well, it was time to go more carefully now. He had approached the outskirts of the town again, and the first houses were looming up before him. Far to the right he saw the big camp-fire around which he had led his men when escaping from the town. Bringing his horse down to a walk, he moved carefully in between two houses, halting frequently and listening carefully. The Cossack pony pulled impatiently at the bit every time he halted, tossing its shaggy head and dancing around.

The first thing was to get some information. Probably the best place to get it would be in the vicinity of the big camp-fire near which he had caught a momentary glimpse of Colonel Nagoi. He slowly circled toward the light of the fire, screening himself by the intervening trees and houses.

There seemed to be half a hundred men at least around the fire, judging from the shadows that passed and repassed in front of its blaze. Some of them were singing. He could hear the melody with its accompaniment on a wheezing accordion. He recognized the song, a very famous old Russian song, entitled "Cossack, Where Are You Going?"

So interested did he become in the more distant camp-fire that he forgot for a moment to watch things nearer at hand. A sudden shout almost at his elbow brought him back swiftly to his immediate surroundings.

A heavy, dark figure loomed out of the dusk and shouted at him again in an authoritative voice. The man seized his reins. Lifting the heavy Cossack whip, the *nagaika*, Davies cut viciously at the shape before him. The man dropped the reins with a scream, throwing up his arm to protect his head.

The scream was the signal for the darkness to come to life. The earth seemed to erupt shadowy forms.

Davies, rising high in his stirrups, disengaged his lance from the bucket and loop. With the butt of the lance he smashed at several figures that leaped to his horse's head, jabbing at them fiercely and making many hits, judging by the howls of pain. But more figures succeeded them.

Spurring his horse at them, Davies drove with the point of the lance, swinging it rapidly. He lunged forward with the point and drawing it back, struck again and again to the rear with the butt. Men gave way before him but more rose up. His lance became caught in some one's body, and he could not disengage it. Raising the terrible *nagaika* again, he laid about him, heavily, smashing at heads and shoulders and wielding the weapon like a flail. The Cossack pony screamed and kicked.

Suddenly something whistled out of the darkness overhead and settled around his shoulders. He struggled frantically to rid himself of it. It was too late; a rope slipped down around his arms pinning them to his sides; it was jerked tight. He felt himself being yanked out of the saddle over the pony's back. He fell heavily to the ground. Over him fell and tripped a mob of men, growling like wild beasts, a peculiar savage growling that reminded him of the pack of hounds on his father's ranch—the pack that had killed one of their number under his eyes once, with that same bestial, low growling.

He felt blows landing on him, heard shouts and yells above him. Suddenly the weight removed itself from his body. He lay bound on the ground. His attackers were standing stiffly at attention around him. Some one, evidently an officer, had stopped the proceedings.

Torn and bleeding, he was lifted up and half led and half dragged toward the nearest house. The interior was lighted up. As the tramp of feet echoed on the wooden porch the door was flung open. Standing in the bright light from inside, his small body crouched forward like an animal ready to spring, his great head looking like some monstrous deformity in the light, was Colonel Nagoi.

"I am very happy to see you again, my friend," his whining, snarling voice broke the silence. The Cossacks who held Davies fell back instinctively, as if in fear.

In the meantime Sergeant Duggan was stretched out on the ground, in the grain room of a stable, his eyes closed, and with blood slowly caking over an ugly wound in his head. His captors were not quite sure whether he was dead or not, and decided to wait until daylight before reporting his capture. In the meantime they sat in a circle in an alleyway between the horse stalls, smoking and drinking tea.

It was Corporal Nadonsky's sudden desertion of the party that had brought Duggan to this pass. He had followed the Russian American closely as he pivoted his horse and galloped away at the time the man had flashed the lantern on the *sotnia* of Cossacks and its leader.

"Here! Where you goin'?" Duggan had called after him, but Nadonsky made no reply, only whipped up his horse.

He fled away among the houses bordering the road and lost himself between several buildings. Duggan had drawn up perplexed, listening for a while, then deciding that it would be better to rejoin the major.

As he turned his horse he heard men shouting and following him. Riding quickly into the yard of a small, square, log building, near at hand, he drew his horse up into the shadow of its walls and waited for five or six minutes. He did not wait in idleness, but occupied himself with something that had to do with the roof of the house. A shouting, yelling mob of men went past as he waited.

When the coast seemed to be clear, he had made for the road again. Scarcely had he set foot on the highway when a figure rose right up at the ground at his horse's feet, growling something unintelligible. Other figures, prone on the ground near by, took up the growling chorus. To Duggan's dismay, he found that he was in the center of a bivouac of men, surrounding him on all sides.

The man at his horse's head asked him some question. Duggan made no reply. The man peered up at him. Duggan attempted to ride him down. Suddenly the whole bivouac was swarming around him. He fought as in a dream. The whole world seemed to be trying to pull him from his horse. Suddenly he felt a terrific blow and then felt himself slipping, slipping quietly as if he were floating down some dark river. Then all was oblivion and vast silence.

Davies, sitting on a long wooden bench, his hands tied behind him and the rope fastened to the bench, watched Colonel Nagoi strut back and forth. The American watched him with a slight trace of amusement, which was slowly bringing the light of madness to the Russian's eyes.

"My friend"—the sing-song, whining snarl of Nagoi's voice became more unpleasantly vibrant as he talked—"I have promised myself some rare sport with you. I have many pleasant and delicate little attentions ready to bring to your notice; you would be flattered did you know the amount of thought I have given to your case, I and my Chinese assistant."

Clapping his hands, Nagoi shouted something through the open doorway. The huge form of the Chinese whom Davies had seen in Nagoi's anteroom appeared. His hands were lost in the capacious sleeves of his padded jacket. He bent his head as Nagoi spoke to him in Chinese. In the eyes of the Oriental was that came calm, reflective, almost gentle look that Davies had observed before.

The Chinese came over to him. Reaching out one long fingered yellow hand, he touched Davies' shoulders and chest, then ran his hand around his neck, finally squeezing his arms. His eyes were gently speculative; he might have been some doctor examining a patient.

The Chinese nodded. He said something to Nagoi, his voice very matter of fact.

"My assistant here is a very skilled practitioner; he says that you would last a long time with the delightful pastime of the Death by One Thousand

Slices." Davies' face was impassive, but his brain was working fast. He had once seen in Shanghai a series of photographs illustrating the "Death by One Thousand Slices." It was not a pretty set of pictures.

Nagoi turned again to the Chinese, giving him some instructions. The man withdrew, nodding assent. A voice came from outside. Davies raised his head—that voice was familiar!

Nagoi answered impatiently.

Into the room stepped Captain Grineff, the young Russian whom he had met on the train. Grineff gazed at him as if he had never seen the American before. He saluted Nagoi and handed him a message.

Nagoi grunted something that sounded like "Khorashaw!" after reading the paper.

The Chinese entered with a package wrapped in silk. Unrolling it, he laid on the table a glittering array of cunningly designed knives.

"You see them?" Nagoi turned to Davies. "They are very pretty, are they not? It will go, oh so slowly! First he will start on your face—think how the girls will love you with your nose cut off and your ears gone and your lips cut away!"

Davies looked at him in contempt.

"Oh, go to hell, you infernal little monkey!" Davies' voice was bored.

It was like a red rag to a bull. Nagoi threw back his head and screamed out something in Russian. He frothed at the lips. Coming closer to Davies, he leaned over, shaking his fist in his face and shouting a stream of abuse in Russian.

Davies gathered himself, tightening up his muscles as he sat tied on the bench. His feet were free. Nearer and nearer came the Russian, his words coming so fast that they fairly tripped over each other.

Suddenly Davies leaned back on the bench. His legs gathered under him. His feet leaped forward like a catapult. Fair and square on the chin he caught the colonel. Nagoi shot back across the room as if propelled by a battering ram. He crumpled up weakly at the feet of the Chinese by the table.

Then a surprising thing happened. Grineff, who had been a silent and seemingly disinterested witness of all that had happened, gave one look at the unconscious colonel. With the swiftness of lightning he leaped toward Davies, drawing a small dagger from a gold encrusted sheath that hung at his belt.

Before Davies knew what had happened, he felt the ropes which bound his hands dropping to the floor.

Grineff pointed out the open door. The Chinese, who had watched without a flicker of emotion disturbing his olive features, slowly came toward them, a short knife in his hands. Davies crouched and then propelled himself at the huge bulk of the man, expecting a hard tussle.

He drove heavily at the Chinese. To his surprise the fellow dropped like a log. There is no one more pathetically vulnerable to Anglo-Saxon fists than the average Oriental.

Turning to Grineff, Davies grasped his hand. Grineff pushed him away, pointing to the door. Flinging himself out on the porch, Davies saw three Cossacks sitting under a tree in the yard, quietly smoking. They looked at him in surprise but made no move to stop him.

He hurried out of the yard into the street, running and stumbling until he found a group of horses tethered to a fence. He helped himself to one of these. In a few seconds he was galloping away. There seemed to be no outcry or excitement behind him.

Orienting himself, he sped toward the place where he had left the two men. He located the haystack without much difficulty. To his low whistle Daniels responded with a glad shout.

"By God, Major, I thought they'd got you surer than hell." His voice sounded immensely relieved. Then, quietly, "Did you see anything of Duggan?"

"Not a sign—blamed near got done away with myself. I'm afraid Duggan has been captured with Nadonsky. We're too few to rescue them. All we can do is to ride hell bent for election until we strike the railroad and keep along it until we hit our own people. Then we can come back and show these infernal people a thing or two. I hope to God that madman Nagoi doesn't kill the two of them before we get back."

Knowing that the railroad lay over to the left, Davies headed in that direction with Daniels and Schneider, plying whip and spur at full gallop. It was going to be a close call if they were to save Duggan and his companion.

Meanwhile Duggan was slowly regaining consciousness, his head throbbing like some great engine. For a long time he could not remember anything except the fact that he had started on an expedition after some maps with Major Davies. He sank back a little relieved. He knew that Davies would look after him. Then as his brain began slowly to function anew, he recalled the entrance into the town and the flight from the Cossacks. For the life of him he could not remember any events leading directly up to his capture. He was much puzzled trying to figure out how he had become separated from the rest of his comrades.

Judging from the smells, he was in a stable, or near horses somewhere. He tried to raise his hand to his throbbing head and found he was bound securely. All was darkness around him.

After what seemed hours of being alone there in the dark, when he was nearly fainting from thirst and weakness, he heard voices near at hand. A door suddenly opened, admitting daylight.

The light so hurt his eyes that he was unable to keep them open. He heard several men enter. They pulled him roughly to his feet and half dragged and half carried him outside and across a courtyard. They entered another building and led him up a staircase, coming at last to the second floor where he was shoved into an antechamber. Standing inside the door was a tall Cossack officer in a white Astrakhan hat.

The far end of the room was screened by heavy red portieres. Behind these he could hear voices talking in Russian. One voice was strangely familiar. Where had he heard it? Of course, on the train, it was that Cossack officer who had talked and had the drinks with Major Davies. What was his name? Yes, Grineff or something like that.

The voice seemed to be pleading for something. Another voice broke in, a peculiarly penetrating voice, sort of snarling, and whining at the same time, like a cat's. The second voice rose in excitement and anger, its high snarl became more noticeable. Finally it shouted out some command.

There was a scream which ended with a sickening sort of a gurgle, and a noise like that made by a meat ax on the chopping block—a thud and all was silent.

Duggan, looking at the Cossack officer, saw the fellow grinning wickedly, his slant Tartar eyes shining with a strange light.

After a few seconds in which Duggan heard a sound as of something heavy being dragged across the floor, the curtains parted and a bland, smooth faced Chinese came into the room, dressed in long flowing robes. He carried something that gleamed dully in his right hand. Seeing Duggan, he quickly concealed it behind his padded robe. Staring at him, Duggan noticed that the Chinese face was bruised and puffy. Duggan quickly conceived an immense distrust for this bland Celestial. He strained at the bonds which secured his hands behind him. Twisting and turning his wrists, he tried to loosen the ropes.

The Cossack officer in the anteroom called something through the curtains. The snarling cat-like voice responded in sharp command.

"Next!" whispered Duggan to himself as the Cossack beckoned to him. The sergeant, with one wary eye on the Chinese, followed through the curtains. As he passed through, out of the tail of his eye he saw the bulky form of the Celestial uncoil like a snake and rise to full length.

"I wish to God Major Davies was here," thought Duggan wistfully as he turned to face what lay before him.

After ten minutes' hard riding, Davies and the two with him saw ahead of them the telegraph poles which marked the railway, and in a few minutes rode up to the narrow ribbons of steel which ran from Moscow to Vladivostok, over mountains and rivers, and steppes and forests, across Europe and across

Asia—over five thousand miles of steel rails.

The fact that the Trans-Siberian Railway was fit to rank with the Great Wall of China as a stupendous engineering feat bore little weight with Davies at that moment. What he wanted was a train. Scanning the railroad line in both directions, he could see no sign of anything moving. The only thing to do was to ride in the direction of the American forces, hoping to flag a train when it did go by. Low lying clouds obscured what little moon there was, and the night was almost pitch black. The steel rails stretched away beside them, gleaming faintly in the darkness, their cold silence undisturbed by any faint hum of approaching traffic.

The three rode silently, occupied with their thoughts, Davies being sunk in worry over his two men. Of the maps he thought little. What were a few pieces of paper in comparison with the lives of two soldiers? After his own experience with Nagoi and his maniacal depravity, he shuddered to think about what might be happening to good old Sergeant Duggan at that very moment. Impatiently he spurred up his horse and they moved forward more swiftly at the gallop.

His head sunk low, Davies did not see the lights of the station ahead of them until Daniels called his attention to them. Speeding up their hard breathing horses, the Americans rode up to the place, finding a small wayside station with a single light burning in a small room at one end.

On a siding stood a train of five or six flatcars and a locomotive with sparks coming from its smokestack. The engine cab was deserted. There seemed to be no one around. Davies at last found the engine crew snugly ensconced around a steaming samovar sipping tea in the rear room of the station. In a weird mixture of English and pidgin-Russian reinforced by an authoritative voice and the aggressive gleam of his pistol, Davies finally prevailed upon the crew to move out.

Abandoning the horses to the station *narcharlnik* who accepted them dubiously, the three Americans climbed on to one of the flatcars and the train started, heading out with enough ringing of bells and blowing of whistles to raise the dead.

They had not been traveling more than ten minutes when the train pulled into a siding. Davies, going forward to investigate, found the engine crew making themselves comfortable around a hastily built fire, with water being made ready to boil for tea. Expostulating with them, he was unable to get any satisfaction. They simply pointed down the tracks and shrugged their shoulders. After waiting, with what patience he could muster for what seemed like hours to him, Davies finally discovered the reason for the delay, when a ray of light flickered along the rails followed by a humming sound which grew into a roar, as a big passenger train rushed by and disappeared into the darkness.

The engineer and fireman reappeared, and in the most leisurely fashion started to get up steam again, having neglected the fire while waiting. This consumed another half hour. Finally they set forth again.

Davies had grown absolutely dulled, hoping against hope that he could get back to Duggan in time, but beginning to feel like a Russian, who can readily resign himself to anything with a shrug of his shoulders. It was just as well that he grew more philosophical. They had scarcely started when there was the sudden roar of escaping steam. The train stopped again.

Davies found the engine crew standing by the track, gazing at the locomotive and shaking their heads. Something had gone wrong again. The decrepit engine, mishandled for years, had broken down.

There was nothing to do. Davies and the two men made themselves as comfortable as possible while waiting for daylight. The hours dragged through. Davies dozed now and then; Schneider snored loudly and vehemently; Daniels stared off into the gloom, his head bent, his thoughts heavy with worry for his friend Duggan.

A shout roused Davies from a nap. Daylight had come. Daniels was dancing around like one demented, pointing down the road. There, in the early light of morning, Davies saw a group of men in olive drab uniforms walking slowly along in full pack, carrying their rifles. Behind them to the right and left he saw other groups. Still farther back on the road was a larger body, and behind them in the distance a long column of American infantry flowing along the road in that shuffling, seemingly slow gait of the doughboy on the march.

Hurrying down to the road with his two men, Davies waited until the advance guard had passed and the main body came up, Colonel Borrow riding at its head.

Very briefly Davies explained the situation to the colonel.

"—and if you'll let me take all the mounted men in the regiment I can move forward rapidly and find the two men before that devil does them up."

"Surely," boomed the colonel, and calling to his orderly, he instructed him to go back and get Major Davies' horse, at the same time notifying all mounted men to report up front immediately.

The orderly sped away. In a few seconds the first horseman came up, an orderly. He was followed at intervals by mounted messengers and more orderlies. Soon a large group came from the headquarters company and a final group from the machine gun company, with a few stragglers drifting in from the trains. Altogether Davies mustered nearly forty men. All of them were armed with the pistol and most of them carried rifles. The most part of them were ex-cavalry soldiers.

Taintor, Davies' orderly, came galloping up with Peggy, his thoroughbred mare. Swinging into the saddle happily, Davies found that Peggy seemed enormous after the Cossack ponies. He borrowed a pistol from some company officer, his own having been seized by the Cossacks. He picked out two men who didn't look very capable and had them dismount and turned their horses over to Daniels and Schneider.

The men lined up; Davies gave them "Count fours!" and quickly moved them out in column. Going by the colonel at a trot, he saluted and heard a cheery "Good luck!" shouted after him. Leaving the foremost elements of the advance guard behind, he settled down in dead earnest to eat up the miles that lay between him and the Cossacks.

He had not gone far when he saw before him the dust raised by a small squad of Cossacks galloping madly away. He grinned as he saw them, figuring out that they had been sent out in pursuit of him the night before.

After an hour's swift progress he saw ahead of him the golden dome of the cathedral in the town. In a few more minutes he was among the houses on the outer edge of the place. His long column of mounted men stretched behind him, a businesslike looking outfit. Looking around at them proudly, he was confident that with them he could clean up ten times their number of Cossacks.

Not wishing to run any needless risks, he sent forward a small patrol under charge of Daniels, who soon reported back, stating that the Cossacks were friendly and that the way seemed clear.

Major Davies decided to risk it. He trotted boldly into town keeping a sharp lookout to right and left. The groups of Cossacks he saw here and there waved to him cheerfully.

Turning sharply into the main street, he swung up the hill before the barracks where he had held his original interview with Colonel Nagoi. All seemed to be in confusion. There were no sentries before the great gate with its arrogant double headed eagle staring down superciliously.

Dismounting and throwing his reins to his orderly, he called Daniels and Schneider and climbing the stairs, entered the small anteroom with the red curtains screening the far end. The anteroom was deserted.

He pushed the curtains aside and stepped into the larger room where he had held the fateful interview with the snarling voiced Colonel Nagoi. Daniels and Schneider crowded in after him, pistols in hand. There was an exclamation from Daniels. Davies turned.

The two soldiers were gazing in horror at something on the floor.

Coming closer to where they pointed, white faced and grim, Davies stared in silence with them. A long, oblong pool of blood lay on the floor. The three men looked at each other silently, the same thought in the mind of each. Without a word they left the room.

They sought through the building but found it completely deserted. Finally they entered the courtyard in rear. Here they found a sick Cossack lying on a pallet of rags. He could speak a little broken English.

"Yes, the *polkovnik* was gone. How long? Maybe short time. Which way?" He pointed out toward the southern edge of town, shrugging his shoulders.

"*Americanski* soldier? *Da, da*," he nodded his head. Where? He didn't know, maybe with *polkovnik*. *Da*, just one soldier, maybe with *polkovnik*, maybe not.

With this meager information Davies returned to his waiting troop. There was only one American soldier with the Russians. Who was it, Nadonsky or Sergeant Duggan? What had happened to the other?

After watering his horses and having saddles adjusted, Davies led the troop out toward the southern extremity of town. A wandering *moujik* at the edge of town confirmed the report, showing by signs that a big bunch of Cossacks had gone through that way a short time previously. The tracks in the dust further showed that a large body of mounted men had passed through. The *moujik* further conveyed the important information that there was an *Americanski* soldier with them, very pale and sick looking.

The horse droppings along the road indicated that horsemen had passed not more than fifteen or twenty minutes previously. Davies, with his longer legged American horses, knew that it was only a matter of time until he outstripped the Cossacks with their small mounts. He settled his troop down into a steady trot, knowing full well that it would wear down the enemy eventually. Sending out an advance guard with careful instructions, he began patiently to follow the trail so plainly outlined before them. With all his worry for the safety of his two men, he was joyous to have a cavalry command behind him once more. And Peggy's free, square trot was certainly a relief after the choppy, short legged gait of the Cossack horses he had been riding.

The road wound along deep in white dust. A few hundred yards from town it entered deep woods, silent except for the occasional call of some bird or the indignant chattering of a gray squirrel.

After a mile of this they came out into open country again. The road wound through green carpeted meadows and around the bases of small hills.

Carefully estimating the time he had been traveling and comparing it with the speed he knew the Cossack ponies could make, he reasoned that he should be running into the enemy very quickly. And very suddenly the joy that had been his in leading this long column of mounted men over this beautiful country deserted him as if by magic. A sudden pall descended upon his spirits, like some gray blanket of foreboding. He tried to throw off the feeling of oppression that seemed to fetter him in icy chains. What in the mischief was the matter anyway?

His troop had left the shelter of a fir wood some hundreds of yards in their rear. They were at a walk, moving down into a small valley that rose on the far side by smooth stages to another wood in front.

He tried to analyze the deepening feeling of apprehension that had come over him. It was a plain feeling of dire foreboding. His advance guard ahead was in plain view riding among the trees on the far side of the valley. They had already combed the woods ahead and were signaling back that all was well.

Some sixth sense was evidently warning him that all was *not* well. He wanted no impediments thrown in his way toward rescuing his men and punishing Colonel Nagoi. Colonel Nagoi? The snarling, tiger-like little man. He frowned in puzzlement. Some idea was trying to make itself heard in his mind. What was it? Tiger? There was some connection with the word "tiger." A sudden picture flashed into his mind of the old *polkovnik* on the tiger hunt. What was it he had said?

"The *tigre de Siberie* always hunts his hunter!"

By God, that was it!

He turned swiftly in his saddle and looked behind. His men were riding along quietly heads to the front. Galvanized into sudden action he shouted, "Form fours! Trot! March!" and watched his wondering men trot obediently up into sets of fours.

"Gallop! March!" he shouted and the troop speeded up into the gallop. Several of them looked back to see what the major was staring at in the rear.

Their startled eyes beheld the flash of sun on steel, a long line of glittering lance points breaking out of the woods behind them, followed by a solid double rank of shaggy horses ridden by silent Cossacks. The line extended the whole width of the meadow; over two hundred men were galloping down upon them, the farthest flanks of the Cossack line already circling so as to catch the Americans in flank. On they came, their horses' hoofs deadened in the soft meadow grass.

The Americans, with their faster horses, were pulling away from them. Davies led them into the trees, executed a column left so that his troop paralleled the Cossack line, and signaled:

"Fight on foot! Action left!"

A line of olive drab figures swarmed to the ground, rifle and pistol in hand. They swept forward to the edge of the woods. The busy click of breech blocks filled the air.

"Fire at will!" shouted Davies.

A scattering volley rang out, followed by a rapid hail of well directed fire.

The Cossacks checked suddenly; horses reared and ran out of ranks, riderless; men were dropping. Suddenly the Cossack line broke and fled in all directions, the men firing under their horses' necks and across the saddles in all sorts of attitudes. Firing from the saddle with rifles is picturesque but not very deadly. An occasional bullet pinged overhead, and that was all.

"Cease firing," ordered Davies, and the wood occupied by the Americans grew silent except for the occasional whine of an enemy bullet.

Davies knew very well that the Cossacks were not retreating. They were simply practising the tactics of the "Lava," the famous old fighting maneuvers of the nomad horsemen of the steppes—cavalry tactics older than Genghis Khan himself.

Sure enough, the fleeing men suddenly formed into groups which came charging back, firing as they galloped.

Waiting until they came close enough, Davies gave the command to fire. Again that deadly hail of bullets broke forth from the woods. Watching carefully for evidences of any outflanking movements, Davies studied the terrain in front of him and at the sides. In front, the fire of the Americans was emptying many saddles and knocking down fleeing horses which struggled and threshed in the long grass of the meadow.

Again the Cossacks broke their formations, dissolving into clouds of wildly galloping riders. These clouds broke and reformed, firing to the rear from their saddles. Their tactics would have been bewildering to any regular cavalry attacking them with the saber. To a bunch of cool American riflemen prone on their stomachs, firing steadily and calmly, the Lava formation was nothing to get excited about.

Men continued to drop from the saddles and horses to go down until the green of the meadow was covered with dark forms of the bodies of horses and riders.

Davies studied the field carefully and spied at the far end a single small figure on a white horse, standing statuesquely on a knoll. The large head and small body of the solitary horseman was distinguishable even at that distance. Davies leveled his glasses upon it to make doubly sure.

He nodded. Yes, it was Colonel Nagoi.

The Cossacks were milling around now, the heart seemingly having gone out of their mounted attack. They began to head back for the shelter of the woods. Davies hoped that they would not attack dismounted with rifle fire. He was outnumbered four to one. He gave "Cease firing" so as not to waste precious ammunition.

Something happening on the knoll occupied by the solitary figure of Colonel Nagoi attracted his eye. A lone Cossack had approached the single figure from the rear. Davies stared in amazement, then directed his glasses on the two to make sure that he saw aright. For the lone Cossack had thrown a rope around the colonel and was prodding him forward with his lance—bringing him toward the Americans!

The strange pair came nearer and nearer the American line. Davies shouted a warning as he saw rifles go up to pick them off.

"Why, it's Nadonsky!" he called to Daniels and Schneider, busy reloading their pistols near him. "And he's bringing in that damn' Nagoi brute!"

Corporal Nadonsky could be seen very plainly, attired in full Cossack uniform, galloping behind Colonel Nagoi, pricking him with the lance point whenever the frightened looking commander tried to argue with him. They were headed straight for the American line.

In a few seconds they galloped up across the valley the Cossacks watched, curiously silent and inert. Nagoi was pulled from his horse by the nearest soldiers and stood, a rope around him, the other end of which was held by Corporal Nadonsky. The corporal saluted unperturbed.

"I left you to go after this fellow, Major," he reported.

"Good work! Where's Duggan?"

"Back there with the Cossacks; he's all right, a little bruised up. This dog"—and Nadonsky pointed a contemptuous thumb at Nagoi who quailed under his eye—"this dog was about to have him killed before you entered the town and scared him away."

Across the valley a Cossack officer, accompanied by a soldier who carried a white flag on his lance point, started for the American line, trotting across the intervening space.

Davies turned to Nagoi, who glared at him like a veritable trapped tiger.

"You seem to have gotten yourself into trouble," he said quietly. "You shouldn't try your funny little tricks on Americans." The Cossack officer with the white flag rode up. Davies beckoned to him; he dismounted, and, bowing, strode forward.

"My comrades sent me to tell you that we have no quarrel with the Americans," he stated briefly. "We have been obeying the orders of That One." He pointed to Nagoi. "Our hearts are not in it. We would like to be friends with the brave soldiers you have shown yourselves to be."

"That suits us," Davies nodded. "Call out your men and take care of your dead and wounded. Send over my sergeant right away."

The Cossack officer saluted, bowed again and, going to the edge of the woods, signaled across the valley. The Cossacks came out into the open, stacked their lances and carbines and rode slowly across the meadow to the American side, forming a large half circle below the firing line.

Out of their ranks strode Duggan, his face pale but his eyes alight. As he went by Nagoi, he stopped in front of him.

"Why, you poor piece of cheese," he remonstrated, his voice indulgently reproving, "how come you set yourself up as a little Napoleon and try and get rough with us? That ain't no way to act a-tall, a-tall." And, shaking his head, Duggan reported to Davies who grasped his hand and shook it without a word.

"Sure was scared about you, Sergeant," said Davies simply.

"Kinda got scared about myself once or twicet," he confessed, grinning.

"Did they get the maps from you?"

"No, sir, I shoved 'em under the eaves of a little log house back there in the town just before they jumped me. I can get 'em when we go back."

Daniels came up and banged Duggan on the ribs.

"You poor son of a gun," he said feelingly, "I sure thought them birds had done for you," and Daniels' eyes were misty as he spoke, sheepishly and awkwardly.

Nadonsky smiled down at Duggan from the saddle where he still sat holding Nagoi's rope in his hand. Davies looked at the Cossack commander somewhat puzzled. He wasn't supposed to be taking Cossack prisoners. But Nadonsky spoke up, saying something in Russian to Nagoi. The colonel trembled and looked at the faces of his men gazing up at him stonily from the great half circle below.

Nadonsky gave a jerk at the rope. Before Davies could interfere, he had jerked Nagoi off his feet and dragged him directly in front of the whole Cossack force.

Davies started to protest. Duggan spoke up.

"He had that guy Grineff chopped down," he said.

The American officer nodded comprehendingly and said nothing more.

Nagoi crawled to his knees and then up to his feet while Nadonsky rose in his stirrups and addressed the horde of shaggy looking men before him, in ringing forceful Russian.

A shout went up from the Cossacks.

"What is it all about?" Davies asked the Russian officer who had brought the white flag.

"I don't know. I do not think your man on the horse likes our Colonel Nagoi," explained the officer seriously.

Another shout went up. Suddenly the Cossacks whipped up their horses. Nadonsky put spurs to his mount. Again Nagoi was jerked from his feet. He screamed loudly as he fell and was hauled over the ground by the galloping horse. He screamed again and again as the Cossacks followed Nadonsky, raising their terrible *nagaikas* and cutting down at the shrieking howling figure on the ground.

There was something animal-like about the howls of the figure being dragged along behind the galloping horse. He was soon surrounded with a black cloud of Cossacks, growling and striking. The whole pack disappeared into the woods.

"Good Lord!" exclaimed Davies. "That was terrible! What was it all about?"

The Cossack officer standing beside him nodded his head.

"I understand now," he explained. "This Nagoi was once a convict on Sakhalin. He was—what do you say?—executioner, and was sentenced to death by the other convicts of whom your man was one. That is all," and the Cossack shrugged his shoulders. "It is all very regrettable," he said mildly, "but then, Nagoi was an extremely unsympathetic type." He lighted a cigaret. "Yes," he continued reflectively, "he was verree, verree impolite fellow, that man Nagoi!"

Duggan, standing near by, turned gravely to the Russian.

"Them's hard words, stranger," he objected. "I wouldn't go so far as to say he was impolite—jest a tiny bit temperamental, I'd say."

Straight at the closed window he hurled it.

The Czarina's Pearls

IT WAS A QUIET LITTLE SUPPER, that winter evening early in 1914. But, like a pebble cast into a still pool, the waves of that supper traveled far, and were noted at widely scattered points. Among other places, they penetrated into the secret bureaus of a building in Berlin, into the quiet chambers of a chancellery in Vienna, and into the upper rooms of a certain unassuming Downing Street house in London.

The Villa Rode in St. Petersburg lent itself to quiet suppers, having, as it did, a number of discreet little private dining rooms where almost anything might happen and often did.

There were three of them around that table, the most noticeable being a burning-eyed, fanatic-looking, tall, thin figure in peasant costume with silk embroidered shirt. He had a thatch of unruly hair, a tangled black beard and flowing mustache. It could be none other than Rasputin himself.

Next to him sat a fleshy, blue-black jowled man dressed in the green and silver of an officer of the Imperial Suite, a deep-voiced and hearty fellow whose eyes were just a shade shifty and frightened-looking.

The third member, a stolid, blockily-built personage, glanced at the other two from time to time, with something like contempt peering forth from his small, hard blue eyes; eyes that stared forth humorless and arrogant from a bullet-shaped head surmounted with a brush of stiff and pompadourish hair.

"So far it is nothing but talk, talk, talk," spoke up this last one, his Russian sounding strangely harsh and guttural. "Germany does not want talk, it demands proof. Where is the proof?" The arrogant one struck the table with his clenched fist so that the other two looked at him, worried.

The fat one in the green and silver of the Imperial Suite leaned forward, licking his lips nervously. "Your excellency forgets that so far the proceedings have been interfered with by an almost diabolic series of happenings—"

"It is true," the man in the peasant boots and blouse spoke up in a deep and resonant voice, "the hand of God seems to be against us."

"You Russians!" and there was contempt in the harsh voice of the stocky, stiff-haired one. "You Russians! Whenever your own incapacity becomes too evident, you blame it on the hand of God. Who is working against you? Who has upset your plans? Kill him without mercy!"

The other two looked at each other, startled. Finally they nodded to each other.

"He has been drawn against us by accident and by the influence of the Czarina's newest lady-in-waiting, Natalia Feodorovna," the imperial officer said. "She is the one who had charge of the pearls."

"Kill her, too," spoke up the blocky man brutally.

Both his listeners shook their heads.

"No, it will not be necessary, the Okhrana can handle Natalia's case." And it was noticeable that when the imperial officer mentioned the name of the dread Russian Secret Service he lowered his voice and glanced about.

"It is Prince Michael who must die," he continued.

"Yes," echoed the bearded man in the Russian peasant costume. "And Natalia, the little vixen, must have her pride humbled. Leave it to Grishka. She shall be taught humility." His deep-socketed eyes glowed savagely.

For Rasputin himself, the most powerful individual at the Russian court, had been flouted and tricked.

It had all started a few days before when a certain lieutenant went on duty as officer of the Palace Guard.

II

THE IMPERIAL BODYGUARD

OVER ST. PETERSBURG A LEAD-COLORED SKY pressed down like a heavy blanket. The Neva was frozen solid and exhaled an icy chill toward the huge, frowning bulk of the Winter Palace sprawled along its bank. The Czar and his family were at home, as could be seen by the huge imperial standard rippling lazily from the tower.

In a large hall within the palace stood a tall young lieutenant of Red Hussars, a broad-shouldered, slender-waisted figure in scarlet dolman and gold-embroidered pelisse. There was a suggestion of restrained and smoothly functioning power about him, like the strength of a giant jungle cat.

His tawny, sleepy, wide-apart eyes stared curiously aloft at the enormous bronze and crystal chandeliers, then gazed along the hall through the arched entrance to another hall and still another at the end of which he could see the silent cat-like pacing figures of the Cossacks before the heavy door of the inner apartments, the dwelling place of the Czar.

Lieutenant Prince Michael Doblestni had absolute responsibility for the safety of the Czar's person for the next twenty-four hours, no light responsibility in view of the fact that attempts had been made on the ruler's life no less than three times in the last year.

No sound disturbed the silence of the palace except an occasional subdued cough, or the whisper of some one of the many footmen in crimson coats and knee breeches.

He studied his men, lithe tall fellows, booted and spurred, their sabers at the carry, the long scarlet saber knots swinging as they paced their posts gravely and quietly.

Enigmas to him were these Russian soldiers, stolid respectful fellows. He knew soldiers and loved them and had spent many happy years in their company. But those were the lank, loose-jointed men of his uncle's American cavalry regiment. With this uncle, the brother of his American mother, he had spent many happy vacations, riding and marching along the Mexican border.

He smiled. "Mike," the American soldiers had called him; while these sternly respectful men never addressed him except as "*Vashe Blagorodie*"— "Your Honor." Undoubtedly the Russian cavalry regiment was more colorful, but he missed the American cavalrymen's humanness and humor.

The early darkness of midwinter came on. Dim lights sprang out of the shadows here and there. It was his first tour of guard duty there and he was rather overwhelmed with the seriousness of it. Should any one enter through his sentinels and harm any of the imperial family, the Russian officer's code left only one course of atonement open: he must take his own life.

The whole great gloomy palace seemed to be listening and watching, with its pad of silent feet and its whispers.

Dawn was heralded by the arrival of the cleaners, red-trousered, white-shirted men, a long line of them advancing over the floors, working industriously and silently.

A trace of his Slavic ancestry remained in young Prince Michael, a form of superstition for which he laughed at himself but which he invariably heeded. He always started the day by counting anything that appeared in numbers over five. If the score came out seven or eleven or any multiple of those numbers he felt that the day was begun under good auspices.

He counted the cleaners, breathing a sigh of relief as he totaled their number to twenty-one. He wondered how dependable these cleaners might be. He knew that it was the custom of the Czar to walk through these halls at eight o'clock, on his way out for a walk. What could prevent one of these cleaners from smuggling in a bomb or a revolver and making an attempt on the life of the ruler?

Then the lieutenant shook his head, smiling at his own state of nerves.

It was nearing eight o'clock. A stir and rustle in the halls between his hall and the inner apartments betokened the expected passage of the Czar. The red-trousered cleaners came back, carrying their mops and buckets.

Idly, wishing to verify his chances for the day again, the young officer counted them. Startled, he sat bolt upright in his chair and rubbed his eyes, rapidly counting them over a second time.

There were only twenty of them! One was missing, left behind in the inner hallway through which the Czar would come any moment now!

The lieutenant paused, a horrible fear gripping his heart. It was his first tour of guard duty. There were many guards on duty in the two great halls which separated him from the inner apartments. Surely it would be looked upon as impertinence on his part if he rushed in and demanded a search of those two halls.

There was a stir and bustle about the doors leading to the Czar's private quarters. A file of Cossacks had ranged themselves on either side.

For a second a struggle went on between his more fatalistic Slav ancestry and his more dynamic American blood.

The American in him triumphed. Calling his orderly, he strode rapidly toward the inner apartments.

Several Cossack sentinels looked at him in surprise. There was nothing in that hall behind which a man could remain in concealment. Into the next he went.

The bustle about the door of the Czar's suite continued.

The second hall contained several great pieces of bronze statuary, one of which, an equestrian figure, flanked the entrance nearest to the door at the Czar's chambers. Like a hound on the quest, the Hussar officer went for this.

Cowering behind it, with some dark object in his hand, crouched the form of the missing cleaner.

As the lieutenant rounded the base of the statue the man rose, his eyes ablaze with fanatic resolve, his two hands around the dark object. With this he did something, drew forth a pin or adjusted it in some fashion and, leaning backward, threw it at the scarlet-clad officer before him.

The lieutenant of Hussars dodged the missile which was whirring strangely. Then with the speed of thought he leaped for the thing, a cubical box in some dark metal, and grasping it, ran across the slippery floor toward the nearest window.

The thing in his hands continued to whir. As he ran he gazed at it fascinated, wondering what second it was going to explode and blot him out.

He was within five yards of the window now. The thing in his hand stopped whirring and clicked suggestively, once and again. With all his force he threw it, heaving it straight at the closed window.

The heavy small iron box left his hand, described an arc, struck the windowpane and splintered it, passing through.

A sudden rumbling roar from outside announced the explosion of the infernal machine. Splintered glass flew about the hall.

Turning swiftly, the lieutenant shouted and pointed at the man behind the statue.

One of the tall Cossacks ran with drawn sword, leaping like a cat on the cleaner. There was the hungry flick of a blade, a stifled moan and the assassin sank down, coughing blood.

The hall suddenly filled with men. Officers and soldiers of the guard appeared as if by magic. A great shouting and hubbub arose. It was stilled by a commanding voice.

"*Smeer'na!* Attention!" shouted a huge, red-clad Cossack, straightening the black Persian lamb skin cap on his head and freezing into immobility.

The silence of the tomb succeeded the hubbub that had taken place.

A short, bearded man, wearing the uniform of the Preobajensky Guard Regiment with his cap set on one side of his head rather jauntily, stepped forward and asked a question, looking sadly at the body of the cleaner.

Men pointed at the lieutenant, standing stiffly on the outskirts of the crowd.

"What has happened here?" asked the bearded man, his eyes gazing in kindly fashion into the face of the Hussar officer.

The lieutenant wildly tried to remember the ritual of a guard officer's reply to the Czar.

"In the guard and on the posts of your imperial majesty—" he stuttered.

"Yes, yes," the voice of the bearded man interrupted, "what happened?"

Prince Michael told his story in as few words as possible, still not sure that he had not transgressed all the laws of the palace guard.

"But that was splendidly heroic!" The bearded man turned toward the tall Grand Duke at his side.

"Splendid, your majesty!" echoed the Grand Duke, an uncle of the Czar.

"And your name?" The Czar turned again to the lieutenant.

"Lieutenant Prince Michael Doblestni, of the your imperial majesty's regiment of Hussars of the Imperial Bodyguard," returned the lieutenant.

"Oh, you are the officer who has been so much in America?" The Czar looked at him kindly. "You have done a courageous thing this day." Suddenly it came over the Hussar officer that living or dying meant very little to this gentle-mannered ruler of Russia, that he was honestly more interested in the proof of courage on the part of one of the officers of his guard than he was in his own narrow escape from death.

"You have done a splendid thing, and it shall not be forgotten," said the Czar, and turned away.

Nor was it. After a needed afternoon's sleep, he went to the quarters of his regiment, to be greeted by a great ovation. Dinner had advanced not over half an hour when a Cossack officer of the guard was introduced and bowed low to the lieutenant.

"Her imperial majesty sends her grateful thanks to Lieutenant Prince Doblestni and requests the pleasure of his company at dinner at eight o'clock this evening."

III

RASPUTIN

THERE WAS VERY LITTLE TIME TO LOSE. Accompanied by the Cossack guard officer, Prince Michael, clad in the scarlet and gold of the Red Hussars, drove rapidly to the Winter Palace.

At the far end of the great salon, standing near an open fire, was the Czar. Seated near him, her gray eyes kindling with a welcome, sat the Czarina, tall and stately and beautiful. A fresh-cheeked girl, whose merry eyes belied the stateliness of her carriage, was the Grand Duchess Tatiana.

Bowing low over the hand of the Czarina, Michael heard her murmur some words of praise and rose to find the eyes of Nicholas fixed on him in kindly fashion. Greetings being exchanged, he was introduced for the first time to another member of the party, a slim, dark-haired girl with clear eyes and a sensitive, beautiful face alive with vitality and a sort of suppressed eagerness.

There was something challenging and at the same time deeply friendly about her eyes, so clear, frank and understanding, that his pulse drummed in his ears.

It was the new lady-in-waiting to the Czarina, Natalia Feodorovna Goldouriki, the daughter of Prince Feodor. So dazed and thrilled was Michael with the beauty and charm of the girl that it was not until later that he noticed the really remarkable rope of pearls she wore, a huge triple strand of perfect jewels.

He marveled as he finally looked at them, so beautiful were they, the sheen of each pearl tinged with a faint glow of pink, like a lucent globe of solidified mist bathed in the warm rays of the setting sun. It seemed fitting that the beautiful rope of pearls should so sinuously adapt itself to the curves of her slender figure, glowing against the satin whiteness of neck and bosom, following the curved loveliness of her breast and dropping almost halfway to the tapering gracefulness of her dainty feet and ankles.

As they rose to enter the dining room, an *aide-de-camp* of the Czar joined them, a Captain Barjensky. The dark green and silver of his uniform fitted loosely over his somewhat too evident curves. He was one of those big men whose weight quivers on them like jelly, whose jowls are always blue-black. He had a deep and hearty voice that lacked very little of being convincing.

The girl Natalia frowned a little when he entered and kept a carefully averted face when he talked, as he did almost constantly.

"Those are beautiful pearls you are wearing, Natalia Feodorovna," whispered the Hussar lieutenant to the girl at his side.

"Yes," she agreed in a low tone, and her voice was a delight to the ear, low and with a musical throb to it. "They are her majesty's. I wear them to keep them in health. They are beautiful, but oh, so heavy; and they mean so much responsibility!" Her tone expressed weariness.

"Keep them in health?" Michael looked puzzled.

"Yes," whispered the girl. "You know that pearls 'die' when they are worn by some people and unfortunately her imperial majesty is of the type who cannot wear them for any length of time. Only on rare occasions does she wear them. Immediately afterward they begin to grow pale and it is necessary that they be worn by some one else who can make them recover."

"His majesty tells me that you have been long in America," the voice of the Czarina came to the ears of Michael Petrovich.

"Yes, your imperial majesty, with my uncle, a colonel of cavalry."

"And what do you think of the American cavalry?" asked the Czar.

"They ride and shoot amazingly well, your imperial majesty."

"Better than my regiments?" asked the Czar, his face showing interest.

"I think they are better practiced in dismounted firing with the rifle."

A quick look of disapproval flashed from Captain Barjensky's eyes and he said: "It would he impossible for any cavalry in the world to shoot better than the regiments of your majesty's army."

Prince Michael flushed a dull red, realizing that he had made a *faux pas* and angry that this fat captain had taken it up so quickly.

"It is so difficult to get at the truth when one is Czar," Nicholas said quietly, and cast a kindly glance toward Michael.

There was a murmured word at the outer door, then a deep, vibrant voice boomed out a greeting.

"It is Grigori!" exclaimed the empress, clasping her hands and staring earnestly at the door. The Czar nodded absently. The Grand Duchess Tatiana frowned. Natalia shuddered a little and lowered her head. The stout *aide-de-camp*, Captain Barjensky, rose respectfully.

A man of strange appearance stepped into the room. He was tall and thin. His black hair descended in curly ringlets to his shoulders, great burning eyes stared out of an abnormally pale, unhealthy-looking face half covered by a tangled black beard and flowing mustache.

He was dressed in a white, silk embroidered shirt, worn after the Russian fashion, long, dark velvet trousers and soft peasant shoes. The man radiated a queer, hypnotic power, so that his presence in the room affected every person in it. Michael felt his attention fixed on the newcomer sharply, as though he were attracted by some powerful magnet.

"Rasputin!" whispered Natalia to him, and there was a world of fear and dread in her tone.

Michael had heard much of this strange character and none of it good. According to the gossip of the mess, he was an adventurer of the worst type, who by the exercise of hypnotic power and some healing ability had gained an ascendancy over the Czar and especially the Czarina, through his seemingly marvelous ability at keeping the young Czarevitch Alexei in health. There were other rumors, about the Czarina, which no one spoke aloud.

Grigori Efimovitch Rasputin, originally a horse boy and then an itinerant *starets* or wandering holy man, had come from Siberia. No one knew much about him. Some said that he was in reality a gifted man of God, others that he was an incarnation of the Anti-Christ. There was no denying that the Czar and Czarina were as wax in his hands.

"You have seen Alexei to-day? He looks better?" the Czarina leaned forward anxiously, staring at the strange Rasputin as though he held the keys of heaven and hell themselves.

"Fear nothing, Alexandra Feodorovna," the voice of Rasputin boomed forth like the tolling of a bell, "so long as I am with thee, no harm shall come to the little Alexei. Grishka can save, Grishka can cure, Grishka can bring peace."

He used the familiar form of salutation, the "thou" of the second person singular. It went unnoticed by all save Michael Petrovich who looked with astonishment on this coarse peasant monk with his thick bright red lips and penetrating eyes, this man of whom so much evil was spoken that it was feared that he would drag down the imperial family and end the rule of the Czar over Russia. Without further greeting, Rasputin sat down at the table, and wolfed a pear.

For a moment the young officer felt the piercing regard of this strange

Rasputin probe deep into his soul. It was as though his secret and inmost thoughts were turned upward for this man to gaze upon.

"Oho!" said Rasputin. "So here is the brave little officer who risked his life for the Czar. You will go high, young man, but not without Grishka. You will plan, Grishka will change."

When the uncouth monk removed his eyes from Michael's, it seemed as if the beam of a powerful and blinding searchlight had been suddenly shifted. His gaze was now fixed on Natalia, at Michael's side.

"And here is my frightened little pigeon again," the monk exclaimed, "the little pigeon who will never look into Grishka's eyes. Look at me, my dear, and find peace as so many of your friends have found it."

But Natalia continued to keep her head bent, and her eyes fixed on her plate. Her face was pale and she trembled a little in dread and horror. Suddenly Michael felt a great surge of anger against this uncouth peasant, and a great wave of desire to protect this girl against the so-called holy man.

"Is it compatible with your alleged state of holiness to show so much interest in young girls?" Michael said softly, and looked squarely into the queer eyes of the monk.

A great silence fell on the table. The Czarina nervously clenched her fingers. The Czar looked up, mildly worried. Captain Barjensky, after staring as though unable to believe his ears, smiled maliciously and nodded his head. Natalia raised her head quickly and shot a glance full of warning at Michael.

"Ho, ho, ho!" Rasputin leaned back and stretched his legs, laughing with all the abandon of a drunken peasant. "Our little hero is a fighting cock. We will cure him of that. We will teach him to appreciate Grishka's holiness." He gave a sidelong glance at Michael that was less a threat than a calm announcement of retribution to come.

A constraint fell upon the table. Michael Petrovich cursed himself for having let his tongue get away with him. He had made a powerful enemy, right at the Czar's table, and at the outset of his career. Rasputin stared at the ceiling as though he had already forgotten the incident. But from tales he had heard, Michael was under no delusion as to Rasputin's powers of forgetfulness.

During the remainder of the evening he was ignored by all save Natalia.

"When shall I see you again?" he whispered as he was taking his leave.

"You will be at the ball next Wednesday?" she answered quite simply.

"Yes."

"We will meet there," she said, then a look of something like anxiety came into her eyes. "Be on your guard against Rasputin," she whispered.

• • •

IV
THE CZAR'S BALL

ON WEDNESDAY NIGHT MICHAEL DROVE UP to the Jordansky entrance of the Winter Palace, a rich, high-collared fur coat covering his scarlet Hussar uniform.

A stream of brilliantly uniformed officers flowed toward the great staircase above, from which could be heard the stirring notes of a military band. The court costumes of the ladies, shimmering in silks and glittering with jewels, made an effective background for this spread of color.

Michael drifted along with the crowd, bowing here and there to officer friends. Gazing about the great ballroom his eyes sought through the enormous scene for some sight of Natalia's dark hair and slim figure.

It was a bewildering scene, made more brilliant by the great mirrors which doubled the vastness of the halls. The mirrors reflected the sheen of marble, the gleam of thousands of lights, the shimmer and sparkle of jewels and the glitter of the gold and silver of the officers' uniforms.

Suddenly there was a hush as black-coated, gold-chained masters of ceremonies tapped on the floor with slender ivory wands, forming an alleyway through the great crowd.

From the bandstand came the majestic flowing notes of a march. Down the alleyway, the Czarina on his arm, came the Czar, in the uniform of the Ismailoffsky Regiment of the Guards.

Following them came foreign ambassadors and their wives, grand dukes and grand duchesses, and admirals and generals. It was a brilliant group as it came finally to rest and the dancing started, with a waltz.

In that great crush, trying to find any individual was like hunting for a needle in a haystack. But Michael persevered until at last he saw her, superbly slim and graceful in a cream-colored ball dress which set off her figure proudly. She was talking to some old dowager covered with jewels when Michael approached and leaned over her hand.

At last they were in the Pompey gallery, where the crush was less.

As he gazed at the fresh loveliness of her, a great rage against Rasputin rose in his heart, an anger against the elderly, dirty-bearded *muzhik* whose power was so formidable.

"I am grateful to you," she said hesitantly, "for your reprimand to Grigori Rasputin the other night. But you must not risk yourself against him. Sometimes I think he is more powerful than the Czar himself!"

The solicitude in her voice set Michael's blood to hammering in his ears. "I fear for you, Natalia Feodorovna." He lowered his voice and bent over her. "Tell me, are you in great danger from him?"

She nodded, a sudden flicker of dread showing in her eyes for a second, then raised her head proudly.

"I would kill myself before I allowed that beast to touch me," she said very simply. Michael looked sideways at her tense, earnest face.

"Personally, I would far rather have you alive than dead," he remarked dryly.

And suddenly for no explicable reason, the two were smiling at each other. It was good to be young and handsome and beautifully dressed, a guest at the emperor's palace with the music of a Viennese waltz throbbing a half delirious, half intoxicating undertone in the distance. For a moment, such is the natural resilience of youth and beauty, they forgot Rasputin and the evil which surrounded them and found joy in each other's nearness.

They had seated themselves on a divan on the far side of the statue. Voices coming from the other side suddenly cut in on their gaiety.

"And you think it will come this summer?" a man's voice asked gravely.

"As sure as there is a God in heaven war will come this summer, your imperial highness. It is talked of openly in Berlin, it is known in the very cafés that the war plans of the General Staff are perfected to the smallest detail."

Natalia shivered, and again there crept into her eyes that frightened, strained expression.

"Oh, they're always talking war," murmured Michael reassuringly.

Natalia raised her head suddenly, her eyes tragic, her hand went to her throat, she started to say something, then shook her head and was silent.

"What were you going to say?" asked Michael, his voice chaffing. "What load of sorrow is oppressing your young soul?"

"It is no laughing matter," she said simply and her eyes bore out the statement.

"*Prahsteets!* Pardon!" he said.

"It is nothing." She smiled a little sadly. "Only I am so close to their majesties . . . A young girl should not know so much of horror and tragedy . . . And I can tell no one—I cannot even help!" She flung her hands outward in a helpless gesture, poignantly sad in its abject hopelessness.

"Natalia Feodorovna, will you accept me as a friend?" asked Michael.

"But surely."

"Won't you call upon me for help?"

"I cannot!" she moaned.

Michael said boldly: "Whatever it is, you must tell me instantly; I insist on aiding."

Having some of the average woman's liking for being bullied, and being overburdened with her heavy knowledge and helplessness, she took comfort at the assured note in his voice.

"There will be war this summer," she whispered, leaning forward, "war with Germany and Austria; and—and—" She plucked nervously at the string of pearls about her throat.

"Yes?" encouraged Michael.

"And Rasputin has sold himself and his influence to Germany!"

Michael looked at her gravely.

"Are you sure of this?" he asked.

"Absolutely."

The music of the military band came floating through the Pompey gallery playing some stirring march. Michael stiffened in his seat.

"I am glad you have confided in me," he said. "It may mean the lives of the men of my regiment, the lives of the men of many regiments." He stared into space, unseeing.

"But I need help, oh, I need help," she half moaned, nervously twisting and untwisting her fingers.

Michael reached forward, clasping the nervous hands in his own firm grip.

"I am here to help," he said, and patted her hands feeling an electric thrill transmit itself from the soft, tapering fingers. For a moment she allowed her hands to rest in his, a glorious moment which made them both a little breathless, then she gently disengaged them.

V

CHALLENGE

"THE CZARINA IS A GERMAN PRINCESS, as you know," she said hurriedly as the soft color flooded her face. "The pearls that you saw me wearing the other night are hers, not part of the Russian crown jewels. Rasputin wants them."

"Rasputin wants the pearls of the Czarina? But why?"

"Yes, Rasputin has to have them," she leaned forward eagerly, her voice thrillingly low. "You see, he must show his power to the satisfaction of his employers in Berlin. They will not reward him or trust him fully until he has secured the pearls of the Czarina, as a gift. And—and—the Czarina is half inclined to give them . . . as a price for the health of Alexei." Natalia threw up her head proudly. "Her majesty is first and foremost the mother of her children, whatever the world may whisper!"

"I know that," Michael returned gently.

Natalia smiled at him in gratitude and went on.

"Once he has the pearls, it will do two things—prove to his German employers that he is worthy of their powerful support, and"—her eyes clouded angrily, she clenched her hands—"prove to the Russian nation that he is the honored confidant and friend of the Czarina—and perhaps more."

Michael looked up sharply as the full implication dawned on him. The radical and revolutionary elements of Russia had gained enormous ground. What a weapon these pearls would put into their hands, should they appear around the greasy neck of Rasputin! What a powerful lever it would give the Reds to overturn the throne, with such proof added to the widespread whispers!

"Have you the pearls in your apartment at the palace now?" he shot at her so suddenly that she was startled.

"Yes."

"How much longer will you be wearing them for her majesty?"

"Perhaps two weeks."

"Is it possible for you to plead illness and go to your estates, taking the pearls with you?"

"Yes, I have taken them with me before."

Michael nodded, his eyes narrowed in thought. Suddenly he looked up.

"There is only one thing to do," he said calmly. "You must take them with you and go, immediately, tomorrow. And I—God help me—I must rob you of them and put them in hiding."

Natalia gazed at him white-faced. A slowly dawning admiration for the daring and the brilliancy of the scheme came into her eyes. Michael shrugged his shoulders absently.

"It is a duty," he said simply, "a duty for Czar and for Holy Mother Russia."

"What is this that is a duty for Czar and Holy Mother Russia?" a sharp voice broke in on them. There, not three paces away stood Captain Barjensky, the stout *aide-de-camp* of the Czar gazing at the two of them with what could only be characterized as a particularly unpleasant smile upon his face.

But Michael Petrovich, after the first dizzying second of alarm, was more than equal to the occasion. He rose and bowed.

"The duty of which I spoke is the duty of an exceedingly beautiful lady-in-waiting to show kindness to an officer of his majesty's Hussars."

"Oho, I see." The unpleasantness of Captain Barjensky's smile was not diminished one whit, rather augmented. "What form, may I ask?" And the sneer that lay under his words was too patent to be missed. "What form, may I ask, will this kindness take?"

"That question," said Michael very calmly advancing two paces, "merits only one answer." So saying- he raised his arm very swiftly and with the open palm of his hand slapped Captain Barjensky across the open mouth.

"Oh!" returned Barjensky, as calmly, and drawing forth his handkerchief daintily wiped at his face. Returning the handkerchief to his pocket, he bowed very formally.

"That leaves the situation in this wise," he said, and the self-control of the man was a marvelous thing to see; "that in addition to your duties to his imperial majesty and Holy Mother Russia, you have a third duty to perform."

"Quite so," nodded Michael, "a duty which I shall be very happy to discharge the moment you send your seconds to call upon me."

"Thank you, Prince Doblestni," said Barjensky, bowing very formally.

"At your service," Michael returned in French. Then as though the existence of the captain were forgotten, he turned to the pale statue in marble that was Natalia Feodorovna and offered her his arm. "Shall we go in to supper?" he asked.

As they walked sedately and quietly down the long Pompey gallery, Natalia looked up at Michael with fear in her eyes.

"Don't you see," she whispered, tightening her hold on his arm, "don't you see that that was done purposely?"

"No doubt," replied Michael.

VI

RASPUTIN'S THREAT

THE FOLLOWING AFTERNOON MICHAEL CALLED on his mother at her apartment and found her proud at his new honors, but worried and anxious about the Rasputin affair. A gracious white-haired lady, she had lived so long in Russia that she was nearly as much Russian as American.

"I have sent your father a message about the decoration; he will be pleased," she said.

Michael Petrovich shrugged his shoulders. "Precious lot he will care," he answered.

"In his way he cares very much," she said, her eyes troubled, "and I believe that he will be proud and happy. That your father and I get along so poorly does not alter the fact that you are his son and that as his son he is very proud of you."

Michael Petrovich thought of the trim, precise, rather cold-eyed retired colonel of Hussars, his father, and shook his head.

"After all, my son," she said gently, "it was much better that you did not marry that peasant girl, Maria Ivanovna."

"Granted," he said a little impatiently, "but there was no need of driving me from home with such bitterness. It was only a silly boy's first love."

"Yes, but you know how proud he is of his ancient family."

Again Michael shrugged his shoulders. It was not a subject that he cared to dwell upon. He had been seventeen and romantically absurd.

His mother's eyes clouded with anxiety.

"Your father's cousin, General Sabladoff, called me up to-day telling me to warn you that Rasputin meditated some evil against you. He said to beware especially of a Captain Barjensky."

"I know," nodded Michael. He had guessed as much; and he determined not to tell his mother of the approaching duel.

Taking his leave, he decided to walk to his own quarters. The early darkness of winter had descended upon the city as he strode along, his hands deep in the pockets of his military overcoat, his head bent reflectively in his fur collar. It was not until he turned into a darker side street, a short cut to his own quarters, that he became aware of some one following him.

Ahead of him a few yards the street suddenly turned sharply at an angle of forty-five degrees. Once around the projecting corner he sped swiftly into the nearest shelter, a porter's lodge-gate. Here he stood silently, squeezing himself against the shadows and waited.

In another minute his pursuer rounded the corner, and stared down the empty street, nonplused. After a moment or two of searching examination, the man, a short, squat fellow, dressed like a petty tradesman, hurried on.

Michael followed cautiously on his trail, taking care to keep concealed. The fellow hastened on toward Michael's own quarters, stopping occasionally in puzzlement or in the hope that he might sight his quarry again.

Near the entrance to the building Michael heard him whistle softly. Another figure detached itself from the shadows and the two conferred at length, watching the street narrowly as they talked. After a time they both nodded their heads and the first man started off again. The second man stood staring up at the unlighted windows of Michael's apartment.

Michael ducked past and followed the first man into a well-lighted street filled with automobile and *droshky* traffic and many pedestrians. After several blocks the fellow suddenly turned into a café called the "*Chorny Koshka*"— the Black Cat—a restaurant of the better class much frequented by officers.

Without a second's hesitation, Michael strode into the entrance and found himself in an inconspicuous waiting-place by the cloakroom door.

After about three or four minutes a waiter came out and nodded to the squat fellow who waited in the hall so impatiently. In another minute there came another figure through the doorway, a stout man in evening clothes, wiping his mouth with his napkin as he came along.

The two men conferred for a moment or two. The man in evening clothes looked impatient and annoyed. The other was evidently making excuses.

Finally the man in evening clothes turned back to his dinner. The other went swiftly out of the door and into the street.

Michael Petrovich strolled homeward very thoughtfully; for the man in evening clothes was stout Captain Barjensky of the Czar's staff.

At his own quarters, Michael found no trace of the second spy. Lieutenant Drenadoff was awaiting him with a car and an invitation to dine at the Villa Rode.

Absent-mindedly Michael followed his friend and fellow officer into the famous restaurant.

Scarcely had the two seated themselves at the table when there was a great clatter and hubbub outside, accompanied by shouting and the sound of blows; then Rasputin, half drunk, teetered in with a beautiful young woman on his arm.

Loudly demanding wine, the drunken "holy man" ordered the gypsy orchestra to play one of his favorite airs. He rose unsteadily and advanced to the center of the floor where, all of a sudden, he started to dance, leaping gracefully and easily and whirling about, keeping perfect time to the gypsy music with the stamp of his great boots. In his dancing he suddenly came to a stop before the table occupied by Michael and Drenadoff.

"Oh, ho!" shouted Rasputin drunkenly. "So here is the young fighting cock again! My little officer will have his spurs cut if he is not careful. Already has Grishka humbled one person to-day, the proud Natalia—"

Michael uncoiled like a steel spring and towered over the drunken *starets* threateningly. "You lie, you beast!" he stated, his eyes blazing wrathfully.

"No, no, Grishka does not lie. The beautiful Natalia Feodorovna will—"

Michael lunged forward, smashing with all his force full into the fleshy red lips. The tall peasant staggered for a second under the impact of the blow, then fell backward in an ignominious and startled heap.

The place was immediately filled with shouts and screams. The orchestra stopped playing suddenly. Waiters came running up, aiding the fallen Rasputin to his feet.

Michael Petrovich stood where he had delivered the blow, his fist clenched, his tawny eyes blazing with anger, his nostrils white.

Rasputin, helped up by the hands of the waiters, stood on his feet, blood flowing from his cut lips, his eyes red with anger.

"You have raised impious hands against a man of God," Rasputin shouted. "Long and terrible shall be your punishment!"

"Heed well what I say, Grigori Efimovitch!" Michael's voice flicked like a steel saber. "Let there be another move on your part to annoy her and I will kill you with my hands!"

There was a silence in the restaurant as he finished speaking and turned contemptuously on his heel.

At the door of his quarters, Shnitskin, his orderly, met him.

"A woman to see your honor," announced the man.

VII

WOMEN SPELL TROUBLE

A WOMAN TO SEE HIM? HE STOPPED, SURPRISED. It could not be his mother; she never visited him without invitation. He could think of only one woman who could possibly come. It must be Natalia Feodorovna with some important news. Suddenly he found his heart singing within him.

Entering the long hall quietly, he pushed aside the curtains of his drawing-room and stepped within. A girl stood against the table at the far end. His greeting died on his lips. For it was not Natalia Feodorovna who stood waiting for him.

The girl who smiled at him from the opposite end of the room was a peasant girl, dressed in her Sunday finery; her broad, rather pretty face and healthy skin could not disguise the fact that compared to Natalia she was like a cart horse alongside a racing thoroughbred. She was full of an animal vigor, but she had stubby, toil-roughened hands, she was lumpy and short, her coarse ankles and broad feet were clumsily shod in some product of the village shoemaker's art.

There was about her a half defiant, half uncertain air as she waited.

"Maria Ivanovna!" Michael tried to keep the displeasure from sounding in his voice. "What are you doing here in St. Petersburg?"

It was none other than the peasant girl from his village, the girl who had been the cause of his father's anger.

As Michael spoke there flashed through his mind a series of disconnected pictures: himself as an awkward youth, four years before; the village dance to the music of balalaikas and accordions; Maria Ivanovna, the village belle and himself, the son of the *barin*, strolling to kiss under the willows by the river; his father's discovery of the incipient affair, which resulted in Michael's being driven away to Cadet School.

"I am visiting my uncle," she answered. "And—I hoped that you had not forgotten your Masha." Again she looked at him with that cunning, half uncertain, half defiant air.

"But, Maria Ivanovna, you know our little friendship was nothing but a boy and girl affair and that it is best forgotten," he said kindly.

"Yes, I know." Her eyes grew hard. "You are like all men, kiss and forget." She put her hands on her hips and raised her chin, shaking her head defiantly. Her voice grew more shrill: "A fine one you are, with your pretty uniform and your sword, to kiss a girl and win her heart and then go away and leave her!"

"Maria," Michael broke in quietly, "you are at least three years older than I am. When I was seventeen, in the village, you were at least twenty. You know as well as I know that a girl of twenty is far wiser than a boy of seventeen."

She flounced her shoulders angrily and sneered, "So you've turned into the preacher nowadays?"

There was a discreet cough outside and a shuffling of feet. Shnitskin appeared on the threshold.

"What is it?" called Michael.

"Your honor, there is a lady wishing to see you," said the orderly and Michael's mind subconsciously registered that in making known Maria Ivanovna's presence, his man had not used the word "lady."

"Who is she?" and Michael knew as he asked, who she was.

"She won't give her name, says she's got to see you right away."

Michael looked worried. How the mischief was he going to get rid of this Maria Ivanovna?

She settled the vexing question for him.

"I can make myself scarce," she said flippantly, "if that's what's upsetting you. Have you got a place I can sneak into?"

Without a word he pointed at the entrance to his bedroom which opened off the little salon. She picked up her hat and disappeared, closing the door after her.

It was Natalia Feodorovna, as he knew immediately despite the heavy veil she wore. She came in timorously, looking about her, her fingers twisting nervously. He seized both her hands in his, kissing them respectfully and waved her into a chair. She removed her veil and looked at him with eyes in which worry and deep trouble shone forth.

"I had to come," she said breathlessly. "I could not get in touch with you in time. There was no other way. . . . I need help so!"

"I know, I know," soothed Michael, casting an anxious glance behind him at the entrance of his sleeping quarters. If only that infernal girl would stay there!

"Something has to be done immediately, to-night. Rasputin has talked the Czarina into giving him the pearls; he has told her that the Czarevitch Alexei will suffer grave harm if she does not, and she has finally acceded. Tomorrow evening at five o'clock he comes for them—and at six o'clock, as I know, he goes to the German Embassy!"

Michael drummed silently on the arms of the chair.

"To-morrow morning Drenadoff goes on duty at the palace. He will trade tours of duty with me. Will you have the pearls in your possession?"

"Yes, until she calls for them. . . ."

"Then you will have to say that you have been robbed of them, and in the meantime you will have to turn them over to me at the palace."

Natalia looked frightened, then drawing her breath, nodded.

"It is the only way," she whispered, looking at him anxiously, "but it is a fearful risk you run!"

Natalia sank back in her chair, looking about her for the first time since she had entered the apartment. Suddenly she stiffened in her chair and gazed past Michael toward the door of the sleeping chamber.

"Oh!" she said, then sat very primly in her chair, her face a mask.

Michael, not daring to look around, heard a step behind him.

"Well, goodbye, my dear," said the breezy voice of Maria Ivanovna. A stubby-fingered hand patted his cheek affectionately, and the peasant girl, her hair and her clothes very ostentatiously disarranged, went out of the door, her eyes gleaming with malice.

The door slammed and all was silent.

TO BE CONCLUDED NEXT WEEK

VIII

THE DREAD SECRET POLICE

"I MUST BE GOING." Natalia arose, her voice a little constrained and her eyes avoiding him, but her head held high. He could not see the pain and the deep hurt she tried so hard to conceal.

Michael stood up frowning.

"There you go, just like a woman, jumping to conclusions—and invariably the worst conclusion!" His voice could not be called gracious by any stretch of the imagination.

She raised her eyebrows in well-bred surprise.

"Conclusions?" she answered very sweetly, but oh, so distantly. "Conclusions? I am not interested in the slightest in drawing conclusions. But I really must be going. I have been here too long as it is."

"If you would please allow me to explain—"

"I am sure that your explanations could be of no possible interest to me," she interrupted, putting on her gloves and adjusting her veil.

"Very well," Michael bowed stiffly, "so let it be. But remember, I will be on guard at the palace at eleven tomorrow. What time may I expect you with the pearls?" His voice was cold and matter-of-fact, his manner business-like.

"I—it will have to be some time during the day. I will seize what opportunity I can."

"Good. But we must not be seen together for a second. I will be in the third hall from the inner apartments. Come through that and drop the pearls, wrapped in something, behind the statue of Peter the Great, on the left as you enter. I will be near by and will pick them up after you have left. Is that clear?"

"Yes," she said, and swept toward the entrance, stopping underneath the parted curtains. "Thank you so much for your loyal aid to the Czar and to Mother Russia." With that she swept out, her head disdainfully high, her bearing full of hauteur, too much hauteur. Had Michael known more of womankind he would have known that her haughty bearing was a shield to hide her pain and hurt pride.

"You plotted to steal the pearls of the Czarina!"

But Michael, being pretty much of an average male idiot, knew none of these things and sat nursing his wounded feelings like a bear with a sore tooth until finally he realized that it was time to think about the job he had in hand.

He called up his mother and asked for Piotr, the old family servant, who had come up from the estate. Then he got in touch with Lieutenant Drenadoff, and got the permission of the regimental commander for the exchange of days of duty.

The next steps he took carefully, one of them being to take his second-best overcoat and cut a slit in the inside pocket, first making sure of the good state of the inner lining of padded silk.

Next he gave his orderly, Shnitskin, some very particular and detailed instructions and made that somewhat thick-headed individual repeat them until he knew them by heart.

Thereafter he wrote a note to Natalia, explaining Maria Ivanovna's presence in his quarters. He tore up the note and wrote another. Finally with the third writing he was satisfied and despatched the missive.

The next morning he went on guard with his detachment of Red Hussars. But it was not until after lunch, about two o'clock, that Michael's long watch was rewarded by the sight of Natalia's slim form walking very sedately through the inner hall. She came on into his hall, then with a very pretty imitation of the confusion of a lady whose garters need attention, she slipped for a second behind the statue of Peter the Great. She came forth after what had all the appearance of a momentary adjustment of her stocking. No one could have found anything untoward in the perfectly natural action, and the soldiers on duty scarcely looked up as she passed by, returning Michael's salute with a distant bow.

Thereafter the lieutenant passed by the statue and leaned down to adjust a spur which was dragging loosely. It was none too warm in the big hall and as Michael rose he slipped his hands into his pockets. Something exceedingly sinuous and slippery dropped down through a slit in his second-best overcoat pocket and spread itself out behind the padded silk lining.

At three o'clock his orderly called, bringing his best overcoat, as he had been ordered, and carried away the second-best with the slit in the pocket to Michael's quarters, where he folded it and packed it into a suitcase which he strapped and locked and left in the middle of the floor. After that, Shnitskin went forth to execute the other commissions he had been instructed to perform.

At five o'clock old Piotr, his white beard and hair giving him an air of apostolic sanctity, came by Michael's quarters and let himself in with a key. After a few minutes he left, carefully locking the door again.

At seven o'clock that evening an officer came to the Winter Palace to relieve Michael and he was ordered to report to his regimental commander—under arrest.

The order was disquieting enough in all truth. He hoped against hope that it was nothing but some complication over the impending duel.

A light was on in the colonel's office as he entered the courtyard of the barracks. Drawing a deep breath, he mounted the stairs and entered the room. Facing him, next to Colonel Prince Zaikin and three other officers, sat the portly form of Count Mirzanka, the head of the dread Okhrana, the secret police of the Russian Empire.

Michael drew in his breath sharply, ready for the worst.

"Good evening, gentlemen." He bowed formally, first to his colonel and then to Count Mirzanka and the three unknown officers. One of these last had sheets of foolscap paper before him and pen in hand. It was to be a real examination, with questions and answers recorded. Michael was waved to a seat.

"We wish some slight information from you, Prince Doblestni, to aid in clearing up a mysterious robbery at the Winter Palace." Count Mirzanka's voice was smooth and friendly, the sort of voice to draw confidences from an oyster.

"Did you, at any time to-day, speak to or see one of the ladies-in-waiting to her imperial majesty, one Natalia Feodorovna Goldouriki, while you were on duty at the palace?"

"Yes, I saw her some time during the afternoon. I did not speak to her. She passed through the hall where I was stationed. I bowed to her," returned Michael composedly.

There was a moment's silence, broken only by the scratching of the pen. A significant look passed between Count Mirzanka and one of his aides.

"How far were you from her when she passed through?"

The question was asked very quietly.

Michael shrugged his shoulders.

"Twenty or thirty paces," he replied.

"You are sure you exchanged no words with her?"

"Your excellency!" Michael's voice was hard as steel.

"Your pardon," apologized Mirzanka coolly. "I was not doubting your word; it was simply to ask you to refresh your memory. Nothing else, of whatever nature, passed from her hands to yours at this time?"

"I have said that we were fifteen or twenty paces apart," said Michael somewhat impatiently.

"Yes, yes, of course," soothed the smooth voice of the questioner. "Did you send any package forth from the palace at any time during the afternoon?"

"No," replied Michael promptly, thinking fast. They undoubtedly knew of his orderly's coming there. "No, I sent no package out of the palace."

"Did your orderly report to you at any time during the afternoon?"

"Why, yes; he brought my fur-lined overcoat when it began to grow colder."

Count Mirzanka half closed his eyes, glancing sidewise at the aide nearest him. "Did he take anything away with him on his departure?"

"Naturally, he took my silk-lined overcoat back with him."

As he said these words, Michael suddenly saw the weak link in his chain and began to think hard and fast before the next question should come.

An old military adage of his American cavalry school days came to him: "When in doubt, take the offensive."

"May I ask," he inquired, and simulated very well a half-puzzled, half-impatient frown—"may I ask the purport of all this questioning? And may I ask"—his voice took on a sharper note—"why I have been subjected to the indignity of being placed in arrest?"

His colonel sat with his shoulders hunched over; Count Mirzanka and his three aides looked a little flurried.

"That will be revealed in due time," answered the inquisitioner finally. "To continue with our questioning: Where is that silk-lined overcoat now?"

Michael had his answer ready.

"That I cannot say. It should be at the tailor's if my orderly obeyed my instructions."

"That is all the information you can give concerning this overcoat?"

"Certainly. I have not been at my quarters as yet to see if my instructions have been carried out."

The scratching of the pen filled the ensuing silence for a moment.

Count Mirzanka leaned over and whispered something to one of his aides. The officer rose and stepped out. Michael knew exactly who would appear with him when he returned, and looked up with well-acted surprise when the officer returned with his orderly, Shnitskin, his sleepy eyes filled with alarm.

The orderly stood in the middle of the floor, stiffly at attention, in that strained, muscle-stretching, slightly tremulous position of attention required of the Russian soldier.

"What were the orders you received from your officer this morning?" Count Mirzanka asked the man.

"Your honor, his honor told me to come for his overcoat to the Winter Palace at five o'clock and bring his fur-lined overcoat. Yes, your honor, that's what he told me."

The soldier stood strained and waiting very much in the attitude of a man expecting at any moment to hear a command that he be taken out and shot.

"Yes? And what else did he tell you?"

"He told me to take his hunting suit to the tailor's and to—"

"You dolt!" Michael's voice broke in sharply. "I told you to take my overcoat to the tailor's and to pack up my hunting suit for the country!" His eyes blazed with indignation.

There was a stir and commotion among the assembled officers.

"If you will please not interrupt the questioning," reproved Count Mirzanka in an annoyed tone.

"Your pardon, but it is aggravating to be beset with such stupidity," answered Michael, frowning.

"Yes, your honor," chimed in the orderly, anxious to right himself and feeling guilty under any circumstances, "it was as his honor the lieutenant says; he told me to take his overcoat to the tailor's and to pack his hunting suit for the country. Sometimes I make mistakes," he added naively.

"That was not what you told us a few minutes ago!" thundered Count Mirzanka, half rising in his chair.

The orderly quailed before the anger of this unknown official, but his own officer was there, and it must be as his own officer had said. "I sometimes make mistakes, your honor," he explained. "It was as his honor the lieutenant says. I'm sorry, but I got mixed up."

Count Mirzanka and the aides looked at each other helplessly for a second while Michael frowned at his servant.

"What did you do with my hunting suit, then?" growled Michael.

"I—I took it to the tailor's, your honor."

Michael threw up his hands helplessly, as much as to say, "What can any one do with such stupidity?"

"You will please not interrupt," admonished Count Mirzanka again, and returned to his questions.

"What then did you do with the overcoat?" he went on.

"I'm sorry, but I packed up his honor's overcoat in his suitcase," said the orderly.

"What became of the suitcase?" went on the relentless question.

Shnitskin turned pale.

"It was stolen," he said in a die-away voice.

"Stolen!" thundered Michael in good imitation of angry astonishment.

"You will please not interrupt," droned Count Mirzanka's dry voice. "What were the circumstances of its loss?" he asked the orderly.

"Your honor, I left it packed in the apartment. S-s-sometimes I forget to lock the door"—he cast a worried glance at Michael, who watched him grimly—"but I'm sure, your honor, I locked the door while I went to the tailor's. When I came back the suitcase was gone."

Again Mirzanka and his aides looked helplessly at each other. They whispered together for a moment.

"All right; that is all; you can go," said the count to the orderly, who, in his anxiety to be gone, saluted and made an about-face, nearly falling over in his haste.

When Count Mirzanka turned again to Michael his face had grown harder.

"Prince Doblestni"—his voice had the rasp of steel in it—"I can play with you no longer. I know, on unimpeachable authority, that Natalia Feodorovna Goldouriki came to your quarters last evening after you returned from the Villa Rode. I know, further, that you two plotted to steal the pearls of the Czarina—"

"I beg your pardon, excellency," Michael rose angrily, "but you know nothing of the kind. You forget that I am an officer of honorable family, possessed, moreover, of great wealth, and that the lady you mention is situated in like estate."

"Granted," replied Count Mirzanka, and his voice was very smooth, "but you have overlooked one important fact."

"Yes? That cannot alter the conditions in the slightest, whatever it is," returned Michael.

"Yes, my friend; you forget that we have already examined the lady—and you probably do not know that she has told us everything!"

Michael stared steadily at the Count Mirzanka for a space. They knew infernally little, he reflected, if they had to use an old police trick worn as threadbare as that one. There was something like contempt in his voice as he answered.

"In that case," he said, "it will be self-evident to you, Count Mirzanka, that as an officer and a gentleman, you owe both the lady and myself an apology for linking our names with this affair!"

Count Mirzanka and his aides were plainly flustered. Even the recorder of the proceedings looked up startled. Colonel Prince Zaikin raised his head for the first time and smiled.

But the head of the Okhrana recovered his aplomb quickly.

"Yes?" he said. "If there is an apology due, then it will certainly be forthcoming. But in the meantime"—he bowed ironically—"I will call in Natalia Feodorovna Goldouriki." He turned to one of his aides and motioned toward the rear door of the office.

IX

A MINE IS EXPLODED

NATALIA ENTERED, HER FACE PALE, but her head held high. Michael and his colonel rose and bowed as she set foot in the room. Michael hastened to offer her a chair, which she accepted, nodding distantly, her eyes fixed in a sort of fascination on the officials of the dread Okhrana.

"I have just told Count Mirzanka that if you have told him all, as he states, he then owes us both an apology," said Michael very swiftly, before he could be interrupted.

"You will please not speak together," said the count angrily, but it was too late. Natalia knew the situation and what was expected of her in a lightning flash.

Count Mirzanka placed the index fingers of his hands together and spoke very slowly.

"We know the whole story now," he said, "lacking a few very unimportant details. We know that you"—he addressed Natalia—"visited Prince Doblestni in his quarters yesterday afternoon. We know the conversation that took place between you in which you two agreed to remove her majesty's pearls from the Winter Palace. We know that Prince Doblestni asked to have his guard tour changed so as to be on duty at the palace to-day. We know that the pearls were in the possession of Natalia Feodorovna, that they passed from her possession into Prince Doblestni's, that they were carried out in an overcoat by the prince's orderly, that they were placed in Prince Doblestni's quarters and from there disappeared. We intend to know the rest." His voice had taken on an edge of steel.

Suddenly he half rose in his chair. Pointing his finger at Natalia, he thundered, "If it was not for the purpose of plotting the theft of the Czarina's pearls, why did you visit Prince Doblestni alone in his quarters?"

The implication was too patent to be missed. Natalia flushed scarlet and then her cheeks drained themselves to a marble whiteness. She raised her head proudly and sought for words.

Michael rose, crouching like a cat and stepped two paces forward, his eyes blazing.

"That was a vile question, vilely put!" His voice shook with suppressed anger. "I will answer it. I have the honor to be engaged to the lady to whom you have addressed your insulting question. She agreed to meet me at my quarters, that we both might repair to my mother and call upon her, telling her the news!" He paused to let his words sink in, forbearing to look at Natalia Feodorovna. As he waited, a lightning flash of comprehension came over him. Why had he not seen it before? He continued, a contemptuous note in his voice:

"There was a third person there, a young woman from my father's estates, with whom I had once had a youthful affair. That this woman, seized with sudden feminine spitefulness, should run to you with the wild tale you have acted upon, is something strange and incomprehensible. Gentlemen, I begin to see in it deeper things than are here disclosed. I begin to see in it more powerful influences than can be spoken of. This, taken in conjunction with other things, makes me believe, gentlemen, that you are acting at the instigation of forces disloyal to his imperial majesty. It makes me believe, gentlemen, that my life and my honor are being attacked because of my proven loyalty to the Czar!"

Count Mirzanka and his aides stirred uneasily. It was a simple matter to become involved in the bad graces of highly placed personages in this intrigue-ridden city and court. There were two powerful factions, one loyal to the Czar and the Empire, Russian to the core; and another, represented by Rasputin and the influences behind the monk, working toward the undoing of the monarchy.

Colonel Prince Zaikin growled deeply under his breath and looked with admiration at his lieutenant. At his first words Natalia had flashed a startled gaze at Michael, then had maintained a quiet, expressionless mask of her face, staring straight to the front, unseeing.

Mirzanka whispered with his aides. There was much shaking of heads among them and more whispering. He turned and asked a question of Colonel Prince Zaikin, who rose, nodding, and went out the rear door, followed by the three aides. Michael stiffened suddenly to attention as he saw Count Mirzanka remaining behind.

"Look here, my children, I am old enough to be your father," Mirzanka said, his voice kindly, and he placed a hand on Michael's shoulder and smiled down on Natalia. "I know why you have done this thing, that it was done from the highest motives. You don't have to tell *me* why you did it. I think you have done a splendid thing. Only I must know how it was done and where the pearls are now, that is all, and the incident will be closed and forgotten and things be as they were before."

Once a policeman, always a policeman, thought Michael swiftly and shook his head.

"The sooner, my dear count, that you get rid of all ideas of our complicity in the purloining of the Czarina's jewels, the sooner will you find the right trail and crown your efforts with success."

"That is final?" asked the count, and there was an ugly glitter in his eye.

"What else could it be?" asked Michael.

Mirzanka turned on his heel sharply and called in the other officers. The four of them conferred together in whispers. Colonel Zaikin returned and chewed his mustache, glaring at these representatives of the dreaded Okhrana with no perceptible friendliness.

One of the aides finally left, leaving Count Mirzanka whispering with the other two. Five minutes dragged into ten, and ten into fifteen and twenty before the absent aide finally returned with a sleepy-looking man dressed like a clerk, who carried a blank book and some papers and a seal.

Count Mirzanka returned again to the couple sitting so quietly together at the far side of the room.

"It is very regrettable," he said, "that we have to annoy you so much, but it is only by exhausting the possibilities of one set of clews that we can turn to another, and as you say, Prince Doblestni, hope to crown our efforts with success."

Michael could not guess to what new devilishness this preamble was leading.

"You see, the finger of suspicion points at you two so strongly that the matter has to be taken seriously," continued the count. "It is a very powerful web of circumstantial evidence that surrounds you two. On the other hand, you have explained each and every one of your actions together and singly in a logical fashion. You see I am trying to be just," he smiled generously, then his face hardened again.

"But at the risk of seeming rude, I must point out that I am informed you have only met this lady-in-waiting to the Czarina on two occasions: once at his imperial majesty's table and once at a court ball. It seems a very short time in which to propose marriage and to be accepted. *That*, I might say, is the weak point in your nearly perfect alibi. If you are engaged, then of course you two intend to marry."

"Of course," nodded Michael, suddenly seeing what was to be proposed.

"Then," went on Count Mirzanka smoothly, "in order to clear you both of this regrettable suspicion, you would not mind complying with a small formality?"

Michael glanced sidewise at Natalia's firm profile, trying to discover if she understood, as yet, what was about to be proposed.

"It is but a little thing," laughed Count Mirzanka easily, "a simple form that will not take five minutes."

He waved to the small, sleepy-looking man with his papers and his blank book and his seal.

"Yes?" Michael inquired.

"Yes. The state will be enabled to accept your protestations of innocence, with pleasure, if you and the young lady will perform the marriage ceremony before witnesses, thus establishing your good intentions and proving that your relations with her are what you say they are!"

X

DISASTER

MICHAEL DID NOT DARE LOOK AT NATALIA NOW. Out of the corner of his eye he saw the girl flinch slightly, as though some one had struck her, and he caught a low-toned "Oh!" of mingled horror and astonishment.

Seeing Count Mirzanka's eyes studying her intently, Michael hastened to provide a diversion.

"My dear count," he said, "there are several reasons which militate against so hasty and irregular a wedding. A young girl of rank is entitled to a proper wedding with her family and friends about her. In the second place she will have to resign her position as lady-in-waiting. And in the third place, it does not meet with our plans, which were to be married in the presence of both our families and with the concurrence of the officers of my regiment."

"All very agreeable," nodded Count Mirzanka, "but the circumstances being what they are, I can state to you that this ceremony to take place at once will be the only proof that you two are not accomplices in the theft of the Czarina's jewels."

"It might be a tactful thing," Michael answered levelly, "to allow the two principals in this affair to have a word together concerning their destinies."

Count Mirzanka looked at them sharply, then rose, the others with him. "Certainly . . . I might say that we none of us feel that it is a very hard fate to which we are subjecting you!" He smiled and bowed in courtly fashion before he followed the other officers from the room.

As Michael turned he found Natalia staring straight ahead, nervously lacing and unlacing her fingers. She did not look at him.

"We seem to be between the devil and the deep sea," he said. "If we don't marry, we are considered guilty. If we do marry"—Michael paused, then went on—"you have me tied to you for life."

Natalia replied nothing, did not look at him, but sat as if carved in stone.

Michael regarded her curiously, then shook his head.

"And I imagine that the latter alternative can't be a very pleasant prospect for you," he said gently. She looked up at him quickly, started to say something, then bit her lip and kept silent.

"In case of discovery, I will take all the blame," he said.

She threw up her head proudly. "It is not that I fear discovery for myself, but the jewels would be found. Rasputin will receive them and terrible harm will come to the Czar and to Russia."

"I will not be party to forcing a young girl into marriage with a man she scarcely knows. Why," he said thoughtfully, "we have only seen each other three times!"

"Yes, we have only seen each other three times," she repeated absently.

For a moment Michael stared at her. Then he rose, and bowing low before her, raised her hand to his lips.

"Will you do me the honor of marrying me, Natalia Feodorovna, until this crisis is past? Afterward, you will be free to have the marriage annulled should you so desire."

Natalia stared straight in front of her, her eyes clouded. Finally she leaned backward as though greatly weary.

"Yes," she whispered, "I think it is best, best for their imperial majesties and best for Russia that we do this thing."

With this decision she seemed suddenly to have achieved serenity; her face molded itself into steadfast lines of quiet courage and she rose.

Michael bowed deeply, and called Count Mirzanka. The official entered, studying the impassive faces of the two young people before him.

"In order to put an end to what seems to be a form of malicious persecution, we are agreed to do as you request, Count Mirzanka, on one condition."

"And that is?"

"That no word of this is allowed to leave these walls. It would not be fair for Natalia Feodorovna's position at court to be imperiled. Let the matter be kept secret until we can publish it ourselves. Are you agreed to that?"

"Yes, yes." Count Mirzanka's tone was a little testy. His plan had failed and he was beaten, being maneuvered besides into a very awkward position. "I give you my word of honor that no word of this shall escape."

"Good. Call in your men," Michael said shortly, and in a moment the clerk-like fellow with the papers and the seal came in, followed by a longhaired, bearded Russian priest in gold-embroidered vestments.

There, with the colonel of Michael's regiment and the officers of the Okhrana as witnesses, the matter-of-fact clerk scratched down the necessary data, asked questions of the tall youth and maiden who stood before him so quietly, asked for each of their signatures and the signatures of the witnesses, placed his official seal upon the paper, and rose to depart after giving a copy to Michael. The priest in his turn went quickly through the services of the Russian Church.

"Congratulations are in order, I presume," Count Mirzanka asked dryly. Michael bowed, unseeing and half unhearing. Natalia's face was almost of marble whiteness, but her eyes were serene and untroubled.

"If you are now through with us, we may go?" asked Michael formally.

"Yes, yes, indeed." Mirzanka clicked his heels and bowed. His under officers bowed in the same cold fashion. It was Colonel Prince Zaikin, the regimental commander, who came up to the two as they started out the door, who followed them into the hallway.

"Beastly rotten business; wanted you to know I had nothing to do with it," he grumbled, patting Michael on the back affectionately; then, lowering his voice, "but look out for them, look out." He glanced around fearfully. "This is only the beginning!"

The two did not speak as they drove away in the *droshky*, too occupied with their own thoughts.

Michael finally cleared his throat. "And where shall I take you, Natalia Feodorovna?" he asked gently.

"It is my duty as your wife to go where you wish," she answered in a low voice, still not looking at him.

A sudden dizzying throb went through him. Here was this gloriously beautiful creature, his, his wife! He half turned toward her, his hands outstretched. The sight of her clear, cold profile arrested his gesture. Reason came to his aid and steadied him down.

"You know you are free to do as you wish. Shall I take you back to the Winter Palace?"

"I am no longer at the Winter Palace," she said evenly. "Her majesty's major domo informed me to-day that it would be advisable for me to return to the country for a rest."

Michael looked up sharply. So matters had reached that pass? He knew that Natalia was an orphan; that her nearest relative, an old aunt, had her estates in a district many days away toward the Black Sea. The girl literally had no nearer place to go.

"I shall take you to my mother," he said quietly; and she flashed a quick glance at him, then lowered her eyes. Leaning forward, he instructed the driver, and the man turned his team in the street and drove away in the new direction.

His mother, charming and gracious, received Natalia with open arms.

Michael told briefly what had happened. Suddenly he saw his mother's eyes beckoning him to leave, and leave he did, with a very lively suspicion that Natalia was crying her heart out on his mother's shoulder before he had closed the door of the apartment.

Thoughtful and preoccupied, he drove to his own apartment.

"Some one to see you," said his servant, and Michael entered to find Piotr, his mother's gray-bearded servant, awaiting him.

Michael stared, astounded.

"Piotr!" he exclaimed. "Why have you not gone with the overcoat to your brother's village?"

A vague dread seized upon him as he spoke.

Old Piotr waved his arms hopelessly.

"*Barin*, there were no pearls in the overcoat when I returned to your mother's apartment with it."

Michael stared at the man, unseeing, his face grim.

So the jewels of the Czarina were actually stolen after all!

XI

THE SWORD WHICH DID NOT GLEAM

TO AVOID THE NETWORK OF ESPIONAGE which he felt closing about him, Michael did not remain long in his own quarters, but instead spent the night with Lieutenant Drenadoff, his best friend in the regiment.

Drenadoff willingly agreed to act as second in the forthcoming duel with Barjensky. For the necessary other second he got Count Merdinoff, a distant cousin of Michael's, who was a captain in the Black Hussars.

The three repaired the next day to Michael's quarters, where two exceedingly solemn officers in the dark green of the Imperial Suite waited upon them. Michael lounged in dressing gown and slippers in his bedroom while the conference went on in the drawing-room. Merdinoff tiptoed in, looking very serious.

"I never heard of such a thing," he complained. "As the injured party, Barjensky has elected swords. We had to accept. Can you handle the sword at all?"

"Assuredly," returned Michael Petrovich, absorbed in his concern over the missing pearls. "Sword, ax, or crowbar."

Merdinoff looked at him in astonishment.

"You're a cool one," he remarked. "Then all is settled. In view of his majesty's regulations against dueling, it has been deemed advisable to meet very secretly. Therefore we have chosen the vacant private dining room of the Black Cat Café."

Michael looked up quickly. The Black Cat Café? That was where that spy had reported to Barjensky the other night. Something queer about that rendezvous. Undoubtedly Barjensky had proposed it.

"All right," he nodded. "When?"

"This afternoon at three o'clock."

"Unusual hour for an affair of honor," Michael remarked calmly.

Merdinoff shrugged his shoulders.

"Barjensky's seconds have kindly offered to provide the dueling swords," he stated.

"Very nice of them," grunted Michael. "How about some lunch?"

It was about lunch time, and the three of them went forth and ordered their meal at the Black Cat Café so as to be on the ground.

His two seconds, who eyed Michael gravely throughout the meal, tacitly forbore mentioning the approaching duel until after the coffee had been served.

"You know," said Drenadoff uneasily, "Barjensky is supposed to be the best swordsman in the Guards. He won several prizes and was entered at the last Olympic. Have you ever fought in an affair of honor, Michael Doblestni?"

"Not even in an affair of dishonor—as yet," returned Michael.

"Have you had any practice with the dueling sword?"

Michael shrugged his shoulders. "A little under my father, a little under Cesar of Paris, and a little under Brindetto of Rome. Due to my American blood, I've always preferred the pistol," he added, "as Barjensky probably knows."

Both men looked at him with new respect in their eyes. After all, Cesar and Brindetto were the premier *maîtres-des-armes* of Europe, heading the French and Italian schools respectively. They even looked a little pleased, as if to say that this might be a contest and not a slaughter after all.

The lunch had dawdled along. It was close to three o'clock. The door opened, and Barjensky entered the restaurant, followed by his two seconds. The three green-clad officers halted, a little surprised at finding their antagonist before them, but clicked their heels and bowed formally.

The three cavalry officers, two scarlet-clad Hussars, and one in black and silver, rose and bowed with equal formality.

A worried-looking proprietor directed them to the private dining room upstairs, where the table had been pulled back against the wall, allowing a large cleared space.

"There is a rear entrance, your honor," he assured Captain Merdinoff, "in case of any fatality; also, I have a doctor here, as you ordered."

A bearded, solemn individual stepped up, owlish behind his great heavy-lensed glasses.

"At your service, gentlemen," he bowed.

Michael leaned negligently against the table near the entrance. At the farther end of the room Captain Barjensky gazed out of the window into the street below. The four seconds conferred together in low, hushed tones. Michael smiled to himself at the cold and professional interest the doctor displayed in him.

Upon a side table near the opposite wall lay the two triangular-bladed swords, their steel gleaming coldly and dispassionately.

"It has been adjudged best that you both strip to the waist," Captain Merdinoff came up. "We have ruled that honor will be satisfied by the first drawing of blood."

"All right"—and Michael removed his scarlet *pelisse* and dolman, his fine linen shirt and his undershirt. He stood forth, his skin glowing with healthy living, the muscles moving easily under the skin like the muscles of a cat.

Again the seconds conferred, this time examining the swords, testing them for weight and balance, comparing them until finally both pairs of seconds declared that they were entirely satisfied.

The two principals were then called, and stood facing each other coldly, while the senior of the seconds took the dueling swords, laying them across his arm, hilts outward, and offered them first to Michael, his opponent being the man who had chosen the weapons.

Michael selected the nearest and strode back to his place, testing the blade and flexing his wrist.

There was a sudden subdued knocking at the door which interrupted the further discussions of the seconds, and they all turned as the doctor opened the door and took a letter from some one.

"It is for Lieutenant Prince Doblestni," he announced solemnly, and Michael took it, wondering who could be writing him at this strange place and hour.

"Your permission, gentlemen?" he asked, and, as all present bowed in response, he broke open the seal.

The letter was in an unfamiliar handwriting.

YOUR HONOR:
   Do not allow yourself to be touched by the sword of Captain Barjensky. The tip of his weapon will be coated with a deadly poison, fatal to life if introduced into an open wound.
                                                              A FRIEND.

Michael read through the letter again without a flicker of any sign showing in his face. He drew from his coat a gold cigarette lighter, embossed with his coat of arms. Flipping it open, he touched the tiny flame to the letter, seeing it burn to ashes before he ceased.

Captain Merdinoff, who considered it necessary to use the French language in such an affair as this, drew himself up stiffly.

"*Messieurs, êtes-vous prêts?*" he demanded.

"Ready as hell," said Michael in English, and took his place. He thought the letter was a cowardly and untruthful attempt to shake his nerve. Nevertheless, he watched Captain Barjensky narrowly.

That individual had his sword in hand. The afternoon sun, gleaming through the window, glittered over the sword blade and made every inch of it shine like molten silver. Then Captain Barjensky turned his back and reached into the pocket of his breeches. Again he faced his antagonist. The sun glittered over his sword blade, making every inch of it shine like molten silver—except the last two inches, near the point.

These two inches were dulled, looking more like heavy lead than glittering silver.

Something had suddenly dimmed the bright sheen of Captain Barjensky's sword-tip.

As for Michael, standing in his place, sword in hand, he was thoroughly angry. The glitter of the steel of his sword-blade found its counterpart in the glitter of steel in his eyes. He flexed his wrist once or twice as Captain Barjensky faced him, then bent the blade against the floor. He frowned as the limber steel whipped back into place, frowned and examined the blade. All four seconds watched him anxiously.

"The blade is not satisfactory?" asked Captain Merdinoff.

"I like not the feel of it," grumbled Michael, and tried it again, seeming more dissatisfied than before.

Captain Barjensky watched him through narrowed eyelids, silently, as a cat watches its prey.

"No, I do not like this blade," announced Michael definitely, then went on, his voice smooth: "Perhaps, as these are Captain Barjensky's weapons, he would not mind exchanging with me."

Some sort of a spark leaped to the eyes of Barjensky and was as quickly extinguished. He stood as a mail carved from marble.

The seconds, who had sole charge of such niceties of dueling, conferred a moment in whispers.

"Most assuredly," finally announced Merdinoff, "the seconds of Captain Barjensky agree. Allow me," and he took the blade from Michael, handing it to the senior of Barjensky's seconds.

In like manner Captain Barjensky's blade was taken from him. He watched it impassively, and as impassively received the exchanged weapon.

Michael Petrovich took the new sword in his hand and swung it by the hilt slowly up so that the point was on a level with his eyes. There, on the point, was a thin layer of greenish paste.

He found Barjensky's eyes fixed on him, a secret fear mirrored in their depths. Michael stared for one revealing second at the man, until Barjensky's eyes dropped and he turned pale. Then Michael smiled contemptuously.

"I find there is no difference in the feel of the blades, after all," he said, "and will exchange again if Captain Barjensky will be so accommodating."

Barjensky's jaw dropped for a second. He stared in amazement. His hand trembled as he received back the poisoned blade.

"But I wish to register a protest against the combat being ended at the first blood. It is my desire to fight it to the end," said Michael very firmly.

"*A toute outrance*?" asked Captain Merdinoff.

"To the bitter end," answered Michael in English.

Captain Barjensky could do no less than accede, although the seconds were displeased and argued against it. But Michael was stubborn and won his point.

The two antagonists, very much of the same height, both stripped to their waists, sainted each other gravely and both fell into the position of readiness, their blades touching, while Captain Merdinoff held the two points aloft with his own sword.

"You are ready, *messieurs*?" he asked for the last time.

Both nodded.

"Then God have mercy upon you!" he said, crossing himself with his free hand. "Commence!" and he withdrew his saber.

The two blades leaped at each other like living things. At the first rasp of steel against steel Michael knew that he had an experienced swordsman as an opponent.

They both played cautiously, each feeling out the other's strength and skill. The steel blades slid delicately along each other's length, Barjensky shifting from tierce to quarte and back again, and Michael meeting each essay with a faint flick of the wrist in riposte.

Suddenly Barjensky disengaged, his blade slipped in and out like a snake's tongue, now under, now over Michael's guard in an effort at a double feint.

It was at that precise second that Michael, having gauged his man, suddenly took the offensive and cleared his opponent's blade out of line, following this up with a steady, remorseless attack, driving resistlessly at Barjensky's hairy chest.

The room was silent save for the breathing of the two men, the rasp and whir of the blades, and the stamp of a foot as one shifted or gave ground.

Barjensky, who had started with a confident air, knowing he only needed to scratch his opponent, began slowly to lose his assurance. A faintly worried look came into his eyes. Again and again he parried the slender steel point that sought his blood so remorselessly, but it was only by a narrow margin each time that he cleared the blade.

Once Barjensky's sword slipped through Michael's guard and came dangerously close, so close that it was within an ace of cutting the skin. The exultant, lightning flare in Barjensky's eyes died down as Michael made a swift riposte and lunged in sixte. Barjensky recovered, but grew more wary. His breath was coming more laboriously, while Michael scarcely breathed as yet.

Then with a single desperate motion Barjensky lunged and missed, standing for a fraction of a second fully extended, at least a third of his sword extended out and past Michael's body. It was too good an opening to be missed, and Michael drove swiftly at it.

He felt the point of his sword bite home, felt it thud against bone, and then saw the blade shiver and snap off, leaving only about a third of it in his hand.

There was a groan and a slowly welling stream of blood from Barjensky's chest. A half maniacal glare came into the doomed man's eyes. With the end of the steel sticking out from his chest he drove at Michael with the poisoned blade.

There was a shout from the seconds, and Michael heard the sound of footsteps, saw dimly that they were trying to come between the two opponents; but he watched nothing save that flying point, seeking to leave its poison in his body.

With his shortened blade he parried it again and again away from his chest and from his right arm, only to have it stab at his groin, whence he cleared it by only a fraction of an inch. He was lighting at a fearful disadvantage, but a cold rage possessed him, a cold rage that cleared all his faculties and made him move with the deadly certitude of a well geared, well oiled machine.

Catching the poisoned blade on his foreshortened length of steel, he deflected it high above him and closed with Barjensky, under the sword, stabbing viciously. The blow was driven home and the short broken steel ran through the *aide-de-camp's* chest.

The sword fell from Barjensky's grasp and tinkled faintly on the floor. Michael withdrew his reddened stub of a blade and leaped backward, waiting. Slowly the heavy *aide-de-camp* collapsed to the floor.

Calling his seconds, Michael pointed to the remnants of greenish paste on the point of his opponent's weapon.

"Tell the gentlemen who are acting as seconds for Captain Barjensky that they unknowingly owe us an apology. If you and they will examine the tip of this blade and have an analysis of this green paste made by a chemist, they will understand what I mean," Michael said, handing over the sword, then turned and dressed himself.

There was a shocked silence behind him. The two seconds of Barjensky stared at the sword-blade and at each other. The doctor rose from the body of the fallen man, shaking his head.

Michael's head suddenly went up and he listened intently at the creak of footsteps outside the door and the faint whispering of several voices. Quickly he strode to the window and looked out. Down on the street below he saw the blue and silver of police uniforms.

"I think we'd better be going," he said to his two seconds and led the way to a small service door at the rear.

As he reached this there was a sudden pounding on the main door of the room and a shout:

"Open in the name of his imperial majesty!"

"May I assist you gentlemen?" Michael asked Barjensky's seconds.

"It is not necessary; we have powerful influence, no harm will come to us," spoke up the elder of them, and Michael followed his seconds through the small exit just as the great door burst open and a crowd of police poured into the room.

The back stairs were dark and evil-smelling. He came out into the kitchen, and made his way to the alley.

XII

RASPUTIN STRIKES

AT HIS QUARTERS HE FOUND THE TELEPHONE RINGING. It was a strange voice, a man's voice which struck some familiar chord of memory, though for the life of him he could not place it exactly.

"Is this Prince Michael Petrovich Doblestni? Yes? I am instructed to tell you that your wife is safe in the care of Grigori Rasputin and will be returned to you in exchange for certain articles of which it is not necessary to speak. I am to tell you further that if you do not return these things to Rasputin himself by noon to-morrow, the lady will be prevailed upon to join Rasputin's inner circle." The voice stopped and there was silence at the other end of the wire.

Michael stood as one turned to stone, remembering that infamous inner circle, that *seraglio* of high-born women and peasant girls who were compelled to surrender to this crude peasant.

"Just a moment," returned Michael, forcing his voice to remain calm and steeling himself to an ordinary tone. "I am prepared to do my share, but I have no guarantee that my wife will be returned unharmed. This is the most that I will do: I will place the articles in the hands of a third party who will agree to deliver them at eleven o'clock to-morrow. When he notifies you he has the articles, my wife must be sent to me immediately."

There was a long silence on the other end of the wire, but finally the voice spoke again.

"It would depend, of course, on the reliability of the third party you mention. Have him call up this number," and he gave the telephone number. "If he proves satisfactory the lady will be sent to your quarters immediately after, but a guard will be placed over the building until the jewels are in Rasputin's hands."

"That is satisfactory to me," responded Michael and hung up.

For a full moment he leaned against the table, his eyes closed, cold beads of sweat on his forehead as he envisaged the desperate situation in which he found himself. He did not dare to think of what might be happening right now to that clear-eyed, comradely girl who had been so strangely married to him.

A swift call to his mother confirmed the fact of Natalia's disappearance, in response to a message supposedly from him.

Hurrying into overcoat and cap he went forth, his face set in grim and purposeful lines. Hailing a *droshky* he directed the driver to take him to a well-known restaurant. Here he paid the man and entered, but went right on through, leaving by another door and seizing another carriage. He repeated the maneuver several times.

Furtively, he made his way into the office of a beady-eyed little man called Sherpov and conferred long and earnestly with that individual, leaving as secretly as he had come, finally regaining his own apartment.

He wasted not a moment, but set forth boldly and openly, going to the barracks of his own regiment where he found Colonel Prince Zaikin in the act of leaving. The two men talked long and seriously together and finally Michael took his leave.

The plan was laid, but now came the hardest part, the waiting to see whether it would operate. The big test would come within the next few minutes. If they sent Natalia to him as they had agreed, then the way was clear. Whether the shrewd peasant suspicion of Rasputin would be aroused remained to be seen.

Michael paced the floor anxiously, watching slow minute after slow minute ticked away by the clock.

Finally Michael's tortured nerves could stand the strain of waiting no longer. Slipping a pistol in the pocket of his overcoat, he hurried forth, hailing a car and directing the chauffeur to proceed to the house of Sherpov, the little beady-eyed man whom he had sought out and conversed with so seriously earlier in the day.

He had need to worry, did he but know it, for at that moment Natalia, alone and frightened, cowered in a corner of the infamous "little room" of

Rasputin's apartment at 64 Gorokhovaia.

It was a cleverly worded message they had brought her, and she had flown eagerly to serve her husband. Now she was dazed and pitiful, her whole world cast down in ruins about her, her slim body shaking with sobs, the fabric of her girlish dreams likely to be rent at any moment by that coarse and evil-smelling peasant whose heavy footfall she awaited with despair and terror.

Vainly had she searched the room for something with which to take her own life or to defend herself, but it was bare of anything save the little table and the crude iron bed. Ironically enough, portraits of the Czar and Czarina stared forth coldly from their frames on the wall.

Outside, the little group of loiterers which constantly hung about the entrance quickened into sudden life as a big car drove up with Rasputin lolling in its rear seat. The bearded peasant *starets* waved cheerfully in response to their greetings, his eyes watery and his legs a little unsteady as he strode up to his apartment.

Pushing his way through the fawning crowd, Rasputin entered the dining room and greeted his group of women and called loudly for more wine.

As he gulped down the Madeira he glanced with gloating anticipation at the door of the little room which stood closed and silent.

Without paying any attention to the women who flocked around him, he rose and stretched, yawning prodigiously.

"Ho, now to the taming of the little pigeon!" he growled deep in his chest and smoothed out his tangled beard as he strode to the door of the little room. He opened the door brusquely and as brusquely closed it behind him. In the silence which followed, the listening women heard the click of the lock as it was made fast.

Rasputin turned from locking the door of the little room and stared into the darkness, seeing nothing but a faint shadowy figure crouched down in the corner.

"Fear me not, little dove. I come but to lead your soul on the true path," his voice rang forth sonorously, and he struck a light, applying it to a candle resting upright on the small table.

The feeble rays caught hold of the wick, flickered once or twice, and then burned with a more steady glow, casting a faint light on Natalia where she huddled, white-faced and trembling.

Nothing could be heard save his heavy breathing. Then slowly, his long fingers clenching and unclenching avidly, he stepped nearer until his hot breath was almost in her face.

"Fear me not, little dove," he breathed hoarsely and his hands dropped on the smooth slope of her shoulders. She shrank back and screamed, a despairing, heart-rending scream.

Her piercing cry was answered by a mighty shout coming from outside in the dining room, a shout echoed by feminine shrieks. Something hard and heavy struck the door with a jar that nearly tore it from its hinges. Again and again the heavy body smashed against the thin door until with a splintering crash it fell inward and Michael leaped over the debris.

For a second he paused, accustoming his eyes to the dim light, seeing in a swift flash the slim figure of his beloved, a dizzying glimpse of dark hair and dark eyes. Then he leaped at Rasputin with a roar of a man enraged past all bearing.

His powerful arms seized the form of the peasant, picked it up bodily and threw it across the room where Rasputin tumbled in a sprawling heap, whimpering like a whipped cur.

Natalia fled to her lover and Michael seized her by the waist, bearing her to the door. There was a confusion and shouting in the outer room. Several men had appeared and were blocking the way. Sweeping Natalia behind him with his left arm, Michael drove at the face of the nearest, smashing exultantly full into the bearded chin and shouting as the man collapsed.

There was a dim tangle of heads and bodies through which Michael bore savagely, sweeping Natalia with him. He gained the outer door and slammed it closed behind him full in the face of his pursuers.

The waiting chauffeur started his engine and they were off down the street with Rasputin's household buzzing like a beehive in impotent anger behind them.

Once in his own apartment Natalia sank into his large chair, her eyes glowing with thankfulness and gratitude as she watched her lover, who paced back and forth, his face still white with the rage that had possessed him.

"But won't he follow here?" she asked, timorously.

Michael shook his head.

"No, not even Rasputin would dare to abduct a man's wife from his own home, but he will send the police to guard against your escape.

"Thank God, you're out of that hell-hole at any rate," he said feelingly, then looked at her, a question in his eyes. As he studied the clear, unsullied beauty of the girl, the questioning look left his face and was succeeded by an air of immense relief. He had been in time.

Natalia did not look worried, her eyes were filled with serene contentment, a contentment founded on the confidence she had in this quiet-voiced man of hers.

Michael was not as confident as he seemed, knowing that his plan had not reached its fulfillment as yet and would not until eleven o'clock the next morning.

But of this he said nothing as they drank their tea and ate the supper which Shnitskin brought them. Their conversation slackened as midnight approached.

It was Michael who finally spoke up, pointing to the door of the bedroom.

"You shall sleep there," he said, "and I will rest on the couch in the dining room."

Her head came up quickly and for a second her eyes stared enigmatically into his. Then she bowed her head in submission, saying nothing as she softly entered the bedroom and softly closed the door behind her.

In the morning, as eleven o'clock approached, Michael grew more and more agitated, going often to the window and looking into the street where the stolid police still held their posts, pacing up and down before the apartment house as before a beleaguered city.

Sharply on the hour, the beady-eyed Sherpov was waiting in the anteroom of Rasputin's house, carrying under his arm a package wrapped in black velvet.

Rasputin, his lip swollen, his eyes red and one of his arms in a sling, came forth from an inner room and nodded grumpily at the little Jewish banker-jeweler.

"You have them?" he asked gruffly of Sherpov, who nodded his assent, and they repaired into an inner room where Sherpov spread out the black velvet and reverently displayed a great triple strand of pearls, which flowed under his hands like a river of frozen moonlight flushed with opalescent fire.

The dirty-bearded *starets*, his misfortunes of the night before forgotten at sight of this great wealth which spelled a nation's doom, clutched the pearls greedily and let the pinkish globules flow through his hands, sensuously enjoying the feel of them.

"I am to get a receipt for them," said Sherpov, timidly.

"A receipt?" Rasputin glared at him. "No," he thundered, "no such thing!"

"But," expostulated Sherpov, "I must have a receipt or the money." The little man set his jaw stubbornly.

"What talk is this of money and receipts? These pearls are mine. A gift from the empress herself!" shouted Rasputin, banging the table.

"There is some mistake." Sherpov was frightened but stubborn. "These are my pearls from my stock, made up on the order of Prince Doblestni!"

Rasputin stared at him unbelieving for a moment, then his shrewd brain began to grasp the import of the jeweler's words, and he saw that he had been tricked.

"Hold these," he shouted, and rushed to the French-type telephone where he gave orders that the woman in Prince Doblestni's flat should be seized immediately. Slamming the telephone back on its stand he rushed down the stairs, leaving the terrified jeweler standing gaping at him. Calling to several men who lounged about the courtyard, Rasputin leaped into a waiting car and shouted directions to the driver.

In the meantime as eleven o'clock approached Michael paced the floor, his bearing more and more nervous.

At ten minutes to eleven there was a clatter of hoofs in the street before Michael's house and a squadron of the Red Hussar Regiment, his own squadron, came to a halt. Two of the trim Hussars with handsome capes dismounted from their horses and entered the building, watched curiously by the police officers. After a few minutes the two Hussars returned with Michael, who mounted his waiting horse and moved out with his squadron for the morning's exercise.

At a quarter after eleven a police car drove up, discharging two or three officials who excitedly demanded of the men on guard whether the lady in the flat had departed. The police on duty there said, "No," and the officials immediately grew calmer.

In another minute there came the car used by Rasputin and it stopped with a shriek of brakes while the tall, bearded peasant-priest leaped out. Without exchanging a word with any one he hurried up the stairs, knocking violently at Michael's door. Behind him came his companions, four or five men he had picked up in his courtyard.

It was Michael's orderly, Shnitskin, who opened the door and stood respectfully at the view of the famous Rasputin. The peasant pushed by him, his eyes smoldering with anger, and strode into the drawing-room. There was no one there. Without a word Rasputin flung open the door of the bedroom, snarling like a savage beast.

Scattered on the bed and chairs was some feminine wearing apparel, a skirt and blouse and some other articles. Of Natalia there was no sign.

The whole flat was searched, but aside from the orderly and a Hussar friend, whom he was entertaining in the kitchen, the place was vacant.

Knocking these men out of his way, Rasputin departed like some savage bear, growling deeply in his beard.

Down at the railway station a tall Hussar officer and his slim and rather beautiful orderly, muffled in a large Hussar cape, seated themselves in their compartment, just as the train began to move out.

"On my father's estates," said Michael, "Rasputin cannot follow. There we can find peace."

"Yes," said Natalia in a low voice, "and perhaps a little happiness." For a second she glanced into his eyes. It was a glance as revealing as a flash of lightning.

"You mean—" his voice throbbed joyously.

Again she flashed that look at him and suddenly those two found no need for words.

It was after a half an hour of smothered whispers and joyous silences that Michael frowned in thought.

"But I have to go back," he said, "and find the jewels of the Czarina."

Natalia shook her head, and reaching into her soldier blouse she drew forth a package wrapped in linen.

"It was I who stole the pearls from your flat," she said. "I was afraid that harm would come to you and oh, my dear," she cried, "I want no harm to come to you, ever!"

Back in St. Petersburg the German ambassador waited vainly for Rasputin to appear with the Czarina's pearls. Sherpov, hugging his precious imitation string tightly, scurried back to his shop where he found an envelope crammed with thousand-ruble notes, more than enough to repay him for all his trouble. And on that train speeding away to safety two very happy people laughed and whispered tenderly together.

The Dumb Bunny

"I'M TELLIN' YOU, BO, we're so far out of the line of travel that the War Department has plumb forgot us!"

Snyder threw a peeled potato into a tubful of water and vengefully attacked another one. "Yes, sir, we're so far away it ud take ten dollars' worth of stamps to send us a postcard."

Snyder stared with unfriendly eye at the Siberian village and the mountains and the forests beyond it, mile after mile of trees which marched resistlessly until at last they were defeated by the Arctic Circle and dissolved into the Siberian tundra.

"What are we here for anyways?" growled the other cook's police.

"What are we here for! Ain't nobody knows, not even the President hisself. All I know is we're goin' to be in pretty much of a jam if these Bolshies decide to act nasty."

"Oh, you're always crepe hangin'," retorted the other man crossly. "We got fifty doughboys here an' a good many thousand rounds of ammunition. Ain't nobody goin' to bother us none."

"Yeah!" Snyder was heavily sarcastic. "That's what you say. You're like all the rest of these war babies. If you'd put in as many hitches as I have, you'd know somethin' about soldierin'. . . ."

Are you tryin' to say that Lieutenant Jennings don't know nothin' about soldierin'?"

"I'm sayin' jest that!" retorted Snyder emphatically. "Jest because he wears a couple of pieces of tin on his shoulders ain't no sign he knows how to be an officer. Where'd he learn his soldierin', answer me that!

"I'll tell you where he learned it. He learned it sittin' on the quarter deck of a four-line escort wagon. He spent all his time manicurin' a set of Missouri jar heads. Jennings was swingin' the business end of a shovel cleanin' up after a team of mules when I was workin' the bolt of a rifle against goo-goos an' Moros an' greasers. . . ."

"But he sure knows how to razz a bunch of men," interposed the other man.

"Sure he does; no man can be a mule skinner that ain't got a good line of cuss words. But when you said that you said everything. Why look at this here camp"—and he pointed out of the door of the shed down the village street to the far end where a row of brown khaki tents showed near the church—"here we are with our kitchens down at this end of the village and all our spare ammunition stored in the Y.M.C.A. hut in the next room. And what happens?

"Three times a day the hull outfit comes down here armed with nothin' better than mess kits leavin' all the rifles at the other end of town in the tents guarded by a couple of men. What's to prevent a gang of Bolshies gettin' next to that and jumpin' us while we're at chow? Didja ever hear of Balanguiga? No? I thought not. If Lieutenant Jennin's had been in the Army instead of the Quartermaster Corps he'd a heard about it.

"Yeah, Balanguiga was the name of a town in the Philippines. An' there was an outfit of doughboys there like we are here. An' what happened to them? I'll tell ya what happens to them. Their cook shack, like our'n was on the other side of the *barrio*. And they leaves their rifles behind 'em an' goes to chow jest once too often. An' a swarm of Bolo men hacks 'em to pieces."

The other man stared down the length of the village street.

"Yeah," he answered doubtfully, "but these here Bolshies ain't so much."

"No? Maybe you ain't been usin' your eyes like I have lately, an' maybe you ain't noticed that there's jest about twict as many Bolshies here in this town as there was when we come."

"Yeah, they do seem to be thicker than they was," agreed the other man slowly.

"An' more'n that, they got a real leader, too, a guy that don't miss nothin'. It's that fellow Kusmitsky, I mean. You know what I found out about that baby? I found out he ain't no more a coal miner than I am. That guy was an officer in the Tsar's old army and turned Bolshevik after the revolution. Believe me he ain't missin' many tricks.

"And it's him that's bringin' in these men all the time. I heard this mornin' that there's forty or fifty more of 'em comin' over from Vladimora tomorrow night. An' when them babies gets here that means we're outnumbered about four to one. An' believe me, there'll be hell poppin'.'"

First call for retreat sounded from the other end of the village and both men glanced up from their labors as the soldiers began to pile out of their tents and line up preparatory to retreat inspection.

"Why don't you say somethin' to Jennings about it?" asked the other man, a worried frown on his face.

"Fat chance!" Snyder's tone was scornful. "When you been in this army as long as I have you'll learn that it don't pay to shoot off your face with a gratuitous issue of advice. I know jest about what'd happen if I sound off to Jennings. He'd have me doin' kitchen police the rest of my natural life.

"Here he comes now lookin' all pleased with hisself. He'll go in now an' get slicked up an' go callin' on that Natasha woman. The blame lunkhead don't know that she's Kusmitsky's sweetie an' is just playin' him for a sucker for what information she can get out of him."

Both men watched as Jennings, having finished his retreat inspection, came striding down the village street, paying no attention to the sullen glances from the hairy, bearded Russian miners who lounged about, hands in pockets.

The air still quivered to the exceeding pungency of his remarks as he upbraided his outfit for the state of their equipment and their manner of executing "Present Arms." He swaggered into the quarters he shared with "Doc" Evans, the little Y.M.C.A. man, and threw his belt and pistol holster on the table with the air of a man who has done a good day's work and is satisfied therewith.

"Doc, I never seen such a bunch of dumb-heads as I got in this outfit. But believe me I sure read 'em the riot act tonight!"

Doc Evans glanced up from the book he was reading and peered with near-sighted eyes at the officer before him.

"Yes, yes," agreed the little man absently, and a worried frown appeared above his horn-rimmed glasses. "They're not such bad boys," he said lamely, "they're nothing to worry about, but there is something that is worrying me, Lieutenant."

"Yeah?" returned Jennings sarcastically, "you're always in a stew about something, Doc. What's on your mind this time?"

The little Y.M.C.A. man, his oversized uniform hanging on him in awkward folds, carefully marked his place in the book he had been reading, then rose and went to the door where he stared down the length of the village street.

As usual its muddy width was darkened here and there by idle groups of rough-looking miners and peasants who moved aimlessly in and out of the various log *izbas* and gathered in little, low-voiced, gesticulating knots.

Doc Evans' eyes rested on them indifferently for a moment and then he glanced aloft at the sky and sniffed the air.

"Lieutenant, I'm worried about all these soldier boys," he said. "There are all the signs of a cold snap coming on and they've got nothing but those thin cotton tents and no stoves or anything to keep them warm."

Jennings in the meantime had filled his canvas wash basin with water and was vigorously scrubbing his face. He looked up, his face dripping, and grunted in disgust.

"Too bad about them poor soldier boys," he commiserated ironically. "I ain't their dry nurse. A little cold ain't goin' to hurt 'em none. Besides, what kin I do about it? There ain't no stoves to heat them tents and that's all there is to it."

"I was thinking . . . perhaps . . . you could set them to work building some kind of huts and they could make fireplaces out of rocks and clay and maybe keep themselves warm."

"Yeah, an' let's buy 'em some gold-plated foot warmers an' some solid ermine pajamas an' some eiderdown quilts," jeered Lieutenant Jennings.

"Ye-e-s, but . . ." expostulated Doc Evans weakly.

"Yes, but," mimicked Jennings, rubbing his face with a towel. "They'd ought to put you in the army nurse corps where you coulda tucked the boys into bed every night 'stead of makin' you a Y.M.C.A. secretary! You're all right, Doc, so long as you 'tend to your knittin', you jest keep on runnin' your weekly vaudeville show an' dolin' out your cigarettes an' chocolate an' leave it to me to look after the soldiers. That bunch of lunk-heads ain't worth worryin' about."

Whatever else the little Y.M.C.A. man had to say he kept to himself and went back to his reading with a sigh, only glancing up when Jennings at last finished his toilette by putting on a clean blouse and was ready to set forth.

"Where are you going, Lieutenant? It's nearly supper time," he reminded.

"Where am I going, he asks," marveled Jennings. "Where the blazes do you s'pose I'd be goin' all slicked up like this? I'm goin' where I'll get a good bellyful of chow an' a good drink or two an' a chance to talk with a good-lookin' girl."

Doc Evans' brow became a little clouded. He shook his head.

"Better look out for these Russian women," he advised.

"Yeah," jeered the lieutenant. "Listen to what's givin' advice about women. Doc, all you learned about women you studied from books. Me, I been learnin' 'em first hand for thirty years an' I'll go on learnin' 'em that way."

Then seeing the little man sitting there rather forlornly alone, Jennings had a qualm of conscience.

"Why don't you mosey along down to Natasha's house after dinner an' sit there an' chin a while? There'll be some singin' an' it'll do you good to get away from these here poor neglected soldier boys for a while."

"I may do that," said Doc Evans surprisingly enough.

He watched Jennings set his hat at a jaunty angle on his head and depart down the village street. From the open doorway Doc Evans saw the tall figure of the lieutenant swinging through the groups of miners who gave way at his approach and grew silent until he passed by.

But many more eyes than those of the Y.M.C.A. man were upon the American officer as he stopped at a small log *izba* set back from the road and strode to the gate of the house where Natasha lived with her father, the school teacher. The door opened to Jennings' knock and for a second the girl's figure showed against the candle light. Then Jennings passed in and the door was shut.

Doc Evans stood in the doorway of the log building and continued to gaze into the fast gathering dusk. In the darkening shadows there was much quiet going to and fro of dim figures and much furtive gathering of small knots of men whose voices came subdued in the silence of the evening.

Something soft and damp fell on Evans' hand and he looked up to see the first snow flakes of the season drifting silently down in the night. From the far end of the village came an occasional burst of laughter where the soldiers were getting out mess kits preparatory to coming the length of the village for their evening meal.

From the far end of the building where Evans stood came the clatter of pots and pans where the cook and cook's police were even now ladling out the supper.

Doc Evans turned away from the door and went into the large hall which occupied the center of the building. The former storeroom converted into a Y.M.C.A. hut was a cheerless looking place in spite of his attempt to brighten it up. Four or five rickety tables stood about the center, a rough stage occupied one end and a decrepit pool table stood disconsolate near one wall, flanked near at hand by an equally battered and decrepit looking piano.

Back of a small counter were the shelves on which reposed tobacco and cigarettes and chocolate and such other articles as were dispensed by the Y.M.C.A. A few dog-eared and ancient magazines completed the amusement facilities for the soldiers in this far-off place.

It was Doc Evans' kingdom, the place he ruled—but its sight brought no joy to him. He stared somberly over its bare cheerlessness and a sigh escaped from him.

The truth of the matter was that Doc Evans, as old as he was, had been among the first to heed the call to arms. But a firm but kindly medico, after examining his teeth and general physical get-up, and after determining his age, had shaken his head.

Doc's earnest desire to get into the war had finally landed him in the Y.M.C.A. And now he found himself out in the farthest flung outpost, doling out cigarettes and chocolate and arranging a weekly entertainment, treated with faint contempt by the officers in command and with easy tolerance by the soldiers.

"He ain't the preachin' kind and don't run the holy Joe stuff on us," was their kindest word of praise, Other than that the men treated him as part of the system and let it go at that.

But Doc Evans was discontented in the narrow confines of his kingdom. The fact that he was a learned man and had been a professor of history in a leading college would have made no difference to the men around him, even had they known it, which they did not.

Among these brawny, husky fighting men Doc Evans' meager frame and near-sighted eyes ranked him as a non-combatant. And the knowledge was as gall and wormwood to his soul.

The still of evening was broken in upon by the gay voices of the soldiers, who, with much clatter of tin cups and mess kits, were surging down the street on their way to supper. The clatter was quickly succeeded by a grim and purposeful silence as the hungry soldiers attacked the heaped-up provender.

Again Doc Evans sighed and turned to his task of lighting up the oil lamps which did their best each evening to dispel the gloom of this somber hall. He completed this task as the first of the soldiers hurried in.

"It's colder than all blazes!" announced the newcomer, starting a cry which was taken up by succeeding men as they came in shivering.

"How about a fire, Doc?" they demanded.

And, assent having been given, they carried in armloads of wood and built up a roaring blaze in the sheet-iron stove which Evans had managed to salvage from somewhere.

More and more men came into the cheerful glow until the hall resounded to their talk and laughter. Doc sought out his own supper and ate it in lonely silence in his room, thereafter staring out into the village again.

The snow was now falling in great, soft flakes and its blanket was laying an eerie silence over the hills and fields and woods. And through the silence he heard the distant tinkle of a *balalaika* from the schoolmaster's house where Lieutenant Jennings was taking his ease even now.

Some qualm of conscience made Evans look into his amusement room but it was plain to be seen that he was not needed there. The pool table was occupied, the phonograph was going, a group of men were singing by the stove, two or three card games were in progress and the evening was well started. Without a single backward look he strode toward Natasha's house.

He received a warm and typically Russian welcome. Jennings' confident face and capable figure was next to Natasha at the table and they both smiled a cheerful greeting, the pretty Russian girl dimpling at him in hospitable fashion. Her father, the old schoolmaster, poured him a stiff measure of vodka and Natasha resumed her playing on the *balalaika*, interrupting her music to make an occasional remark in broken English.

Scarcely ten minutes had passed when there came a knock at the door, and they all looked up as a tall, bearded Russian strode in.

"Hello, Kusmitsky," greeted Jennings—while Doc Evans bowed formally.

Kusmitsky was an arrogant sort of a man with something masterful about him at the same time. Bending low, he kissed Natasha's hand, greeted her father and then turned to Jennings.

"Eet is moutch snow tonight," he remarked as he vigorously pumped Jennings' hand.

"You said it, bo," returned Jennings easily. "How's tricks?"

This last was beyond Kusmitsky, but he smiled amiably enough, and then sat on the other side of Natasha, who eyed him with keen interest. Under the flurry caused by her father's refilling the vodka glasses, she shot a single low-voiced question to Kusmitsky, speaking in Russian.

"Is everything ready, Serge Ivanovitch?"

"*Da*, yes," nodded Kusmitsky, "the comrades have arrived from Vladimora this evening and are hiding at the church all armed and waiting."

"And they will first seize the rifles from the camp and then attack the soldiers in their clubhouse?" she asked.

"Careful," he warned. "They may understand us."

"Oh, the big ox doesn't understand a word of Russian and the little dumb bunny is too hopeless to understand his own language." She shrugged her shoulders contemptuously and went on: "And it is agreed that I am to invite the big ox to meet me at the dance at the inn at nine o'clock?"

"Yes, we want him out of the way so that the soldiers shall be leaderless," answered Kusmitsky. Then, lifting his glass, he turned smilingly to Jennings and Doc Evans. "Your verree good health," he toasted in English, and drank down the fiery liquor.

"How," said Jennings, and gulped his down with equal celerity.

But Doc Evans' thoughts were far away and he sipped his drink slowly and then, while Serge Kusmitsky engaged the little Y.M.C.A. man in labored conversation, Natasha turned to Jennings.

"Is eet that you would like to dance tonight?" she asked very prettily.

"Sure," responded Jennings heartily, "when it comes to dancin' I'm there like a rubber duck!"

"A rubair duke?" She looked slightly puzzled, but then went on: "Eef it ees that you like to dance tonight I go to the little inn—you know the one verree close to the railroad. You will come there at nine o'clock and dance with me, yes?" She smiled deeply into his eyes.

"Will I? Try to keep me away!" said Jennings emphatically. "Is Serge goin' to take you down there?"

"Yes, we go verree queek now. You will coom later at nine o'clock? Yes?"

"Sure," responded Jennings, hiding his slight chagrin at not being invited to accompany her, but making the best of it in any case. Glancing at his watch he saw it was already a quarter to eight. "Guess we'd better be moochin' along then, if you an' Serge is headin' out."

He rose. Doc Evans, seeing that he was departing, also made his excuses and the two headed out together.

Doc Evans shivered a little as the chill of the outer air struck his spare figure. It had grown much colder. The snow was still falling, however, and effectually blanketed the village and half concealed the houses. Behind them the church loomed up dark and silent and gave no sign that it housed some fifty or sixty men, all armed and waiting.

To one side of it lay the American camp deserted save for a single sentry and the corporal of the guard and his two or three men. Even Jennings noticed the cold as the two of them headed for the Y.M.C.A. hut at the farther end of the town.

The village lay dark and sinister behind them as the two entered into the warmth of the hut, its heavy log walls retaining the heat of the single large stove. The men were singing, oblivious of any danger that might threaten them.

"Lieutenant," said Doc Evans wistfully as he eyed the busy amusement room packed with men all warm and comfortable, "I certainly don't like to see these boys go back to those cold tents tonight. As far as I can see there's a blizzard coming on. And you know, when it gets cold in Siberia it gets cold and those men are going to suffer in those unheated tents."

"That's their hard luck," grunted Jennings. "What are you gonna do about it? We ain't got the stoves to heat 'em up."

"Why, I was thinking," said Doc Evans diffidently, and in his nervousness he took off his horn-rimmed glasses and polished them with his handkerchief as he blinked nearsightedly at the officer. "I was wondering if we couldn't use this big hall of ours for a sort of barracks. There's room enough for all of the men with their cots and belongings, and they could keep warm and dry in here."

Jennings paused in his labor of changing into a cleaner shirt and glanced through his open doorway at the lighted hall, studying the problem.

"I dunno as that's such a dumb idea after all, Doc," he said after a while. And this was a great concession from Jennings, for in his mind soldiers and tents went together as naturally as ham went with eggs. "Yeah, Doc, that ain't such a dumb idea after all. I'll think it over tonight and look into it in the mornin'."

"But it's going to be cold tonight, Lieutenant," persisted Doc Evans.

"Aw, another night won't hurt that bunch of bums none." Jennings' tone was easy as he finished his changing and drew on his overcoat preparatory to setting forth for the dance. "I'll look into it in the mornin', Doc," he repeated. "Don't sit up for me. I'm liable to be late." And with that he was gone.

Evans stared after him, his eyes brooding. He was in for a lonely evening, but that did not depress him so much as the thought of those men in the cold damp tents at the other end of town. He thought a little bitterly of his dreams of war and glory and compared them with the actuality. Why! He was unable even to secure the removal of a handful of men from one end of town to the other!

The bitterness of his own helplessness struck him anew and his shoulders sagged wearily as he turned into the amusement room and moved listlessly through its crowded confines. It was time to issue any last calls for cigarettes and tobacco and chocolate.

As he went toward his counter he barked his shins against a row of long, heavy boxes that were piled in the shadow, and cursed out the thoughtlessness of the men who had piled the reserve ammunition in the exact spot where he stumbled over it almost daily.

As for Lieutenant Jennings, he had long since found himself a horse and was on his way to keep the date with Natasha. The snow had stopped falling and the full moon had risen, flooding the fields and woods with silvery light so that Jennings' horse picked his way easily as he pursued the narrow road that led toward that small house near the foot of the hill which happened to be the Russian equivalent of a roadhouse.

The soldiers had long since discovered that vodka was to be had there, and they gave it their patronage on pay days in spite of the unsavory reputation of the place. To Jennings' credit, be it said that he had never before entered the inn. Therefore, he studied it curiously as he approached, finding it a dark, low building half concealed under the shadow of a hill.

The road wound around, crossing a cleared space from whence he had a good view of the house, and then plunged into the woods again before it circled up toward the building. Arrived there, he saw no one about but dismounted, nevertheless, tethering his horse to the post, meanwhile glancing back from whence he had come, noting that open space where the road was in view for a few yards.

He turned then toward the building.

It was a cold night as only nights can be cold in Siberia. He knocked at the door and waited. Then, as there was no response, he tried the handle, but the door would not give to his efforts. Knocking again, more sharply, he heard this time the sound of footsteps dragging slowly and grudgingly toward the door from inside.

At the same moment he thought he saw a shadow detach itself from the corner of the house and disappear toward the rear, but could not be sure as he turned his attention to the person inside. Whoever it was, was slowly taking down several bars.

And then the door opened, disclosing a gnarled and twisted figure of a man whose head was sunk so low on his shoulders that he seemed in truth to have no neck at all. The fellow's huge hands and arms nearly swept to the floor, they were so long, and he seemed to rest like an ape on his knuckle bones as he stood there, a sinister figure in the faint glow of the candle which illumined the room behind him.

Jennings' hand dropped down towards his pistol holster and he stood there a second undecided whether to enter or not. But the cold was growing more penetrating and the man inside had opened the door wider and invited him to enter.

Jennings had another shock when he heard the fellow's voice. Its notes were shrill and querulous, like the tones of a peevish child or a woman in pain, and created a most extraordinary effect upon him, so disproportionate was the reedy voice to the bulky body of its possessor.

Jennings entered, glancing about him for a trace of the girl he had come to meet. But there was no one else in the long, low-roofed room as far as he could see. Well, he reasoned, the Russians had no idea of time anyway.

The place was crude enough, its floor nothing more than hard packed clay. At one end was a large brick stove of the regular Russian peasant type, upon whose broad top the entire family could sleep with comfort in the extremely cold weather of the Siberian winter.

Several rough pallets, a crudely hewn table and chairs and the presence of many soiled tin plates and cups showed that a fairly large number of people frequented the place. At either end of the large room two doors led into the rear.

Jennings looked about, wondering where the musicians were and the other guests at the dance, but figured that, Russian-like, they would be late, too.

Jennings looked around at the cluttered dirt and disorder with distaste, finally turning to the ape-like man who stood watching him from little, reddish, pig-like eyes.

"Well," said Jennings irritably, "snap into it. Fetch me some vodka. Savvy?"

The Russian understood the one Russian word and hurried out to the rear somewhere, returning with a bottle and a none too cleanly glass, accompanying it with a large round loaf of the heavy, slightly sour tasting black bread of the Russian peasant, the famous *tchorni kleb*.

Conquering his repugnance for the dirty glass, Jennings poured himself a good three fingers of the colorless fluid and tossed it off. The warm glow of the vodka induced him to a more cheerful frame of mind. He half rose as a knock came at the door, and straightened out his belt and smoothed back his hair.

But the person admitted by the ape-like creature was very far from being Natasha. The newcomer was a stocky, gray-haired Russian in peasant dress who had very bright red cheeks and extremely bright eyes. He carried a broad bladed axe in his belt.

It was not until he came within the radius of the candlelight that Jennings noted that the fellow's forehead was branded deeply with a Russian letter. It came to the American suddenly that he had heard of Russian murderers at the prison island of Sakhalin being branded by the jailers.

And this fellow certainly looked like a murderer. Jennings didn't like a bit the way the fellow fingered his axe. But the newcomer bowed first to the *ikon* corner in Russian fashion and then to the ape-like man and finally to Jennings.

Thereafter he seated himself inconspicuously against the wall and sat there silent, his hands in his belt. But Jennings felt the man's bright eyes fixed on him and it made him vaguely uncomfortable.

He poured himself a fresh drink of vodka, but scarcely had he tossed it down when there came another knock at the door and this time it opened to admit a half dozen men, an even worse looking lot than the one already present. They were shaggy-haired, long-bearded fellows, dressed in rags and tatters of clothing and very evidently long strangers to anything faintly approaching soap and water.

They came in silently, their eyes taking swift appraisal of the room and the lone American officer. They bowed as the first man had done and like him said no word as they squatted here and there on the floor and against the wall. Like the first man who had entered they each carried a sharp, broad bladed axe.

The vodka was beginning to take effect on Jennings and he scowled at the silent men who sat around staring at him from the shadows. There was something uncanny about their fixed regard and he had the feeling somehow that they would spring on him if he so much as turned his back.

"You're a pretty tough-looking bunch of babies," he addressed them scornfully, "but here's somethin' that'll tame you if you start anything funny."

He pulled his .45 Colt from his holster and laid it on the table in front of him. The silent Russians watched him gravely, but they made no movement. He called for more vodka and as the fiery stuff began to work in him he more or less forgot the passage of time. He also ceased to bother about the Russians lined against the wall.

Nearly an hour passed and he had lost count of the drinks. He pushed his pistol to one side to make room for another glass. Then as he filled it and started to raise it to his lips, the ape-like man jostled him, spilling half the contents of the glass.

It was at that precise moment that things began to happen. The candle was suddenly knocked out, leaving the cabin in darkness. Powerful arms settled in a strangling hold around his throat. Other arms pulled his feet out from under him. He kicked and bit and tried to strike out.

The table went over with a crash and a heavy weight of smelly bodies bore him to the earth. In a second his hands were jerked behind him and tied, and his feet knotted together.

A voice shouted something in Russian above him. A match spluttered in the gloom and the wavering light from the candle again illumined the room. The disreputable looking men who had entered the cabin were grouped about him, but a new figure had joined them.

Jennings blinked his eyes as he stared up into the face of Serge Kusmitsky, who gazed down upon him coldly.

"What the hell are they tryin' to pull on me, Serge?" Jennings growled, trying to heave himself up to a sitting position. But a firm hand pressed him back to the earth again. Serge Kusmitsky rubbed his hands together.

"I am verr-ee sorr-ee, my friend," he said, "but I had to use, how do you say it—harsh measures."

Jennings suddenly lay still. "What's your game?" he demanded.

"Oh, it ees nothing. It ees very simple. Come, I will explain it to you," said the Russian.

He growled some order to the men standing about. They immediately lifted Jennings' bound form up into a chair, handling him as lightly as though he were a child. From this position he glowered around at his captors noting that one of the axe men had his pistol.

"Well, go on!" snarled Jennings. "Shoot!"

"No, it ees not a question yet of shooting," replied Serge Kusmitsky. "It ees that I have had to use—how do you say?—a ruse. This evening everything it was so beautifully prepared. All the comrades were concealed in the church waiting until nine o'clock when your men would all be at their club, as they were every day. But you, my friend, you were too clevair for old Serge. What did you do? At half past eight o'clock you ordered them into the big, strong building with the heavy log walls. And what do we find—nothing but empty tents. So-so, you were too clevair and Serge and his comrades could not go up against that strong building with your men inside with all their so deadly guns and all their ammunition. . . ."

Jennings stared amazed at the Russian. A great light began to dawn upon the lieutenant.

"Why that lousy little bum of a Doc Evans," he muttered under his breath. "Blamed if he didn't slip one over after all!"

". . . and so, my friend," continued Serge Kusmitsky, "it is necessary that I coom down here with my comrades, away from your men and secure their surrender by other means less dangerous"—here Serge interrupted himself to issue an order and then continued:

"And so, my friend, I have you here and all my men are here. . . ."

Jennings raised his head and listened to a sound that had puzzled him before, a sound which had resolved itself into the stamp of many booted feet and the mutter of many voices and he realized that the Russian spoke the truth.

"Yeah, I get you, you blankety-blank double-crossing son of a son," retorted Jennings with considerable asperity, "but now that you've got me here what's the next move?"

"It ees nothing, my friend, it ees nothing except that you will write a little order to your sergeant telling him to bring the soldiers immediately, leaving their guns behind. . . ."

"And your plug-uglies will shoot them down like dogs when they arrive!" snorted Jennings. "You can go plumb to hell!"

"No, no, they will not be shot, I promise you that. Maybe we will take them prisoners, but they will not be shot. I'm sure you will be verr-ee reasonable."

The Russian called something over his shoulder. There was a stir and movement by the stove and Jennings saw the most villainous looking of the Russian axe men doing something with a bellows and a slender piece of red hot steel.

Jennings stared at the man uncomprehending until the fellow approached with the steel gleaming wickedly. At the same minute heavy hands tightened on his arms and a rope was slipped around his shoulders while his head was forced back.

"You see, my friend, we are desperate men ready to do anything for the cause," purred Serge Kusmitsky's voice, "and while I re-ee-gret to hurt you, you must be reasonable."

Jennings felt the glow of the hot steel approaching his face.

"At first it ees only the right eye we will burn out," said the remorseless voice of the Russian.

Something like an electric shock went through Jennings as he listened to the purring, growling words of the Russian. Nearer and nearer came that devilish steel. He had a vision of himself going through life blinded and a vast horror surged through him.

In another second the damage would be done and he would be blinded for life. His brain was working frantically. The Russian had promised not to shoot his men. Maybe the men would get wise. Perhaps he could warn them in the note.

"Stop! I'll do it!" he yelled, as he tried to avert his head from that deadly red-hot, steel bar.

"So-oo," came the Russian's voice and the steel was suddenly removed from its uncomfortable proximity of his right eye, "you will be sensible. *Ochin chorashaw*. Verree good."

And suddenly Jennings found his right hand being released and a pen and ink placed before him and a square of paper. He glanced around desperately, but saw only a glittering axe poised above him and Serge's revolver leveled at him.

"There," he said as he signed his name and sunk back dejectedly as the paper was taken up and examined by Serge who then folded it and gave it to a messenger.

Jennings sat there under guard as the slow minutes dragged by. He was sunk in the deepest of dejection, but his ears were strained for a sound of his approaching men.

The full horror and enormity of what he had done smote him like a wave and he would have given his right hand to undo the cowardly thing he had done.

From the sounds outside he knew that Serge's followers were already in position, hiding in ambush ready to pour their murderous fire into the unsuspecting ranks of his men.

A half hour passed and then another—while he strained for every sound. When at last he began to believe that his letter had been interpreted correctly and that his men had saved themselves he heard a shout from outside and a stir as of many men.

Suddenly the door was flung open and in strode Serge Kusmitsky. Behind him shambled a familiar figure and Jennings looked up to see the meager form and heavy horn-rimmed glasses of Doc Evans.

It gave him quite a start, but Jennings managed to find his voice.

"Where the hell did you come from?" he blurted out, glancing at Serge Kusmitsky.

Two husky Bolsheviki guards were behind the little Y.M.C.A. man and Jennings noted that they kept him covered with their rifles.

"Oh, I just rambled on down ahead of the outfit," said Doc Evans quietly. "Sergeant Wilkins received your note, but he'll be a little slow about getting here. . . ."

"Why ees that? Why does he not coom?" broke in Serge.

"Well, you see it's like this," explained Doc Evans in his dry, matter-of-fact voice. "Just as he was about to start, some reinforcements came, a company of two hundred and fifty men with three officers. . . ."

"What!" shrieked the Russian. "And where are they now?"

"Oh, they're coming behind. . . ."

"It ees a lie!" yelled Serge Kusmitsky, his eyes blazing.

"All right, if you don't believe me keep an eye out on the road."

Serge Kusmitsky whirled about and flung himself at the door followed pell-mell by the other Russians. Unseen and unnoticed Doc Evans slipped out his knife and cut the cords that bound Jennings. The tall lieutenant staggered to his feet, followed to the door and stared out.

Gazing down the hill he saw first many groups of Bolsheviki scrambling up towards the building, streaming out of the woods and glancing fearfully behind them. As his eyes traveled along they came to rest on that small section of road across the clearing.

And then his heart bounded as he saw good solid olive drab figures sweeping along, rifles on shoulder in column of twos. They were moving down the road in a steady stream crossing that open space, man after man of them, squad after squad and platoon after platoon.

Serge Kusmitsky turned about, panic on his features, and shouted something in Russian. The men about the building began to race towards the rear. Just as Serge prepared to follow them, little Doc Evans ran out with upraised hands.

"You run into certain death that way," he said jerking his head back up the hill. "The whole crest is lined with soldiers. You are surrounded, you and your force. Best thing you can do is surrender, Serge Kusmitsky."

And Serge Kusmitsky decided that this was the best thing he could do after hearing the rattle of several rifles barking from the hilltop and seeing his fleeing men stream back.

They were all docile enough now, those Bolsheviki and willingly and anxiously threw down their arms.

But Jennings blinked his eyes as he saw Sergeant Wilkins leading the American force with no more than some forty men behind him.

But those forty men swiftly and efficiently surrounded the disarmed Bolsheviki and herded them down the hill while Serge Kusmitsky was bound and retained as prisoner.

"But—but where in blazes is that company of reinforcements," inquired Jennings staring about him.

Serge Kusmitsky peeked down through the trees, endeavoring to locate them, as well.

"There's isn't any company," responded Doc Evans, and grinned over to where Sergeant Wilkins stood, superintending the herding of the prisoners into column. "You see that stretch of open road there between the trees?" he continued. "Well, I asked Sergeant Wilkins to march his men across that in column of twos and then run them back out of sight behind the trees to march over it again so that they just passed and repassed. And then we sent a few men up on top of the hill to chase the Bolshies back in case they started up there."

Jennings stared at him unbelievingly for a moment. Finally he nodded his head.

"You ain't so dumb after all, Doc," he admitted, "but where in hell did you dope out such a scheme as that?"

"Oh, I read it in a book," responded Doc Evans and then without exchanging further words with Jennings, the little Y.M.C.A. man strode over to Serge Kusmitsky.

Doc Evans reached up and caught hold of the Russian's beard.

"Look here, you renegade, when you see Natasha again, you tell her that funny little dumb bunny isn't so dumb as he looks!"

The queer part of it was that Doc Evans was speaking perfect Russian!

The Western Front

TREASON

TO BE SITTING AT THE *RAT MORTE* DRINKING CHAMPAGNE and listening to the throb and hum of violins was my lot that night. It doesn't seem a very noble lot when you figure that men were dying like flies in the trenches just a few hours' journey from Paris. But I was on duty nevertheless. As a matter of fact I had just come off a big case. You'll probably remember the case of the four bankers at Bordeaux, a case which we solved, much to the astonishment of the French. At any rate I was pretty tired and in no particular mood for the feverish gaiety of Montmartre. It must have been about eleven o'clock that the *garçon* at my table slipped a note into my hand.

Thinking it was one of those little *billet-doux* sent over by a hopeful and enterprising *cocotte*, I glanced at it carelessly. But my carelessness vanished quickly when I saw it was from the Old Man himself. Glancing

for GLORY

over it hastily I shoved the note in my pocket. Cameron was out on the floor dancing with a neat Belgian blond, Waite had found a gang of friends at another table, while Truby was sitting beside me solemnly sipping away at a glass of champagne.

"Goodbye darling, I must leave you," I hummed.

"What's up?" asked Truby sharply.

" 'The trumpet calls and I must go,' " I continued.

"In other words, the Old Man isn't going to give us one evening off," said Truby in deep disgust.

"Not even the beginning of an evening," I said. "He wants the whole gang of us. I'll beat it on down to headquarters, you flash the high-sign to Waite and Cameron and the three of you go by L'Abbe and pick up Gregory. *C'est entendu?*"

"Yes suh, we won't be no moah than five minutes behind you," said Truby and on that I slid out, leaving behind me the throb of violins and the air full of confetti and the popping of wine corks.

Collins was at the wheel of my car, half-asleep, but he quickly snapped into it when I told him headquarters wanted us. We went down that hill of Montmartre like a bat out of hell and in very few minutes were rolling up the

Champs Élysées. We arrived at headquarters in no time at all and I beat it up to the colonel's office.

The colonel didn't waste much time in getting down to business.

"Hello, Steele," he said, "take your weight off your feet and have a cigarette."

"All this overwhelming courtesy," I said, "being the prelude of sending me off on a tough job."

"Sometimes, young fellow, you show almost human intelligence," returned the colonel, blandly snapping his lighter open and lighting my cigarette for me. By that gesture I knew that it was a particularly tough job.

"I hate to put you back on it so soon," began the colonel, "especially after you and your gang have done so beautifully on that Bordeaux job. . . ."

"Crocodile tears, Colonel, crocodile tears," I answered. "Spill the dirt, Colonel, and I'll be on my way."

He grinned and opened some papers before him on the desk.

"You've got about twenty minutes to get going," he said. "It's a front line job. One German spy who seems to be demoralizing an entire division."

"Where is it?" I asked.

He told me and then went on:

"Old General So-an'-So is in command, but he won't bother you much as he's still too bewildered to know what it's all about."

"Who's the chief-of-staff?" I asked quickly.

"Colonel Hezekiah Norton."

"Umm," I grunted, "and what's his specialty?"

The colonel looked at me with a quick, sidelong glance.

"Just a wee bit fussy. Thinks he should be a brigadier general and is inclined to be impatient with the new army."

"West Pointer?" I asked.

"No, Spanish-American War, one of the crimes of '98."

I began to see why the colonel had been so zealous in lighting my cigarette.

"And this German spy?"

"Fellow by the name of von Drakenfels. Seems to be playing fast and loose with the division. Writes impertinent letters to the chief-of-staff and roams at will around the area kidding the whole works."

"Sounds interesting," I said, and listened to some footsteps on the stairs. "Here comes my gang now. We'll motor down I suppose?"

"Suit yourself," said the colonel. "Goodbye and God bless you," and he shook my hand with unusual solemnity.

"Why the tragic note, Colonel?" I asked. But this time he didn't smile.

"Watch your step, kid," he advised me seriously. "This man von Drakenfels is a bad actor. He's bumped off three of the divisional intelligence officers already," and the Old Man patted me on the back in a fatherly sort of way and went to the door with me.

We hit that divisional P.C. just at reveille, after a tough all night ride, the last port of which was on a shell-torn road, sandwiched in between miles of trucks going one way and ambulances going the other. I wasted no time in reporting to the chief-of-staff. He certainly was a venomous old bird and acted about as friendly as a rattlesnake. I was in no terrifically friendly mood myself, having been on the job day and night for the past month on that infernal Bordeaux case. Although I had gotten a lot of pats on the back, a D.S.M., a Commander of the Legion of Honor, and three or four other decorations out of it, all the medals and ribbons in the world didn't make up for lack of sleep. But in the army, a colonel is a colonel, and I stood up, clicked my heels and saluted the Old Boy in my best military manner.

"Who the hell are you?" snarled the old fossil.

"Captain Steele, sir, military intelligence section; general staff, ordered to report to the commanding officer of this division by V.O.C.G." I rattled off the formula glibly enough but sagged a little on one leg, for I was beastly tired.

"Intelligence section, general staff!" snarled the old brute. "And you don't even know how to stand at attention! Just another ninety-day wonder!" He glared at me.

God knows I didn't want to be there messing around his old division and I didn't like the war anyhow. I had left a perfectly good ocean-going steam yacht in New York harbor, a very commodious Long Island estate, a fine string of polo ponies, a hunting lodge in the Shires in England, and a shooting box in Scotland to join this blame war and help my ungrateful country. And it made me kind of sore to be snarled at by this copper-nosed old war-bird who had been doing squads right all his life at some dinky little army post. But none of this showed. I looked as wooden as regulations required, rolled up my eyes and said, "Yes, sir."

"I don't see what headquarters means by sending a young squirt like you down here," growled the colonel. "They might at least have sent me a major instead of a wet-nosed captain!"

You know how it is with those old dyed-in-the-wool regular army birds. They figure brain cells by what a man has on his shoulders and not by what he might have above his ears. But there was no use arguing with old Hezekiah. I sagged on the other leg and got another dirty look.

"Hr-r-umph!" exploded the old fossil. "If headquarters insists on sending wet-nosed kids down here I'll have to insist on having them supervised by senior officers of rank and experience. Orderly! Send for Major Harkness!" The orderly snapped out a salute and beat it on out. "Major Harkness," said the Old Boy to me heavily, "is divisional intelligence officer. You will work under his direction."

I suppose my eyes opened wide, for this was counter to my instructions. For the gang I had brought down was known as "The Flying Squadron," and we were sent anywhere we were needed and given *carte blanche* to work on our own without any hampering orders from local authorities. More than that, we had the right to call on even a major general for such help and assistants as we needed. But there was no use trying to argue with this old billygoat. Maybe after all this, Major Harkness would turn out to be a good guy and we could work along as friendly as peas in a pod.

But my first view of Major Harkness dashed those hopes to the ground. He wore gold pince-nez, did this Harkness bird, and his humorless eyes glinted forth from behind them with all the scintillating hardness of a plateful of cracked ice. He ignored the hand that I stretched out to him when we were introduced, but unbent like an icicle in a furnace when the Old Man spoke to him. I put him down as a one hundred per cent Yes Man, and let it go at that.

"Major, you will take charge of this young man and his personnel and instruct him in his duties. That's all."

Harkness nearly bent in two bowing, and then jerked his head at me to follow outside. My gang was waiting for me in the big staff car, and I must admit that they were an unsanitary looking bunch, big Truby and that lanky Cameron and the ungainly Gregory and that little chipmunk of a Waite, all of them sprawled around in the car trying to snatch what sleep they could.

This Major Harkness looked at them with a frosty eye. Then his jaw set and he spouted.

"It must be very hard to leave the bright lights of Paris and come down to real soldiers," he said cuttingly. Now I don't care how much they knock me, but it made me a little hot under the collar to hear those loyal, hard working birds run down by this stuffed shirt.

"Oh, I don't know, Major," I said mildly enough, "all of us were pulled out of the front line trenches and we're sort of battle scarred veterans with two or three Distinguished Service Crosses amongst us and four or five citations. You see, we were with the First Division in the first push." I knew this would hit him hard, for this baby hadn't been over very long judging from the air of him.

"I see," he said very shortly, and led me to his dugout, where he gave me all the dope he had concerning this von Drakenfels. I must say it wasn't very much.

"Now what I want you to do, Captain—" he started in very arrogantly.

"Now what you want us to do, Major," I interrupted him, "is like the flowers that bloom in the spring, tra la." I was getting madder and madder.

"What the devil do you mean by that?" he barked at me, his eyes frosty behind their horn-rimmed glasses.

"It has nothing to do with this case," I barked right back at him. "I am sent down here by orders of the commanding general to work independently on this case. You're supposed to furnish co-operation and not direction. . . ."

He gave me a dirty look did Major Harkness and started to rise from his camp chair.

"We'll see about that," he said with a gleam of something akin to pleasure in his eye. "The first thing I'll do will be to report you for insubordination."

"And the second thing you'll do, Major," I said very quietly, "will be to pack up your troubles in your old kit bag and trudge the weary road to Blois where they are supposed to reclassify square pegs out of round holes. Read that, Major," and I flipped out my confidential orders.

He read them all right and turned kind of a sickly green.

"Of course, of course, Captain, I want to do all I can," he blustered around, and I felt a little ashamed at being so hard-boiled.

"Oh, that's all right," I said, "the main thing is to get the job done and for the love of Mike let's do it without going haywire on non-essentials."

And then the bird changed his tune so quickly that he kind of disgusted me, I must admit, just a touch of slave psychology, if you know what I mean. Anyway, I got rid of him as quickly as I could and picked me out a nice smelly dugout about half way between Division P.C. and the front line trenches. This done, I went back and woke up my sleeping beauties and told them to stand by while I conferred with the adjutant. He was a pretty decent bird, a trim, snappy West Pointer, and when I told him I wanted Collins, our chauffeur, assigned to the telephone switch board and Lieutenant Gregory to the Machine Gun Battalion and the other three at Brigade Headquarters, he snapped into it and issued the orders immediately.

The first job I tackled was the examination of the descriptive list and officers' records. From these I picked out a few that looked as if they might furnish leads. The second thing I did was to circulate around amongst the regimental intelligence officers and pick up all the dope possible.

It didn't take me long to figure out that this fellow, von Drakenfels, had the division just about buffaloed. He certainly had played fast and loose with them. The fellow was brazenly circulating about the division doing incalculable harm. Not an order was issued that did not find its way to the enemy. The movement of any sizable body of troops was immediately subjected to a devastating fire from the German heavies. The arrival and departure of any officers of rank was immediately commented upon by scornful letters from this same von Drakenfels.

I saw two or three of these letters. They were written on American Army stationery in a fine copper plate hand. It did not take me long to figure out that the fellow was posing as an American officer, for there was no other explanation for the ease with which he knew the decisions taken at various headquarters and officers' meetings and staff conferences. There was a ray of hope, for the fellow was undoubtedly afflicted with the megalomania of his caste and possessed all the supercilious contempt for his antagonists that was common with many of his prototypes in the German army. With a man of this type it might be possible that the fellow would get so cock-sure and over confident that, given enough rope, he would succeed in hanging himself.

I was pretty weary as I rambled back to my dugout and cajoled a hard-boiled cook into turning me out some chow. Having gathered in so much information I decided to let it simmer awhile in the back of my head. I find that the good old bean if switched to something else will sometimes solve its own problems. With this object in view I hauled a book out of my musette bag and propped it up on the ammunition box before me while I tucked away corned Willie and dry bread and coffee. It was a blame interesting book by Raphael Sabatini called *The Justice of the Duke*.

I was right in the middle of an interesting page when I heard somebody come in behind me and a heavy voice boomed in the dugout.

"Nero fiddling while Rome burns!" The voice was heavily sarcastic and I turned around to find the chief-of-staff, old Colonel Hezekiah Norton himself, glaring at me. My candle flickered as he dropped the blanket over the dugout entrance, and for a second there was no sound except the distant dull boom of our guns strafing the enemy cross roads. The Old Boy was across the dugout in two strides and grabbed my book away, snorting like a hippopotamus as he read the title.

"Bah! Reading while a war's going on all around you! *The Justice of the Duke*. If there was any justice in headquarters they'd send someone down here who'd spend his time running down this German spy instead of reading trash! What you ought to be reading is a book on how to catch German spies!"

"I don't take much time for reading, Colonel, except while I eat," I said wearily. "I work pretty steadily at this game and I find that my brain operates more clearly when I relax once in awhile and think about something else. That's pretty sound psychology, Colonel. You should try it some time."

"Psychology hell! I'll believe in psychology when I see it capture this von Drakenfels. And the only reading I believe in for young officers is a hard study of war tactics and regulations. You'd better by a damn sight get some results around here before you sound off about psychology! Results! Captain, results are what count!" And grumbling deep in his throat, the old walrus flung himself out of the dugout. I finished my cup of coffee and decided to ease myself down for a few minutes on my cot and think things over. As I started to do this I saw a square of white paper pinned to my blanket. It was written in fine, copperplate script.

"My dear Captain Steele," it read, "pray consider me entirely at your service in your praiseworthy attempts to put an end to my pernicious activities. I am indeed honored that a group of officers should be sent all the way from General Headquarters to occupy themselves with my unworthy self. I am hoping that you will prove yourself of higher mental calibre than the estimable but somewhat inept gentlemen against whom I have been pitted so far. It must be confessed that their somewhat clumsy efforts to capture me have been so easily evaded that the game is becoming slightly boresome. Accept, my dear Captain Steele, the assurances of my highest consideration."

The note was signed "Erich von Drakenfels."

I must say I had to grin a little bit. I flopped down on the cot and went over the notes I had made on the personnel records of the officers of the division. They had not yielded very much with the exception of two. One of these was a Lieutenant Carl Solberg, born in Brooklyn of German parents, previous occupation a bookkeeper. The other was a Captain Hugo Stempful, who was born in New York City of an Irish mother and a German father. Both of them spoke German flawlessly and made no bones about it, and both of them were in positions which gave them access to affairs at headquarters, Lieutenant Solberg being attached to the division staff as an assistant intelligence officer while Captain Stempful was a regimental intelligence officer. Both men entered the service via the officers' training camp. Lieutenant Solberg had been employed by a dry goods firm while Captain Stempful had been in a Wall Street brokers' office.

Deciding to have these two birds looked into, I moseyed on up to Division P.C., when I flashed an inquiring glance at Collins, who was already installed on the switch board.

"Any dope, Collins?" I asked.

"Yes, sir," Collins frowned, "about five minutes ago somebody calls up, kiddin' me, and says if my boss, Captain Steele, needs any more readin' matter he'll be glad to supply it. Before I can locate him he rings off laughin' fit to kill. I dunno who he is or what it's all about. . . ."

I knew who it was. So von Drakenfels was trying to be funny, was he? But all the same he must be pretty confident to sound off like that, proving to me that not only did he know that Collins was my man but also that he was keeping a pretty close watch on me.

But I had little time to stew over this, for old Hezekiah Norton bellowed my name out of the inner office and I dutifully went in there to see what all the shouting was about.

"Look at this!" shouted the old dodo, shoving a piece of paper at me. "Read this and see what's going on at division headquarters on the eve of a big drive!"

So I read the blame thing. It was written in the same copperplate script.

"Felicitations upon the thoroughness of the new sleuth from General Headquarters," it read. "His charming *naiveté* is only equaled by his devil-may-care *insouciance*, and he should go high in the councils of the American army! Sorry that I have to relieve you of these few unimportant papers *mais c'est la guerre!*" Of course, it was signed "von Drakenfels."

"And that isn't the worst of it!" spluttered the Colonel. "He's taken the operation orders for tomorrow's attack! Taken them right out of my despatch case! Do you understand? Right out of this office! Do you understand? What in blazes are you going to do about it?"

"He's a tough egg, Colonel, but . . ."

"Yeah!" Old Hezekiah was openly contemptuous. "Tell me something I don't know. Your job, young man, is to catch that blankety blank spy without any hemming or hawing. Where are you going to do it?" He hammered the table. "Our attack is scheduled for tomorrow morning . . . if von Drakenfels gets those orders over to the Germans it means we're cooked. When are you going to grab that fellow?"

"Colonel," I said, "you've been trying to catch this man for two weeks. I've only been here about six hours. All the same, sir, I'll have him for you tonight." And with that I executed an about face and moved out, front and center, leaving the old dodo staring after me with his jaw hung open.

In cases like this, half an hour's quiet reflection is worth five or six hours of running around in circles, and I headed back for my dugout. On the way I noted a quiet stir and movement throughout all the area, with fresh troops filtering through from the rear, regimental P.C.'s showing signs of unusual activity, details of men bringing up ammunition and supplies and the medicos fussing around and setting up new dressing stations.

Back in my own dugout I saw my book, *The Justice of the Duke*, lying face downward on the top of the empty ammunition box. Never in my life did I leave a book open and face downward in that shape, and I wondered idly who had been reading it in my absence. Picking it up to close the covers I found a square of paper underneath it.

"My dear Captain Steele," read the note. "Obviously you are a civilian officer in need of the advice of a professional soldier. War is a highly complicated and involved game, requiring intense effort and study. My advice to you, as a young man just starting his military career, is to read less of Raphael Sabatini and more of Field Marshal von der Goltz. Follow my advice and I am sure you will become a more worthy opponent than so far you have shown yourself. Accept, my dear Captain Steele, the assurances of my highest consideration. . . . Erich von Drakenfels."

I grinned again. This bird von Drakenfels must be cuckoo to waste so much time in running around and writing notes to people. I resolved to give him a lesson in military conduct.

Scarcely knowing what I did, I picked up the book again and glanced at the story I had been reading. As I read along, something clicked in my brain and suddenly I saw my way clear before me.

I headed forth for division headquarters finding that it was getting toward late afternoon. Glancing at my wrist watch I found that there were not many hours left if I was to succeed in grabbing von Drakenfels before midnight.

I had hardly gotten inside the place when Collins gave me the high-sign and called me over to the telephone.

"Somebody's tryin' to get hold of you, sir," he said. I clamped the phone to my ear.

"Is this you, Johnny Crawford?" asked the voice.

"Johnny Crawford himself and none other," I answered trying hard not to get excited for when I get excited I stutter a little bit. It was Gregory who was speaking at the other end of the wire, Lieutenant Gregory, one of my best men, speaking in the telephone code which had been agreed upon for the day.

"I've got that requisition all filled out and signed," his voice went on.

"Which form do you mean?" I asked in return, barely repressing that infernal stutter.

"Form eighteen, B," returned the voice. "Shall I bring it up?"

"Br-br-bring it up," I returned unable to keep the stutter out of the last few words. The telephone at the other end was hung up and I waited with what patience I could muster. For as plainly as though he had spoken outright, Lieutenant Gregory at the other end of the wire had informed me that he had a report of such exceeding importance that he could only make it in person. Yes, the net was closing around von Drakenfels.

The minutes dragged along. After some twenty minutes had passed I couldn't stand it any longer.

"Where the devil did that call come from?" I asked Collins.

"From the machine gun battalion P.C.," he answered, "and it's about time that the Lootenant was showin' up. It ain't so far from the machine gun battalion P.C. but what he could make it in ten minutes fast walkin'."

Another ten minutes passed by and I couldn't stand the strain of waiting any longer and headed forth toward the machine gun battalion P.C. Half way there I rounded an abutting wall in the communication trench and found some stretcher bearers and a group of men gathered about a form lying huddled on the ground.

One look was enough.

It was Lieutenant Gregory with the back of his head blown out.

The job had been done with a pistol evidently, fired from near at hand for there were powder marks on the head. It was far away out of reach of an enemy sniper. The trench walls were high at this point. Gregory had been murdered just where the trench turned at an angle. It was plain to be seen that the assassin had lurked just around the turn and had fired at Gregory as the lieutenant had passed by, hurrying on his way to headquarters with his important information whatever it was.

I knew that the telephone wires were tapped. But this fellow von Drakenfels was almost uncanny. Not only had he kept Gregory under surveillance but he knew instantly, in spite of the code message, when my lieutenant started for headquarters to report information. Von Drakenfels had struck with brutal swiftness.

Investigation disclosed that no one had seen the murder. The body had been found by a ration detail.

News travels fast even in a division of twenty-seven thousand men and I could sense the boiling anger in this division as the men became aware of the fact that von Drakenfels had added another cold-blooded murder to his other crimes.

I hurried straightway to Gregory's dugout. Here I found everything in disorder. The contents of Gregory's musette bag were scattered all over his cot, his note book was gone and his code diagrams had been taken. On the table, secured by an empty bottle, was the inevitable note. I snatched it up with an impatient hand.

"Sorry," it said laconically, "but this fellow unfortunately became a nuisance to me. So far you, Captain Steele, and your aides Cameron, Waite and Truby are safe. I don't consider your combined brains worth wasting a bullet upon! Yours cordially, von Drakenfels."

And that was that. My job now was to find out what poor Gregory had started to report. One of the machine gun officers had seen him about ten minutes before he was shot. He told me that Gregory had brought up a doughboy prisoner to the battalion P.C. at the point of a pistol and turned him over to a guard. . . .

"What's become of that prisoner?" I asked.

He had been sent toward Divisional P.C. in charge of two military police.

"Did Lieutenant Gregory give any explanation of the arrest of the soldier?" he asked. The adjutant shook his head. I noticed the sergeant major standing by looking as though he wished to say something.

"What is it, Sergeant?" I asked.

"Nothing much, sir, but I noticed that Lootenant Gregory had a rifle grenade in his other hand when he brought that bird up here in arrest and the rifle grenade looked kinda funny because it was in two pieces, hollow like as though it was empty."

That was the exact hint I needed. Suddenly I knew what Gregory had tried to report to me. He had paid with his life for discovering von Drakenfels' method of getting his messages across to the German trenches. They were fired in rifle grenades over No-Man's-Land. That much was learned by Gregory's death.

Evidently the German spy had confederates amongst the soldiers. It was important to find out what had become of the fellow whom Gregory had captured and sent back with the two M.P.'s. It didn't take more than twenty minutes' search to locate the two M.P.'s. Their bodies stabbed again and again, by what must have been a trench knife, were found in an empty dugout between the machine gun battalion P.C. and headquarters. Of the prisoner they had been escorting there was not the slightest trace. He had disappeared in thin air.

Reports of the two additional murders ran through the division with all the swiftness of bad news. I wouldn't have given a snap of my fingers for von Drakenfel's life if he had been captured by any one of the twenty-seven thousand officers and men of that division.

I got word immediately to Waite, Truby and Cameron, telling them to watch out along the front line trenches for rifle grenades. I also notified division headquarters, going up there and telling the colonel myself.

"What is it now?" snarled old Hezekiah. "What are you going to do, wait until every man in the division is murdered before you find that blankety blank German?"

I tried hard to keep from stuttering I was so blame mad, but went on with my report in spite of it.

". . . and Colonel, I'll have to ask you to call a conference of all the divisional intelligence officers tonight at ten o'clock to meet at the machine gun battalion P.C."

The colonel growled at this, but made a note nevertheless on his memorandum pad.

"What in blazes you want with a conference I don't know," he grumbled, "and besides, the machine gun battalion P.C. is pretty close to the enemy lines to assemble so many officers."

"That's just the reason I'm holding it there, Colonel," I said, and lit out before the Old Man had a chance to ask any questions.

Waite, Truby and Cameron were assembled outside when I appeared.

"What about those two birds, Lieutenant Solberg and Captain Stempful?" I asked.

Waite reported nothing unusual concerning Solberg, but Cameron spoke up.

"I went through Captain Stempful's dugout," said the slow-speaking, slow moving lieutenant, "and I found his pistol barrel fouled from a recent shot, also only four cartridges in his magazine instead of five."

"Good," I nodded, "keep on watching them both." And then I detailed them each to a sector of the front line, keeping that part that was held by the machine gun battalion for myself.

"I'll watch out there," I said, "but for Pete's sake, you three keep your eyes and ears open. That fellow von Drakenfels is going to try more murder sure as shooting. . . ."

"You'd bettah kinda watch yoh step yohself, Captain," advised Lieutenant Truby, the soft voiced southerner. If this heah von Drakenfels knows that you done put a crimp in his gettin' his messages ovah with rifle grenades he's goin' to act right peevish."

The others echoed this warning, but I shrugged my shoulders impatiently.

"I'll watch my step," I stated. "The first thing I'm going to do is to investigate the strip of trench held by the machine gun battalion. Along there our trenches are nearer to the enemy than any other part of the line. Keep in touch with Collins at headquarters. Turn up at the conference at ten o'clock." And with that I headed towards the machine gun battalion sector once more.

Supper hour had come and gone and darkness was descending. I went blithely on my way, unaware of the fact that the word had already gone out for my death. How it went forth no one seemed to know, but it was preceded by a buzz of excitement through the division. Word came to everyone almost simultaneously that the German spy had at last been sighted and recognized. It came by telephone and by word of mouth; it flew on mysterious wings so rapidly that in a very short space of time almost every man in the division was seeking the man described so carefully in the message.

"Von Drakenfels is posing as an American captain in the intelligence service," went the unvarying warning, "he is a stockily built, red faced young officer, who suffers from a slight impediment in his speech when excited. Don't take any chances with him, if he puts up the slightest resistance to arrest, shoot and shoot to kill!"

It was a diabolically clever move at that, and I went cheerfully on my way towards the machine gun sector blissfully ignorant of the fact that an almost perfect description of me had been broadcast to the division as the description of a man who should be shot down on sight like a mad dog.

The worst of it was that every soldier in that division was so filled with rage at the German spy that he was determined to take the law in his own hands should he meet with the fellow who had caused so much grief to the division.

I went on my way ignorant of the danger that surrounded me and thinking of the conference I had called tonight. Everything depended upon that conference, for I was certain that von Drakenfels would be there in person.

The hard problem would be to make the German spy, who would undoubtedly be cleverly disguised, expose his true colors amongst all the officers who would be gathered there. But I had evolved a scheme for this and had made my arrangements to carry it out.

Thinking more of the problem ahead of me than the route which I was following, I rounded the jutting trench wall just as a light flashed from the interior of a dugout. It was only a second's flash as the blanket before the entrance was raised and dropped again, but in that second I must have stood outlined in the lantern's rays.

The trench was plunged into darkness again, but I heard an exclamation ahead of me. Some instinct of danger made me pause a second when suddenly I felt powerful arms gripping me and felt the muzzle of an automatic pistol shoved into the pit of my stomach in no gentle manner.

"Hands up!" rasped an unpleasant voice in my ear, and I obeyed quickly. The beam of a flashlight leaped out in the darkness and played for a second on my face and form and then was flashed off again.

"By God! We've got him!" rasped that unpleasant voice again, and the pistol muzzle was shoved more deeply into my stomach.

"Who are you, fella?" asked a voice out of the darkness.

"Ca-ca-captain S-s-ss-steele"—my tongue became twisted in my excitement and anger at this abrupt hold up, and I stuttered out the words—"m-m-m-m-military intelligence s-s-s-sec-section ge-ge-ge-general headquarters. Who are you and wh-wh-what do you m-m-m-mean bub-bub-bub-bub-by holding me up in this fashion?" I was mad clear through. But the ominous silence which greeted my words chilled me instantly.

"Guess there ain't any doubt about it now," came a voice from his right.

"Not on your tintype there ain't—short, stocky, red faced and stuttered when he's excited—" rasped the unpleasant voice again. "Hey Mr. Boche spy, we kinda got you this time. . . ."

"You men are crazy!" I expostulated.

"Yeah? Crazy like a fox," retorted the man who was holding the gun in the pit of my stomach; then addressing his companions. "What'll we do with the ——?" he asked.

"Now we got him, can't take no chances on his gittin' away," returned the unpleasant voice. "Best thing is to give him the works before he pulls any funny stuff."

"Hadn't we better take him to some officer?" asked the first voice uncertainly.

"Some officer, hell!" retorted the unpleasant voice. "Ain't no use beating about the bush. Crack down on him and get it over with . . ."

"Listen here, you men"—the gravity of my situation had steadied me up and given me control over my twisted speech—"you are making an awful mistake. Take me to an officer and let me identify myself . . ."

As yet I did not realize the peril in which I stood, being much less concerned about my own life than I was about this danger of interruption to my carefully laid plans. Much depended on them, the success of my entire mission.

A silence greeted my words.

It was broken by the voice of the man who held the pistol.

"He speaks purty good United States," he commented uncertainly.

"Yeah? He speaks purty good United States! What d'you suppose them Germans is? Nitwits? O' course he speaks purty good United States. They ain't sendin' over any guys that talks like Dutch comedians to act as spies. Crack down on him and get it over with!"

"I tell you, you are making a mistake you men—" I began.

"Stow that chin music, you —— Heinie, or I'll knock all your front teeth down your neck!" threatened the unpleasant rasping voice, then went on, "gwan, Slabsides, crack down on him! You got the pistol!"

"Yeah," answered the other uncomfortably, "but it kinda seems to me we'd ought to wait and be sure. . . ."

"Sufferin' tripe!" exploded the other. "Here! gimme that gat!"

I stood with every nerve and muscle paralyzed.

There was a movement in the darkness in front of me. The pressure of the pistol muzzle against my stomach was relieved for a second. A frightful calm descended upon me. I waited for death without any other feeling than a numbed indifference, my brain picturing the pulling of the trigger and the explosion of the shell, with the .45 automatic bullet tearing and rending its way through my internal organs. The pistol muzzle was again pressed into my stomach.

"This is where you get yours, you —— squarehead!" rasped the unpleasant voice. There was a ringing in my ears and I heard the man's voice as from a vast distance.

"The blankety blank lousy gat is clogged!" growled the man in front of him.

Suddenly my faculties cleared as if by magic. I brought my arms down from over my head and struck blindly into the darkness, putting the full force of my body behind the blow.

Someone went down before me. A yell went up from behind me and more forms appeared in the darkness. A huge fist swung at me out of the blackness, scraping my face cruelly. I drove at the vast bulk of someone in front and smashed again and again until the man collapsed with a grunt.

Hands were clawing at my shoulders and head, and I spun about and struck in the darkness.

Suddenly I heard an authoritative voice call out. There was a flash of light. At that second I felt a jarring blow and must have passed out.

I dimly remember being dragged along and hearing a confused roaring in my ears. Again I became aware of the light, a glow which became stronger and stronger until at last I could dimly see. I found myself tied in a chair with a row of faces in front of me and someone dousing cold water on my head. A voice was speaking above me.

". . . So it seems to be pretty conclusively proved that we have got our man at last," said the voice. "First we have his forged orders bringing him to the division. Secondly we have found on his person a notebook in German. Thirdly, we found these codes which are unknown to us and are undoubtedly the latest codes of the German general staff!" I looked up dizzily and made out the gold pince-nez of Major Harkness who was standing above me holding some paper in his hand. He was the one that was doing the talking.

Looking about I saw that I was in the machine gun battalion P.C. and that the place was filled with the divisional intelligence officers, amongst whom I saw Lieutenant Solberg and Captain Stempful, both of them staring at me unwinkingly.

"You can see," went on Major Harkness, "that this fellow answers perfectly to the description of him broadcasted this evening, for he is short and compactly built and red faced. The two men who arrested him state that when accosted he stuttered very badly in his surprise."

I saw conviction grow in the eyes that were staring at me. They were cold eyes, all of them, and I read no mercy in their depths.

"Have you anything to say, Captain von Drakenfels?" Major Harkness turned his gold pince-nez upon me, and his cold blue eyes gleamed frostily behind them.

Again that telltale stutter twisted my tongue as it always does when I am excited.

"W-w-what time is it?" I asked.

Somebody growled, "ten-ten," and I closed my eyes.

Suddenly attention was turned away from me as a terrific racket came from outside. Machine guns were playing a devil's tattoo with the rattle and roar of automatic rifles forming an accompaniment while the deeper boom of high explosive shells furnished the bass. Several of the officers looked worried.

Louder and louder grew the racket while those nearest the door started out. In another second they suddenly rushed back into the room.

"The Germans are in our trenches!" they yelled.

The words were hardly out of their mouths before there came a deep toned shout and a clump of boots. The doorway was filled with bulky figures clad in field gray and wearing queer shaped coal scuttle helmets.

A German officer strode into the room.

"Shoot down these swine!" I heard him order. Obedient, his soldiers crowded in and spread out, leveling their rifles at the inmates of the room.

The American officers stood as if turned to carved statues. There was silence for a space. It seemed as though those Germans would never fire. Suddenly a high pitched voice broke the silence.

"Stop! *Schweinhund!*" screamed the voice in German.

The German officer looked at the man above me, startled. *"Wehr sind sie?* Who are you?" he asked brusquely.

"Ich bin Erich, Freiherr von Drakenfels," returned the voice arrogantly. The officers in that room stared uncomprehendingly at Major Harkness. I jerked my head towards him.

The German officer at the door clumped across the room, his face shadowed within the coal scuttle helmet. Arrived before this Major Harkness who had just announced himself as the Baron von Drakenfels, the German officer did a surprising thing. For suddenly he shoved an automatic pistol in the stomach of the pseudo Major Harkness.

"Hands up!" growled the German officer, and then spoke to me out of the corner of his mouth. "Well, suh," he said, "it kinda looks as though we all done got ouah man. Come on over here Waite and untie the Captain."

Thank God! the adjutant had carried out my orders!

It took that group in there a full minute to realize what had happened, and it took them several minutes to realize that the whole thing was a put up job. It was the adjutant from divisional headquarters who came up rubbing his hands gleefully.

"A pretty good bunch of fake Heine soldiers I turned out for you, Captain, eh?" he asked. But I was busy watching the play of emotions showing itself on von Drakenfels' face as he stood there, his wrists linked together with a pair of handcuffs.

"Well, Herr Baron," I said, "perhaps now you'll stop writing me those sassy letters."

"I admit to the mistake of having underrated your capabilities," he said, bowing formally. "May I ask you how you conceived this scheme?"

Old Colonel Hezekiah came puffing in then, his jaw open in surprise.

"Yes, Herr Baron, I'd be glad to tell you. You probably remember a certain book of fiction in my dugout. It was, as you remember a collection of stories called *The Justice of the Duke*. Had you read one of those stories instead of writing me a sassy letter you would have found that one of Cesare Borgia's spies was captured by this same ruse away back in the days of the

Renaissance. Sometimes it pays to read fiction, eh, Colonel?"

But von Drakenfels said nothing as he was marched away, and the colonel said even less.

But the Old Man borrowed my book before I returned to Paris and, confound his tintype, he hasn't returned it to this day!

The Road Without Turning

THE TWO MEN WERE SOMEWHAT SIMILAR IN APPEARANCE, both being rangy in build and tall. But the German looked like a professional soldier. Kurt von Kelnitz always sat erect in his chair and wore his field gray as though he had been poured into it. On the other hand the Britisher, behind the desk, slouched in his khaki with that elaborate carelessness which gives an English officer the air of having only recently donned the uniform and of being willing to doff it as quickly.

"What a heavy footed fellow that sentry is," complained Von Kelnitz, breaking the silence.

The British officer nodded, and the two of them listened, their faces turned toward the corridor just beyond the door. Out there a sentinel walked steadily. His footfalls receded thirty paces down the hall, where he made an about-face and returned, the solid clump of his boots growing steadily louder until he passed the door.

From the courtyard at the far end of the corridor there came the crash of grounded arms and the staccato challenge and reply as the midnight guard went through the centuries-old custom of the Transfer of the Keys. Both men glanced at the clock, the British officer furtively, the German calmly.

Again that oppressive silence fell between them. It was broken only by the sound of the scratching of the pen as the German officer finished his letter. At last he signed it, folded it and placed it within the envelope, writing the address in precise fashion. His face impassive, he handed it to the British officer.

"You will see that it reaches her, Dick?" he asked.

"Of course," said the Britisher hastily and placed the letter on the desk with a trace of awkwardness.

The German glanced about the small stone-walled room.

"It's a picturesque old place, this Tower of London," he said, and there came a glint of amusement into his eyes. "Picturesque, ancient and outmoded, like your creaky old British Empire, Dick."

The Englishman, Major Richard Fortescue, smiled at the sally.

"Remember, Kurt, before the war, at the Embassy in Berlin, that big argument we had concerning the relative potency of schnapps and Scotch whisky?" he countered.

The German officer removed the monocle from his eye and twisted it about between finger and thumb.

"Will I ever forget the headache that next morning! *Ach! Du lieber Gott!* It felt as though it had been hit by a battering ram, that head."

"You were a *Leutnant* of Uhlans then, Kurt, and a bachelor. It must have been after I left that you married. Tell me, were you married before or after the war?"

"Before the war," responded the German. "We were married secretly, for I did not have the permission of his Majesty."

The British officer glanced down at the envelope on his desk.

"She was French, was she not?"

"Yes, she was. We met in Berlin, while she was visiting distant relatives. I fell madly in love with her, finally persuading her to marry me. She had no immediate relatives except a younger brother, and so there wasn't *that* kind of interference."

"In spite of that, it must have been a little complicated," said the Britisher. "How about your corps of officers? Tell me about it and tell me what happened to you at the outbreak of war."

The British officer handed him his cigar case, from which the German selected and lighted one, bowing from the waist in thanks. After carefully clipping the cigar with a small gold clip attached to his watchchain, he lighted it and took a long puff before replying.

"As you say, Dick, the marriage was a little complicated. I ran the risk of a court-martial for marrying without the permission of the Kaiser. I also risked the displeasure of the corps of officers for selecting a wife from what was soon to be an enemy country. But that was not all."

The German flicked the white ash from the end of his cigar and stared reflectively at the end of the glowing tip. Major Fortescue glanced in furtive fashion at the clock, looking quickly away again. He cleared his throat nervously.

"Tell me about it, Kurt, from the beginning. You have never told me your experiences at the commencement of the war, and I have often wondered if you found an opportunity to get into action with your Uhlans."

Kurt von Kelnitz needed little urging.

Yes, it had been a little complicated, that marriage. At first the girl was none too willing to hurry things, and there were legal formalities to be gone through. But they were married quietly out at one of Berlin's suburbs just before the girl returned to France.

At the time there was much talk of war between their countries. He had received several letters from her until the war situation grew more tense and it was forbidden to correspond. Thereafter he did not hear from her. Yes, he had led his Uhlans into battle.

His regiment was one of the first to be ordered to the frontier and was sent up to the north.

He felt exceedingly joyous that day, and when word came at last, ordering them across the frontier, his men cheered loudly for the Fatherland and the Kaiser. They crossed over with the entire regiment singing.

Kurt was only a *Leutnant* then, but he had absolute confidence in his platoon of some twenty-four lances. They carried the tubular steel lance and wore the flat topped, black leather *Schapka*, the distinctive Uhlan headgear. They were well mounted, his men, on sleek Hanoverian horses, standing fifteen two hands high, the least of them. The cavalry orders were to work in cooperation with the machine guns and the armored motor cars. This he did not like so well, for he wanted opportunity to lead his platoon thundering gloriously against the enemy.

For the first few kilometers they saw no sign of the French. They reasoned that the enemy forces had been withdrawn from the frontier.

Kurt's platoon was flung out as a scouting force in advance. He trotted them along the road and through the woods, passing through the cobbled streets of gray stone villages whose inhabitants remained concealed behind shuttered windows. Despite his light heartedness and the thrilling sense of adventure that possessed him, the silence and the deserted appearance of the countryside began to oppress him as something slightly sinister.

Moreover, he was worried about his wife. Somewhere along the line upon which he was marching lay the château of Sevrey-sur-Aisne, where "Mademoiselle" Odette de Sevrey lived with her younger brother, Vicomte de Sevrey, whom Kurt had never met. It had been weeks since he had received a letter from her, since the war situation had become menacing. Naturally enough, he was worried and anxious to see her again.

What troubled Kurt more than the silence from his wife was the fact that the château of Sevrey-sur-Aisne lay right in the path of the enormous German thrust toward Paris.

So much, however, was Kurt the soldier that, despite his personal feelings, he could not help but thrill to the realization that he was an integral part of that thrust. To his right and left, as far as he could see, squadrons were breaking out of the woods and crossing the fields and sweeping onward in a wave of horsemen. Behind him the earth trembled to the tramp of hordes of infantry and reverberated to the clank and heave of great guns. *Der Tag* had arrived and the Fatherland was on the march!

Some eight kilometers behind the frontier they had their first brush with the enemy. His *Feldwebel* called his attention to the farmyard ahead of them at the turn of the road.

"If it is permitted to speak, *Herr Leutnant*"—the slow spoken Bavarian pointed to the farmyard. Kurt von Kelnitz signaled a halt.

"Speak up, and be quick about it!" Kurt barked impatiently.

"*Herr Leutnant*, truly—I think—it seems there are enemy soldiers in that farmyard!"

Scarcely had the words left the *Feldwebel's* lips when something pinged viciously into the bark of a tree near at hand and in another second they heard the crack of a rifle. The *Leutnant* drove his platoon to the shelter of the trees on the side of the road and rode forward himself to reconnoiter, keeping close to the edge of the woods. The *Feldwebel* had spoken truly, for now Kurt could see men in blue coats and red breeches moving about the barnyard.

He watched the spurt of dust from the muzzles of the rifles they were firing. He turned to give orders to his platoon when he heard the clank and creak of machine gun carts coming up the road behind him. Their commander, a fat and pimpled officer, came trotting up. The officer was not too fat, however, to make quick work of getting his guns into action, and in a few seconds two Maxims were chattering from the edge of the woods and the red trousered enemy had disappeared from view.

Taking advantage of the situation, Von Kelnitz galloped his platoon across the intervening space in open order and arrived at the farmyard to find three or four dead and several wounded Frenchmen. It was his first sight of enemy casualties and he rode on sobered by the view.

He noted on his map that the road he was following would eventually take him within two or three kilometers of the Château de Sevrey-sur-Aisne. His platoon was well out on the right of the regimental patrol sector. Upon climbing a hill he saw, still farther to the right, a platoon of the Death's Head

Hussars in their gray fur busbies. He waved to their officer and received a punctilious salute in reply. They were lighter men on lighter horses, those Hussars, and personally he was of the opinion that his own husky Uhlans could account for twice their number of Hussars—which is what a young officer should think.

In the late afternoon an action developed somewhere off at the left. Then for the first time he heard the thud and smash of the artillery in action. He found his men listening gravely to the sound, all of them soberly elated. A few minutes later, after throwing out pickets, he halted the platoon and watered horses at an inn whose frightened landlord served his men with good red wine and bread which they ate and drank with their sausage. The fighting on the left died down. Toward dusk there were sporadic bursts of rifle fire, but distant and of no consequence.

That night they bivouacked in an abandoned mill and fed their horses from sacks of grain. The *Leutnant* inspected his outposts between dawn and daylight. He had placed four double sentry posts on duty—one outside the mill, one to the right of the village, one to the left, the fourth one in front at the edge of the woods. Toward morning he heard the rumble of heavy gunfire from the north. Stopping to listen to this for a moment, he continued his inspection.

It was when he was approaching the outpost to the right of the village that he was brought up short by a sharp challenge:

"*Wer da?*" growled the sentry, and Kurt heard the snick of a breech bolt.

He had placed no sentry here and, after identifying himself, he strode up to the man. It was Private Klimtsig of the third section.

"What are you running around all over the place for, you fool?" he stormed.

"But, *Herr Leutnant*"—stammered Klimtsig—"but there is something wrong at the post at the edge of the woods. I heard a groan come from there and they do not answer when we call."

Wasting no further words on the sentry, the *Leutnant* drew his Luger and ran toward the point. It was dark at the edge of the woods and he snapped his flashlight. Its beam showed him two bodies sprawled on the ground. The two Uhlans, Shultz and Willer, with their throats cut from ear to ear. Their weapons were gone.

The platoon was ominously silent when they heard the news. After burying their comrades the next morning they went on with a new spirit of hatred among them. Plainly, reasoned the *Leutnant*, it had been the work of Frenchmen of the same type as those armed civilians who had prowled about the armies of 1870. The *Leutnant* registered a vow that it would go badly with any civilians whom he found with weapons in their hands.

With a few brushes with a small patrol of enemy cavalry to enliven the next day, they continued on, dropping back once into the regimental support and being sent forward again. The fighting now grew heavier in the north and raged all of one day and far into the night. Word finally came that the French and English had been driven back.

"Did you run into any English patrols?" asked Major Fortescue, interrupting the German officer's even toned recital of his experiences.

"Not then, Dick, but several days later," replied Kurt von Kelnitz, listening to the clatter outside in the corridor as the sentinel was changed, and continuing his story as the receding clump of the heavy booted, relieving detachment diminished down the corridor and lost itself in the courtyard. The German glanced at the clock, noting that it was 2 A.M., at which time the second relief went on post in most armies.

No, he had not seen any British troopers, but he had heard that the Death's Head Hussars at his right had had a brush with a squadron of British Dragoons in which the honors were about evenly divided; they both drew swords and charged, coming to collision in the middle of the village street.

About this time the *Leutnant* was growing anxious for a sight of that château which sheltered his wife. Fortunately, his regiment shifted its sector toward the right, and at last he found himself leading his platoon to the Aisne River, crossing below the village and the Château de Sevrey-sur-Aisne.

Several kilometers away he saw the tall, gray stone towers of the château, with their conical pointed roofs rising above the village. His heart skipped a beat or two as he gazed upon the roof that sheltered his beloved. He was riding at the time through a scattering of houses at the edge of a stone quarry on the far bank of the Aisne. His scouts were well forward and to the flank, but as he passed the mouth of the quarry he heard the crack of a rifle from the edge of the woods to the right of the road, not three hundred meters away.

Almost simultaneously with the rifle's crack he heard a grunt behind him and turned to find his *Feldwebel* staring stupidly at his right side. Something dark was spreading over the man's tunic.

"If it is permitted to speak—*Herr*—*Leutnant*"—coughed the *Feldwebel*, and suddenly with a horrified look in his eyes the poor fellow swayed out of his saddle and slumped heavily to the ground.

His horse snorted and reared aside.

Some one caught the frightened animal while the *Leutnant* drew his Luger automatic and, waving to his men to follow, galloped toward the point whence the shot had come. His men crashed into the trees on either side of him as he rode through. There was no trace of any one in the woods and no sign of a living thing until he leaped his horse out on the far side of the woods at the edge of a slightly sunken road which bordered the field.

Here he came upon three of his men surrounding a young Frenchman with a bicycle. As the *Leutnant* arrived, one of the Uhlans stabbed at the youth with his lance, but the young Frenchman warded off the blow by catching the steel point in the spokes of his rear wheel. At the *Leutnant's* shout the Uhlans gave back and one of them dismounted quickly and searched the Frenchman. There was no weapon upon him.

The other Uhlans rode in, reporting that they had found nothing. He'd hidden it well somewhere, no doubt. Suddenly the memory of that agonized look in the *Feldwebel's* eyes rose up in the *Leutnant's* mind. With it came that memory of the sight of his two Uhlans with their throats cut. Something like a red mist enveloped him and he felt his temples throbbing. As from a distance he heard his voice issuing commands.

A section of the Uhlans dismounted swiftly, dragging their carbines from their boots. An *Unteroffizier* was binding the youth's hands behind him and backing him against a tree. There was something unreal and dream-like about the whole thing. The *Leutnant* found the eyes of the young Frenchman fixed upon him with something a little proud and a little contemptuous in their depths. There was no sign of fear or cringing as the section of Uhlans lined up with their rifles. The young Frenchman looked up at the sky and around at the trees. The *Leutnant* remembered, strangely enough, the beauty of that summer afternoon and knew what the man before him was thinking.

It was all over so swiftly that the *Leutnant* scarcely knew what had happened and he stared rather stupidly at the huddled body at the foot of the tree and felt his eardrums still ringing to the crash of the volley. Like some detached spectator, he watched while the *Unteroffizier* placed his pistol to the ear of the fallen youth and fired the "mercy shot."

Mechanically Kurt von Kelnitz reached for the articles the *Unteroffizier* had removed from the pockets of the slain youth. There were three or four letters, a small leather covered notebook, a sterling silver cigaret case with some design upon it and a monogrammed handkerchief.

Leaving the body to lie where it fell, he led his men back to the road again and resumed his march toward the river crossing.

He was still in a daze from the swiftness of the tragedy he had just witnessed, but was suddenly brought back alertly to the present by the crackle of rifle fire from the far side of the bridge just ahead. Halting his platoon, he waited for his scouts to gallop in. They came, reporting a small enemy force on the far side of the bridge in an old factory building.

The fire grew hotter as he listened. Another one of his scouts rode in, reporting that the two men and horses on the point of the advance group had been killed and were lying on the approach to the bridge.

Dismounting his Uhlans, he led them forward behind the shelter of some piles of firewood and gave them order to fire. Scarcely had their carbines begun to bark when the return fire from the enemy broke out along the far bank and back among the houses. Such strength did it develop that he shortly gave the order to cease firing and withdrew his force from its exposed position.

Back among his horses he drew forth his map and carefully plotted the coordinates of the enemy position across the river and wrote them down on a message blank, being careful, however, to delimit the area so as to exclude the château. This done, he wrote a message in two copies, tore it from his notebook and dispatched two messengers.

Across the river the rifle fire died down and the area gave signs of being evacuated by the enemy. Normally he would have followed up with his platoon, but the messages he had sent made this impossible and he was forced to wait.

It was nearly twenty minutes before he heard the sound for which he waited, the deep toned barking of fieldpieces far to the rear. This was succeeded by the sound of the passage of swiftly hurrying missiles in the air overhead and the boom and crash of exploding shells on the luckless village across the river.

It moved like clockwork, that barrage, sweeping with steel fingers from the river's edge up through the village to the edge of the hill whereon rested the château. All in between those limits was a churning inferno of riven stone and shattering steel and quick rising clouds of dust and torn timbers. That deluge of steel rained out of the sky for thirty pitiless minutes and then ceased as abruptly as it had started. It was as simple as turning off the spray of a garden hose.

Heading his platoon, he rode over the bridge and stared in wonder at the smashed village. Roofs sagged crazily and houses leered drunkenly through what was left of windows and doors, while the street was pitted with shell holes and cluttered with beams and fragments of building stone. Over the whole desolation a heavy dust hung suspended in the still air, while from several half obliterated buildings tongues of flame licked out and spewed forth clouds of smoke which cast a pall over the scene. Here and there, bodies lay amid the wreckage, but there were few of these. Evidently the inhabitants had vacated the place before the bombardment had started.

Picking his way carefully through the debris, he led his platoon up the hill toward the château and arrived to find the great iron gates locked and bolted. Two carved stone lions stared down indifferently. Peering through the iron bars, he could see people scurrying here and there beyond the moat. There seemed to be many people about, both in the courtyard and in the park, for he could see past the angle of the nearest tower, down into the park, whose green of lawn and massed trees was relieved here and there by the white marble of graceful statues.

One of his men hammered on the gate with his lance butt, demanding admission, until a white faced and trembling concierge nervously unlocked and flung wide the iron portals.

The *Leutnant* rode in first, looking eagerly around the courtyard and at the long windows, hoping to catch sight of his wife, but the people he had seen had disappeared by now and there was no one in view except a nervous servant who stood by the great door in livery and knee breeches.

The *Leutnant* paid no attention to this man, but dismounted and strode through the entrance hall, carrying his saber under his arm.

It was a stately hall in which he found himself, with its white marble staircase stretching up to the right and great doors opening into a marble floored salon on the left. He caught an instant glimpse of portraits and statues lining the walls before he heard a light footstep on the stairs.

Turning about, he looked up and saw his wife standing there above him. He took a single quick step forward, his hands outstretched, but dropped them to his sides and stood very straight as she came slowly down the last few steps and stood before him. Clicking his heels and bowing low from the waist, he waited for her to speak.

"I had thought, Kurt, to welcome you to the château under happier circumstances than these," she said. Her voice was low and full of pain.

"This war that has come between our countries," he said, "is there any reason that it should come between us?" But she made no reply to this, only swayed a little on her feet as though feeling faint.

Then came a clatter and a racket in the courtyard, and he stood to attention and saluted as several staff officers and the brigade-general strode briskly in.

His squadron was assigned to guard this headquarters and for the next few days he was on duty at the château. It was after his arrival that the first check to the German advance had come. With victory almost in their grasp, the German army had been held from the prize. And all due to the stupidity of one man, that fool of a *Leutnant-general*.

"Against stupidity even the gods themselves fight in vain," Kurt quoted. Yes, so it was.

At any rate the lull gave him time to see his wife and to attempt to win her to his way of thinking. She was horribly distressed, for her younger brother whom she adored had disappeared the day the Uhlans had arrived. She was distraught with worry over this and his task was to attempt to comfort her on this score and to prevail upon her to leave this war torn area. For, as he had told her, the château was doomed and there was no safety for her in France, for the armies of the war lord were invincible. To the suggestion that she travel to his own home in Germany she demurred hotly, having no wish to be a lonely French woman amid hostile Germans.

They compromised at last upon Switzerland.

She was extremely downcast at the prospect of leaving the château, for she was the *chatelaine* and in obedience to age old custom the people of the surrounding farms and villages had sought sanctuary behind the medieval walls of this old stronghold. Because of this she had remained at her post alone, her brother having disappeared on the approach of the Uhlans.

Altogether it was a very sad time, this strange honeymoon of theirs with the war between their two countries to sadden them and the uncertain future making them anxious. And in addition to these things the thought of her brother was on her mind day and night.

"He is a little wild, is Raoul," she told Kurt, "but I have been a foster mother to him. Please try to find a trace of him and send word to me immediately that you hear anything."

There was little time left. Orders came, sending his squadron once more upon the march. That night the officers gave them a banquet in the great hall and many deep toned German toasts were drunk to the pale and none too happy looking bride.

It was a strange banquet, by candlelight in the marble hall, with the faces of her ancestors staring down from the walls in grim disapproval, and the officers of the staff and of the regiment massed in their alien uniforms.

"And your colonel and your officer corps, they made no objection, Kurt?" asked the Englishman curiously.

"No"—the German shook his head—"she was very beautiful and *that* they understood," he answered; and then he added, "Also, she is of high and noble family."

The time was short, for the regiment was to march at midnight. He said goodbye to her from the saddle two hours later and rode into the darkness, leaving her behind with her promise that she would make her way to Paris and from there to Switzerland. She would write to him.

And write she did, for her letters came to him down in front of Amiens and out to East Prussia, where he was sent for several exciting months, and back again to the solemn corridors of the Greater General Staff building in Berlin, where he was put in the intelligence section.

It was known to his chiefs that he had spent many years in England and it was evident that he looked more English than German and could pass anywhere for an upper class Britisher. These things made it almost foreordained that he should be picked for important espionage duty when the time should arise and the need become great.

And that need became great a month or two before the Battle of Cambrai. Word had filtered through to the Greater General Staff that the British were experimenting with some new instrument of war. Increasing reports of this came in, but there was no knowledge as to what form this new instrument would take. And to be forewarned is to be forearmed.

Three higher officers, one after the other, had failed to discover any information of these new instruments until at last one day the *Leutnant*, now promoted to *Rittmeister*, was called in by the chief of his bureau and given orders to prepare to go in disguise and find out what was behind these rumors.

"My word," interrupted the British officer, "you had rumors about the tanks that far ahead?"

"Surely," returned Kurt von Kelnitz, selecting a fresh cigar.

There was during this pause the tramp of feet in the corridor and the eyes of the British officer slid quickly around to the clock again. The German officer stared at it as well, noticing subconsciously that it was 4 A.M., the time for the third relief to go on post. There was the clatter of grounded arms, the low question and answer of the relieved and the relieving sentinel, the crisp orders of the corporal of the guard, and the old relief marched away while the new sentinel began his unhurried, steady footed march up and down the corridor.

The German officer lighted his cigar, then continued his story:

It was to find out about those infernal tanks that he, a baron and a *Rittmeister* of a proud regiment of Uhlans was to be sent forth like any common spy. And here Kurt von Kelnitz quoted a sonorous German saying: "Forward you must go, for backward you can no longer turn."

Besides that, his duty was to obey orders and it was for the Fatherland. Moreover, and here was a grain of satisfaction, his designated route led him through Switzerland. He would have opportunity to spend a few days with his bride.

He had clicked his heels, saluted and gone forth to make his preparations. Two days later he was with his wife. *Ach*, the loveliness of those four days by the lake!

(Kurt von Kelnitz quoted Schiller and became absent minded until the ash of his cigar dropped to his knee and brought him back to the present.)

She was beautiful and gracious and lovely and those few hours stolen from the war passed all too quickly. With her he left his suitcase containing his uniform and his decorations, all except one—the *Ordre pour le Mérite* which he wore on a ribbon around his neck.

"Kurt, you didn't tell me that you had won the *Ordre pour le Mérite*," interrupted Major Fortescue.

"Surely, and placed around my neck by his Majesty himself," answered the German composedly, and went on with his story, neglecting to state how he had won the highest decoration that a German officer can receive.

His wife clung to him on his departure from Switzerland, making him promise to write frequently; and he gave his word of honor as a German officer to write at least once a week. He was provided by his chiefs with an American passport under the name of Thomas Spaulding and it was agreed between them that he should write his letters to her addressed Mrs. Thomas Spaulding, Geneva. There was little difficulty in getting out of Switzerland and into France, for the German "underground railway" was extremely efficient.

He spent a day idling on the boulevards of Paris, sitting at the Café de la Paix where two or three people chatted with him of seemingly inconsequential matters before he departed for Boulogne. He underwent a rigorous examination from both British and French authorities at Boulogne, but his papers were perfect and there was little suspicion attached to traveling Americans at this time.

So complete had been the preparations made for him that his English accent was ascribed to Boston and he was provided with a fraternity pin and letters which purported to show that he was a graduate of Harvard.

Upon arrival in London he got in touch immediately with the chief of the German espionage system in Great Britain and lunched openly with him at Berkeley's and dined and danced with one of his assistants, a very beautiful woman, at the Savoy and the Cecil. It was at the former place that he had a narrow escape when one of the big footmen in knee breeches and silk stockings showed signs of recognizing him.

In spite of the fact that in former days he had handed the footman many a shilling tip in exchange for his hat and stick, he managed to look through and beyond the fellow with an assumption of indifference that seemed to convince the footman that he had made a mistake. After that close shave Von Kelnitz, who was now Mr. Thomas Spaulding of Boston, U.S.A., ran no further risks of that nature by appearing at his former haunts.

It was after his third or fourth day in London that a vague uneasiness began to descend upon him and he found himself filled with a species of jumpy, nervous watchfulness for which he could not account. He feared that it was some sixth sense trying to warn him that he had been discovered and was being watched. It was nothing tangible, but there constantly grew on him the feeling that he was being shadowed. He sought to shake it off by changing lodgings and for a few hours would succeed in finding a little surcease from the nervous strain only to have it recur.

He took to glancing behind him as he walked through the crowded streets, but in no case was he able to pick out any one individual who seemed to be shadowing him. While he was in London the chief of the German espionage service in Great Britain informed him that three of his most trusted agents had been arrested and removed within the past week. This did not operate to increase Kurt's store of confidence and he found himself growing heartily sick of his task, anxious to be done with it. Many and many a time he sighed for the cheerful jingle and steady thud of his squadron of Uhlans trotting behind him.

He waited anxiously for a letter from his wife in response to his own letter informing her that he had arrived safely. Her letter came at last, but it did not succeed in improving his spirits, for to his mind it sounded a little strained and cold and perfunctory. It might have been, he reasoned, that his soul was too filled with anxiety, too overburdened with the anguish of loneliness and worry for any letter from her to succeed in cheering him up and he might have been oversensitive. But at any rate he was more oppressed after her letters than before.

After all, for a man like him, accustomed to the gatherings of his gay fellow officers, it was a harsh fate to be out here alone on a dangerous mission in which discovery would mean an inglorious end at the hands of a firing squad.

Another letter from her came before he left London and this was couched in the same strained and perfunctory fashion. He grew a little alarmed and wondered what might have happened to chill her. In casting over possibilities the thought of that German uniform he had left in her charge returned to plague him. It occurred to him that she might have found something in the pockets that had upset her. But he had little time to speculate on these matters, for the information he had been seeking had come in volume enough to permit him to make his next move.

In other words, he had found out that the strange new weapons of war, which had been rumored, were actually in being and were reported present somewhere on Salisbury Plain. It was said that they were being tried out there behind a great wall of secrecy and heavy cordons of guards. There was nothing for him to do then but to go to Salisbury Plain and attempt to discover the secret.

He made his preparations very carefully, walking from his quarters with stick and gloves as though taking a stroll. Thereafter he rode in a tram for many squares, to alight and dart away in a taxicab. He ordered the driver to take him to the Whitechapel district, where he circled about and pursued a devious route until he was certain that any pursuer must be thrown off his scent. He finally paid off his driver, worked his way through a rabbit warren of streets and hailed another taxicab, which deposited him near the point where his own motor car with a trusted driver was awaiting him.

They slid out of London after dark, speeding toward Salisbury Plain at a good forty miles an hour. It was after they were well out of the glare of the city lights that he first noticed the headlights of that car which followed him so persistently. Mile after mile it followed behind him until at last he ordered his chauffeur to turn out his light and dart down a side road.

Obedient, the chauffeur did as he was directed and they fled along a country lane and made a detour of many miles between high hedges before they came again to the main highway. He looked back as they struck the main road and relaxed with a sigh of relief as he saw no sign of those annoying headlights.

But his relief was short lived. They had made scarcely a quarter of a mile when he noted a deeper shadow on the side of the road. Turning to watch it, he saw it moving silently along behind them. His pursuers had simply waited with lights out at the road junction of the most likely turn into the main road.

He confessed that something like an icy hand closed over his heart as he saw that relentless black shadow speeding along behind him, but "he must keep going forward for he could no longer turn back."

That infernal following car stuck closer than a brother. They were getting too uncomfortably near to Salisbury Plain now to permit of anything going wrong. Luckily the car with which Von Kelnitz was provided was a fast one; he needed every bit of speed he could manage for the next few minutes. Selecting a convenient turn in the road, he ordered the chauffeur to drive the car at the highest speed of which it was capable. Accordingly it shot down that length of road and around another turn at over a mile a minute.

Before the other car had a chance to pick up speed they managed to increase the distance to over three times what it had been. Meanwhile Von Kelnitz gathered his possessions together and clung on the runningboard. Again they rounded a turn.

"Now slow up!" he called, and the car was throttled down to a safe speed.

"Go like the devil as quickly as I jump!" he commanded.

He leaped out and rolled down a convenient bank while his car gathered speed and disappeared in the darkness ahead. Crouching there in the shadows of the embankment, he heard the following car thunder by overhead. After a safe interval of time had passed he arose, shook the gravel and dust out of his clothing and struck into a copse nearby. Here he unrolled his bundle and changed his clothing in the dark, hiding his neat tailored suit under a log and dressing himself in rough workman's clothing.

With a smear or two of grease on his face, with his hair rumpled up and with a soiled neckerchief knotted about his throat he was changed into a British navvy. His costume was complete even to a rough stick and a half empty bottle of liquor in one coat pocket and some bread and cheese wrapped in a newspaper in the other.

Thus disguised, he struck out for the nearest village. That night he slept in a straw pile on the outskirts of the village. The next morning he entered the village pub and, flinging a shilling or two on the bar, demanded bloaters and tea in excellent cockney dialect. Here he posed as a working man seeking employment, confessing boldly that he had drunk himself out of his last job.

This was all in keeping with the role he had assumed and the innkeeper and his servant and two or three hangers-on in the bar accepted him for what he was, treating him with the instinctive caution of villagers to the stranger within their midst. This was well enough, and he ate his meager breakfast in more or less comfort, considerably excited within himself at the nearness of his goal and the great prize in the way of information that lay so close.

All went well and he found himself feeling secure enough, until, happening to glance out of the window, he noticed the keeper of the pub in shirt sleeves and apron leaning against the gate, deep in conversation with a constable who had ridden up on a bicycle. As the two talked together Von Kelnitz saw the keeper of the pub jerk his head back toward the bar, pointing his thumb over his shoulder at the same time. The policeman leaned his bicycle against the hedge and came on up the path.

The rough looking navvy sprawled at the side of the table felt a clutch of fear go through him as the man entered the doorway and stared him up and down. He bore the scrutiny without flinching as far as any outward sign appeared, but inwardly he felt hot and cold chills run up and down his spine. It seemed an eternity before at last the policeman strolled toward him.

"Look 'ere, my man," said the policeman. " 'Oo are you an' wot are you a-doin' of in these parts?"

"Wot am Hi a-doin' of?" answered the navvy in honest indignation. "Carn't yer see wot Hi'm a-doin' of? My nyme's Halfred 'Iggins—"

"Well, 'Iggins, 'ow about showin' me some hidentification pypers?"

"Blimey! 'As it got to the pass where a honest workin' man carn't go abort a-lookin' fer a job without bein' held up by hevery hamateur polyceman along the road? What pypers d'ye want to be lookin' at? 'Ere they are. Look 'em over while Hi finish my meal."

So saying, the navvy handed over several greasy papers, treating the policeman with lofty indifference as that official glanced through them. The navvy munched solemnly at his breakfast until his well worn papers, which included among them a food card giving his local habitation and his name, were read through by the newcomer.

The German espionage system was nothing if not thorough. The policeman read the papers through laboriously and finally handed them back with a grunt.

"But look 'ere, my man, you'd best not be seen loafing about this district. Wot with the work bein' done by the military on Salisbury Plain stryngers aren't welcome. So finish yer breakfast and be on yer way."

"Right-o," returned the navvy cheerily.

But after leaving the village he circled back to the road again and kept on his way toward the plain. All that afternoon he lay up in a group of trees by the side of the road and watched heavily laden motor lorries go by. After dark they still continued to come and he crept nearer the road, watching for one that would be sufficiently slow for him to scramble aboard. At last his opportunity came—a huge lorry whose sides and top were covered with canvas. He swung himself up on the tail gate and down inside. He found the floor covered with bales of burlap sacking. Several of these bales were broken and he managed to conceal himself among the loose sacks. The motor lorry jerked and clanked along for what seemed to be an interminable length of time, but at last it drew up and lanterns flashed about it.

The rays of light from one of these fell on the interior of the truck and some one, whom Von Kelnitz judged to be a soldier, stuck his head in and made a perfunctory inspection. Then permission to go on was given and Von Kelnitz sighed thankfully as the machine resumed its progress. He felt it being backed into some sort of shed. The driver departed.

Pushing the sacks aside, Von Kelnitz rose and peered through the curtains, finding that his truck was one of a long row of military lorries parked in a huge shed. A sentinel appeared every five minutes or so, making his rounds, but Von Kelnitz figured out his posts and the time it took him to cover them and slipped across the opening of the shed and into the dark shadows on the far side.

There were more sheds to the right and left and directly ahead of him were great piles of forage covered with canvas. Moving along in the shadow of these, he worked along the line of buildings until he came to a group that was more strongly guarded and brilliantly lighted.

It was impossible to get by this cordon of sentries, but here, he reasoned, must be sheltered those secret machines which he had come to discover. There was little of the night left him by now, and he sought for shelter and a hiding place for the day. This he found in a pile of forage. He climbed up and under the canvas, arranging a place where he would be able to see the entrance of those strongly guarded buildings.

There he slept until he was aroused by a great clanking, roaring sound and awoke to find it was broad daylight.

From this concealed observation he thrilled at the sight of his first tank, a huge, oblong, steel box on peculiar caterpillar treads that came lurching and grinding out of the shed in front of him and waddled off across the field. It was followed by another and another until the air was heavy with the gas from their exhausts.

As each one passed he made a mental note of some fresh characteristic until as the last one waddled out of sight he had an accurate description of the cumbersome and the deadly looking machines, their armament, their construction and as much as he could gather of their interior arrangement and crews from one that halted and underwent some repairs not thirty yards away.

He was highly elated at his success so far. Here was the jealously guarded British secret which, transmitted to the German High Command, meant a great source of danger removed from the Fatherland. He was too keen a military man not to realize the potentialities of those great armored beasts and the overwhelming effect they would have upon startled infantry.

The next step was to get away with his information and send it to Berlin as quickly as possible. There was no hope of getting out of there before dark. He observed that practically every one was in uniform and even the workmen wore military overalls and seemed to be soldier mechanics.

All that day he lay stretched out under the canvas, cold and hungry and thirsty but borne up by the knowledge indelibly imprinted upon his brain. Night came at last and he stole from shadow to shadow, slipping through an inner line of guards by crawling on his stomach and coming at last to the outer line. Here he found barbed wire in front of him and worked along it, becoming panicky as he found no means of getting through. At last he came to a small gate guarded by a single sentry. The sentry was none too alert and Von Kelnitz was desperate. The consequence was that the luckless soldier, expecting no trouble from his rear, was suddenly knocked into oblivion and Von Kelnitz found himself outside the barbed wire.

Laying a course as best he could from what he remembered of the countryside, he walked all night until at last, more by good luck than anything else, he struck the main road to London. Not deeming it safe to resume his own costume, he hailed a passing char-à-banc and paid his fare into London.

So successful had he been that he decided to take a chance and made his way boldly toward the small hotel from which he could get in touch with the proper agents for transmitting his important information to Berlin.

As he stepped into the entrance hall of the hotel a heavy hand was dropped on his shoulder. He was swung about and felt the cold steel of handcuffs clicking into place over his wrists. . . .

"So that's my story, Dick," concluded Von Kelnitz, grinding out the remnants of his cigar. "But what puzzles me is how your people captured me so quickly. How soon after my arrival in London did they know of my presence?"

"About two days, Kurt," returned Major Fortescue gravely.

"And you shadowed me every moment thereafter?"

"No, not every moment. I must admit we lost you from the time you left that motor car near Salisbury Plain until the time you hailed that char-à-banc that carried you back to London."

"That char-à-banc had one of your men aboard?" asked the German.

"It had a group of our men aboard. It had been cruising up and down looking for you for twelve hours."

"That was very keen work," said the German admiringly, "but I still can't understand how you pierced my disguise. I was considered very clever."

"Oh, there were any number of ways," returned the Britisher noncommittally.

His eyes were a little haggard as he glanced at the clock. The hour hand pointed to 5 A.M. His ears were strained, listening to a sound which stirred in the courtyard, a sound compounded of the crash of grounded arms and the answering of men to a roll call.

"Yes, Dick," said Kurt von Kelnitz, quietly, "the time is very short. I cannot tell you how I appreciate your kindness in all that you have done for me, especially in sending for my uniform. Do you suppose my wife will understand why I wanted it?"

"I don't believe so, Kurt," said the Britisher gently.

The German nodded, satisfied, and then a slight frown gathered on his forehead.

"Do you know, Dick, that this uniform explained a little to me why my wife's letters seemed strained and perfunctory?"

The Britisher looked up swiftly.

"Yes," continued Von Kelnitz. "I told you, if you remember, that I feared she might find some letters in the pockets. Those letters were in the pocket when I left the uniform with her. And now the letters are no longer there."

"Have you been carrying on an affair with some one else, Kurt?"

The German shook his head gravely.

"No, nothing like that, but those letters and a leather covered notebook I had carried since that day when I ordered the execution of the young Frenchman near the bridge at Sevrey-sur-Aisne. They were the letters and the notebook that were taken from the pockets of the dead man."

The Britisher stared at him.

"You see, Dick, the letters belonged to him and were addressed with his name, and the notebook contained notes in his own handwriting."

"And the name?" asked the Britisher.

"The letters were addressed to the Vicomte Raoul de Sevrey—the brother whom she worshipped."

A silence fell in the room. It was broken at last by Kurt von Kelnitz's voice:

"So you see, Dick, it's pretty much of a mess all around. Never did I mention her brother's death to her, nor the fact that I was instrumental in that death. That she should discover that he had been killed was inevitable, but it was only due to my forgetfulness in leaving his notebook and letters in the pocket of my tunic that told her the whole truth. And so I fear that I am passing out of her life, leaving hatred instead of love behind."

There was pain on his features and the Britisher looked away, his eyes haggard.

Suddenly both men raised their heads. For a second they stared into each other's eyes. There was panic in the eyes of the Britisher; nothing but a cool acceptance of fate in the eyes of the German. A sound was coming from the courtyard. The sound grew in volume and resolved itself into the steady, disciplined tramp of many feet.

The Britisher's face went white. Kurt von Kelnitz nodded quietly to himself.

"You have been good to me, my friend," he said simply and rose as there came an order to halt, then the crash of grounded arms outside the door. "I've only one thing more to ask of you, Dick, and that is that you will send this"—he jerked a ribbon, from which hung a decoration, from the inside of his blouse and laid it on the table—"that you will send my *Ordre pour la Mérite* to Odette. Her address is under the name of Mrs. Thomas Spaulding, No. 13 Bahnhof Strasse, Geneva. You will do this?"

"Of course, Kurt," whispered the Englishman.

Both men were standing up as the door opened.

"They have come for me," said Kurt von Kelnitz, and extended his hand. The Britisher took it. Of the two he was the more unnerved.

"By God, Kurt—I'm sorry—it's rotten luck. I'd rather"—something like a sob choked his utterance.

"It is nothing, my friend. Forget it. Goodbye and thank you." And Kurt von Kelnitz, *Rittmeister* of Uhlans, Baron and *Freiherr* of the Kingdom of Prussia, convicted spy, clicked his heels and bowed stiffly from the waist.

He strode briskly to the door, where an officer, a chaplain and the guard stood ready to conduct him to the firing squad that even now was waiting at an angle of the courtyard wall.

After what seemed an eternity of silence the Britisher flinched as there came the dull sound he had dreaded. For a long time he sat staring at the wall.

"Poor old Kurt! What a beastly business!" he whispered to himself at last.

He reached with a hand that trembled into the drawer of the desk. He brought forth a long official envelope that contained the papers relating to Kurt von Kelnitz. From among these he pulled a faintly scented square of notepaper. It was inscribed in spidery characters. In clear and careful English it denounced Kurt von Kelnitz as a German spy, told the name under which he was hiding and the place where he might be found. The envelope was postmarked Switzerland, the return address was 13 Bahnhof Strasse. It was signed "Odette de Sevrey."

"What a *beastly* mess!" repeated the Britisher, his face haggard, as he drew forth another envelope from the drawer of his desk. "And how rotten sorry she'll be if she ever discovers the truth!"

And again he read that report of the French Sûreté upon the Vicomte Raoul de Sevrey:

"This individual became suspected of treasonable traffic with the Germans shortly before the outbreak of the war. On evidence that he was selling information to pay debts in gambling, to which he was addicted, orders to arrest him were sent to Sevrey-sur-Aisne after the outbreak of hostilities. Evidently he became apprised of these and fled from his domicile. It was reported that he made his escape by exchanging clothing with a French peasant youth. Due to this ruse it was for many months believed that de Sevrey was dead until he was reported in Belgium in the following year. In June of 1916 he was arrested by agents of the Sûreté, tried and convicted of being a spy in German pay. Executed at Fort Vincennes, July 30th, 1916, as a traitor to France. Information secret and confidential. Relatives not notified."

The Britisher stared at the coldly official wording of the document.

"*What* a beastly mess!"

Out in the courtyard a man with mop and pail cleaned up some stains. The members of the firing squad, as was the custom, were excused from all other duties for the day.

OFF-TRAIL PUBLICATIONS
Specializing in the era of American pulp fiction
offtrailpublications.com

History

THE THING'S INCREDIBLE!
THE SECRET ORIGINS OF *WEIRD TALES*
By John Locke • 310 pages, $24 (softcover), $35 (hardcover)

A sweeping revisionist history of the founding of *Weird Tales*, one of the most influential pulp magazines. Its first two years (1923-24) was a period of tumult and controversy unequalled in the pulps, before or since, an experience so painful to its creators that they immediately banished their memories to secrecy, their silence suppressing the story for almost a century. Here is the true saga, the unraveling of the many twisted threads which have bound the creation of *Weird Tales* in mystery. This is the grand story of the establishment of a radical, new magazine in the early 1920s—the immortal *Weird Tales*.

PULPWOOD DAYS: Volume 1: Editors You Want To Know
Edited by John Locke • 180 pages, $16

*Numerous articles from the writers' mags by and about pulp editors, with ample biographical profiles. Editors include: Frank E. Blackwell (*Detective Story, Western Story*), Ray Palmer (*Amazing Stories, Fantastic Adventures*), Edwin Baird (*Weird Tales*), and many more.*

PULPWOOD DAYS: Volume 2: Lives of the Pulp Writers
Edited by John Locke • 250 pages, $22

This unique collection mines the writers' mags for those articles in which pulpsters looked back on the glories and hardships of the pulp racket. These are hardboiled writing stories from the Pulp Era—when the greatest time in history to sell fiction—the 1920s—was suddenly followed by one of the worst—the '30s. Twenty pieces. Includes new profiles of authors Arthur J. Burks, Tom Curry, Steve Fisher, Hapsburg Liebe, Chuck Martin, Harold Masur, Tom Thursday, Paul Triem, Jean Francis Webb, and many others. Over 100,000 words of pulp history.

Adventure

THE GOLDEN ANACONDA: And Other Strange Tales of Adventure
By Elmer Brown Mason • Introduction by John Locke
10 stories, 260 pages, $20

Fantastic and horror-laden stories set in the exotic corners of the world known to their globe-trotting entomologist author. Includes all five Wandering Smith stories from The Popular Magazine; *and five tales from* All-Story Weekly. *All published, 1915-16.*

HOBO STORIES
By Patrick & Terence Casey • Introduction by John Locke
6 stories, 332 pages, $20

The Caseys were two brothers from San Francisco who broke into the pulps while still teenagers. Within a few years, they had conned their way into the prestigious pages of Adventure. Hobo Stories *reprints their series of exploits of a teenage hobo and his dog from* The Saturday Evening Post *(1914) and* Adventure *(1916-21). Included is their story of a teenage pulp writer from* Romance *(1920); and a lengthy introduction which explores the lives of the Caseys and the origins of their hobo stories.*

THE OCEAN: 100th Anniversary Collection
Edited by John Locke
20 stories, 234 pages, $18

Munsey's The Ocean *(1907-08) was one of the first specialized pulps, a sea-story magazine. The best adventure stories are included here, along with 30+ pages of nonfiction material: a history of the pulp, and extensive author profiles.*

J. Allan Dunn

OUTDOOR STORIES
By J. Allan Dunn • Introduction by John Locke
3 stories, 190 pages, $16

Presented are all three of Dunn's tales from the ultra-rare Outdoor Stories *(1927-28). These gripping adventures, set in the exotic places of another day, rank with Dunn's best. The featured story, "New Guinea Gold," is an epic tale of friendship, survival and revenge. Included is a history of* Outdoor Stories, *a biography of editor Edmund C. Richards, and an examination of Dunn's role in the magazine.*

THE PERIL OF THE PACIFIC
By J. Allan Dunn • Introduction by John Locke
Complete 5-part serial, 168 pages, $14

Dunn's Japanese invasion epic is future history, published as a five-part serial in People's *in 1916, but set in 1920.* Peril *pits a force of American irregulars armed with futuristic technology against a relentless naval empire bent on conquest. Dunn uses San Francisco and California's Central Coast as his main settings, drawing upon his well-traveled past more than in any other story he ever published.*

THREE SOUTH SEAS NOVELS
By J. Allan Dunn • Introduction by John Locke
3 stories, 360 pages, $20

Dunn began his fiction career as a South Seas specialist. These three early works established him as a fan favorite in Adventure *magazine. Includes Dunn's first full novel,* The Island of the Dead *(April 1915); also* The Gold Lust *(November 1915) and* Beyond the Rim *(July 1916). Enjoy these colorful epics of modern-day buccaneers who behave a lot like their olden-day counterparts.*

Weird & Weird Detective

THE WEIRD DETECTIVE ADVENTURES OF WADE HAMMOND
By Paul Chadwick

Vol 1: 10 stories, 180 pages, $18 • **Vol 2**: 10 stories, 172 pages, $18
Vol 3: 10 stories, 202 pages, $18 • **Vol 4**: 9 stories, 232 pages, $18

Wade Hammond complete in four volumes. In these chilling adventures, all from the classic 1930's pulps, Detective-Dragnet *and* Ten Detective Aces, *freelance investigator Wade Hammond battles a series of weird enemies. Some of the best of '30s pulp fiction.*

GROTTOS OF CHINATOWN: The Dorus Noel Stories
By Arthur J. Burks • Introduction by John Locke

11 stories, 194 pages, $16

The complete adventures of Dorus Noel from All Detective Magazine *(1933-34). Burks' Manhattan Chinatown is a place of dark mystery, riddled with secret passageways, menaced by hatchetmen. Introduction discusses the history of* All Detective *and the career of the Speed-King of the Pulps, Arthur J. Burks.*

CULT OF THE CORPSES
By Maxwell Hawkins • Introduction by John Locke

2 novelettes, 150 pages, $13.95

Two weird detective stories from Detective-Dragnet *(1931) by a forgotten master. Introduction discusses the weird-detective trend of the early '30s, and the career of Maxwell Hawkins.*

DOCTOR COFFIN: The Living Dead Man
By Perley Poore Sheehan • Introduction by John Wooley

8 novelettes, 178 pages, $16

Weird stories from Thrilling Detective, *1932-33. A former character actor who faked his own death, Doctor Coffin runs a string of mortuaries by night and fights crime at night. One of the strangest detective series.*

Weird & Weird Detective

THE MAGICIAN DETECTIVE: And Other Weird Mysteries
By Fulton Oursler
Introduction by John Locke
7 stories, 210 pages, $18

> *Fulton Oursler was one of the great editors of his time, ruling over the Macfadden publishing empire for two decades. But stage magic was his first love. In this collection of early fiction, Oursler's bewitching imagination takes flight in tales of magic, murder and mystery. Featured is an exploration of the astonishing career of Fulton Oursler.*

GHOST STORIES: The Magazine and Its Makers
Edited by John Locke
Vol 1: 19 stories, 256 pages, $24 • **Vol 2**: 15 stories, 272 pages, $24

> *Macfadden's* Ghost Stories *(1926-31) presented haunted tales in every exciting arena: the Western Front, gangland, aviation, the Klondike, the circus, etc. The personnel behind* Ghost Stories *were a fascinating group: poets and scholars, war heroes and war correspondents, adventurers and Bohemians; a few became prolific pulpsters; a few became bestselling authors. And a few led haunted lives. Vol 1 includes the history of* Ghost Stories, *bios of every editor, and every Vol 1 author. Vol 2 includes bios of every Vol 2 author, every cover artist, and a gallery of all 64* Ghost Stories *covers.*

Weird & Weird Detective

SUPER-DETECTIVE FLIP BOOK: Two Complete Novels
From the pulp *Super-Detective*:
"Legion of Robots" (November 1940) by Victor Rousseau • Introduction by John McMahan •• "Murder's Migrants" (March 1943) by Robert Leslie Bellem and W.T. Ballard • Introduction by John Wooley
2 short novels, 174 pages, $18

> Super-Detective *started as a Doc Savage-like adventure pulp, then changed format to hardboiled detective. The* Flip Book *features a novel from each of the two phases with intros exploring the historical background.*

FROM GHOULS TO GANGSTERS: The Career of Arthur B. Reeve
Edited by John Locke
Vol 1 (fiction): 21 stories, 264 pages, $20 • **Vol 2 (nonfic)**: 260 pages, $20

> *Reeve was the leading American detective-story writer of the early 20th Century, with his scientific detective, Craig Kennedy. The astonishing breadth of his career is explored for the first time here. Vol 1 includes a cross-sction of fiction from all phases of career, including many never-before-reprinted pulp stories. Vol 2 provides a 40-page biography; an extensive Art Gallery of cover repros, interior illos, ads, etc; a 75-page guide to Reeve's work in all media; and more. An "excellent piece of scholarship"*—MYSTERY SCENE, *Spring 2008.*

Gangster

GANG PULP

Edited by John Locke • 19 stories, 294 pages, $24

*Hardboiled stories of the criminal underworld from the first year (1929-30) of the gang pulps: Gangster Stories, Racketeer Stories, etc. These violent tales came under immediate censorship pressure; the history is explored in an in-depth essay. "A remarkable work of popular-culture scholarship"—*MYSTERY SCENE, *Fall 2008.*

IF SHE ONLY HAD A MACHINE GUN
Crime Stories by Richard Credicott

Introductions by Dave Credicott & John Locke
Edited by John Locke & Rob Preston
18 stories, 360 pages, $20

The complete stories of one of the best gang-pulp authors. Includes gang stories from Racketeer Stories, Mobs, *etc., wildly entertaining tales of mob intrigue and mayhem, and the violent whims of molls; and detective stories from* The Dragnet, Dime Detective, *and others. All from 1929-33. A complete biographical profile offers rare insights into the pulps during the early years of the Depression. As a special feature, Dave Credicott provides reminiscences of his father's life.*

CITY OF NUMBERED MEN: The Best of Prison Stories

Introduction by John Locke
12 stories, 278 pages, $20

During Prohibition, famed publisher Harold Hersey turned America's disintegrating prison system into the hardboiled Prison Stories *(1930-31). Included are stories from all issues of this rare pulp, the startling history of* Prison Stories, *cover gallery, and "Tales of an Ink-Stained Wretch," the first comprehensive biography of pulp publishing's most colorful character, Harold Hersey.*

Gangster

THE GANGLAND SAGAS OF BIG NOSE SERRANO
Volume 1: Dames, Dice and the Devil
Volume 2: Horses, Hoboes and Heroes
Volume 3: Hell's Gangster
By Anatole Feldman • Introductions by Will Murray
Each: 4 novels • **Volumes 1-2**: 266 pages, $20 • **Volume 3**: 224 pages, $18

The complete Big Nose Serrano novels from Gangster Stories, Greater Gangster Stories, *and* The Gang Magazine, *1930-35. Feldman was the best of the gang pulp authors, and Big Nose was his most inspired creation, the berserking king of Chicago gangsters.*

QUEEN OF THE GANGSTERS: Volume 1: Broadwalk Empire
Introductions by David Bischoff & John Locke
8 stories, 234 pages, $18

Tough, rough, remorseless stories from the first woman hardboiled crime fiction writer; from gang pulps like Gangland Stories, Racketeer Stories *and* Mobs. *Margie Harris slammed her typewriter like a machine gun, mowing down good guys and bad guys alike; shooting them, knifing them, blowing them up—lacing her prose with metaphysical commentary on the destinations of their damned souls. This is the first time her work has been collected. Introduction from bestselling author David Bischoff.*

www.ingramcontent.com/pod-product-compliance
Lightning Source LLC
Chambersburg PA
CBHW030403020726
47493CB00003B/929